THE NOMINEE

Rev. 2d Ed.

A LUCIUS WHITE LEGAL THRILLER

ALAN P. WOODRUFF

THANK YOU READERS

Thank you for buying and reading my book and I sincerely hope that you enjoy it. As an independently published author, I rely on my readers to spread the word, so, if you like my book, please tell your family and friend. And if it's not too much trouble, mention me on your social media pages and **post a review on Amazon**. If you would like to tell me your opinion directly, please visit my website – **www.alanpwoodruff.com** – and send me a message. If you have a question, I will respond as soon as possible.

PROLOGUE

Pellets of rain the size of birdshot and driven almost horizontal by the hurricane wind hammered the Angler Lounge. The shutters, battened against the storm, rattled as each new gust assaulted the popular gathering spot overlooking the marina. The late-season tourists, and most of the residents of the Florida Keys, had complied with the evacuation order. Inside the lounge, two dozen hardy residents of Vaca Key continued their time-honored tradition of ignoring both nature and the government. The violent timbre of the storm, roaring like a locomotive, was lost in the gaiety of the hurricane party.

An old man—pale and gaunt—stumbled through the weathered wooden door and leaned stooped against the wall, fighting to catch his breath. Water from his yellow slicker and scraggly gray beard gathered in a pool at his feet as he struggled to stand erect.

A large man, one of the local charter boat captains sitting at the end of the bar, nudged his companion and motioned to the old man with a tilt of his head. His companion glanced toward the old man, shrugged a message of no recognition, and returned his attention to the game of liar's poker.

At the pier outside the lounge, the old man's decrepit commercial fishing boat crashed against the pilings. The two men in the wheelhouse were thrown violently against the bulkhead as the crashing waves battered the boat. One of the men held a powerful flashlight that illuminated the cabin deck where the other man was hammering a pry bar between the worn timbers. At any moment, a wave could obliterate the cabin, but the smuggled cargo they sought made the risk worth taking.

Inside the lounge, the old man shuffled slowly across the room. He was bent forward and rocking slightly from side to side as if still fighting the storm on the deck of a boat. On the other side of the room, he reached for the back of the booth to steady himself before collapsing onto the bare wooden seat.

A waitress dressed in shorts and a halter top reluctantly left the crowd at the bar and approached the booth. The old man moaned and wiggled a finger of his gnarled hand, signaling the waitress to come closer.

"Hey, Diane," someone shouted from the vicinity of the pool table.

"Hold your horses," the waitress shouted back as she leaned closer to the old man and asked, "What's it gonna be?"

"Ayuda," the old man muttered, barely more than a whisper, as if the act of speaking required considerable effort.

"I can't understand, sweetie."

"Ayuda me," the old man muttered again before his head fell forward, his chin resting on his chest.

The bartender shouted, "What's he want?"

"Beats me," Diane responded as she turned and headed back toward the bar. "I couldn't understand what he said. But whatever he wanted, he's had enough. He's passed out."

&

Eight hours later, the worst of the storm had subsided. Beside the pier, the battered remains of the old man's fishing boat rose and fell with each wave. The last of the partiers stumbled out the door of the lounge, and the bartender began turning off the lights. The waitress approached the old man and tapped him on the shoulder. "Let's go, old-timer. Time to leave."

The old man remained motionless, slumped against the corner of the booth.

"Come on, fella. I'm tired, and I wanna go home," she pled, gripping the old man's slicker and pulling him toward her.

The slicker slid off his shoulder and opened across his chest.

"Oh, God!" she screamed at the sight of the old man's blood-soaked shirt.

1.

The bailiff knocked twice on the door to the judge's chambers and boomed, "All rise."

Judge Jason Caldwell, his black robe flowing behind him, took his place behind the polished walnut bench that occupied half the width of the courtroom. "Be seated," the judge said.

On the side of the courtroom beside the jury box, a door opened and the somber-faced jurors filed in. Some of the jurors looked at the judge. Others looked at the floor. None of them looked in the direction of Lucius White and his client.

A faint smile formed on the lips of the state's attorney, Paul Parker. Lack of eye contact with the defendant is usually a good sign for the prosecution.

The government's case was strong, but it was based entirely on circumstantial evidence. The defendant, Howard Marshall, was in financial trouble. He had recently purchased a million-dollar policy on his wife's life, and he had fought with his wife on the night she was murdered. The murder weapon was never found, but the state's ballistics expert testified that the gun was of the same make and model as a gun owned by Howard Marshall—a gun the defendant couldn't account for.

"Has the jury reached a verdict?" Judge Caldwell asked in a deep voice that echoed in the stillness of the courtroom.

For Paul Parker, it was more than just another trial.

After a series of losses in high-profile cases, Parker needed a conviction. The victim was a prominent woman from an old family. Old money and a socialite victim meant volumes of press coverage, and, with an election coming up, Parker wasn't taking any chances. Over White's objection, Parker had called eleven witnesses to prove what could have been established with three. But that only gave White more opportunities to raise doubts about the prosecution's case.

The one thing Parker had been unable to establish was Howard Marshall's location at the time of the murder. In fact, he had an alibi, but jurors tended to be less than sympathetic to his defense: "I couldn't have killed her because I was with my mistress at the time." And since the mistress had refused to testify, even that defense was without value.

The victim, Susan Marshall, was also having an affair, but putting the victim on trial was never a good idea in a brutal murder case, especially when the victim was active in most of the major charities and civic organizations in the county.

For Lucius White, Marshall's attorney, it had all come down to jury selection. An acquittal seemed out of the question. But, with a little bit of luck, one of the three divorced men, one the victim of a bitter divorce brought by a cheating wife, would ignore the evidence and hang the jury. Then he would have a chance to plea bargain for an acceptable sentence.

White scanned the faces of the jury. Being sequestered in the economy-class hotel down the block from the courthouse, unable to see their families for the duration of the three-week trial and five days of deliberation, could not have been what they expected when the trial began. White could see that the deliberations had taken their toll. The jurors were tired, maybe even angry, and wanted to go home

"Yes, Your Honor," the jury foreperson said, so quietly that the judge and gallery had to strain to hear her. She was a small, unimposing woman in her mid-sixties. She had gray hair and wore a floral pattern dress that made her seem like everyone's grandmother.

For White, she was the ideal foreperson—unlikely to have much influence over the other jurors and lacking in the strength to force a divided jury to reach a verdict. Three times the jury asked for portions of the testimony to be reread, and several more times they asked the judge for further instructions. Some of their concerns seemed to favor the prosecution, but the majority of them appeared to favor the defense. Those were the makings of a hung jury and a mistrial. White remained cautiously optimistic. But he also knew what it meant when a jury did not look at the defendant.

All eyes remained on the jury as the bailiff retrieved the verdict form from the foreperson and delivered it to the judge.

After five days of deliberations, the media had the odds for a hung jury at seven to five. The announcement that the jury had reached a verdict wasn't a good sign for the defense. A few reporters exchanged excited whispers. White put a hand on his client's shoulder and whispered something in his ear. His client frowned and lowered his head.

In the first row of the gallery, the parents and sister of Susan Marshall clutched hands. Her sister said a silent "Yes." Her father stared at Howard Marshall. His eyes showed a mixture of contempt and revenge.

Judge Caldwell glanced at the verdict form, without giving any indication of its contents, and returned it to the bailiff. Judges shouldn't care who prevails in any case they preside over, and Judge Caldwell took that mandate to an extreme. He had a reputation for neutrality and formality.

The courtroom echoed with the click of the bailiff's heels on the polished wood floor as he crossed the room and returned the verdict form to the foreperson.

The gallery grew hush.

"The defendant will please rise and face the jury," Judge Caldwell said. The words were so familiar to the judge that he said them with no emotion and no recognition that the rest of the defendant's life was about to be determined.

Lucius White rose. At the other end of the defense table, Harry Harris, White's partner, sat up straighter in his wheelchair. Between them, the defendant bowed his head and uttered a short prayer before standing.

If the old adage, "juries vote for the attorney they like the best," was true, White's client had a chance. At six feet, two inches tall and one-hundred-ninety pounds, White was too slender to be considered a physically imposing figure. Nor would he be described as handsome. His leathery face was creased and weathered. His nose, broken in a childhood accident and reset by his father, was not quite centered beneath his dark eyes. His walnut-brown hair, now graying at the temples, was worn long and unkempt, in a rugged western way reminiscent of his formative years in Ketchum, Idaho. But he had an intangible presence, a don't-tread-on-me look, and a voice, deep and resonant, that couldn't be ignored. Clients never doubted that they were in good hands, and juries knew he could be trusted.

"Madam foreperson, will you please read the verdict."

"We the jury…" she began before pausing and coughing. "In the matter of *State of Florida v. Howard Marshall*, on the charge of second-degree murder, find the defendant…"

The forewoman coughed again and cleared her throat. Silent tension consumed the courtroom.

The pause seemed to continue forever as the forewoman looked nervously at the gallery.

"Not guilty."

The gallery erupted, and the spectators immediately began debating the verdict.

Marshall dropped to his seat and gave a sigh of relief.

Harris reached around their client and pumped White's hand.

Parker dropped his head, stared vacantly at the legal pad on the table in front of him, and crumpled the sheet of paper that held the notes for his intended victory press conference. His assistant put a hand on his shoulder and whispered something in his ear. Parker pursed his lips and shook his head.

The reporters who filled the courtroom rushed for the exit, ready to position themselves with their camera crews for the post-trial interviews on the courthouse steps.

"Order," Judge Caldwell demanded, pounding his gavel.

The jurors looked at each other. None of them seemed to know what they were supposed to do now.

"Order," Judge Caldwell demanded again.

Slowly, the remaining spectators returned to their seats. Judge Caldwell surveyed the gallery, glaring fiercely at anyone who wasn't moving fast enough to satisfy him.

"Ladies and gentlemen of the jury," Judge Caldwell said, "the court thanks you for your service. The defendant is released and free to go."

Another swing of the gavel and it was over. A year of preparation, three weeks of trial, and five days of jury deliberations, and just like that, it was over.

The empty feeling of finality that always overwhelmed White at the conclusion of a grueling trial, like the feeling of Christmas morning after all the presents had been unwrapped, would come later. It always did. For now, he was all smiles as he received the renewed hugs of his client and the congratulations of well-wishers.

As the crowd cleared the courtroom, Parker walked to the defense table and extended his hand. "Congratulations, Lucius. It was a good fight."

"Thanks, Paul. You did a good job."

"Apparently not good enough," Parker said without humor. "Maybe next time."

"Maybe," White said. There was no emotion in his voice, just an acknowledgment of what Parker had said. Parker turned and headed for the door.

&

As was his custom, Lucius White waited until the courtroom was empty before preparing to leave. He was returning the last of his papers to his briefcase when a voice behind him said, "That was a hell of a closing argument, Lucius. Maybe the best I ever heard."

White immediately recognized the voice of Graham Brochette, US attorney for the Middle District of Florida. He turned and extended his hand. "Coming from you, I take that as a compliment."

"I mean it, Lucius," Brochette continued. "I never thought you'd get the guy off."

"It helps that the US attorney wasn't prosecuting the case."

Brochette frowned and responded with an uneasy silence. He knew what White meant. It was no secret that White believed that most of the federal prosecutors had the ethics of reptiles.

"Parker was more concerned with how his case was being reported in the press than with how it played to the jury."

"I'm sure he did what he thought was right."

"He did what was right for himself, not what was right for the state." White put the papers he was holding into his briefcase and leaned forward with both arms outstretched and his hands on the edge of the counsel's table. "Nothing pisses me off more than an incompetent government prosecutor."

"You should like that. It makes your job easier."

"I'm not interested in making my job easier. I only expect them to play by the rules."

"And you don't think the government plays by the rules."

"I didn't mean that the way it sounded."

"Yes, you did. Everyone in my office knows how you feel about the ethical lapses of government prosecutors."

White's decision to become a criminal attorney, and his loathing of the government, were the almost inevitable product of the experiences of his youth. He was only sixteen when his father, an outspoken opponent of all government, was arrested on dubious charges of conspiracy and criminal trespass on government property. White wasn't allowed to attend the trial, but everyone in the community knew about the fabricated testimony by paid informants and others who had made deals to avoid prosecution. His father died in prison two years later, stabbed in the back by a drug dealer. There was no investigation of substance, and the drug dealer was released less than six months later, almost two years before he was first eligible for parole.

White, by then an eighteen-year-old high school senior, knew it was more than a coincidence. He knew, as an article of faith, with the certainty that a devout Christian believes in the Holy Trinity, that the government was responsible for his father's death. It was a memory that haunted and drove him. It was with him every moment when he was preparing for a trial. He tried not to think about it, but it was now too much a part of him to be ignored. After a minute, he realized what he was thinking and returned his attention to Brochette.

"I noticed you in the back of the courtroom," White said, acknowledging Brochette's presence during closing arguments. There didn't seem to be any reason for the US attorney to be observing a state court proceeding, but there hadn't been time to think about it during the trial. Now the strain of the trial was replaced by another thought. Why is Brochette here? Whatever the reason, it wasn't likely to be good news. The question was, who was going to be on the receiving end of the bad news.

"Congratulations on your nomination to be deputy assistant US attorney general," White said, filling the silence while he searched for something in Brochette's eyes that would explain this obviously intentional encounter. "They couldn't have chosen a better man."

Brochette nodded an acknowledgment of the compliment. For a moment, he didn't say anything as his eyes moved around the empty courtroom. White knew that Brochette had something important on his mind. It wasn't like him to avoid an issue, however sensitive it was, with a meaningless conversation such as the one they were having about the trial and Brochette's nomination. White sensed that whatever Brochette had on his mind was painful for him to discuss and he couldn't be rushed. White sat on the end of the counsel's table with his arms folded across his chest and waited.

Finally, Brochette took a deep breath and faced White. In his eyes, there was a look of distressed angst. "I need your help. My son has been arrested."

2.

Lucius White was not given to excess in his personal life, but his success allowed him to enjoy a full measure of comfort at work and home. His physical environment was a reflection of his personality. He was as passionate about preserving the symbols of cultural history as he was about protecting the dignity of the law—both of which he feared were falling victim to social change. He was especially proud of his offices, which, as a result of his efforts, were listed in the National Registry of Historic Places.

The offices of Lucius A. White & Associates were located in a converted warehouse on the edge of the Caloosahatchee River and four blocks from downtown Fort Myers, Florida. The warehouse had been built late in the eighteenth century—land title records were not clear as to the exact date, and it was largely irrelevant to all but the title company—to store goods shipped by boat into the small community on the site of what had once been a frontier fort maintained by the Union army during the Civil War. Until early in the twentieth century, Fort Myers remained isolated from the main populations of Florida— by the Everglades to the east and by Charlotte Harbor and the Peace River to the north—and the waterfront was an active part of the town. In the 1920s, the railroad arrived in Fort Myers, and shipborne trade began an immediate and precipitous decline. Over the next sixty years, the water-front warehouses slowly succumbed to the ravages of time, neglect, and decay. By early in the 1980s, only the warehouse that now housed White's offices and apartment survived. Eventually, it had become the property of the city, seized for unpaid property taxes, and was scheduled for demolition as a public nuisance. The city was more than happy to sell the derelict building to Lucius White.

After more than a year of restoration, the warehouse had been completely gutted and refurbished. All that remained of the original warehouse were the red brick walls and the giant oak beams that supported the original floors and ceiling. The remainder of the building had been painstakingly restored using the same tools and construction methods used to build the original. No detail had been overlooked. A blacksmith's furnace had been built on the site to make nails the way they had been made in the early frontier days. Floor planks had been cut on an original steam-powered saw that White acquired for his project and later donated to the city historical museum.

The first floor of White's warehouse was occupied by his firm's main reception area, the offices of White's associates, the conference room, and the file storage room. The clerical staffs worked in the center of the first floor under a two-story atrium.

The offices of Lucius White and his partner, Harry Harris, and their administrative assistants were located on the mezzanine. A wide balcony extending from the mezzanine and surrounding the atrium contained the rows of shelves that made up the firm's law library. Most legal research was now done on computers, but White had a special fondness for his library. For him, the library was more than a place to research the law. He loved the rows of books, the mahogany tables with their Tiffany table lamps and the quiet that embraced the library. It created a link to the past when the practice of law was still a noble profession.

Between the offices of White and Harris was a windowless conference room, generally referred to as the War Room. It was here that they met as a team, the attorneys and their clients, when analyzing the complex facts of major cases or preparing cases for trial. The War Room was the beating heart of the firm.

In the middle of the room was an oval oak conference table surrounded by eight leather chairs. At one end of the room was a white marker board. The side walls of the room were covered with corkboard. Early in every case, seemingly random facts were recorded on white cards and posted on the corkboard walls. As patterns later emerged, facts were transferred to colored cards, each color representing facts that related to different events.

&

When White and Brochette stepped off the elevator onto the mezzanine, they were met with a clutter of assorted boxes and loose tissue paper. Leslie Halloran, with whom White shared the apartment that occupied the entire third floor of the warehouse, was busy helping Grace Matthews, White's administrative assistant, hang the office Christmas decorations in preparation for the firm's upcoming gala.

Brochette could not avoid smiling whenever he saw Leslie. Few men could. But few men stopped at a smile. Brochette was nothing if not a complete gentleman; a graduate of the "look but don't drool" school.

Leslie wore her thirty-nine years with style. Five feet, six inches tall and one hundred twenty lithe pounds of Irish womanhood. Shiny brick-red hair that cascaded recklessly in soft curls over her shoulders and halfway down her back. A crème brûlée complexion was the perfect setting for her large hazel eyes. A trim body with full breasts and shapely legs, honed by years of competitive tennis, and a Nordic-

Track ass. But the first thing people recognized about her was that she radiated happiness. It was a quality so different from White, who, to all but his closest friends, always seemed serious, almost dour. He could be open and caring, but it was a side of him reserved for only a few.

Today Leslie was wearing a halter top and short shorts that accentuated her best qualities. Even by the casual standards of White's office, her attire was extreme—but the holiday season was made for exceptions. Leslie stood, kissed White, and greeted Brochette cheerily. "Graham! Happy holidays. What brings you down here?"

Brochette forced a smile. "I have a little business to discuss with Lucius."

"Oh. What kind of business?"

Brochette ignored the question and changed the subject. "I heard that they closed most of your clinics."

Leslie stepped back and looked at Brochette. The look on her face suggested she wasn't sure what he meant. Leslie had spent the last five years as a public interest lawyer representing AIDS clinics who were suing the federal government for funding that was always promised during election campaigns but was never delivered.

"It's too bad. I hear you were doing a great job." She had never opposed Brochette in court; he was far too important to be bothered with a case that only presented a question of administrative law. But she was well known to the attorneys in his office, and he had genuine respect for her and the work she was doing.

"I've been helping out at the legal-aid office since the clinics were forced to close down."

"I'm surprised Lucius hasn't put you to work for him. According to my staff, you're a fearsome litigator."

"We've talked about it," Leslie said, glancing at White to be sure he was paying attention. "I haven't been able to convince Lucius that women are just as capable of representing criminals as men." They didn't teach subtlety at Leslie's law school.

"That doesn't sound like Lucius."

Leslie laughed. "Don't get me started."

White wrapped an arm around Leslie and kissed her on the cheek. "Do I have to remind you that I'm standing right here?"

Leslie kissed him back before returning her attention to Brochette. "You tell him, Graham. Maybe my ever-loving chivalrous pig of a boyfriend will listen to you."

Brochette smiled. "I think I'll stay out of this one."

Leslie chuckled. "Coward!"

Before anyone could say more, the elevator door opened and Harry Harris rolled out.

"Harry!" Leslie shouted happily as she ran to him and gave him an exuberant hug.

Brochette watched the display with a look somewhere between curiosity and disapproval. It wasn't as if his opinion made a difference to anyone present, but as a government lawyer he was accustomed to more decorum. As the scene between Leslie and Harry extended, Brochette became aware that he was about to ask a significant favor of a lawyer whose style was entirely foreign to him.

"He's been in hibernation since the trial began," she said. She seemed to be addressing her remark to Brochette. "He's my big teddy bear."

Harris blushed. "She takes care of me like a daughter."

Leslie suppressed the sudden sense of sadness she felt at Harry's statement. Before joining White, Harris was a highly regarded trial attorney. His practice, and life as he knew it, was cut short when a drunken teenage driver broadsided his car, killing his wife and child and leaving him a paraplegic. The loss of his family—and the realization that he would be confined to a wheelchair for the rest of his life—sent Harris into a deep depression. He became addicted to painkillers, antidepressants, and alcohol. Eventually, he was abandoned by all his friends and colleagues—all except Lucius White.

White saw him through rehabilitation and eventually brought him in as his partner. In time, Harris's physical scars healed, but his mental scars had not. Before the accident, his stock in trade was pure theater, gestures, postures, and dramatic movements within the well of the courtroom. One moment he would rant and roar like a revival tent preacher. The next moment he would speak so softly that the jury had to lean forward to hear him. He was Hamlet with a briefcase, but his early attempts at trial practice following his accident only served to remind him of his physical limitations. Although he no longer had the confidence to try cases, Harris was still an extraordinary tactician and investigator. He never forgot a fact and was an expert at managing mountains of documents. These qualities made him the perfect second-in-command for White and mentor and sounding board for White's young associates.

Leslie's reflections were interrupted when White said, "Harry, if you're finished trying to steal my girl, I'd like you to join Graham and me."

Harry followed White and Brochette into White's office and closed the door.

A cherrywood conference table surrounded by four black leather Herman Miller chairs on swivel bases dominated the center of White's office. The sitting area at the end of his office contained a large, sea-green leather sofa and matching love seat, each placed against the walls in one corner. A wood-and-glass corner table and two matching end tables, each with a modern brass lamp and a glass-topped coffee table framed the sofa and love seat. The floors, like the floors throughout White's apartment, were hand-laid oak covered with Persian carpets, predominantly maroon in color and in varying traditional patterns. The interior walls were covered in grasscloth. Paintings of sea-birds and waterfront scenes, all originals by renowned local artists, adorned the walls. Noticeably absent were any of the diplomas and court admission certificates that adorned the vanity wall of most lawyers' offices. Such self-aggrandizement was not part of White's persona.

Brochette took a seat on the sofa as Harris rolled his chair to his customary position beside the conference table. White crossed his arms and half-leaned against, half-sat on the edge of the table. "Graham has been telling me about a little family problem. His son was arrested in a drug bust in Matlacha—out on Pine Island."

Harris ignored the formality of an unnecessary, and ultimately meaningless, statement of condolences. Brochette could feel sorry for himself, or his son, on his own time. Harris had work to do. He pulled a legal pad to the edge of the table and asked, "What have they charged him with?"

"Possession with intent to distribute," White said. His bored tone made it sound like just another fact. He might as well have said, "carnal knowledge with two pigs and a goat." He and Harris had seen it all. For them, criminal charges were no longer about acts. They were merely labels, references to the sections of the penal code that define the elements of a crime, the things the prosecutor has to prove, and the sentences that could be imposed.

"Cocaine?" Harris guessed.

"Yeah."

"Weight?"

"Two kilos."

Harris made a long whistle. "That's serious weight. The

feds are likely to take jurisdiction, and anything over five grams carries a mandatory sentence of ten years to life."

"I know. 21 USC 841. If my son is convicted, he'll probably get life."

"Was the coke pure, or had it been cut?"

"I don't know. The lab report isn't back yet."

"That's damned serious," Harris said. It wasn't a fact that had escaped anyone else's attention.

Brochette nodded in a way that could have signaled either agreement with White's answers or admiration for Harris's well-targeted questions.

Without looking up from his legal pad, Harris said, "State or federal?" This was the threshold question in all drug cases. State and federal courts are subject to different procedural rules and have different standards for negotiating plea agreements. But most importantly, the federal sentencing guidelines impose much harsher penalties than are commonly imposed by state courts for the same drug-related offenses.

"The raid was conducted by the sheriff."

"Is the case going to stay in state court?"

They all knew that US attorneys have the authority to take over any drug case, but Brochette exercised his discretion sparingly. Over the objection of the junior attorneys in his office, recent law school graduates who commonly develop their trial skills on drug cases, Brochette maintained a policy of not asserting jurisdiction over state drug cases unless they involved major dealers. But this time things were different. With his son involved, Brochette had a conflict of interest and needed a good reason to leave the matter in state court.

White glanced at Brochette and saw the troubled expression on his face and understood the need to rescue Brochette from his dilemma.

"It should stay in state court," White said. "Paul Parker is up for reelection next fall, and he won't want to give up what could be a high-profile drug case. Besides, there doesn't seem to be any aspect of the case that would be of special federal concern."

Harris stopped writing and looked at White. They both knew that the case met all the requirements for a transfer to the US attorney. White shook his head imperceptibly, and Harris understood his message. "Not now, Harry."

White and Harris returned their attention to Brochette, whose face was growing increasingly taut and pale. Until then, Brochette had, as any parent would, apparently only thought of the arrest in terms of what it meant for his son. White's summation forced him to analyze the facts as an attorney. Two kilograms of uncut cocaine was significant by any standards, and Pine Island was known as a place from which high-speed boats traveled to rendezvous with passing freighters and low-flying aircraft to pick up shipments of drugs from South America. The potential for smuggling charges was obvious, but smuggling meant automatic federal jurisdiction.

Brochette hung his head, unable to face White and Harris. Thoughtfulness? Denial? Shame? It was hard to say. It's one thing to know something intellectually. It's something else to hear it from another authority. Without looking up, Brochette said, "David claims he didn't know anything about the drugs. He was sharing a house with another guy, Tom Jackson. Jackson has a record of drug-related arrests. That's all I got from the arrest report."

White waited for Brochette to continue when he suddenly realized the significance of what Brochette had said. He pulled a chair from the conference table and sat facing Brochette. "Let me guess. You haven't talked to your son."

"It's complicated."

White and Harris exchanged puzzled looks.

Harris returned to his notes and was about to add something when his hand twitched and his pen slid across the table. "*Damn*," he muttered, glancing around the table to see if anyone had noticed. As Harris reached for his pen, White studied his face. It wasn't the first time Harris had experienced problems with his fine-motor control, and White had already discussed the problem with his friend.

"Sorry," Harris said, avoiding White's concerned look.

White continued to study Harris. He knew something was wrong but was loath to consider the possibilities. None of the alternatives were good, and he needed Harris as much as Harris needed him. Finally, White returned his attention to Brochette. "When was your son arrested?"

Brochette seemed to be occupied with an examination of the pattern in the Persian carpet in front of the sofa. Finally, be responded in a voice that was hardly more than a whisper. "Five days ago."

White looked up from his legal pad. "Five days!"

White's expression made it evident that he had another question in mind. "Why did you wait so long?" White rolled his pen between his thumb and index finger as he waited for an explanation.

As an experienced attorney, Brochette had to know what White was thinking, but he wasn't ready to explain the reasons for his delay. "As I said, it's complicated. But mostly I waited because I needed you. Jurisdiction will be here, and you know the local players."

White ignored the plea implicit in Brochette's tone. "Tell me about your son."

Brochette leaned forward, resting his elbows on his knees and staring at the floor as he gathered his thoughts. "This isn't easy."

"Take your time."

Brochette seemed to be devoting his attention to the carpet at his feet as if it would help him choose his words. "First of all, David doesn't know I'm his father."

White controlled his impulse to catch his breath. Harris stared at Brochette as though he was not sure that he had heard Brochette correctly. Brochette continued to hang his head, seemingly gathering his thoughts, and courage, before continuing. "David's mother got pregnant my final year of law school. I didn't know about it until a little more than a year later."

White was momentarily startled by Brochette's revelation and quickly thought through what he knew about the US attorney. Old political family with social standing and nothing to prove. Honors graduate from the University of Tennessee and Vanderbilt Law School. Started as a state prosecutor. Joined the US attorney's office and spent five years there building a reputation as a competent litigator. Transferred to the Department of Justice Office of Public Corruption and spent another five years investigating and prosecuting government corruption. Resigned to take the position as U.S. attorney for the Middle District of Florida.

White stored his thoughts away and returned his attention to Brochette.

"By the time I knew about David, she had married someone else, a guy named Richard Shepard, who thought he was David's father."

White glanced at Harris, hoping to see some indication of Harry's thoughts about where Brochette's disclosures were taking them. Harris responded with an almost imperceptible shrug. It was obviously stressful for Brochette to talk about his son and the circumstances of his birth. Trying to hurry him wasn't going to help, so they remained silent as they waited for Brochette to tell the story in his own time.

"Shepard was killed in an automobile accident when David was eight. That's when his mother told me I was David's real father."

"It must have been difficult."

Brochette took a deep breath and exhaled. "I had my suspicions when I first found out about the pregnancy."

White studied Brochette's face, searching for some sign of the anxiety he knew Brochette was feeling. Sharing his secret couldn't be easy, especially under the current circumstances. Brochette seemed to know what White was thinking. "Don't get the wrong idea about his mother. We weren't in a serious relationship... or even an exclusive one."

"Still..."

"Yeah," Brochette agreed with White's unspoken words. "It was a little difficult to deal with."

"What made his mother come to you after all that time?"

"It wasn't money... if that's what you were thinking. Her husband's insurance left them with enough to get by."

"Then why?"

"She just thought I should know. She never asked for anything, but I felt responsible and started sending her money."

White responded with a subtile nod, just enough of a movement to indicate his understanding. "When did she tell David?"

"That I was his real father?"

"Yeah."

"David's mother and I stayed in touch, and we talked about telling him several times." The quivering of his jaw suggested that Brochette was struggling with painful memories. "I thought we should tell him. But that may have been my paternal ego talking. We agreed that we should tell him sometime, but the timing never seemed right. It wasn't until David was in high school that she came to me for help."

"What happened when he was in high school?"

"He got mixed up with the wrong crowd and started using drugs. Marijuana mainly. He may have been using other stuff. I don't know."

"Was he ever arrested?" White asked as Harris continued jotting notes.

"Once… for possession… when he was a freshman in high school. That's when his mother came to me. She knew I was a government attorney and asked for my help. I made some calls, and they let him off with community service. They expunged his record when he turned eighteen."

"Any problems after that?"

"By his junior year, he was getting out of control. He started ignoring school, cutting classes, and hanging out with his friends until all hours of the night."

"How do you know that?"

"As I said, his mother and I stayed in touch."

When White didn't ask anything else, Brochette continued. "In the spring of his junior year, two of his buddies, a couple of older kids he'd gotten involved with, were arrested. They were over eighteen, so they were sentenced as adults—five years each. I don't know if it was because of what happened to his friends, but after they went to jail he straightened up. For a while, it seemed as if he wanted to do something with his life.

As he told David's story, Brochette began to relax and he faced White. "When he graduated, he decided to study criminal justice. I don't know how or why he made that decision, but I admit that I was pleased. Unfortunately, his performance as a high school senior was too spotty to get into a decent college, so he started at Hillsborough Community College. He got an associate's degree and transferred to Florida State. Then, in the middle of his junior year, he quit."

"What did he do then?"

Brochette swallowed hard and looked away. Either the memory was too painful, or the truth was something he didn't want to deal with. Whatever the reason, White knew there was more to the story than Brochette was going to disclose—at least not yet. Was it something Brochette was trying to hide from himself, or something Brochette was trying to hide from White? He couldn't tell which and stored the thought away for future consideration.

Brochette seemed to finish collecting his thoughts and continued. "He pretty much dropped out of sight. Now I know he spent most of the time bumming around the Florida Keys."

"Have you spoken to him since his arrest?"

"I'm not sure it would be good for me to be too close to the situation right now."

It wasn't an answer to White's question, but White knew what Brochette was trying to say.

Brochette moved uneasily on the sofa as White and Harris looked at each other in silent communication. With nothing more than an almost imperceptible nod, they made a decision, and White broke the silence. "We'll require an initial retainer of $50,000." White had long since ceased being embarrassed about asking for such a large retainer for what seemed like a routine drug case.

Brochette relaxed and extended his hand. "I'm very grateful."

3.

As the elevator door closed behind Brochette, White walked to the railing of the mezzanine and leaned against it with both arms outstretched. He had never taken a case without first meeting with his client, and he was trying to understand why he had made an exception for Brochette's son. Brochette was little more than an acquaintance, a professional colleague at best, so friendship wasn't the reason. And nothing Brochette had told him about the case made it particularly interesting. But he had a feeling, something that he could not explain, that this was going to become much more than a simple drug possession case.

White put his thoughts aside and headed across the mezzanine to his assistant's desk.

Grace Matthews had worked for White ever since he had come to Fort Myers after graduating from law school. Long before he could afford a full-time secretary, let alone a qualified legal secretary or a paralegal, he had advertised for a part-time helper to do routine filing and typing. Matthews was still in high school when she appeared at his office and, with confidence far beyond her years, claimed the position. What she lacked in skills, she made up for in determination, and she made it clear in her interview that White had no choice but to hire her. She'd been a fixture in White's firm ever since, quickly establishing herself and taking over all the details of running their little office. Now there were times it was unclear who worked for whom.

Matthews was tall and slender with mocha skin and

large black eyes. She was thirty-three years old but looked much older. A bad marriage to an abusive husband, over but not forgotten, had left her bitter and distrustful. White supported her throughout her ordeal, a kindness she repaid with her unwavering loyalty. She was protective as an old hen, and when she was at her desk outside of White's office, she was the undisputed guardian of the manor.

"Please open a file for David Shepard," White said.

Matthews looked confused.

"He's Graham Brochette's son."

Matthews nodded.

"And ask Horse to come up here."

As Matthews reached for the telephone, White returned to his office and sat on the sofa beside where Harris remained parked in his wheelchair.

"All right, Harry," White said. "What's going on?"

Harris turned away from White and began thumbing through his notes of the meeting with Graham Brochette. "What do you mean?"

"You know what I mean. The pen," White said as he searched his friend's eyes for some clue to whatever had caused him to drop his pen. "That's the third time you've lost control of your pen in as many days."

"It's slippery."

"Bullshit. When's the last time you saw your doctor?"

"A couple of months ago," Harris said, still looking at the table and shuffling his papers in an apparent effort to put an end to the conversation.

White knew it wasn't true, but chose not to say anything. Instead, he waited, letting the silence build.

"All right," Harris said, looking up from his notes. "It's been a while… but I'm fine."

White continued to wait, watching Harris's eyes.

"I'm fine," Harris insisted, refusing to return White's look.

"I want you to see the doctor."

"When did you become my mother?" Harris said. His attempt to express annoyance was contradicted by the hint of appreciation that was in Harris's eyes.

"When you became my father." It was unnecessary to say anything more. Although only ten years older than White, Harris was the major stabilizing influence in White's life. Harris understood, perhaps better than anyone, the forces that drove, and sometimes consumed, White. Before his accident, Harris had been much like White, motivated to the extent of compulsion. His accident, his fall into the grip of depression and drugs, and his recovery had changed his perspective.

A knock on the doorjamb and the entry of his investigator saved White from dispensing any further unwanted advice.

"I saw Graham Brochette downstairs," Horse said. His face was a picture of strain and concern.

"His son has a little problem," White said.

"He told me about it when he was leaving."

"I want you to pick up a copy of the police report, then go down and see what you can dig up in Matlacha."

Harris watched the exchange between White and Horse with mild consternation. "And I suppose you expect me to sit on my ass and hold down the fort." His voice left little doubt about his desire to participate in their new case.

In spite of his importance to White's firm, Harris rarely left the office except to cover routine motion hearings or sit second chair at White's trials. White justified the limitation on his active participation in investigations by emphasizing the importance of Harris's role in managing the work of White's associates. But Harris was, with increasing frequency, dropping hints that he wanted to be more active.

White considered Harris's statement for a minute before asking, "Are you up to paying a visit to Lou Hamilton?"

Lou Hamilton was a retired police officer who stayed in touch with everyone he ever met. He was the ultimate source of reliable inside information, as well as unreliable gossip if that was your thing. The local law enforcement agencies had more leaks than a pack of dogs with bad kidneys, and Hamilton knew where every dog lifted its leg.

Harris grinned at the prospect. "Me? You're going to let me do some real investigative work?"

White rolled his eyes toward the ceiling and let out a long sigh. "Yes, Harry. I'm going to let you do some real investigative work."

Harris continued to smirk at the discomfort he knew White felt when confronted with his excessively protective concern for Harris's circumstances. "I think your poor old invalid partner can handle that little task."

"Good. See if you can get with him tomorrow."

"What are you going to do?"

"First thing in the morning, I'll go over to the jail and have a chat with our new client."

4.

When the meeting with Horse and Harris ended, White left the conference room and trotted up the stairs to the apartment he shared with Leslie Halloran. It was rare for him to be home before the middle of the night, and he relished having the time to enjoy the home he had so carefully planned.

The apartment occupied the entire third floor of his warehouse. It consisted of two large bedroom suites and a spacious open-plan living area. At one end of the room was a fully equipped restaurant-grade kitchen. The dining area, with its modern cherry table that could seat twelve, was separated from the kitchen by a marble-topped breakfast bar. The center of the room was tastefully furnished with leather sofas and barrel chairs grouped in three seating areas. Persian carpets covered the dark oak floors. The room had the appearance of an art gallery or museum and could comfortably accommodate large groups. White wasn't active in local civic organizations, but he frequently made his apartment available for fund-raising events sponsored by organizations that served the community's neediest citizens.

At the end of the room opposite the kitchen was a smaller, more intimate sitting area in front of a massive brick fireplace. The fireplace wasn't part of the original warehouse, but it was a necessity for a boy from Idaho. The sixty-foot wall of the main living area was a series of French doors opening onto the wide cypress deck that extended the length of the warehouse. Fourteen-foot-high brick walls were covered with an eclectic mixture of Native American carvings, Ansel Adams photographs, modern art—all originals selected by Leslie—and a few stuffed animal heads. Two large brass sculptures stood in the center of the room.

White's private study occupied one corner of the apartment. More than anywhere else, it was here that White's other side was revealed. The walls were covered with books, mostly history books, biographies, and the classics of literature. His collection of first editions of the classics—he had several dozen—were among his most prized possessions.

&

Sherlock, White's mixed-breed Labrador retriever, a pound hound rescued from the city animal shelter just before she was scheduled to be euthanized, was waiting at the head of the stairs when White arrived. Her tail pounding against the open door sounded like someone knocking. The stairway led from White's apartment to his office on the mezzanine level of the warehouse and down to the first floor where a doggy door gave Sherlock access to the fenced yard between the warehouse and the seawall. Sherlock could easily have come down the stairs to greet White, but she never did. Instead, she preferred to wait in the apartment at the head of the stairs.

White retrieved a handful of doggy treats from the oak kitchen cabinet and held them, one by one, in front of Sherlock's nose. With each offering, Sherlock sat motionless, staring cross-eyed at the treat and drooling on the floor until White said "okay." Each treat vanished in a single gulp, and Sherlock sat patiently waiting for more.

"That's all there are," White explained when the last treat had disappeared.

Sherlock didn't believe him.

"Honest. That's all there are," White repeated.

Sherlock wasn't convinced.

Have it your way. Dogs and women. They both think they can get anything they want with a pleading look and a wag of their tails.

White poured himself a Diet Pepsi—he was a recovering alcoholic and hadn't consumed alcohol for almost seven years—squeezed two slices of lime into his drink, and walked out onto the balcony. He pulled a chair away from the glass-topped table and rolled it closer to the railing where he sat and propped his cowboy boots on the middle rail. The sun was now only a brilliant orange hemisphere on the edge of the western horizon. White never tired of the panoramic view of the river all the way to the Gulf of Mexico to the south and west of Fort Myers.

He was still wearing the suit he wore at the conclusion of the Marshall trial. Behind the facade of the tailored suits and silk shirts that he wore to court—White called it his lawyer's costume—he was still a country boy. He could wear his lawyer costume as naturally as a zebra wore its stripes, but his preferred attire was denim dungarees and a classic light blue oxford shirt. Only his custom-made cowboy boots were a constant. Typically, he would have gone straight to the bedroom he shared with Leslie and changed his clothes. Today he was too tired and preoccupied to care.

The door behind him opened, and Leslie strolled across the balcony to where White sat and leaned over and kissed him on the neck. White responded by kissing her on the cheek. "Mmmmmmm. Chauvinist pig happy to see lady lawyer."

Leslie frowned. "We're not through with that conversation, buddy."

White sighed. "I know."

Leslie sat on White's lap and put her arms around his neck. "You look like something Sherlock would drag home."

At the mention of her name, Sherlock moved closer to Leslie and pawed at her for attention. Leslie obliged.

"It's been a bitch of a day."

"You won your murder trial. You should be happy."

"Just glad to have it over with."

"So why are you so pensive?"

"Is that what I am?"

"Pensive… wistful… introspective…"

White gave her a pained smile. "I get the point."

"Immersed… engrossed… contemplative…"

White laughed. "Enough already." Regardless of what else White had on his mind, he slid easily into the banter that characterized their relationship. She understood his every mood and knew when he needed a play break.

"Dad paid big bucks for my education. I'm entitled to show it off occasionally."

"Does it always have to be at my expense?"

"Only until you tell me about Graham's visit."

White shook his head in mock exasperation. "What am I going to do with you?"

Leslie snuggled closer and whispered in his ear, "You could take me into the bedroom and ravage me."

"That sounds like a plan."

"But only after you tell me what's up."

"How about I'll tell you over dinner?"

"We can do that."

"I don't feel up to cooking tonight."

Leslie pouted. "But I was looking forward to one of the gourmet dinners you always make after you win a big case."

"I'm sorry. But Graham's son's case has me a little pre-occupied."

"That's okay. What did you have in mind?"

"We haven't been to the Lazy Gator for a while."

At the mere mention of Lazy Gator, Leslie bit her lip and fought to hold back her tears. White knew she was thinking about Billy Reynolds, whose cooking had made the Lazy Gator famous. Billy had been a volunteer counselor at the AIDS clinics where Leslie worked until he died of the disease less than a year before. They had been good friends, and his death, inevitable and in the end merciful, had been hard on her.

"It's time to remember the good things."

"You're right," she agreed as she wiped a trace of a tear from the corner of her eye. Slowly a look of wistful exuberance lit her face. "Let's go remember Billy."

"Good plan. Besides, its roadkill night at the Lazy Gator."

Leslie wrinkled her nose as if she had just inhaled some noxious fumes. "It's always roadkill night at the Lazy Gator!"

"Yeah. Fine Southern eatin'," White grinned. "You can always be sure of getting the four basic food groups—dead animal, grease, weeds, and alcohol."

"You say that like you have a right to claim the Old South as your home. You know… you don't exactly fit in among the rednecks."

"Not a problem," White responded. "All I have to do is wear a John Deere cap, scratch my ass, call all animals 'critters,' and drive me a big ol' pickup truck."

Leslie shook her head and rolled her eyes upward. "If my parents knew what their well-bred daughter was forced to endure in the name of love, they'd seriously consider having me committed."

&

The Lazy Gator started life as a fish camp on the western side of the Peace River north of Fort Myers. Its current incarnation as a dining establishment commenced when Billy Reynolds, the nephew of the owner of the land, was released from prison and, having no other job opportunities, began serving sandwiches and beer to fishermen. Soon he was preparing the fishermen's catches in his own unique ways. Over the years, Billy put the training learned while a guest of the state to better use and was soon turning the sow's ear of local wildlife into the culinary equivalent of a silk purse. No signs or other means of advertisement disclosed the presence of the Lazy Gator, but everyone in the community knew how to find it.

The menu at Billy's was as unorthodox as the rest of the establishment—there wasn't one, not even as a listing on a blackboard. For starch, you had a choice of "spuds" or "noodles," never referred to as "pasta." Your vegetable was either beans cooked with a slab of fatback or "greens," which might be spinach greens, collard greens, or dandelion greens prepared subject to Billy's whims and discretion.

The closest you could come to an order of your choice was the entrée: "meat," "fish," or "bird." Having specified your category of choice, you got whatever Billy had available—cooked however Billy chose to cook it. The sole exception to these choices was Billy's Seminole Special; gator pounded until it was tender, sautéed and served covered with a chutney of plums and peaches, making the colors of the Florida State University Seminoles. Billy loved the Seminoles.

More likely than not you dined on local game, birds, and fish, not all of which were necessarily in season at the time. Billy laughingly responded to charges that he was ignoring hunting and fishing laws by claiming that he was merely serving roadkill—animals that had already been killed by motorists—and was doing the state a favor by cleaning up its highways. How this explained the inclusion of out-of-season fish entrées on the menu was never explained, but it didn't matter. Everyone who was anyone in local government was a "member" of the fish camp, and most had probably bagged some game out of season in their own time.

White and Leslie took their usual booth against the wall at the end of the room farthest from the door. Like all the other booths, their seats were bare wood. Billy had claimed that the reason for this was that the addition had been built entirely from the remains of old fishing boats and he wanted to keep everything authentic and natural. It was a good story to justify the rustic interior to visitors, but everyone knew the real reason was that Billy was too lazy to finish the wood surfaces with varnish or urethane.

White ordered meat, greens, spuds, and his customary Diet Pepsi with lime. Leslie ordered bird, greens, noodles, and a beer. It wasn't necessary to specify the brand of beer because the Lazy Gator carried only one brand at a time. It varied depending on the price he could get from his distributor.

"Okay," Leslie said. "Now tell me about Graham."

White took a deep breath and exhaled before announcing, "Graham's son has been arrested. He wants me to defend him."

"Hmmmmmm."

"You don't sound surprised."

"I sort of figured Graham was after your services. It isn't like him to just drop by for a visit."

White nodded.

"What was his son arrested for?"

"Drugs. Possession with intent to distribute, for starters. There may be more."

"How's Graham taking it?"

"About like you'd expect."

"What's it going to mean for his nomination?" Leslie asked, forcing White to confront the question that had been troubling him since his meeting with Brochette.

"It shouldn't mean anything," White said without conviction.

"You know better than that."

"I said it *shouldn't* matter, not that it *won't* matter."

White lapsed into silence as he continued to ponder Brochette's situation. After a moment, Leslie interrupted him. "There's more, isn't there?"

"I'm afraid so," White admitted. "David is only Graham's biological son."

"As in, without the benefit of clergy?"

"Something like that."

"That's not going to help."

"Not if it comes out," White agreed.

"Will it?"

White shrugged. "There's no reason why it should. David's mother was married to someone else when David was born. There's no reason anyone should even put him together with Graham."

"But if it does come out, won't it hurt his chances for the nomination?"

"It might. But that isn't the most immediate problem."

Leslie took a swallow from her bottle of beer. "Oh?"

"If the connection between Graham and his son becomes public, it'll be impossible for the state's attorney to make any kind of deal with David. He'd be accused of bowing to the influence of the US attorney."

"Is Graham going to want to be involved in the case?"

"We talked about that. Right now, the fact that David is Graham's son isn't an issue, and there's no reason why the information should even become public. But Graham can't be involved without exposing the relationship, and that would open him to charges of interference or exercising undue influence."

"Will he be able to stay out of it?"

White shrugged. "We talked about that too. I told him that he couldn't have anything to do with the case."

"Maybe I can help."

They both understood that it was more than an offer of assistance. Leslie's participation in criminal cases was a sensitive subject, and the afternoon's tête-à-tête was still on their minds. White dealt with criminals every day, but he did not like the idea of Leslie having to deal with the same clients. As he usually did when the matter came up, White tried to ignore the issue. "What did you have in mind?"

Leslie made a movement suggesting that she was going to slam her bottle on the table, but she controlled her impulse and set it down gently. "You know *exactly* what I mean!"

White looked for assistance in the grain of the tabletop. In the courtroom, White was always in complete control. But with Leslie it was different. White knew he was being manipulated. It wouldn't have mattered, except that he also knew she was right.

"Sometimes, Lucius, you can be…" She caught herself before she said something she knew she would be sorry for. Instead, she crossed her arms and pouted.

White took a deep breath and exhaled. "You're not being fair."

"I know," she admitted, smiling subtly as if she was sorry for having played the pity card.

"You're good!" he chuckled.

"I know that too," Leslie responded, flashing her eyes coyly as she took a sip of her beer. "But you *are* being a chauvinist!"

"I prefer to think of it as being your loving and concerned boyfriend."

"That's just an excuse."

"I know," White admitted. "Let's see what comes up when I meet with David Shepard."

"Fair enough?"

"And whatever you do, you have to promise to be careful."

"Scout's honor," she said, holding up a hand with the middle finger extended.

"I believe the scout's oath requires three fingers."

"I just wanted to save you the trouble of reading between the lines."

White shook his head and chuckled again.

"So," she smiled. "Peace restored?"

"You just love manipulating me, don't you?"

"It's lost some of its challenge, but I have to stay in practice."

White leaned across the table and kissed her. "I'm lucky to have you."

"Yes, you are," Leslie agreed. "I'm a great catch. I know which fork to use for the shrimp, I can quote Shakespeare, and I still love sex. What more could you want?"

"A little modesty would be nice."

Leslie stuck her tongue out and laughed. "What you see is what you get. Boston in the parlor, and Paris in the bedroom."

"I admit it. You're a great lay."

"Such language," Leslie exclaimed as she gave him her best imitation of a look of shocked indignation.

"My apologies. I keep forgetting that you are a lady of good breeding who would never use such vulgar language."

Leslie laughed. "You're fucking right, I am!"

"What can I do to make it up to you?"

"Take me to bed."

"I can do that! I was just thinking about grabbing your ass and whispering, 'How about it?'"

"I've heard more romantic approaches, but that might work."

5.

Horse slowed his Ford Explorer as he approached the outskirts of Matlacha. At intervals of less than half a minute, bolts of lightning lit the sky, standing for a full second as the coming storm released its charge of electricity. Gusts of wind from the leading edge of the storm bent flat the sea of tall grasses covering the marsh on either side of the road between the mainland and Matlacha Pass.

Massive drops of wind-driven rain began hammering the Explorer. Within moments, he was engulfed in an unusually heavy downpour that cut visibility to less than thirty yards.

Horse pulled to a stop outside a cinder block building. A sign over the door declared it to be the Shipwreck Bar. The name was appropriate. The paint on the outside of the building was peeling in flakes the size of pancakes, and the weathered door at the top of a short stairway looked as if it was ready to collapse at any moment.

Horse retrieved a file from the passenger seat and reviewed the police report of David Shepard's arrest. The Shipwreck Bar wasn't mentioned in the report, but that didn't matter. If you need information on people who live on the fringe of civilized society, you go where they're likely to go. In Matlacha, that was the Shipwreck Bar.

As quickly as it had started, the rainstorm was over. Horse left the Explorer and headed for the door of the bar. He was wearing his usual blend-with-the-locals detective outfit: deck shoes without socks, worn jeans, and an appropriately stained sleeveless pullover worn outside his belt to conceal the 9 mm Glock in the holster at the small of his back.

Three Harley Davidsons were parked close to the building. A sign beside the door proclaimed, "No shoes. No shirt. No problem." Life is simple in Matlacha.

The rancid smell of stale beer and smoke, not all of it tobacco, assailed him as he entered the Wreck, as the establishment was known to the locals. To his right, a worn wooden bar ran the length of the narrow building. The obligatory jar of pickled hardboiled eggs and a container of beef jerky sat on the bar beside the cash register. For patrons with a more discriminating palate, Polish sausages rotated on skewers under a heat lamp.

A pool table sat in the middle of the room like a giant green mushroom. An assortment of tables with unmatched chairs lined the windowless wall to the left. At the rear, a sliding glass door opened to the commercial dock.

The bartender, a short, dark man wearing a dirty shirt and a scowl, glanced at Horse before returning to the chore of washing his bar glasses. His dour expression proclaimed that strangers rarely crossed the threshold of this bar, and those who did weren't welcome.

Three men in jeans and sleeveless denim jackets sat at a table in a dark corner of the bar. Horse couldn't make out the insignias on the backs of their jackets, but he was sure it wasn't an advertisement for Calvin Klein. The conch shell ashtray in the middle of the wooden table was overflowing with cigarette butts. Beer mugs and empty shot glasses, the drinking man's breakfast, sat in front of each man.

Two of the men watched Horse as he crossed the room, slid onto a stool at the end of the bar, and waited. The third man stood and headed for the "Buoy's" room.

Finally, the bartender headed down the bar in a way

that suggested he could have moved faster if he wanted to. "What'll you have?"

"How about a draft? Coors if you have it."

"All we got on draft is Bud." Without waiting for a response, the bartender turned away and began drawing a beer from the tap. "That'll be two bucks," he said as he put the beer down in front of Horse.

"Ah'm looking for a friend of mine," Horse said.

"So?"

Horse laid a twenty-dollar bill on the bar.

The bartender stared intently at the bill before returning his attention to Horse. "Who's your friend?"

Horse slid the bill across the bar, keeping his hand on top of it. "His name is David Shepard."

The bartender's eyes moved from the bill to Horse's face. His greedy look was replaced by one of cautious concern.

At the mention of Shepard's name, conversation at the dark corner table stopped. The bartender's gaze shifted from Horse to the table. Chair legs scraped the floor, and the sound of steel-studded motorcycle boots echoed in the suddenly silent room. Horse looked toward the mirror and watched a man approach.

"Why are you looking for David Shepard?" a voice behind him snarled.

Horse sipped his beer without turning. "I have some business with him."

"What kind of business?" the voice demanded as two more chairs pushed away from the table

"Ah'm trying to locate a mutual friend."

"That right?" the voice growled. "Well, your friend got his ass busted. And we don't need him or his buddy around here."

Horse turned on the stool and faced the other man.

He was about five feet, ten inches and two-hundred-fifty-pounds of what had probably been muscle a long time ago. He was in need of a shave and a haircut. A bath would also have been a good idea. But mostly he needed mouthwash.

The bartender reluctantly concluded that his participation in the conversation, and the reward for doing so, had ended. He cast a last covetous gaze at the bill on the bar and backed away. His eyes never left the man standing in front of Horse.

Horse leaned back, his elbows resting on the bar. His face showed no emotion as he studied the man and, just in case, gauged the distance from his foot to the man's groin. "Do you have something against my friends?"

The man crossed his arms and glared at Horse. "We don't need his kind around here."

"Why's that?"

"We got a good thing going, and the cops leave us alone. People start playing with his kind of stuff, and things get uncomfortable in a hurry. We should'a run them out a town, them and the Asian guy with the Porsche, soon as they showed up."

"Ah guess you don't like the guy with the Porsche."

"Never met him an' don't want to."

"Why's that?"

"His kind is trouble."

"You mean people who drive Porsches?"

"You know what the fuck I mean."

Horse glanced briefly toward the table before returning his attention to the man in front of him. "Tell me about the man with the Porsche."

The man looked at Horse suspiciously. "Who the fuck are you?"

"Who would you like me to be?"

The man said nothing as he apparently tried to decide

how to respond. Lacking any more appropriate answer, he asked, "You some kind of smartass?"

"I don't know. How many kinds of smartass are there?"

"Huh?"

"Forget it." Playing mind games was no fun when only one of the participants has the necessary equipment. "I'm an investigator," Horse admitted. "I work for David Shepard's attorney."

The man stared blankly at Horse before beginning to laugh. "I tol' you he wasn't the heat," he shouted at the other men between guffaws. "Fuckin' investigator," he repeated, pronouncing each syllable separately, and shaking his head.

"So, Mr. Investigator," he returned his attention to Horse. "Why'd you claim you were looking for Shepard when you already knew he was in jail?"

Horse ignored the question. "I'm looking for information on his friend."

"You mean Jackson?"

"Do you know his first name?"

"Tom, Thomas. But we call him Tom-ASS."

"What can you tell me about him?"

"Do I look like a fuckin' information booth?"

Horse examined the man before saying, "No. I suppose not. But you do look thirsty."

The man started to say something, then stopped and said, "You buyin'?"

Horse gave the man a toothy smile. He didn't have any desire to make friends with the man, but it seemed like a reasonable gesture under the circumstances. "I only drink with people I know. My name's Horse," he said as he extended his hand.

The man took Horse's hand. "Well, welcome to the Wreck, Horse. Call me Smitty." He continued to grip Horse's hand in a trial of strength. Horse's response was to continue to smile without any indication he was aware that he was being tested.

With his free hand Horse signaled the bartender with a circle in the air. The bartender put another beer in front of Horse's and his new best friend and took two more bottles to the corner table.

Smitty relaxed his grip, stepped to Horse's side, and leaned against the bar while flexing his right hand. When his circulation was restored, Smitty reached for his bottle, took a long swallow, and said, "What was the question again?"

"What can you tell me about Shepard and Jackson?"

"Oh, yeah." Smitty took another swig of beer and burped. "Morons. Both of them. But Shephard… he was just a wannabe."

"What did he want to be?"

"I don't think he knew. I guess he wanted to be like Jackson."

"And what was Jackson like?"

"Jackson… he had a major attitude problem."

"How so?"

"Just thought he was something special. Figured he was a real bad dude 'cause he worked for the guy with the Porsche."

"Who was that?"

"How the hell should I know? He showed up a couple times. Then Shepard and Jackson would go somewhere with him. When they come back, they were loaded with cash."

"Where did they go?"

"Away. That's all I know."

"When's the last time the guy with the Porsche was here?"

"At least a couple weeks. Maybe a month."

"What did they do when they were here?"

"Nothin' that I knew about. Hardly ever came in here."

"Did you ever buy anything from them?"

Smitty examined Horse suspiciously. "Like what?"

Horse raised his head slightly and inhaled deeply. "Ah can smell a lot of smoke that isn't from cigarettes."

"You sure you're not a cop?"

"Last time I checked."

"Then why do you care if anyone smokes a little weed now and then?"

"I don't care."

"So why you asking all these questions?"

"I'm just a curious fellow… and it's my job."

"Well, Mr. Curious Fellow, down here we mind our own business."

"That sounds like a good way of doing things. And I suppose the sheriff looks at things the same way."

Smitty glanced around the Wreck. He seemed to be deciding whether his companions cared that he was talking to Horse. One man at the corner table held up an empty pitcher. The bartender looked at Horse. Horse nodded his acceptance of the proposal. That appeared to conclude the negotiations and Horse regained his companion's attention.

"We got us an arrangement. We don't blow smoke in his face, and he lets us be."

"And what about Shephard and Jackson. Did they understand this arrangement?"

"If you think they was dealing grass, you need to think again."

"What kind of stuff were they dealing?"

"Got busted with a load of coke."

"And were they dealing?"

"What else would they be doing with two kilos of coke?"

"I heard it was five," a man at the corner table called out.

"Shut up, Mack," the bartender said. "You don't know what you're talking about."

Mack stood up and started toward the bar before one of his companions grabbed him by the belt and said something that couldn't be heard across the room. Mack scowled at the bartender and returned to his seat.

The possibility for an altercation having been averted, everyone's attention returned to Horse.

Horse pretended to have ignored the exchange between the bartender and the corner table and took another swallow of beer before returning his attention to Smitty. "Dealers need buyers. If you fine gentlemen weren't their customers, who were?"

The bartender moved a little closer. Maybe that twenty was still available. "They's no buyers for that stuff around here, but they's plenty of folks up in Myers that's usin' coke."

"Then why were Shepard and Jackson staying here."

"I guess you'll have to ask them."

"Uh-huh. Just one more question. Where's the guy with the Porsche from?"

"Miami… I guess. Plates was Dade County."

"Got a plate number?"

"Didn't pay that much attention."

"What color was the Porsche?"

"Dark blue."

One of the men at the corner table shouted, "It was black."

"Shut up, moron," Smitty yelled back. "It was blue, navy blue."

"What model?"

"What do I know from models? I ride a hog."

"But it was pretty new," one of Smitty's companions called out from the corner.

Horse considered the information for a minute before stepping back and throwing another twenty-dollar bill on the bar. "Another round for my friends."

As he headed for the door, the man at the bar called, "That attorney you work for. He any good?"

Horse nodded. "Yeah. He's very good."

"What's his name?" the man asked. "Maybe I'll need an attorney sometime."

"It doesn't make any difference," Horse said as he walked toward the door. "You couldn't afford him."

6.

Lou Hamilton, now five years retired from the Florida State Police, lived alone in a small cottage at the end of a gravel road on the outskirts of St. James City, a small, misnamed enclave on the south end of Pine Island. His cottage was nestled in a stand of red mangroves on the edge of Pine Island Sound. To the right of the property, a narrow channel wandered from the Sound to the small marina and restaurant that were the center of what passed for a social life in St. James City. Lou Hamilton's battered flatboat rocked gently on the shallow swells that rolled into the canal from the sound.

Harry Harris, who had avoided the morning rainstorm, drove past Matlacha to Stringfellow Road, the only road that ran the north-south length of Pine Island. As he passed through Matlacha, he spotted Horse's Explorer in front of the Shipwreck Bar and felt an influx of acid in his stomach. He hadn't done any investigative work away from the office since his accident. Interviews in the office were one thing; he was on his home turf, and he was generally only responsible for preparing witnesses for trial. But this was different. He knew White was counting on him and he didn't want to disappoint his partner. But at least he had a personal connection to Hamilton. That should make things easier.

Hamilton strolled down the gravel walkway to meet Harris as he rolled off the lift of his modified van. "How the hell are you, Harry?" Hamilton grinned. "I haven't seen you since…" Harris knew that Lou was about to refer to his accident. Guilt at having not tried to remain in contact with him was a common reaction from his old friends. Harris was accustomed to it, but that didn't make dealing with it any easier.

Lou Hamilton was tall and thin. His face was drawn, and he had deep-set dark eyes and a narrow nose. He was born in Presque Isle, Maine, about as far north and east as you can get in the continental United States, and raised in Bar Harbor, on the Maine coast. He retained the distinctive accent peculiar to the region, the languid down-east drawl found nowhere else on earth.

As usual, Lou held a cigarette in the nicotine-stained fingers of his left hand. Harris couldn't remember ever having seen Hamilton when he didn't have a lighted cigarette. Why Lou Hamilton, a four-packs-a-day smoker for more than thirty years, had not long ago succumbed to lung cancer was a mystery that would never be explained.

"It's been a while," Harris agreed, accepting Hamilton's hug. "I don't get around much anymore," he added, patting the arm of his wheelchair.

"Aw, hell, Harry. You're a better lawyer on two wheels than any of these new kids are on two legs."

"Maybe. But juries aren't always that open-minded. It wouldn't be fair to bet my clients' freedom on the feelings a jury might have about a crippled defense attorney."

Hamilton tensed at Harris's reference to himself as a cripple. The description came too close to what Hamilton thought when he first saw Harris in his wheelchair.

"I hear you partnered up with Lucius White," Hamilton said as he led Harris through the kitchen and out to the screened porch at the rear of his house. The screen was superfluous. Lizards and flies passed freely through large tears and helped themselves to the remnants of pizza, at least a week old, sitting in the box on the rusting remains of a patio table.

"Yeah. Lucius and I have been together for a couple of years. I was pretty far gone after the accident." Harris paused as the painful memory returned and slowly subsided, like a wave on the shore. "Lucius stuck by me. He helped me through rehabilitation, got me dried out, and gave me a home. I owe him a lot."

"He's a good attorney."

"And a good friend. I don't know where I'd be without him."

"But you didn't come out here to catch up on old times," Hamilton said as he dropped into a wrought iron chair. "My guess is you're interested in the guys that got picked up in the big drug bust."

"What do you know about it?"

Hamilton shrugged. "Not much."

"Come on, Lou. Nothing happens on the island that you don't know about."

"I hear things," Hamilton said as he shook a cigarette out of the pack on the table and lit up.

Harris waited until Hamilton inhaled and blew three perfect smoke rings before continuing. "What do you hear about the bust?"

"Those boys got some bad folks mad at them."

"What makes you say that?"

"They were set up, pure and simple."

"How do you know?"

"According to the sheriff's deputy, they got your basic anonymous call telling them where to look and what they were likely to find."

"Where did the call come from?"

"I don't know. I hear Paul Parker got the call on his cell phone so they couldn't get a trace on it. It was probably a cloned cell phone anyway. That's how those boys usually do it."

"Those boys?"

"Sheriff figures it was probably some sort of double-cross. The smart money says those guys ripped off a major player and this was payback."

"What smart money is there on Pine Island, Lou?"

"Ain't none, Harry. I'm talking about what the state police are saying."

"Why are they interested in a drug bust out here?"

"Two kilos is a big bust no matter where it takes place. Hell, that's even big by Miami standards. The troopers are talking about it all over the state."

"Interesting," Harris said. "Do you have any particular reason for thinking it was a setup?"

"Just good guesses, as far as I know."

"But if it was a setup, someone had to have a reason for getting Shepard and Jackson arrested. Who stood to gain by it?"

Hamilton shrugged. "I suppose that's something you'll have to figure out."

"What can you tell me about Shepard and Jackson?"

"Not much. They never came down to this end of the island. They've been around for a couple of months. Drunk or stoned most of the time, from what I hear."

"If the authorities knew they were doing drugs, why weren't they picked up earlier?"

Hamilton downed a swig of beer before answering. "Parker and the sheriff have a sort of flexible policy on drugs."

"Paul always was a realist."

"It's more than just that," Hamilton continued. "He used to be a narcotics cop. He put himself through law school while he was on the force."

"I'd forgotten that. Over in Miami, wasn't it?"

Hamilton slapped his thigh and laughed. "I said you were as sharp as ever."

Suddenly Harris closed his eyes, grimaced, and shook his head as if trying to clear water from his ears.

"Are you okay, Harry?"

"Just a little… headache."

"Do you want an aspirin?"

A minute passed, during which Harris fought waves of nausea and pain before he could reply. "No, I'm fine."

"You sure?"

Harris closed his eyes, took a deep breath, and exhaled. He opened his eyes and looked around as if trying to get his bearings. "Yeah. I've just been having these damned headaches lately." He forced a smile that he didn't feel and continued. "You were telling me about Paul's drug policy."

"Oh, yeah," Hamilton said. He eyed his friend suspiciously, seemingly satisfying himself that Harris was okay before continuing. "So, like I was saying, Paul knows where the real drug money is. Why waste the taxpayers' money on folks who aren't hurting anyone but themselves? All we have down here are artists and fishermen. They're not a problem for anyone. As long as they're just using, everyone sorta looks the other way."

"Uh-huh," Harris said. "How long have Shepard and Jackson been here?"

"I don't rightly know. Couple a months, I think."

"Do you know where they came from?"

"Naw. They just showed up."

"They ever been around here before?"

"Not that I know of."

"Have they been dealing drugs locally?"

Hamilton shook his head. "Not that I've heard. They

were just a couple of wasted stoners who shared what they had and didn't bother anyone."

"So why is there all of a sudden an interest in them?"

"They were caught with two kilos of uncut cocaine. That's felony weight."

"But you said you didn't think they were dealing."

Hamilton stood, lit another cigarette, and walked to the side of the screen porch facing the canal. "I said I hadn't *heard* anything about them dealing. There's a difference."

"Do you have any theories?"

Hamilton turned and leaned against a post supporting the roof of the porch. "Harry, you know that recreational weed is as common on Pine Island as ticks on a hound. The law enforcement agencies can't be bothered with small quantities. But the problem's been growing for the last couple of years. I don't know who, but somebody is making it easy to come by. I don't know if it's your boys, and I don't know if it's not. But dealers have been known to fight over territory."

"Do you think that's what happened?"

"If it is, someone was willing to spend a lot of money to get the competition arrested. Two kilos of uncut coke are worth a bundle."

"So you don't think they were set up by some other dealer?"

Hamilton smiled like a child with a secret he was dying to disclose. "Now that's the question, isn't it?"

"And what's the answer?"

"You need to look into the tip Paul Parker got. I think that there's more to it than he wants to let on."

"What tip is that?"

"The way I heard it, someone phoned a tip into Parker about the cocaine. Then Parker sent the sheriff out to arrest your guys."

"Wait a minute. Did you say that Parker expected the sheriff to arrest Shepard and Jackson based on nothing more than an anonymous tip?"

"That's what I heard."

7.

Even before he arrived at the county jail, White had a feeling that something wasn't right. So far, he knew next to nothing about his client and even less about the circumstances of his arrest. His queasiness wasn't based on anything he could articulate; just an overwhelming sense that he was getting into something much bigger than a simple drug possession case. It was the same uneasy sensation he had after the meeting with Brochette, only now it was stronger.

His thoughts returned to what Brochette's son's case could mean for his nomination to be deputy assistant US attorney general. Leslie was right. Things could easily be blown out of proportion. It wasn't as if he and Brochette were close, or that he felt an obligation to save his nomination. But he did respect the man and, more importantly, he felt strongly about the responsibilities of the office to which he had been nominated. They made a good fit in an imperfect system, and he sincerely hoped that Brochette's nomination would be confirmed.

White's thoughts returned to David Shepard when he arrived at the jail. He drove into the parking lot, pulled his pickup truck into a visitor's parking spot, and headed for the main entrance.

At the reception desk, White showed his Florida Bar membership card, signed the register, and handed his briefcase to the desk sergeant for inspection.

"Who you here to see?" the sergeant asked without looking up.

"David Shepard."

The sergeant said something unintelligible under his breath, consulted a three-ring binder, and picked up the telephone.

"Lawyer's here to see David Shepard… Yeah, I'll tell him," the sergeant said, making a note in the visitor's log. "Take a seat. Someone will come to get you."

White retreated to a plastic seat in the featureless waiting area. The only interruption in the monotony of the pale gray walls was the cork bulletin board containing job postings and a half dozen wanted posters. White opened his briefcase and studied his notes of the meeting with Graham Brochette until he was interrupted by the sound of a door opening.

"Mr. White?" the jail deputy asked.

"That's me."

"I'm Deputy Lipshutz. Mr. Parker told us to expect you."

"That's nice of Paul."

"Did the sergeant give you any trouble?"

"I don't think he's had his Happy Meal today, if that's what you mean."

Deputy Lipshutz chuckled as he led White through another door. The ominous clang of steel on steel as the jail cell door closed reverberated down the sterile gray hallway.

The interview room at the end of the hall could have been on the back lot of any television studio. Two chairs faced each other across a steel table bolted to the floor. Bars covered the high window at one end of the room. The walls were the same gray color as the chairs, table, and floor. Two lights in wire-protected fixtures hung from the ceiling, just out of reach of anyone in the room.

David Shepard sat upright in the metal chair on the far side of the steel table. At six feet and one-hundred-fifty-pounds, he was taller and thinner than White expected. His face, still showing remnants of a summer tan, wore a two-day stubble. His medium-brown hair was pulled back in what passed for the beginning of a ponytail. He stared at White with bloodshot eyes, unsure who the visitor was or why he was here.

White pulled a chair from the side of the table opposite Shepard and sat down. "My name is Lucius White. I'm your lawyer."

Shepard's eyes shifted between White and the guard who could be seen through the window of the closed door. "You a public defender?" he asked suspiciously, showing none of the false bravado White expected.

"No. I'm a private attorney," White said as he opened his briefcase and removed a yellow legal pad.

The wary look in Shepard's eyes gave way to an expression that bordered on fear. "Who hired you?"

It wasn't a question White expected, nor one he was prepared to answer. "Someone who's concerned about you."

Shepard continued to stare at White as if he was trying to comprehend what he had just heard.

"Is that a problem?"

Shepard ignored White's question as he stood and began pacing around the room. When he reached the wall, he stopped and, without turning, asked, "How soon do I get out of here?"

"What makes you think you're getting out of here any-time soon?"

"You're going to get me out, aren't you?"

"We'll see."

Shepard turned to face White. "You've *got* to get me out of here."

"Why?"

"Why?" Shepard exploded. "Isn't that what you're here for?"

"I'm here to represent you."

Shepard stared at White as if trying to understand a complex riddle. Slowly he returned to the table and stood opposite White where he chewed on his lip before announcing, "You don't have to worry. I'm not going to make any deal to get out."

As he considered Shepard's comment, the foreboding feeling that accompanied him as he drove to the jail returned. "Why would I worry about that?"

"*Jesus Christ*. Don't you know anything?"

"What am I supposed to know?"

Shepard returned to pacing the room, shaking his head and muttering. "Jesus. Oh, God." Finally, he returned his attention to White and repeated, "You've got to get me out of here."

"You already said that. But that's not something I control. The judge decides whether to let you out."

"But they've got nothing on me. I didn't do anything."

"That's not what the police report says."

Shepard swallowed twice before responding. "It's a frame-up. I didn't do anything."

"According to the police report, you had two kilograms of cocaine."

"That's bullshit."

"And I suppose you've never done drugs?"

"What does that have to do with anything?"

White put down his pen, crossed his hands on the metal table, and stared coldly at his client.

"What?" Shepard demanded.

"David," White began, calm but stern. "Right now, I'm the only person standing between you and the next ten or more years in the state penitentiary. If you want to cop an attitude, that's fine with me. But if you do, you'd better get used to bending over for someone named Big Bubba.

"Now, the next words out of your mouth are going to determine whether you get represented by me, or some public defender who graduated from law school last week and already has fifty cases on his desk. He may get around to you the second Thursday after hell freezes over. So, what's it going to be?"

Shepard remained standing, glaring at White and clenching and unclenching his fists. Anger and panic were fighting each other for control.

After thirty seconds of silence, White picked up his legal pad, put it in his briefcase, and began to close the lid.

"Wait."

White paused and looked at Shepard.

Shepard stared at the floor and remained silent as he shuffled to his chair and sat down.

White remained standing by the door.

Shepard fidgeted in his chair, still refusing to make eye contact.

White waited.

It was an old game. The first one to speak loses. White was a master of the game. It was important that Shepard know who was in charge, so the game continued.

Finally, Shepard looked at White. "What do you want to know?"

White returned to his seat opposite Shepard. "First of all, I don't care what you did or didn't do. It's not my job to judge you. My job is to keep you from being convicted."

Shepard seemed to relax.

"In fact, I don't even want to know what you did."

Shepard raised his head and stared at White. "Why?"

"When your case goes to trial, I may have to let you

testify. You're going to want the jury to let you off, and you may be tempted to lie."

"But…" Shepard interrupted.

White held up a hand. "Hear me out. If I know you're going to lie, I can't let you testify. That's why it's sometimes better if I don't know the truth."

Shepard appeared to be confused.

"I know it may not make much sense, but you're going to have to trust me."

Shepard responded with a look that seemed to indicate understanding, but he remained silent.

"Let's start with how you knew the other guy, Tom Jackson."

Shepard drew back and sat up straighter. "How do you know about him?"

"I read the police report."

"Yeah. I guess you would."

"So?"

"So what?"

"So how did you meet Jackson?"

Shepard looked away, seemingly trying to avoid looking at White. "I hooked up with him in Marathon."

"Where in Marathon?"

"What difference does it make?"

"Just answer my question."

"I don't know."

"Yes, you do."

Shepard looked from side to side, anywhere but at White, as he seemed to search for an answer.

"It's a simple question."

"I met Jackson in jail," Shepard spat. "There. Are you satisfied?"

"It's a start. Why were you in jail?"

"They picked me up for smoking grass. The pecker-heads kept me in jail all weekend."

"What did you do when you got out of jail?"

"I just hung around."

"With Jackson?"

"Yeah."

White scribbled a note and waited. As the seconds passed, the silence took on a power of its own. Shepard shifted nervously in his chair, waiting for White to say something.

"How did you end up in Matlacha?"

Shepard pondered the question as if he was trying to dredge up a long-buried explanation before responding. "We were tired of the Keys."

"But why Matlacha?"

Shepard paid another brief visit to some secret place in his memory before saying, "Jackson said he used to work here."

"Doing what?"

Shepard erupted from his chair and began pacing. "Jesus, man. I don't know. What does that have to do with anything?"

"I'm just asking questions."

Shepard returned to his chair and rubbed the back of his neck with both hands. "I don't know. I didn't ask, and he didn't say."

"You're lying."

Shepard froze. Either the question was unexpected, or the answer contained something Shepard didn't want White to know. Either way, it was important.

"David?"

Shepard said something to himself before responding. "He just hung out here when he was doing dope. He said no one would bother us here."

"What do you mean?"

"He said everyone here uses something, and the cops don't care unless you're dealing."

White suddenly changed the topic. "Tell me about the arrest."

Shepard stared at White. "What do you mean?"

"Where were you when you were arrested?"

"At home."

"Whose home?"

Shepard continued to pace. "Jackson rented the place."

"What happened when the sheriff came to the house?"

Shepard ran both his hands through his hair. When that didn't yield an answer, he shrugged.

"Did they knock, or break in?"

"They knocked."

"Who let them in?"

"I don't know. I guess maybe I did."

"What did they say?"

"They grabbed me and said we were under arrest."

"Just like that? As soon as you opened the door?"

"Yeah. Maybe. I don't remember."

"Did he have a warrant for your arrest?"

"I don't know. I was so surprised by everything."

"Did they read you your rights?"

Shepard fidgeted, looking at the table, walls, and doors, anywhere but at White. Finally, he answered. "Yeah. I guess so."

"What did they do then?"

"They went into Jackson's room and came back with the stuff."

"The cocaine?"

Shepard hesitated as if he couldn't bring himself to acknowledge what had been discovered. Finally, he nodded and, in a weak voice, said, "Yeah."

"Did you see where the deputies found the drugs?"

"We were all in the other room."

"Are you sure you were placed under arrest *before* the drugs were found?"

For half an hour White continued to ask Shepard questions about his time in Matlacha and the circumstances of his arrest. When it became apparent that Shepard's concentration had been exhausted, White placed his legal pad in his briefcase, closed the lid. and stood to leave.

Shepard watched him pack. He seemed to want to say something, but he didn't know what it was. As White knocked on the door, signaling the guard that he was ready to leave, Shepard blurted, "What do you think?"

White turned and, for a moment, thought about David's question. Whatever he said would be meaningless. He simply didn't know enough. Maybe after the next interview he could give Shepard an answer. But that depended on how cooperative, and honest, Shepard was. If he expected Shepard to tell him what he needed to know he would need an incentive. Finally, White said, "You're in deep shit, David. I'll get back to you."

8.

White returned to his office shortly before noon. He crossed the mezzanine and picked up a handful of telephone messages and the cup of coffee that Matthews offered. No matter when White arrived in the office, Matthews had a fresh cup of coffee waiting. Perhaps it was a special kind of telepathy that had grown out of their years together. Or maybe it was true, as Matthews claimed, that it was part of the juju she brought with her from her native Jamaica.

Eric Gaustad, one of White's newest associates, trudged up the open stairway from the first floor to the mezzanine.

"Have you got a minute, Lucius?"

White looked up from the pink message slips.

"Judge Carlin's office just called. He's set an emergency hearing for 2:30 on the Donaldson case. I have a deposition that's going to run all afternoon. No one else is available, and I was wondering if…"

White groaned. This was the kind of office problem Harry Harris usually handled. The fact that Harris could no longer try cases didn't stop him from covering routine hearings, most of which concerned nuisance motions filed by opposing counsel for the primary purpose of increasing their billable hours. Gaustad's request was a reminder of how much they all depended on Harris to keep things running smoothly and allow White to concentrate on their most significant cases.

"Sure, Eric. Come into my office and fill me in."

&

White laid his briefcase on his conference table, dropped the handful of pink message slips on his desk, and wearily sank into his leather chair. He was leaning back in his chair, rubbing his eyes, when Harry Harris rolled into his office, followed by Horse McGee. Harris carried his ever-present coffee cup bearing the words "Hell on Wheels." Strangers, seeing Harris with the cup for the first time, assumed it was someone's idea of a bad joke. In fact, Harris had the cup made for himself as a sort of declaration of his recovery.

Harris rolled to his customary place by the conference table.

Horse folded himself onto the sofa in the corner of White's office.

"How'd the hearing go?" Harris asked.

Still rubbing his eyes, White said, "Judge Carlin is a judicial moron."

"That good?"

White continued, shaking his head. "Ten years on the bench and the man still doesn't understand the meaning of a controlling precedent."

"And you're just now finding that out?"

"I never had a case with him before."

"You've gotten too accustomed to dealing with federal judges."

"At least they know the law."

"Now you know what the lawyers downstairs have to deal with," Harris said, referring to White's associates and the other lawyers who shared his office, all of whom had offices on the first floor of the converted warehouse.

"The state court judges can't all be that stupid," White said, more a question than a statement.

"No," Harris agreed. "Carlin is in a league of his own."

"At least I know what Eric is up against," White said. "I was beginning to have my doubts about him when he started complaining about Carlin. Now I understand."

White's frustration was so out of character that Harris couldn't help but chuckle.

"Don't laugh," White said. "The next time we need someone to cover an emergency hearing, I'm sending you."

"Oh, no," Harris said, leaning away in mock terror. "Anything but that."

White picked up the stack of messages on his desk—a sign he was through with the topic of Judge Carlin—and began thumbing through them. "So, what do you have?" he asked, glancing at Horse as he finished sorting the pink slips.

"Graham was right about his kid." There was a hint of sadness in Horse's voice.

White leaned back in his desk chair. "You sound disappointed."

"Maybe I am. I was hoping to find something we could work with."

"Or some redeeming quality we could report to Graham," White said.

"Maybe that too. Graham's a good man. It must be tough on him having to deal with his son's problems."

White nodded a silent agreement. "So, what do you have?"

"Shephard's had trouble wherever he's been. Before I went down to Matlacha, I ran a check on him. He's been picked up a couple of times for vagrancy and public intoxication."

"Drugs?"

"Maybe. He'd always finished off whatever he was using, or gotten rid of it before he was picked up. He spent a weekend in the Marathon slammer on a pot charge, but they kicked him and dropped the charges."

"David told me about that. Anything else?"

"Like what?"

"Jobs?"

"Nothing long term. Some bartending. And, for a while, he worked on the crew of charter fishing boats."

White narrowed his eyes at the mention of the boat.

"Legitimate, as far as I can tell. But it's not uncommon for the boat captains to run a little contraband. There could be something there… but it wasn't obvious."

"Check it out," White said.

Harris made a note on the case file "to do" list.

"Any history of violence?" Harris asked Horse.

"Not that I found yet."

"Did you come up with anything in Matlacha?"

"Very little," Horse said. "I started with a visit to a bar that caters to the least upstanding of the locals."

"Anything?"

"Met one of the local bikers. He didn't have much use for Shepard or Jackson. Thought they were both morons and was glad to have them out of town."

"Why?"

"Probably has his own business going."

"Competition?"

"Don't think so. My guess is that the bikers deal in weed. The last thing they need is federal storm troopers messing with their cozy little lifestyle."

"So Shepard and Jackson were operating on their own."

"I didn't say that. I'm not sure they were dealing anything. I don't know if they were doing anything drug-related in Matlacha—except hiding out and getting stoned."

"That's not much."

"No," Horse agreed. "But my biker buddy said someone showed up occasionally in a blue Porsche with a Dade County plate. Then Shepard and Jackson would disappear for a while and come back loaded with cash."

"What do you think?"

"It sounds like they could be couriers."

"Then why were they still holding two kilos of uncut cocaine when they were busted?"

"Maybe they weren't able to complete a delivery."

"Or maybe they decided to go into business for themselves with someone else's inventory."

Horse rubbed his chin and looked at White. "Then they're playing a dangerous game. Ripping a dealer off for two kilos of coke tends to shorten life expectancy."

"You're right. Even Shepard and Jackson can't be that stupid. So the only logical conclusion is that they got busted before they were able to finish doing their jobs."

"Either that or they were being set up."

"But no dealer is going to invest that much in a setup when a fraction of that amount would have the same result."

"There is one other possibility. What if they were being set up by some law enforcement agency. *They* could be using drugs that had already been confiscated—knowing that they'd get them back after the raid."

"That explains everything we know."

"But it doesn't answer the most important question. What agency would have any reason for setting up a couple of stoned, overgrown delinquents?"

White made a snorting sound. "Anything else?"

"I checked out the house where they got arrested. Not much more than a glorified shack stuck back into the mangroves. The landlord said they had the place for three months and always paid their rent on time… in hundred-dollar bills."

White made a note on his legal pad and continued. "Any nearby boat docks?"

"If you can call it that. There was a trail through the mangroves to a thirty-foot pier. There were a couple of rotting lines hanging from the cleats, but no sign of recent use."

"So, you don't think they're running anything by boat?"

"Not with anything they kept at their shack. And I don't think they'd keep a boat at the city marina."

"Can we rule out offshore pickups?"

Horse shrugged. "Doesn't seem likely. What did you get from our client?"

"Not much. He claims he didn't do anything, but I didn't expect him to say anything else. He did say one interesting thing, though."

Horse and Harris waited.

"He said the deputies went straight to Jackson's room and found the drugs."

"So they already knew where to look."

"Seems like it. But I'm not even sure there was anything to be found. No one actually saw the deputies find the stuff."

"Do you think it was planted during the search?"

"It could have been."

"Did David say anything useful?" Harris asked, his pen poised over his pad.

"It's too soon to know what's useful and what isn't. Getting a straight answer from him was damn near impossible. I've had more productive conversations with Sherlock."

White stood and went to the mini-refrigerator behind his desk, retrieved a Diet Pepsi, and, with a look toward Horse and Harris and a glance toward the fridge, asked the others if they wanted anything. They didn't. He popped the top and took a swallow before continuing. "It was almost as if he was trying to follow a script, but I wasn't asking the questions he was expecting."

"Maybe he and Jackson agreed to a common story just in case they got caught."

"It's possible. Find out who's representing Jackson. I want to talk to him."

Harris made another note on his "to-do" list.

"One thing is certain. Shepard's scared."

"When did we ever represent a first-timer who wasn't scared shitless."

"Never happens. But Shepard isn't exactly a first-timer."

"Maybe not. But a couple of days in the local slammer isn't the same as five to ten years in a state or federal prison. The person I met hadn't even started thinking about doing prison time. He wanted me to get him out for some other reason. He was afraid of something that could happen to him in jail."

"Like what?"

"I don't know. He kept saying that I had to get him out of there. But he made a point of saying that he wasn't going to cut a deal."

"Had you asked him about a deal?"

"No. He just spit it out."

"Any idea what he meant?"

"Not yet." White rubbed his eyes as if the act would squeeze some useful thought into his consciousness. "What do you think, Harry?"

"I can't say anything without meeting him, but I don't think they stole the coke."

White leaned back with his attention focused on Harris.

"Lou Hamilton thinks it was a setup." As he spoke, Harris continued to study the police report. "There's no mention of weapons of any kind."

"Two kilos of coke and no weapons. That is odd."

"That's what I think," Harris said. "Also, Lou said the authorities got an anonymous tip telling them where to look, and what they were likely to find."

"That's consistent with what David said about the search."

"But there was something curious about the tip." Harris thumbed the edges of his legal pad before continuing. "According to Lou, the tip was received by Paul Parker and passed on to the sheriff."

"Why would someone call Parker instead of the sheriff?"

Harris shrugged.

"What do you think it means?"

"Maybe something. Maybe nothing."

"I can always count on you to narrow things down, Harry."

Harris chuckled. "Do you want to crack wise or hear what else I think?"

White laughed. "Sorry. Go on."

"If it's a setup, it isn't just about Shepard and Jackson. The way I figure it, two kilos of coke is too valuable to be planted if all you want to do is get someone busted. An arrest could have been orchestrated with a couple of grams. Whoever planted the drugs had something else, something bigger, in mind."

"Like what?"

"It beats the hell out of me. But it could explain David's comment about not making a deal."

"How's that?"

Harris studied his notes before responding. "Did you tell David that his father had retained you?"

"No. I wasn't sure how much he knew about Graham."

"What did you tell him?"

"I said I'd been retained by someone who was concerned about him."

Harris's lips curled into the self-satisfied smile of a man who has just discovered the secret to understanding women. "So…" Harris hesitated before continuing. "For all he knew, you could have been retained by whoever he was working for."

White slapped the table. "Of course! Why didn't I think of that? And he wanted to assure his employer that he wasn't going to talk. But why?"

9.

The sweet fragrance of blue spruce filled the apartment when White stepped off the elevator from his office. Leslie was seated cross-legged on the floor in front of the fireplace, admiring her Christmas tree. "What do you think?"

White surveyed the fourteen-foot tree Leslie had special ordered from a grower in Vermont. "It's a little smaller than I expected," he said with a smile.

Leslie grinned innocently. "I didn't want to overdo it."

Christmas was Leslie's special time, and each year Leslie's decorations become more lavish. The seasonal scenes she created on the deck facing the river were legendary. Every year the deck was featured in one or more local newspapers and brought a nightly flotilla of boats.

"What are you going to do for decorations?"

"I think I'll manage," Leslie said, tilting her head to indicate a dozen boxes of assorted sizes piled against the wall. Every year she celebrated Christmas with new ornaments and a different theme.

"What are we doing this year?" After five years, White had finally learned to stay out of the way.

"This year we're going retro. I found a place that carries all kinds of old-style ornaments. The whole tree will be covered with bubbling lights."

White smiled and shook his head.

"What?" Leslie demanded happily.

White laughed. "You and Christmas."

"Just you wait," Leslie said, returning to the arrangement of the Christmas tree skirt she spent the past year painstakingly embroidering. Each year she embroidered a new tree skirt, which was later sold at a charity auction on New Year's Eve. Last year, her tree skirt had enriched the local drug treatment center by a thousand dollars.

"I'm sure it'll be beautiful."

"You bet your ass."

White wandered to the breakfast bar. "Would you like something to drink?"

"Some white wine would be nice." Leslie stood and crossed the room. White smiled at the sight of her breasts bouncing freely beneath her thin silk pullover. "Like what you see, sailor?" she asked as she slid onto a stool by the bar.

Sherlock followed her and sat at her regular post at the end of the breakfast bar from which she could watch both White and Leslie. Food could come from anywhere. It paid to be prepared.

White opened a bottle of chilled white wine and poured a glass for Leslie before opening a can of Diet Pepsi for himself.

Leslie sipped her wine. "What was your day like?"

"I went to see Graham's son at the county lockup."

Leslie waited.

"I don't know," he said in response to her unasked question. "He wasn't very willing to talk at first... but he came around when I threatened to walk out and leave his fate in the hands of a public defender."

"So he's not entirely stupid."

"Not entirely," White agreed. "But he's not in touch with the reality of his situation either."

"How so?"

"Old story. What's he doing in jail? He didn't do it."

"Did he? Do it, I mean."

White shrugged. "Too soon to tell. He's involved, but I

have a feeling there's a lot more to this than a simple drug bust."

"Like what?"

"I don't know. Right now, it's just a feeling, but Harry agrees."

Leslie took another sip of wine before responding. "Harry has good instincts about that sort of thing."

&

Graham Brochette answered his private line on the second ring. "I hoped I'd hear from you today, Lucius," Brochette began without preamble. *Sometimes I hate caller identification. Doesn't anyone say hello anymore,* White thought as Brochette continued. "Do you have anything yet?"

"Not much. Just some background."

"Have you seen David?"

"I went over to the jail this morning."

"How is he?"

"As well as can be expected. He's anxious to get out."

"That's hardly a surprise."

Something in his voice, something that White knew but couldn't define, caught White's attention. "He's afraid."

Brochette waited longer than expected before responding. "Afraid of what?"

"Afraid of being in jail."

"Oh?"

White waited, certain that Brochette knew something he wasn't saying. He also knew he couldn't force Brochette to reveal anything he wasn't ready to discuss.

Brochette broke the silence. "But they denied him bail at his arraignment."

"Is that what he told you?"

"I told you, I didn't talk to him. That's what his mother said when she told me he'd been arrested. Isn't that right?"

"Not exactly. The state's attorney asked for two hundred fifty thousand. I asked for a new bail hearing, and we got lucky. The judge had a cancellation on his calendar, and Paul Parker agreed to an expedited hearing tomorrow morning."

"That's great," Brochette said. Relief permeated his voice. "I'll put up whatever bond is necessary."

"There may be more to it."

Anxiety returned to Brochette's voice. "What's the problem?"

"David doesn't have any ties to the community, and he's facing serious jail time. He's an obvious flight risk."

"Can you get him released into my custody?"

"Maybe," White said. "But that would mean disclosing your relationship to David. Admitting you have an illegitimate son won't exactly help your nomination."

Brochette paused as if the problem hadn't occurred to him. "I... appreciate your concern."

"It could get messy if anyone wanted to block your nomination."

"I... know."

"Before we commit to disclosing anything, we need to figure out a few things." For ten minutes, Brochette listened somberly as White summarized his interview with Shepard and Harris's theory that the drugs had been planted as part of a setup.

After a long pause, Brochette concluded, "Harry is probably right."

"Probably," White agreed.

"We have to get him out of jail." Brochette's tone made it clear that he was now speaking as an attorney rather than just as a concerned father.

White paused, considering what to say next. *What does he know that he isn't telling me?* White had represented lawyers before, and it was never easy. They all thought they knew everything and questioned every decision. Worse yet, Brochette was a prosecutor who clearly did know criminal law. But his experience was in federal court. Although customs and practices in federal and state courts are similar, experience in one isn't always applicable to the other. White needed to establish the right relationship with Brochette early in the case.

"If you want me to represent David, you'll have to accept the fact that I decide what is and isn't important."

As he waited for a response, White could imagine what Brochette was thinking. United States attorneys are accustomed to being the final authority in their cases.

"Okay," Brochette finally agreed. "But he could be in real danger."

"What danger could he be in as long as he's in jail? If someone is out to hurt him, jail would be the safest place for him."

"I know, but he's…" Brochette suddenly stopped. "Never mind."

"He's what, Graham?"

"It's nothing. Just promise me you'll get David out of jail."

"That may not be possible."

"Why not?"

"He's charged with a major felony. The courts take these kinds of drug charges seriously down here."

"I am a United States attorney. Surely you can convince the judge to release him into my custody?"

"Except you aren't a parent. Only his mother is, and I doubt if the judge will release him to the custody of a parent who lives outside the jurisdiction."

"But I am his father."

"Only right now nobody but you and his mother know that."

Brochette hesitated for a long moment before responding. "Then maybe it's time they did."

"Are you sure you're ready for the consequences?"

Brochette responded without hesitation. "I told you, I'll do anything I have to do to protect him."

"You could be risking your nomination for nothing."

"What do you mean?"

"Disclosing your relationship may not be enough to get David out of jail. Biology doesn't make you a legal parent, and even if you are willing to assume custody, there's no guarantee the judge will go along with it."

"I understand," Brochette said. He had been involved in enough hearings in which he opposed bail to know what the state's attorney was likely to argue.

"And accepting custody makes you involved."

Brochette understood White's concern but said nothing.

White abruptly changed the subject. "Why would David refuse to even consider making a deal?"

When Brochette didn't respond immediately, White prodded, "Graham?"

"He… I… I do not know."

But you know something you aren't telling me.

"We have to get him out." There was an urgency in Brochette's voice that captured White's attention. If it means I become involved…" Brochette's voice trailed off into his private thoughts. "Do what you can. Whether he knows it or not, my son needs me."

You may wish it was otherwise, White thought but didn't say.

10.

Paul Parker was already seated at the prosecutor's table when White entered the courtroom.

Graham Brochette followed White and took a seat in the last row. White moved down the center aisle of the courtroom and uttered what passed for a "good morning" to Parker before laying his briefcase on the defense table. *Why is Parker handling a routine bail hearing?*

Parker nodded to White, but his eyes never left Brochette.

Brochette looked straight ahead without giving any indication that he knew who Parker was.

White finally approached Parker, pulled him aside, and asked, "What's your position on bail, Paul?"

"Same as at his arraignment."

"At his arraignment, David was represented by a public defender," White said with a good-natured smile, a not-so-subtle reminder that he practiced law at a different level than the overworked public defenders. In the courtroom, White and Parker played their assigned roles as bitter enemies, but outside the courtroom, they were friends. They frequently fished together, and Parker was a regular in White's monthly high-stakes poker game. Their politics couldn't have been more different, but Parker always knew where to find snook, and he gambled away sizeable sums with sufficient regularity that his political views could be overlooked.

"What did you have in mind?"

"I'm thinking about a release on his own recognizance."

Parker rolled his eyes and chuckled. "You never give up, do you, Lucius?"

David Shepard, still wearing the orange jumpsuit worn by all prisoners in the county jail, was ushered in by a bailiff and thrust roughly into a chair at the defense table. Shepard was pale and tense as he grabbed White's sleeve. "You've got to get me out of here."

"That's what we're here for."

"You don't understand. You've got to get me out of here. If you don't, they'll kill me."

Before White could respond, the door to the judge's chambers opened. The bailiff sprang to his feet and intoned the time-honored call to order: "All rise. The Court for the Twentieth Circuit of the State of Florida is now in session. The honorable Judge Stanley Mitchell presiding." The bailiff had only uttered a few words when the judge said, "Be seated," waved everyone to their seats, and nodded to the court reporter, indicating that he was ready to go on the record.

"Let's make this quick, gentlemen. Appearances, please?"

White and Parker rose and stated their names and the names of the party they represented.

"Okay. This is a bail hearing for David Shepard, arrested on the charges of possession of a controlled substance, to wit, cocaine, and possession with intent to distribute a controlled substance, to wit, cocaine. What's your position on bail, Mr. Parker?"

"Your Honor, this is a very serious crime. Drugs are permeating every segment of our society and…"

"Cut the crap, Mr. Parker," Judge Mitchell said. "I've already heard my sermon for the week, and there's no one here for you to impress with the righteous indignation speech. Besides, you've used that spiel so many times that I have it memorized. Now. What's your position on bail?"

"Your Honor, the state requests bail in the amount of two hundred fifty thousand dollars."

White was immediately on his feet. "Your Honor. The state's bail request is unjustified. My client has no felony record. His father, United States Attorney Graham Brochette, is prepared to take custody of his son."

At the mention of Brochette's name, Shepard spun around in his chair and stared at his father. Brochette met the stare and held Shepard's eyes as he responded with an almost imperceptible nod.

Paul Parker could not have been prepared for the surprise announcement that Brochette was Shepard's father. For a moment, he stared at Brochette, then shifted his attention to White.

White smiled back at him. *Gotcha.*

The judge slid his glasses down his nose and stared over the edge of the frame, first at White and then at Brochette. As his gaze shifted to Brochette, his jaw tightened. He returned his attention to White and gave him a look that indicated he wasn't happy about the unexpected involvement of a United States attorney.

"In this case, I request that the court release my client on his own recognizance."

"Your Honor," Parker jumped in, still shaken by Brochette's unexpected appearance as a participant in the proceedings. "The fact that the defendant's father is a respected member of the legal community is irrelevant. The defendant was in possession of two kilograms of cocaine when he was arrested."

"Actually," White interrupted, "the *substance* that was seized"—he made a point of not admitting it was cocaine—"was in the possession of one of my client's roommates. It was in a bedroom my client didn't share and over which he had no control."

Parker was about to say something more when the judge raised his hand and addressed Graham Brochette. "Where do you live, Mr. Brochette?"

Brochette stood and said, "My home is in Tampa."

"That's outside the jurisdiction of this court."

"I understand the court's concern."

"I don't normally release a defendant to a location outside the jurisdiction," Judge Mitchell continued as if he had not heard Brochette.

Brochette remained standing without saying anything.

Judge Mitchell removed his glasses and pinched the bridge of his nose. "However, in as much as you're an officer of the court, I believe I can rely on you to properly supervise the defendant." The judge's reference to Shepard as the defendant rather than as Brochette's son, an indication that he wanted the record to show his decision wasn't based on Shepard's relationship to a US attorney, wasn't lost on the parties.

Parker slumped into his chair.

"Accordingly, I'm going to order bail in the amount of twenty-five thousand dollars, cash or bond, and release the defendant to the custody of his father."

White smiled. David Shepard sighed. Graham Brochette gave no reaction.

Judge Mitchell continued. "I am, however, going to place the defendant under house arrest and order that he wear an ankle monitor."

Parker stood, slowly but with some semblance of authority. He seemed to have grown despondent over his loss but now had one last card to play. "Your Honor. An ankle monitor won't do any good. The range of our monitors is only twenty miles. And they use a different radio frequency in Tampa, so they can't monitor him."

Judge Mitchell pondered this new dilemma for a moment before speaking. "Instead of an ankle monitor, I order that the defendant call the probation office once every six hours from a telephone number that can be verified by the probation officer."

White made a note on his legal pad.

"Anything else?"

White stood. "Yes, your honor. My client requests an immediate probable cause hearing."

Parker jumped to his feet. "Your Honor, we're already preparing to submit this case to a grand jury for a formal indictment."

"What do you say, Mr. White?"

"You know what they say, Your Honor. 'A prosecutor can indict a ham sandwich.' We contend that the arrest was improper as a matter of law. That's a question that has to be addressed by Your Honor."

"He's got you there, Mr. Parker."

Parker quickly consulted his files before returning his attention to the judge. "Your Honor, you're already granted Mr. White's bail request. His client will be free until there is a trial. There is no need to burden the court with another unnecessary hearing."

Judge Mitchel slid his glasses down his nose and looked at Parker over the rim. "Is that the best you can do, Mr. Parker?"

Parker opened his mouth and started to speak.

"Save it, Mr. Parker." The judge consulted his calendar. "You're in luck, gentlemen. I have a cancellation on my calendar. Probable cause hearing is set for tomorrow—two o'clock. Anything else?"

"Yes, Your Honor," White said. "Given the short time

before the probable cause hearing, there may be some problem in locating the necessary witnesses... particularly the police officers who obtained the search warrant and the officers who searched my client's home and made the arrest. We ask that the state's attorney be ordered to produce all of these officers at the hearing."

"Any problem with that, Mr. Parker?" Judge Mitchell said in a voice that made it clear he wasn't asking a question.

"No problem, Your Honor."

"So ordered. Anything else?"

"No, Your Honor," White and Parker said in unison.

"Then we're adjourned."

&

As they left the courtroom, Parker signaled White to the side.

"You do like coming up with your little surprises, don't you, Lucius?"

"You mean Graham?"

"Of course I mean Graham!"

"I didn't know you'd be handling the hearing. I'm sorry I didn't have a chance to give you a heads-up."

"That would have been nice."

"Was there something else you wanted to tell me?"

"Yeah. As a matter of fact, there was. The attorney for your client's accomplice called me the morning he was bailed out."

"About what?"

"Bail. What else?"

"I hear you only asked for fifty thousand for him?"

"That's right."

"Why fifty for him and two fifty for Shepard?"

"Shepard didn't offer an incentive for reduced bail."

"And Jackson did?"

Parker shrugged. "He mentioned some things that were interesting."

"What was he offering?"

"I'll let you know when we have a deal."

"Who's his attorney?"

"Diane Lindsey."

White raised an eyebrow.

"You know her?"

"Yeah. She's good."

"None better for drug cases. You might even learn a thing or two from her."

"It's possible. How did he get Diane to represent him?"

Parker shrugged. "Same as anyone else, I suppose. He paid her."

"But how would he even know who Diane is?"

"Maybe you should ask Diane."

"Maybe I should."

White started to leave when he paused and turned. "Do you have a record of the calls Jackson made from jail?"

The question seemed to confuse Parker.

"If he got Diane to represent him, he has to have called someone. Who did he call?"

Parker reopened his briefcase and removed a file. "The jail logs don't show any calls."

"Then how did anyone know he was in jail?"

11.

None of them—White, Brochette, or Shepard—spoke during the short walk from the courthouse to White's office. Before White would be able to represent David Shephard effectively, Shepard and Brochette would have to come to terms with their renewed relationship. As long as Shepard was ambivalent about that, he could not participate effectively in his own defense. Accommodation of Brochette's different roles, both as his father and as a US attorney, was essential, but it was something that couldn't be forced. White just had to wait, but he couldn't wait too long. He needed information, and he needed it quickly.

David Shepard kept his head bowed as he seemed to make a conscious effort to avoid looking at Brochette or White. Brochette occasionally glanced at his son, apparently trying to find something to say. White observed the exchange—looking for clues to the renewed relationship between father and son. He would know soon enough where David stood.

When they arrived at his office, White left Shepard in the War Room and escorted Brochette into his office. Grace Matthews entered, placed two cups of coffee on the table between Brochette and White, and left, closing the door behind her.

"So where are we?" Brochette asked—his first words since leaving the courtroom.

White again summarized what Horse and Harris had learned and his conversation with David at the jail.

"It doesn't sound like you have much to go on."

"Not yet."

"What do you intend to do now?"

"Turn over some more rocks."

"Starting with…?"

"Starting with your son."

"I thought you already talked to him."

"He wasn't much help the first time. Being in jail does that."

"Mind if I sit in?"

White shook his head. "Not a good idea. You two still have some personal problems to work out. I don't think he'll tell me everything I need to know with you in the room. Besides, you aren't his attorney. If you're there, our conversation won't be protected by the attorney-client privilege."

"Of course. But it's going to be difficult to stay out of your way."

"You don't have any choice. Not if you want me to represent David."

"And we have a lot of catching up to do."

"Just be sure you don't talk about his case… or anything that might even be remotely connected to it."

&

"We've just been going over the police reports," Horse said when White joined him, Harris, and Shepard in the War Room.

"Where's my… father?" David Shepard said.

"He's waiting in my office. He can't be here while we talk."

"Why not?" Shepard demanded.

"Because he's not my client, and his presence during

our discussion would mean our conversation wouldn't be protected by the attorney-client privilege. He could be called as a witness against you if you said anything that would help the prosecution."

Shepard started to say something but changed his mind.

White remained standing beside the conference table opposite Shepard. He folded his arms across his chest and glared at David. Shepard avoided looking at White and stared at the open can of orange soda on the table in front of him. White had interviewed enough criminal clients over the years to be familiar with the pattern that characterized their interaction with their attorneys. Invariably it followed the five stages of grief—denial, anger, bargaining, depression, and acceptance. For some it took longer than others, but White had to lead David through the process as quickly as possible. Until he accepted the reality of his situation he would not, or could not, provide dependable information on which White could act.

"All right, David," White's voice interrupted the silence like the command of a drill sergeant. "It's time you told us the truth." It was the challenge that would set the stage for the conduct of the rest of the interview. Would David respond like a lion, with a defiant roar, or like a mouse, with timid avoidance?

Shepard stiffened but continued to stare at his can of soda. "I've told you the truth," the mouse said so softly as to barely be heard.

"But you haven't told me everything there is to tell."

Shepard shifted his attention to White. "Like what?" His eyes seemed to convey a challenge, but his voice was only mildly defiant. White did not say anything for a minute as he tried to decide how to approach his interview with Shepard. He knew what he needed to learn about the facts of Shepard's case. But he also knew that there was more to Shepard's case than a simple case of possession of cocaine. There was something more, something in Shepard's demeanor, that left little doubt that he had a secret to be protected. What was not clear was whether he was hiding a secret that was vital to his defense or merely some unrelated secret from his past that he wanted, or needed, to protect.

"At the jail, you said you were afraid of being killed if you didn't get out on bail. Why did you think that?"

Shepard's hand tightened around the can of soda. "I think someone wants to kill me."

"You think…?"

"Jackson, the guy I was arrested with… He said we weren't safe."

"Why didn't you tell me this when I met you at the jail?"

"I…"

"You thought I was sent by your boss—the person you and Jackson worked for when you were in Matlacha."

"That's not…" Shepard's eyes darted around the room avoiding any contact with the other men. White knew he was trying to make a decision, but he could only guess what Shepard was thinking. Finally, Shepard spoke. "Yeah. Something like that."

"All right. Let's go over this again."

David squirmed but still did not look at White. "What do you want to know?"

"What did Jackson mean when he said that you weren't safe?"

"I… don't know."

White slammed his palm on the conference table. David jumped backward and fell to the floor.

"Get up and sit down," White ordered. David stood

and stared at White. His eyes had a defiant look, but finally he did as he was told.

White glared at David until he was confident that he had his client's full attention. "Get this straight, David. I know you can answer my questions, so let's not have any more of this 'I don't know' crap. Do you understand me?"

David's eyes now showed a mixture of confusion and fear. "Ye… ye… yes."

White leaned over the conference table, getting his face as close to David's as he could. "Yes what?"

"Yes… sir."

"That's better. Now let's start over." White took his seat, reached for a legal pad, and picked up his pen. "I'll ask you again, what did Jackson mean when he said that you weren't safe?"

"He said that punks like us weren't safe from the other prisoners."

"Why?"

David dropped his head and muttered something incoherent.

"Dammit, David. Speak up."

David glared at White and shouted. "He said we were prime meat and we were going to be gang-raped! There! Are you happy now?"

White made a short note and continued as though nothing unusual had happened. In fact, there was nothing in David's behavior that White was not familiar with. It usually took his clients a while to learn that they couldn't hide the truth from White. He was their lawyer, and he couldn't do his job without knowing everything. If it took tough love to get the truth, White was capable of administering it.

White thumbed through his file notes and, without looking up, said, "At the bail hearing you said that I had to get you out of jail or you'd be killed. You just said something totally different." White raised his head and stared straight into Shepard's eyes. "Which is it?"

Shepard hung his head and didn't speak.

"*Dammit*, David! Answer me!"

Without lifting his head, Shepard said, so softly that he could barely be heard, "The rape thing."

"And when we met at the jail you said…" White paused while looking through his notes. "You said, and I'm quoting you, 'You don't have to worry. I'm not cutting a deal.' Why did you say that?"

"Because of what Jackson said."

"What was that?"

"It's too late to make any difference. You've already bailed me out."

"Why is it too late to make a difference."

"Jackson said that people who get arrested on drug charges and then get bailed out can get killed by dealers."

"Why is that?"

"Dealers figure that you must have made a deal, so they make sure that you can't testify."

"How did Jackson know about this?"

"I don't know. He just did."

"And you believed him?"

"He's been around hard drugs more than me, and he's been in jail before. I figured he knew what he was talking about."

White wrote a note and waived a finger calling Horse to his side. Horse leaned over, and White whispered something in his ear. Horse nodded imperceptibly and left the room with the note.

"Okay. So now tell me who your dealer is?"

David leaped to his feet. "*Dammit*. I keep telling you… and everyone else." David stopped to catch his breath before continuing his rant. "I don't have a dealer. I don't have a supplier. I don't have anything. And we didn't have any drugs in the house when we were busted." When he finished, David slumped wearily into his chair.

White made another note then laid his pen on his legal pad and looked at David. "Then this could be your lucky day, David."

David seemed too emotionally spent to understand what White was saying. "Huh?"

White smiled and said, "I believe you."

David stared across the table, apparently not able to believe what he had heard. "You believe me?"

White smiled. "I do."

"Oh, thank God."

"God has nothing to do with it. Now we have to convince a jury."

David was breathing rapidly, and his hands were shaking. "What do I have to do?"

You need to answer my questions, starting with exactly how you ended up in Matlacha."

"I've already told you. Jackson said everyone down there uses something, and the cops don't care unless you're dealing."

"How did he know that?"

"Hell, I don't know. He said he'd been there before."

"What were you going to do for money?"

"I don't know. Tend bar. Do odd jobs. Jackson said that there's a lot of plant nurseries on the island and they always need workers. And besides…"

"Besides what?"

"Nothing."

White scowled and slapped the table. "Besides what, David!"

"Jackson said he was going to be getting some money

from his father. It had something to do with Jackson not talking about some deal his father was involved in."

"What kind of deal?"

"I don't exactly know. Something about an arrangement he had for getting people out of jail."

"Is that all?"

"It's all I remember. We were pretty wasted, and I wasn't paying attention."

As David spoke, Horse returned to the room, whispered something in White's ear, and reclaimed his seat at the side of the table. White flipped through the case file until he found Harris's notes of his meeting with Lou Hamilton. He ran his finger down the page until he found what he was searching for. "Lou Hamilton says neither Shepard nor Jackson had been around until they moved in three months ago." White slid the file in front of Horse and tapped his finger on the relevant notation.

Horse glanced at the file and began to rummage through the notes from his meeting at the Shipwreck Bar.

"What drugs did you have in Matlacha?"

David's lips quivered as he began to speak, then closed as he seemed to think better of whatever he was going to say.

White and Horse exchanged knowing glances. The interview had followed a familiar pattern from vigorous objection to submission.

David returned his attention to his now empty can of orange soda. When he finally spoke, his voice was barely above a whisper. "I had some grass… and maybe a little hash."

"Where did you get it?"

"I still had a stash from when we were in the Keys."

"Where did you get the cocaine?"

"I told you. I don't know anything about that. We never had that stuff in the house."

"But you did distribute cocaine."

Shepard responded with an explosive, "I didn't know there was any cocaine!" A moment later his statement was followed by, "I swear," uttered in a pleading voice that was barely more than a whisper.

White ignored Shepard's outburst and walked to the end of the room, his back to Shepard. "Start from the beginning. What were you doing in Matlacha?"

"We were just laying low. Sometimes a guy gave Jackson some instructions."

"That would be the guy in the blue Porsche?" White was only guessing, but it seemed logical.

Shepard's head snapped up; his eyes filled with fear. It wasn't merely a fear of White. His whole body tensed as if he was getting ready to make a run for safety. His eyes searched for a place to hide.

"Don't bother denying it, David. We already know about him."

Shepard shook his head as though he could still not believe what was happening. "Oh, man."

"What's his name, the man with the Porsche?"

"I don't know. I never talked to him."

"What did Jackson call him?"

"I never heard him call the guy by name. But he referred to him as the Cambodian."

"What kind of instructions did the guy give you?"

Shepard hung his head and ran the fingers of both hands through his shaggy hair. "I don't know. I really don't."

"Who did?"

"Tom."

"Tom Jackson?"

"Yeah."

"And what did you do after Jackson talked to him?"

"We went to someplace where they had a boat. We took the boat to where the guy told Tom to go and picked up a package floating in the water."

"How did the package get there?"

Shepard threw up his hands. "How the hell should I know? What difference does it make?"

White ignored Shepard's outburst. "David, at this point I don't know what is and isn't important. But any detail, no matter how trivial you may think it is, could become important. Do you understand me?"

Shepard gave an exasperated sigh. "Yeah, I suppose so."

"Good. Now, how long did it take to get to where the package was floating."

"Three or four hours. It took a while, maybe a half-hour, to get to open water. Then we ran for a couple of hours out into the Gulf."

"Could you see land?"

"Sometimes we ran north along the coast, but a long way out. Sometimes we went straight out to sea."

"What kind of boat was it?"

"Just a recreational fishing boat. Center console. T-top. That kind of boat."

"How big was the boat?"

"Twenty-five, maybe thirty feet. But it was fast… really fast. It had three big outboards. Tom said the boat could do eighty."

"Were there any other boats around?"

"There were some other boats at the pier where we got the boat."

"What about when you were at sea?"

"I never saw any."

"Did you ever hear an airplane?"

"No."

"How did you find the package?"

"We had GPS coordinates, and the package had a small radio transmitter."

"What did you do with the package?"

"Tom put it somewhere in the cabin."

"What cabin?"

"The cabin where the boat was."

"What did the cabin look like?"

"I don't know. It was dark, and I never went inside."

"It couldn't have been that dark."

"Well, it was. We only went out on moonless nights."

"Do you know where the place was?"

"No. The guy with the Porsche always drove, and, like I said, it was always dark."

"How far from Matlacha was the cabin?"

"I don't know. An hour and a half. Maybe two hours. We went somewhere down the interstate, then down some other highway to a dirt road. That's all I know."

"How long were you on the interstate? Did you pass anything you knew or recognized? How long were you on the other highway and the dirt road?"

"Dammit. I don't know any of that. I was usually stuck in the back of the Porsche, and I couldn't always see out."

"Tell me about the man with the blue Porsche."

A long moment passed before Shepard responded. "I don't know anything about him."

"I can't help you if you don't tell me everything."

Shepard stared at the table and clasped his hands to control their shaking.

"David," White prodded again.

"He'll kill me," Shepard said softly.

"What?"

Shepard slammed his hand on the table. "I said, 'He'll kill me!'"

"Who will kill you?"

"The guy in the Porsche—the Cambodian. He was constantly reminding us that people who crossed his boss had a way of winding up dead."

"Are you sure he referred to his boss?"

"Absolutely. But he also scared the shit out of me. I'm sure he was capable of killing Tom and me if he felt like it."

"Did you get the feeling that he could do anything to you on his own?"

"I don't know. No. I don't think so."

"Which is it, David?"

"I'm sure he could, but I don't think he would. I'm pretty sure someone else ran the operation. But if we crossed him personally, he wouldn't hesitate to kill us."

"Not if we stop him first."

"You can't." Shepard's voice now had the plaintive quality of a lost and frightened child.

"Why not?"

Shepard shook his head, and his breathing raced. His anxiety continued to build as his head sank to his hands.

"David?"

Shepard's head jerked up and stared at White. His eyes were cold and hard when he said, "Because he's connected to the government."

White hid his surprise by looking at his legal pad and pretending to study his notes. "How do you know that?"

"Jackson told me."

"Exactly what did Jackson tell you?"

"He said we were safe because the guy is connected to the government prosecutors."

"What kind of connection does he have?"

"I don't know. Tom just said we didn't have to worry about anything as long as we did what the guy said."

White looked up from his notes. "What makes you

think you'd be killed if you crossed the man with the Porsche?"

"Because that's what happens. The guy with the Porsche takes care of anyone who knows too much."

"How can you be so sure?"

"'Cause I saw him stick a knife in some guy down in the Keys. That's when we figured we had to get out of there."

White scribbled some notes on his pad as he tried to make sense out of David's latest revelation.

"When did this happen?"

"I don't know. A couple of months ago. During the last hurricane."

"Why were you there?"

"Why was I where?"

"Why were you there when the stabbing took place?"

Shepard took a deep breath before continuing. "We were supposed to meet a boat and pick up a package. But a hurricane was coming through, and the captain of the boat we were going to use wouldn't go out. Somehow, they contacted the boat we were going to meet, and it came into the harbor. That's when the guy on the boat was knifed."

White glanced at Horse and Harris. Both responded with a nod and added notes to their case "to-do" lists.

&

White left the remainder of the interview of David Shepard up to Horse and Harry and went to his office to meet with Brochette. Brochette stood as White entered.

"Sit down, Graham. We have to talk."

Brochette hesitated. White's words were not those that were cause for joy. Slowly Brochette sank onto the sofa where he had been sitting. White sat on the arm of the sofa.

"David seems to think his life is in danger."

Brochette clenched both fists and looked away. "What can I do about it?"

"*You* can't do anything about it. What you can do… what you have to do… is let me do what I think needs to be done."

Brochette took a deep breath and exhaled slowly. "What are you planning?"

"I'm not just planning. I've already arranged for security at your home."

"Okay. Why would I have any concern about that?"

White paused, giving Brochette time to prepare himself for the bad news. "You'll be under the protection of Manuel Rodriguez."

Brochette surged to his feet. "*Absolutely not*! I cannot, and I will not, have a felon providing security for my son." Brochette strode authoritatively across the room and leaned forward with both arms against the conference table. "No way."

White watched and waited calmly as Brochette vented his feelings. "Are you finished?"

Brochette didn't move and spoke very softly when he said, "Yes."

"This is the way it has to be. David is a suspect in a major felony. You can't very well use anyone in law enforcement to provide him with protection. And I'm sure you can't afford to provide him with the protection he needs."

"But you're making me indebted to a felon!"

"*Accused* felon. He's never been convicted of anything."

"That's only because he's been represented by you."

"And he's doing this because I'm asking him to. I just expect you to make sure the police know that Rodriguez's men are there to provide protection and shouldn't be harassed."

"I can't control what the police do."

"Of course you can. And don't forget that your son's life may depend on you."

12.

After Brochette and Shepard had gone, White took his accustomed place at the side of the conference table in the War Room and began, "What else do you have, Horse?"

Before Horse could speak, Harry's pen flew across the table.

"All right. What the hell is going on, Harry?" White's voice was a mixture of concern and accusation. "That was the fourth time in as many days that you dropped your pen. And you dropped your coffee cup the day before that."

"I guess I'm just turning into a klutz," Harris said, forcing a smile that didn't hide the anxiety in his eyes.

"When are you going to see the doctor?" White's tone was more demanding than he intended.

"I have an appointment this afternoon," Harris retorted. "Now can we get on with this?"

White gave Harris a final look of concern before nodding for Horse to continue.

Horse began to flip through his notes. "Jackson's from West Palm Beach. He has a degree in business from Florida Atlantic, but just barely. He was more interested in partying and doing drugs than going to class. He spent half his time on academic probation."

"Does Jackson have any record?"

"He was arrested for possession of heroin when he was in college. He was represented by an attorney from West Palm Beach named Richard Barlow. Barlow negotiated the charges down to simple possession. Jackson got probation on a suspended sentence. He was picked up a couple of times in the Keys, but he was never formally charged with anything. He'd get held overnight, then released."

"That's all?"

Horse shrugged. "It's the Keys. Down there, everyone and his brother does some drugs. Unless you're a dealer, the authorities don't care."

"But if he was on probation, any drug-related arrest would be a violation, and he'd be in prison."

"His lawyer, still Richard Barlow, got the arrests reclassified as something else. Drunk and disorderly, Something like that."

"Do you think he was dealing?"

"Small-time, maybe. He had no other visible means of support."

"So, where's the connection to David Shepard?"

"My guess is they got together in the slammer. David and Tom Jackson were both guests of the county at the same time."

"That's consistent with what David said. Anything else to put them together?"

"Nothing definite. They both lived in Marathon at the same time from May 'til September. That's when they left the Keys and landed in Matlacha. If you need any more on that angle, I'll go down to the Keys and see if anything shows up on the radar screen."

"Maybe later," White said. "But it seems that Jackson has had some very effective representation on his drug charges. I'd like to know more about his lawyer."

"I thought you might," Horse said as he picked up another file and started reading. "Richard Barlow. Lawyer in West Palm Beach. Got his degree from Nova University. Went there on the G.I. Bill after he served in Vietnam."

"What kind of a lawyer is he?"

"Mainly immigration," Horse said. "But there's something unusual about his practice. He only seems to handle immigration from Southeast Asia, Burma, Thailand, Cambodia."

White shrugged. "I suppose that's reasonable for someone who served in Vietnam."

"Maybe. According to my source, he also has a guy working for him, a Cambodian you wouldn't want to meet in a dark alley."

White's eyes widened. "Didn't the guy you met at the Shipwreck Bar say the man with the Porsche was Asian."

"And you think one Oriental is about the same as another?"

"It would fit. What do you have on the Cambodian?"

"Nothing. My hunch is the guy may be some kind of enforcer for Jackson's father."

"He makes sure that the good counselor gets paid?"

"At least. But my gut tells me there's something more."

"Like what?"

"When I was at the Shipwreck Bar, a guy I met said that the guy driving a blue Porsche came down there about once a month and took Shephard and Jackson somewhere. When they came back, they were flush with cash."

"Anything else?"

"Ah'm not sure, but ah think there's more to the lawyer's business than just immigration."

"See what else you can find out."

"Ah'm waiting for some people to return my calls."

"What did his father do in Vietnam?"

"He was part of a unit that trained the Montagnard."

White released an audible whistle. "Those suckers were vicious killers. They operated outside any chain of command. It was pretty much every chieftain for himself."

"And they controlled most of the poppy production in that part of Asia," Harris said.

"I thought about that when I found out about Tom Jackson's heroin arrest."

"Look into it," White said. "And…"

Horse and Harris waited.

"What do you think about the story of the boat and the package pickup?"

"It sounds to me like they were taken to Everglades City. That fits the driving timeline."

"That's what I was thinking. And what about the boat?"

"It sounds like they could have had the pickup anywhere along the coast. Or maybe from a boat anywhere within a hundred miles of shore. Possibly even on the south side of the Keys. They're all reasonable places to pick up packages of cocaine. I don't think those facts are going to be very helpful."

"What do you have on the owner of the Porsche?"

"Not much. I checked with the Department of Motor Vehicles. There are three hundred and fifty-four late-model blue Porsches registered in Dade County. No obviously Asian names, but that may not mean anything. Sixty-three of the cars are registered to corporations. I'll see what I can do to narrow the list."

White nodded. "Keep on it. It's our only lead."

13.

White, David Shepard, and Graham Brochette finished the sandwiches Grace Matthews had ordered so they could eat while they prepared for the probable cause hearing. White gathered the wrappers, crushed them into a ball, and threw it into the wastepaper basket in the corner.

"It sounds like we're going to be trying my case now," Shepard said.

White swept the crumbs from the table with one hand and added them to the trash. "To some extent, we are. We're going to try to make the state show that they have sufficient evidence to justify your arrest. We don't have to argue any of our defenses, but they have to convince the judge they have enough evidence against you to justify a trial."

"So what are we trying to get out of this?"

White stopped stuffing files into his briefcase and sat on the edge of the conference table. "First of all, I want to know how all of this happened. Somebody set you up. I want to know who, and I want to know why. I also want to know if you and Tom Jackson are the only targets, or if there is more to the state's case. By making them disclose the basis for their warrant, we may get some clues about who's behind the plan to have you arrested."

"And you think you can find this out at today's hearing?"

"I hope so. You see, in a trial we'll be focusing on evidentiary issues. In a probable cause hearing, there's more opportunity to make the prosecutor disclose his theory of the case. And Paul Parker isn't likely to have prepared for the probable cause hearing as carefully as he'll prepare for a trial. He may let something slip."

At precisely two o'clock the bailiff called the court to order, and Judge Stanley Mitchell took his place behind the bench and waved the parties to their seats as he took his own.

"All right. What do we have here?" the judge asked impatiently.

White stood and waited while all those present turned to look at him. "Your Honor. The defendant contends that his arrest was improper because it was made incidental to an unlawful search."

"How so?" Judge Mitchell inquired in a tone bordering on boredom. In his twenty years on the bench, he had heard it all and nothing surprised him.

"My client was arrested when the police discovered what they *thought* to be cocaine in his home. However, the only basis on which they were in his home was that the court had issued a warrant to search for cocaine."

"Did I authorize the search warrant?"

"No, Your Honor. Judge Carlin signed the warrant."

The judge wrinkled his nose and shook his head. "Go on."

"It's the defendant's position that the search warrant was improperly issued because it wasn't based on sufficient evidence to establish probable cause."

"What evidence was offered in support of the warrant application?"

"The warrant was issued solely on the basis of the affidavit of Officer David Grey. In his affidavit, Grey stated that there was cause to believe that there was cocaine in the home being searched. The basis for that statement was that Paul Parker had informed Officer Grey that there was cocaine at the residence."

When the judge didn't ask anything else, White picked up a copy of a case opinion and read: "'If an affidavit offered in support of a request for a search warrant contains intentional false statements or statements made with reckless disregard for the truth, the trial court must ignore the questionable material and consider whether the affidavit's remaining content is sufficient to establish probable cause. If the false statement is necessary to establish probable cause, the search warrant must be voided and the evidence seized as a result of the search excluded.' This is from Your Honor's opinion in *State v. Davidson*." White started to state a citation to the source of the published opinion when he was interrupted by the judge.

"I'm familiar with the opinion, Mr. White. As you clearly know, I wrote it."

The judge turned to Parker. "Do you have anything to say?"

Parker had to know that his only hope was to divert the judge from the search warrant.

"Your Honor, the question regarding the warrant is moot," Parker said as if the law was so clear that no argument was necessary. "The police officers found something exactly where the informant said they would find it. That alone is sufficient to establish the informant's credibility."

Judge Mitchell glared at the state's attorney. "You'll have your turn. But," Judge Mitchell said, turning his attention to White, "I don't see a problem yet."

White, who had remained standing during the judge's exchange with Parker, said, "The problem, Your Honor, is that Officer Grey got his information from Paul Parker, but Mr. Parker got his information from an anonymous tip that was phoned to him."

Judge Mitchell quickly turned to Parker. "Is that true?"

Parker stood slowly while avoiding looking at the judge. After a long silence, he said, "Yes, Your Honor."

"And you don't know who this tip was from?"

White took his seat, suppressed a smile, and watched as the judge's questions headed just where he had hoped the judge would go.

"Ah... No, sir."

"So, you had no basis for determining the credibility of the witness?"

"His credibility is established by the fact that his information was accurate."

"Nice try, Mr. Parker. But that argument doesn't work in this court." Judge Mitchell sat up straighter and said, "The court finds that the drugs were seized pursuant to a legally insufficient search warrant and are, therefore, inadmissible as evidence."

White stood and began to make an argument.

"Save it, Mr. White," the judge said. "Without the drugs, the state has no case. The charges against your client are dismissed."

Shepard looked at White with a dazed expression. "What just happened?"

"The evidence against you got tossed."

"You mean I'm free?"

"Don't get too excited, David. Only the *state* charges had to be dismissed. The federal rules of evidence are a little different from the state rules. You're still facing federal charges if the government wants to bring them."

"But isn't that my dad's decision?"

Brochette, who had sat through the hearing in the first row of the gallery was now standing with his son and White. "I am sorry. But since you are my son, I will have to recuse myself from anything having to do with you and any charges that may be brought against you."

"What does 'recuse' mean?"

Brochette shook his head. "It means that the decision is going to be made by someone other than me."

Shepard turned his back and walked away. "That sucks!"

"But it's the law."

14.

Early mornings alone on the deck overlooking the river were Lucius White's special, private time. The river, flat and glassy, was a natural tranquilizer. The sky was overcast and rain was in the forecast. Wisps of fog rose from the water surface. Only the occasional cry of a seagull that had ventured upriver from the Gulf of Mexico broke the silence.

White leaned against the deck railing thinking about what little they knew about David Shepard's case. He never expected it to be easy. No case involving two kilograms of uncut heroin could be. But the complete lack of progress was wearing on him. The facts that they had weren't coming together in any meaningful way, and he knew that his client was still not telling him the whole truth. So far they were only feelings born of experience and instincts. He couldn't put his thoughts into words, but he couldn't put them out of his mind.

Sherlock lay protectively at White's feet, listening for the sound of food. White's thoughts were interrupted by Sherlock's tail thumping happily against the deck. When he looked up, Leslie was standing in the doorway. She was wearing a light negligee and, as he could see from the silhouette revealed by the light coming from behind her, nothing else.

"Could I interest you in a little something to start your day?"

White's consideration of the facts of David Shepard's

case was swiftly replaced by more carnal thoughts. "What did you have in mind? Something lustful, I hope."

"I meant breakfast. Something to eat!" Leslie said in a tone meant to deflect White's leering suggestion.

"You'll need to narrow it down a little more than that."

"I won't dignify that with a response," Leslie scolded, laughingly, "because my mother always taught me to be kind to the ill-bred." White rolled his eyes as Leslie continued. "What I had in mind, you dirty old man, is ham and eggs."

"With a side of Leslie?" White asked hopefully.

"Not in this lifetime, you uncouth SOB."

"I don't recall you objecting last light."

"I was obviously suffering a temporary lapse in good judgment. And the fact that I was horny as a gazelle might have had something to do with it."

"So that's all I'm good for, trimming your horns?"

"Do you have a problem with that? You should always go with your strong suit," Leslie said gayly as she turned and headed for the kitchen, giving a pronounced shake of her ass for good measure.

"On that note, I think I'll take a cold shower. Then I'll make breakfast."

&

The telephone was ringing when White came out of the shower.

"Lucius," Horse said when White answered. "My scanner just picked up a sheriff's call that I think we need to follow up on."

"What's it about?"

"The dispatcher just sent a car to check out a site where

a body is supposed to have been buried. The dispatcher said something about the drug dealers from Matlacha."

"David's alleged partner?"

"The call didn't mention names. But I figure it's worth looking into. I'm heading to the site now."

"Call me when you get there."

"Will do."

White hung up and immediately dialed the number of the state's attorney. Paul Parker answered on the first ring.

"Paul. It's Lucius White."

"Imagine my surprise."

"Do you have something you'd like to share with me?"

"I don't know yet. But, yeah. We got a tip that may involve your client's partner. How did you know?"

"A little birdie told me."

"You seem to know a lot of birds."

White ignored Parker's comment. "So, what do you have?"

"I got an anonymous call this morning. He said we'd find Jackson's body in a pit off State Road 80 out toward Alva."

"I thought you still had him in custody?"

"He was bailed out yesterday morning. His hearing was just after Shephard's."

"With Judge Mitchell?"

"No. Adams."

"Why didn't you tell me?"

"Keeping defense attorneys informed about everything that happens around here isn't in my job description."

"Who issued the bail bond?"

"Someone from the east coast. Fort Lauderdale, I think."

"Didn't that strike you as suspicious?"

"I... Hold on a second, Lucius. I've got a call from the radio car."

White was considering the news about Jackson's bail when Parker returned.

"It was a good lead, Lucius. The deputy just called to confirm fresh digging at the site."

"Mind if I take a gander?"

"Mind? Hell yes, I mind. But I can't keep you from looking. Besides, Horse is already there."

"I'll meet you at the site."

&

White pulled his truck off the edge of the highway behind a row of sheriffs' cruisers. A minute later, Paul Parker arrived at the scene and pulled in behind him. In the middle of the field, fifty yards off the highway, two patrol officers stood beside what appeared to be a small mound of freshly turned earth.

Parker was getting out of his car when another cruiser arrived and stopped behind him. A burly lieutenant with an unlit cigar in his mouth and a scowl on his face called to Parker. "What the fuck is he doing here?" the lieutenant demanded, tilting his head toward White.

"Easy, Jack," Parker said. "He's got a right to be here."

"Well, just keep him the hell out of the way."

"He knows the rules, Jack."

"Just make sure he obeys them," the lieutenant snarled.

White leaned against his truck and watched Parker and the lieutenant march across the field. As they neared the group of deputies, the lieutenant began shouting something at Horse. White couldn't hear what was said, but the gestures being exchanged had international meanings. Parker spoke briefly with the deputies before signaling for

Horse to follow him. As they approached his truck, White heard Horse suggest that the lieutenant perform an unnatural and physiologically impossible sex act. Parker chuckled and walked to the side of White's truck. "Jack sends his regards."

"I heard," White said. "It's so nice to be loved."

Parker shook his head.

"What do you have?"

"Not much more than when we talked. It's a shallow grave. We've only scraped the surface away far enough to know we've got one body. We won't know any more until the coroner and the boys from the crime scene unit get here."

"Is it Jackson?"

"Probably, but we'll have to use fingerprints for identification. Most of the face is blown away. It appears that he was shot in the back of the head."

"Any indication that this is where he was killed?"

"Not really. He was tortured too much for it to have taken place here," Parker said as he surveyed the scene one more time before returning his attention to White. "If you know something else, I'm open to suggestions."

&

At one o'clock, the telephone in White's office rang. White glanced at the caller identification and answered, "Yes, Horse. Where are you?"

"I'm still at the scene. The boys from the crime scene unit are about to pack up."

"Did they find anything useful?"

"These guys couldn't find their ass with two hands and a flashlight."

"That bad?"

"Oh, hell. I shouldn't be too hard on him. The dumb deputies had walked all over everything before the crime scene unit arrived. I'd be surprised if they got anything useful."

"What about the body?"

"It's Jackson. And get this, he was beaten pretty badly before he was killed."

"So it didn't all happen at the dumpsite?"

"Not likely."

"Any thoughts?"

"Someone wanted to know what he knew."

"Or what he had told someone else."

"What do you have in mind?"

"Paul Parker said he'd been talking to Jackson about a deal. Whoever killed him may have wanted to know how much he'd disclosed."

&

White's next call was to Graham Brochette.

"Where's David?"

"He's in his room. Why?"

"Jackson's body was found this morning in a shallow grave out in Alva. He'd been beaten and shot in the back of the head."

"*Jesus.*"

"Amen. Whoever they were working for doesn't want anyone talking."

"Do you think they'll come after David?"

"I'd bet on it."

&

As White hung up the phone, Harry Harris rolled into the office. "Horse just called to tell me about Jackson."

"If you have any ideas…"

Harris leaned back in his chair. "I don't think this is only about drugs."

White put down his pen and leaned forward with his arms crossed on his desk. "What makes you say that?"

"We've always been suspicious about the drugs. Two kilos are too much for a dealer to use for a simple frame-up. He'd know that the police would confiscate whatever was used. No dealer in his right mind is going to give away that much coke."

"What are you suggesting, Harry?"

"The frame-up has to have been organized by the authorities. They're the only ones who can get that much coke for a sting. And they know that they're going to confiscate it and get it back."

"Assuming that you're right, what's the connection to Jackson?"

"According to Horse, Jackson was ready to make a deal."

"What was he going to tell Paul?"

"The discussions hadn't gotten into particulars. But we know that Jackson has a history in the world of drugs. He must have been ready to expose someone."

"That sounds reasonable. Now we know that whoever Jackson was working for isn't above murder to solve his problems."

"You're assuming he was killed by whoever he was working for. Maybe the Cambodian."

"Do you have a better suspect?"

"Unfortunately, I do."

"Who?"

"What if Jackson was going to give Paul evidence that would convict David Shepard?"

"*Damn!* That would make David the number-one suspect."

"But only if David knew Jackson was negotiating a plea that involved him."

"I assume you're hoping he didn't know anything."

"That would be my preference. But I have to keep an open mind."

"A suspicious mind is more like it," Harris said as he rolled toward the door. "Are we still on for dinner?"

"Seven o'clock at Clyde's."

15.

"Let's get a move on it, stud," Leslie shouted over the sound of the shower. "We're running late."

"I'll be right out. Would you get me a clean pair of jeans?"

"Get real." Leslie laughed. "Tonight you're going to look like a gentleman."

"And I suppose you expect me to behave accordingly," White snorted as he walked from the bathroom, a navy-blue terry cloth towel wrapped around his waist.

"I've learned not to set my sights too high," Leslie said as she kissed him on the cheek.

Leslie wore a formfitting emerald-green silk sheath slit high on her thighs and cut low enough to show her ample cleavage. The smooth lines of the dress clung to her body. White could see she wasn't wearing anything underneath.

"Surely we have time for a little…"

"You got your appetizer in the shower," Leslie said, ducking away as White reached playfully for her. "But if you're a good boy, I might come up with something interesting for dessert."

&

Clyde's is the watering hole for the Fort Myers power brokers. It is locally said, not without some truth, that every deal of any significance had originated in, or been finalized at, Clyde's. Equally true is the proposition that you had not made it in Fort Myers until Jack, the bartender to the after-work crowd for longer than anyone could remember, knew your favorite beverage and had it on the bar by the time you reached your customary seat.

Clyde's is reminiscent of the era of White's warehouse. It was originally a private home, a mansion by the standards of the day, built in the Victorian style. It had authentic brick walls and hardwood floors. A mahogany bar, imported from an exclusive London men's club shortly after World War II, extended along one wall from the door to the corner of the room and wrapped halfway down the left wall of the room. A large mirror, held in place by a carved mahogany frame, covered the wall behind the bar. A table at the end of the bar held two steamer trays filled with grilled chicken wings and chicken livers wrapped with bacon. A shiny black piano stood in the center of the room.

The evening hostess at Clyde's met them at the door. "Happy holidays," she greeted them cheerily as she hugged White and exchanged faux kisses with Leslie. "Horse and Sandra are in the back room."

"Thanks, Sarah."

The hostess station was decorated with a wreath and a sign wishing all a "Happy Holidays." In front of the hostess station, a parson's table held a large brandy snifter, listed in many restaurant equipment catalogs as "Tip Jar—Extra Large." Bills, none of them smaller than ten dollars, half-filled the snifter.

Leslie whispered, "I'll bet Sarah grabs all the ones and fives before they hit the bottom."

"She can't let anyone get the wrong idea about what's expected at Christmas."

White and Leslie crossed the room, past the piano where Edgar, whose last name no one could remember ever hearing, was playing a medley of Christmas carols. A mixture of the regular after-work drinkers and post-office-party revelers crowded around the piano singing along. Edgar smiled at them through yellowed teeth and said, "Mr. White. Ms. Leslie. Good to see y'all." Edgar had his own brandy snifter on the corner of the piano. White dropped in a large bill and Edgar's smile grew.

"Christmas carols just don't sound right without snow," Leslie whispered to White.

Waitresses and even busboys greeted them by name as they walked through the main dining room. The holidays, known in the foodservice trade as "Big Tip" season, brought out everyone's biggest smiles.

Horse and Sandra Ward were waiting at a corner table in the back room. They had been dating for more than six months, longer by far than White and Leslie had known him to remain with one woman. Sandra had rapidly advanced past the status of Horse's bimbo du jour to something that was becoming serious. Leslie liked her from the moment they met and told Horse he was a fool if he let her get away.

Half-empty glasses and two trays of appetizers, raw oysters and stuffed mushrooms, testified to their early start, or White's and Leslie's tardiness.

Sandra was beaming, and Horse had the look of a new father, as White and Leslie crossed the dining room.

"All right," Leslie demanded happily. "What are you two up to?"

Sandra looked at Horse.

"Go ahead," he said. "You're dying to tell them." His attempt to sound nonchalant was contradicted by his grin.

"We decided to move in together," Sandra said.

"Oh my God," Leslie sputtered.

"I know," Sandra said. "Isn't it great?"

White rolled his eyes toward the ceiling. Horse grinned

and shrugged. White shook his head and reached out and shook Horse's hand. "Congratulations. This is great."

"Yeah. Well," Horse mumbled.

"Who knows," Sandra continued. "One of these days he might even make an honest woman out of me."

"Huh?" Horse said. "Who said anything about that?"

"Oh, come on, Horse," Leslie prodded. "One of you guys has to show a little class."

"Yeah," Sandra said. "When are you two getting married, Lucius?"

Leslie looked at White impishly. "Yeah. When *are* we getting married?"

White glanced helplessly at Horse. "See what you started?"

Horse held his hands up in mock surrender. "Don't look at me. It was her idea."

Sandra hit Horse on the arm with her rolled-up napkin.

White helped himself to an oyster, which he sucked from the shell. Leslie gave him a show-some-class smile. Sandra snuggled close to Horse. He leaned over and kissed her. The season was off to a good start.

Their joy was interrupted by the chirping of White's cellular phone. "Who the hell can this be?" The number on the screen wasn't familiar. He tilted the phone to read the name of the caller. His expression hardened as he read "Coastal Regional Hospital." "Hello," he answered cautiously.

"Is this Lucius White?"

"Who's this?" White asked without confirming his identity.

"This is Dr. Sebastian calling from the emergency room at Coastal Regional Hospital. Am I speaking to Lucius White?"

"Yes," White said impatiently as he mentally sped through the possible reasons for the call. "What's happened?"

"You're identified as the emergency contact for Elgin Harris. Are you a relative?"

It took White a second to recognize Harry Harris's given name. "I'm his law partner. What's happened?"

"Mr. Harris appears to have had a stroke."

White stiffened. "What's his condition?" he demanded.

"He's critical but stable," the doctor said. "He's disoriented and partially paralyzed."

"What's the prognosis?"

"We just sent him up to radiology for an MRI. We'll know more when we get the results."

"Who's the neurologist on call?"

As White spoke, Leslie tugged on his arm. White put his hand over the telephone and said, "Harry's at the hospital. He may have had a stroke."

"My God. How is he?"

"Too early to tell."

Dr. Sebastian returned to the phone. "Dr. Levenson is on call."

"How long will it take him to get there?"

"He's been paged. He should be here within an hour."

"I'll be there in fifteen minutes," White said as he hung up. Leslie started to follow when White stood.

"No," White said. "You guys might as well stay here and try to enjoy your dinner. Too many of us will only be in the way."

"But, Lucius," Leslie begged, a tear forming in the corner of her eye.

White kissed her, assuring her that everything would work out. "I know the chief of staff and the head of neurology. They'll talk to me, and I'll call you as soon as I know anything."

Leslie turned in her chair and watched White walk away. Tears began to form as Horse put his hand softly on her arm. "Lucius is right. There's nothing we can do now. We'll go to the hospital after they've got Harry settled in."

As he walked across the room, White dialed the number of Dr. John Wiley. Wiley was more an acquaintance than a friend, but he had been instrumental in a prior case in which a mutual friend had been accused of embezzlement from Coastal Regional Hospital. If nothing else, they had developed a mutual respect, and Wiley was the best neurosurgeon in Southwest Florida.

&

John Wiley preceded White through the door to the emergency room. The faces of half a dozen patients sitting in the waiting room turned toward Wiley and White as they marched past. One look at Wiley's clenched jaw and the orderlies and nurses stepped aside as he headed for the emergency room nurses' station.

"Where is Harry Harris?" he demanded in a soft but unmistakably firm voice.

The nurse's hands sped over the keyboard. A troubled look came to her eyes. "We don't show a Harry Harris, doctor."

"Check Elgin Harris," White said before Wiley could say anything.

Again, the nurse typed rapidly; her eyes fixed on the screen in front of her. Relief softened her face as she found what she was looking for.

"He's on his way back from radiology."

"Where is Dr. Sebastian?"

"He's in room three, doctor."

Without responding, Dr. Wiley headed down the hallway, followed by White. "Mike," Dr. Wiley called when he spotted another doctor at the end of the short hallway. The other doctor, who White assumed was Dr. Sebastian, turned and walked toward them. "Give me the bullet on…" Wiley glanced at White.

"Elgin Harris."

Dr. Sebastian flipped open the chart he was carrying. "White male; fifty-eight; five-ten; 160 pounds; paraplegic; presented with severe aphasia and disorientation; normal temperature; mild tachycardia; BP 170 over 120; unknown medical history."

"His father died of a heart attack when he was fifty-four," White offered.

"Did he drink?" Wiley asked.

"He was a heavy drinker until a couple of years ago. He also took a lot of pain medication and antidepressants after his accident."

"When was that?"

"A couple of years ago."

"Does he smoke?"

"A couple of packs a day until about a year ago."

"Any recent surgeries?"

"No."

"Do you know what medication he's taking?"

"He's taking something for high blood pressure, but I don't know what."

"Have you noticed any recent changes in his behavior?"

"Like what?"

"Any slurring or garbled speech? Maybe dropping things."

"Yeah. I started noticing some of that a little while ago."

As White spoke, the elevator doors opened, and Harry Harris was wheeled onto the floor and into the examination room. Dr. Sebastian took over the computer at the nurses' station and, with a couple of clicks of the keyboard, was viewing the results of the MRI and studying the radiologist's preliminary report. Wiley and Sebastian huddled in front of the computer screen, speaking softly to each other.

"What's your plan, Mike?" Wiley finally asked loud enough for White to hear.

Before Dr. Sebastian could answer, White gripped Wiley lightly by the arm and asked, "Aren't you going to take over?"

Wiley shook his head. "Mike's in charge of the emergency room. For now, your friend is going to be transferred to the medical service."

White started to say something when Wiley cut him off. "I'll see to it that he's assigned to Dr. Levenson. He's the head of neurology."

White's expression remained uncertain.

"Don't worry. I'll check in on him, but he's a medical patient, and I'm on the surgical staff."

White ran his fingers through his hair. "What are they going to do for Harry?"

"That's where things get a little complicated," Wiley began, his voice taking on a tone of detached competence. He was now speaking as a doctor rather than as a friend. "It looks like Harry has some ruptured capillaries that have allowed blood to seep into his brain. That's probably what caused the coordination problems you've noticed."

"So they've been there for a while?"

"Probably. But that's not the whole problem. Harry has a clot in a major artery. That's what caused the stroke tonight."

"Why would he suddenly have a clot?"

"It's not unusual for someone like Harry. People in wheelchairs frequently develop clots due to poor circulation. If they suddenly get involved in a lot more activity than usual, the clot can break loose and travel to the brain.

Has Harry been involved in anything unusual; anything that would make him more active than normal?"

"He's been spending more time than usual out of the office investigating a recent case."

"That could be all it took."

White hung his head, considering the possibility he was responsible for Harry's stroke. After a moment, he forced the thought aside and asked, "Is there anything you can do about it?"

"That's the problem. For a clot, we'd normally prescribe a tissue plasminogen activator, TPA. It's a kind of a clot-dissolving agent."

"Can't you use it on Harry?"

"We don't know if Harry is still having active hemorrhaging from the ruptured capillaries. If he is, the TPA will kill him."

"So what do we do now?"

"We could run some more tests, but we're running out of time. If TPA is going to work, it has to be administered within a few hours of the stroke."

"What are the options?"

"We can remove the clot with surgery, but the surgery has its own risks. And even if it's successful, there's no guarantee that the hemorrhaging won't kill him anyway."

"Will you be doing the surgery?"

"Yes, if that's the way we decide to go."

"What gives Harry the best chance?"

"There's no right answer to that question. No matter what we do, there are serious risks."

"What would you do?"

Wiley thought for a moment before responding, "I'd cut."

"Then that's what we'll do."

Wiley nodded and headed off down the hall just as Leslie appeared. "How is he?" she asked as she rushed into White's arms.

"He's had a stroke," White said. "Maybe more than one. They're taking him to surgery now."

Leslie's lower lip trembled as she asked, "What can we do?"

"There's nothing we can do now."

16.

Silence permeated his office when White came down the staircase from his apartment at eight o'clock the following morning. It was rare that anyone else was at work this early, but there was something different about this silence. More than the mere absence of office noise, there was a spiritual reverence to the quiet, like the sound of an empty cathedral.

White was startled by the sound of Grace Matthews's sniffles. As he approached her, he saw that her eyes were red and puffy. Used tissues already filled the small brass wastepaper basket beside her desk. For the first time in the eighteen years she'd worked for White, she didn't have a cup of coffee waiting for him when he arrived.

"Horse called and told me what happened," she said between muffled sobs.

"Harry's going to be all right," White assured her in a voice that carried far more confidence than he felt. "I'm going back to the hospital as soon as I check on a few things."

Matthews pursed her lips, holding back the tears.

"We're not going to be here today. Why don't you take the day off?"

"I'd rather stay here. If I don't stay busy, I'll…"

White nodded. "I understand." He squeezed Grace's shoulder and went into his office where he began impatiently sorting through the last of the previous day's messages. He was still staring at the pink slips, unable to concentrate on their content, when Horse entered his office and dropped onto the sofa.

"What have you heard about Harry's condition?"

White paused, taking a last furtive look at the pink slips before tossing them absently on his desk. "Nothing yet," he said as he sunk, exhausted, into his chair. "We spent the night at the hospital. I left about an hour ago to get a shower and a change of clothes. I was just about to go back and relieve Leslie."

"How's she taking it?"

White rubbed his eyes. "Not good. You know how she feels about Harry."

"How we all feel," Horse corrected.

"Yeah," White agreed.

&

White cursed silently as he pulled into the hospital parking lot. Construction of the new medical office building required the closing of half the lot, and the remainder of the lot was already full. After circling for the third time, White pulled his pickup truck onto the grass that bordered the entrance road and left it there.

Tension gripped him as he approached the hospital entrance, partly because of Harris, and partly because he was never comfortable at hospitals. It was a feeling he could never explain, like the fundamental fear people have of dentists.

Outside the doors to the main entrance, visitors puffed nervously on their last cigarettes before entering. An old man in a wheelchair, an oxygen bottle attached to the back and a mask on the old man's face, was pushed up the ramp by an apparently distraught son who feared the worst. The automatic doors slid open, and the old man passed a wheelchair coming the other way. A young woman smiled down at her newborn child as the proud father beamed.

After a quick visit to the cafeteria, where he purchased coffee for himself and Leslie, White headed for the intensive care unit. Leslie opened her eyes and stretched as White entered the waiting room.

"How's he doing?" White asked as he settled onto the sofa beside Leslie.

"They won't tell me anything. The nurse said he's going in and out of a coma, or whatever they call it. He didn't recognize me when I saw him…" Leslie checked her watch, "about an hour ago."

"Have you talked to John Wiley?"

"He's in surgery. He left a message saying that he'll come as soon as he's finished."

No sooner had she spoken than the elevator door slid open and Dr. Wiley stepped into the waiting room, still wearing his surgical scrubs. "Sorry I took so long. The procedure was a little more complicated than I expected."

"He doesn't look good, John," Leslie blurted. "He doesn't seem to be aware of anything."

"Let me check on him. Then we'll talk," Wiley said as he headed into the ICU.

Neither White nor Leslie said anything as they watched Wiley cross the ICU to Harris's bed, examine his chart, and speak briefly with the nurse. When he reappeared, he didn't look happy. "There doesn't seem to be any improvement."

Leslie clutched White's arm. "What does that mean?"

"The surgery itself went fine. He's probably still hemorrhaging a little from some microscopic ruptured capillaries."

"I don't understand," Leslie said. "Can't you do anything?"

Wiley shook his head. "There isn't anything we can do but wait. Either…"

Wiley was interrupted by the ICU nurse. "Dr. Wiley. You better come quick."

"I'll be right back," Wiley said over his shoulder as he hurried away.

A minute later, Dr. Levenson rushed from the stairway door and into the ICU.

Through the window in the door to the ICU, Leslie and White watched anxiously as the doctors and two nurses attended to Harry Harris. Leslie clung tightly to White's arm and said a prayer.

Inside the ICU, Dr. Wiley bent over Harris's face and shouted something at the nurse. A cart with a tray of mysterious instruments was wheeled to his side. In one practiced motion, Dr. Wiley tilted Harris's head back and inserted a breathing tube into his throat. A nurse pushed a cart beside Harris's bed as Dr. Wiley connected the breathing tube to the cart.

Dr. Levenson lifted the lids of Harris's eyes and passed a penlight over them. He looked at Dr. Wiley and said something. Dr. Wiley repeated the procedure and nodded.

Dr. Levenson removed his stethoscope from around his neck and positioned it in his ears. Methodically, he listened to Harris's chest, reporting his findings to Dr. Wiley as he went. Dr. Wiley stepped to the end of Harris's bed where he retrieved his medical chart and began writing notes.

"What are they doing?" Leslie asked helplessly.

"Everything they can," White assured her.

The nurse said something to Dr. Wiley who shook his head. The nurse's expression changed from hopeful to grim.

"Oh, Lucius," Leslie whimpered.

White put his arm around her and squeezed her shoulder. Dr. Wiley looked toward them and said something to Dr. Levenson. Dr. Levenson nodded and Dr. Wiley headed for the door.

"It's not good," he began as he approached Leslie and White. "He stopped breathing, and we had to put him on a ventilator. His heart's beating on its own, but he's not responsive to light."

Tears formed in Leslie's eyes as she asked, "Is he going to make it?"

"It doesn't look good," Dr. Wiley said. "We're pretty sure he's hemorrhaging into the brain. There's nothing more we can do but wait."

&

"Are you sure you don't want to get some sleep?" White asked when they were back in their apartment.

"I… I'll lie down later. I'm still too worried about Harry to sleep."

"Do you need something to eat?"

"Maybe some toast."

White put two slices of bread in the toaster. "How about some tea?"

Leslie forced a smile. "That would be nice," she responded in a voice that said the act of speaking required great concentration.

"It just isn't fair."

White put a kettle of water on the stove. "I know."

"What are we going to do?"

"Just what the doctor said—we wait."

&

When White returned from the hospital, Horse met him at the elevator and followed him into White's office. "How's Harry doing?"

"Not good. No change from last night."

"How's Leslie taking it?"

"Worried. Afraid."

Horse uttered something incoherent, probably something that indicated his expectations about Leslie's feelings, as he dropped to the sofa.

White stood by the conference table, leaning on his hands with his head bowed.

For a minute neither one of them spoke.

Finally, White turned, sat on the edge of the table, and asked, "What do you have?"

"I got a call from one of my sources on the east coast."

"And?"

"The only thing we have to connect Shepard and Jackson to drugs is the guy in the blue Porsche. Right now, I assume it's the Cambodian who works for Richard Barlow. I asked if he knew anything about a Cambodian being involved in the trade."

"And did he?"

"Nothing specific. But a few years ago, a low-level heroin pusher got busted in Fort Lauderdale and tried to cut a deal by pointing a finger at someone up in West Palm Beach. He claimed that his smack was being brought into the country by couriers who got their entry papers through a Cambodian."

"The guy who worked for Richard Barlow?"

"The file didn't have any names, and the investigation didn't go anywhere."

"Why not?"

"The snitch was shot as soon as he got out on bail."

"Quite a coincidence."

"That's what I thought," Horse agreed. "And so did my source. He thought there might be a connection between the release and the murder, so he checked into who posted the bail."

"And?"

Horse knew what White was hoping to hear. "Sorry. There wasn't any connection to Barlow. All I got was the name of the company that posted the bond. It's a small outfit out of Fort Lauderdale."

"Finding a connection to Barlow was probably too much to hope for. Anything else?"

"My friend didn't come up with anything, but he got me thinking. I asked if he could find out about any bail bonds posted by Barlow."

"What made you think an immigration lawyer would have any reason to post bail in criminal cases?"

"Nothing specific. But sometimes dumb-ass luck rears its ugly head."

"What did you find?"

"Barlow's posted bail in quite a few drug cases over the years."

"So he practices criminal law as well as immigration."

"That's what the bonds would make you think," Horse agreed. "But he hasn't actually tried any criminal cases in any county I've checked."

"That's odd."

"Maybe not," Horse corrected. "The people Barlow represents never seem to go to trial."

"Why's that?" White asked, never doubting that Horse would have the answer.

"Most of them either got sweetheart deals for minimum time or had their charges dismissed."

"You said 'most.'"

"A good number of the people bailed out by Barlow have had fatal accidents."

White rolled his shoulders; something he frequently did when taking time to absorb unexpected information. "This is getting interesting."

"And that," Horse said, "is an understatement. Do you want me to look into it?"

"Later," White said before lapsing into a pensive silence.

&

Leslie was curled up against a corner of the sofa when White returned to their apartment. A glass of wine sat untouched on the coffee table.

She stood and embraced White as he crossed the room. Her eyes were red and puffy and had a vacant look of suspended consciousness. Neither of them said anything.

Sherlock slid off the chair opposite the sofa and ambled to them. She climbed onto the sofa and curled up next to Leslie, resting her head on Leslie's lap.

Leslie scratched her behind his ear.

"Even Sherlock knows," Leslie murmured sadly.

White remained silent, waiting until Leslie seemed to have regained some measure of composure before speaking.

"I talked to Dr. Levenson. He said that if nothing changes in the next day or so we should start thinking about a long-term care facility."

Leslie curled herself around White. A river of tears cascaded down her cheek.

17.

Lucius White's annual Christmas party was an event that shouldn't be missed. White wanted to cancel the party, but Leslie convinced him it should continue as a celebration of Harry Harris.

The air conditioners were on full. A fire crackled in the fireplace. Bars were set up in the reception area outside White's office and in his apartment. Tables in the balcony library and White's apartment were laden with food ranging from barbecue to oysters Rockefeller and cracked Dungeness crab.

News of Harris's stroke had already made its way down the legal grapevine. Everyone wanted to know about his condition and prognosis. Even those who had abandoned him in the dark hours following his accident expressed concern and asked where they could send flowers.

Around the room, people were talking about Harris.

"God, that man could play a jury like a violin…"

"Do you remember the Donahue murder trial? Harry got so wound up during closing argument that he jumped up on the defense table and…"

"He was the best damned fisherman you ever saw. He could coax a bass out of any hole in the river."

"So this hotshot lawyer from Miami is making his opening statement, and he's just getting to the big finale when Harry leaned to his side and passed gas. It sounded like rolling thunder."

Diane Lindsey's appearance at 9:00 was preceded by

an explosion of laughter, something that accompanied her wherever she went. Outside the courtroom, she was never mistaken for a lawyer. She was outspoken, loud, earthy, and uninhibited: qualities consistent with her claim—made to those who didn't know better—that she was a professional stripper whose name was Fluffy LeMuff.

Her stroll across the room was followed by the lustful eyes of a dozen men, and the sour looks of as many women.

"Fashionably late, as usual," Leslie said as she greeted Lindsey and they exchanged kisses.

Lindsey laughed. "I had a bitch of a time deciding what to wear."

"You chose well," White offered, admiring her sleek oriental-patterned cocktail dress.

Lindsey curtsied. "Why thank you, sir. You don't think I'm showing too much tit?"

Leslie laughed. "Class, Diane. Show a little class."

"I tried that once, but showing a little tit gets me laid more often."

"You're incorrigible."

"Hey, girl," Lindsey protested. "You've got super-stud here to keep you happy. Some of us are still looking."

Leslie smiled and shook her head as she asked, "Where's Dr. What's-his-name? I thought you two were an item."

"You mean Dr. Slater."

"Yeah."

"That's yesterday's news. We split up about a month ago."

"Why?"

"I found out it's true what they say about doctors: "You are what you treat."

Leslie responded with a puzzled expression as she considered Lindsey's comment. Finally, she smiled. "He was a proctologist, wasn't he?"

Lindsey laughed. "Girl, you got that right."

White and Leslie joined in Lindsey's laughter.

"Why can't I find a nice sensitive, caring guy?"

"They already have boyfriends," White said.

Lindsey laughed again. "You're an asshole."

"You're confusing me with Dr. Slater."

Lindsey shook her head. "So, point me to the eligible men."

"Can we talk for a moment in my study first?"

"As long as you get me a drink on the way."

&

White led Lindsey across the room, stopped at the bar for a Diet Pepsi and a martini for Lindsey, and headed for his study.

Lindsey sat on the love seat in the corner, leaned back, and crossed her legs. White shut the door and sat on the edge of his desk.

"Now I know why the judges love you," White said, smiling as if he had just discovered the Holy Grail. "If you cross your legs like that in court, no one is going to pay attention to anything else."

Lindsey laughed. "You should see Judge Carlin trying to get a look at my pussy."

"I'd just as soon not see Judge Carlin do anything," White said, recalling his appearance before the judge the week before.

"You and every other lawyer in town," Lindsey agreed. "Thank God he isn't in the criminal division. I'd hate to have him on your case."

"Speaking of which…"

"Let me guess. You want to talk about my latest client."

"Your representation of Tom Jackson was somewhat abbreviated."

"It's what happens when your client gets murdered."

"Do you know anything about it?"

"Do you mean, was my client afraid your client would kill him?"

White stiffened at the thought. "Is that what Jackson said?"

"Relax. I can't be a witness because he didn't say anything specific about your client."

"Did you get any sense that Shepard and Jackson had agreed to a story… in case they were caught?"

"No. Why?"

"I don't know. I'm just trying to read between the lines of my client interview."

"Sorry, but I can't help you."

"By the way, how did Jackson come up with two hundred fifty thousand bail?"

"Two hundred fifty thousand? Where did you hear that?"

"That's what Parker wanted for Shepard."

"That's strange. All he wanted for Tom Jackson was fifty thousand."

White absently picked up a letter opener from his desk and began tapping it on his leg. "Why do you suppose he wanted so much more for Shepard."

"You'll have to ask Paul that. The bondsman who contacted me knew Jackson's bail was going to be fifty thousand and had already issued the bond."

"How did anyone know Parker was only going to ask for fifty thousand?"

"I assume some attorney called Paul and that's what they worked out. All I know is I got a call asking me to represent Jackson at his bail hearing. The next day a courier delivered my retainer and the bond."

"And you were only retained to get Jackson bailed out?"

"Uh-huh."

"Who retained you?"

"A bail bondsman in Fort Lauderdale made the arrangements."

"Isn't that a little unusual?"

"Not really. Out-of-towners who get arrested here usually have a lawyer at home. The lawyer doesn't want to have to come here just for a bail hearing, so I cover it for him. I do it all the time. That's why I thought some other attorney had negotiated the deal for Tom Jackson."

"But if you're being asked to represent someone at a bail hearing, I would expect you to be contacted by the attorney who represents your client? Why were you only contacted by the bondsman?"

"I don't know. But I've done this for the same bondsman before. Maybe the attorney just asked the bondsman for a referral and then asked the bondsman to contact me?"

"But it still seems a little strange. I mean, don't you normally discuss a case with the attorney before you represent his client, even for just a bail hearing?"

"Now that I think about it, it seems a little strange to me too."

"Do you know how the other attorney even knew Jackson was in jail and needed bailing out."

"I assume Jackson called him from jail."

White shook his head. "I checked. The jail log doesn't show Jackson making or receiving any calls."

"Then how did anyone know to make arrangements for bail?"

White started to respond as though he was thinking out loud. "We know that Jackson and Shepard had something going with someone who comes to Matlacha from the east coast. Maybe he found out about the arrest and told whoever he works for."

"You'd know more about that than I would."

"How else would anyone know Jackson was in jail?"

"Maybe he'd been arrested here before. There would be a record of who represented him. Maybe someone at the jail called his counsel of record."

"No. This was his first arrest here."

"Ask Paul Parker. Maybe he knows."

"That's an idea. But there's something else I don't understand about your case. When you represent someone at a bail hearing, doesn't the out-of-town lawyer usually file a notice of appearance, so you're not stuck with the case?"

"Usually."

"Did anyone else file an appearance in Jackson's case?"

"No," Lindsey said. White looked at Lindsey as though waiting for a further response. Slowly the implications of White's statement took shape. "What do you have in mind?"

"It was almost as if someone knew there weren't going to be any more proceedings in Jackson's case."

"Do you think someone already planned to kill him?"

"It's possible. According to David Shepard, Jackson knew that some people facing drug charges were being killed after they had been released on low bail. He thought it could be because some dealer higher up the food chain was afraid that a deal had been made for testimony against the dealer."

"Could be," Lindsey agreed before taking another sip of her martini. "The ironic thing is that if Jackson had waited a couple more days, he would have gotten out anyway… when you had the evidence thrown out at David Shepard's probable cause hearing."

"Do you think it would have made any difference?"

"Why do you ask?"

"Think about it, Diane. Some attorney negotiates for a low bail without ever having been contacted by Jackson. Then you're retained for the bail hearing, without anyone else entering an appearance to take over the case. Doesn't that all sound a little strange?"

"Well, when you put it that way…"

"Can you think of anything that might be helpful to David Shepard."

"Like what?"

"Like anything Jackson did or said that I can use."

Lindsey took a sip of her martini. "There is one thing that might be useful. Jackson wouldn't initially consider any plea deal because he was sure that the U.S. attorney would take over the case and he figured he could get a better deal than he could get from Paul Parker. But that was when he thought that it would be taken over by the U.S. attorney for the Southern District. When I told him that Lee County was in the Middle District, he changed his tune. Then he wanted me to talk about a deal with Parker."

"It sounds like he knew something that would only be useful in the Southern District. Do you have any idea what it might have been?"

"Not a clue."

"What about the deal with Paul Parker? Do you know what Jackson was offering?"

"Just a general outline. He wouldn't give me any specific facts until we had a deal in place."

"What do you know?"

"He said that he knew something about some drug dealers who were murdered after they got released on bail."

"Was Parker ready to make a deal?"

"We hadn't finalized anything before the bail hearing."

"But he was considering it?"

"He hadn't said 'no.' But he also wasn't willing to agree to anything until he knew exactly what he was getting in exchange."

"What do you think your client had?"

"All he told me was that he could name names."

"The people he got the coke from?"

"That's the strange thing, Lucius. He swore the coke had been planted. He said they never brought coke to the house."

"That isn't the same as saying he never dealt coke."

"I don't know. But, as I said, he wouldn't say anything until we had a deal in place with Paul."

"What do your instincts tell you?"

Lindsey put her drink down on the coffee table and looked at White. "This is going to sound crazy, but I think he knew something about cases being fixed."

"*Jesus*. Where did that come from?"

"I… I'm just reading between the lines, but… I'm sure he had something to do with drugs. I don't know what it was, but it was something."

"What makes you so sure?"

"Every time I tried to get him to talk about drugs, he clammed up. He was scared."

"Of his drug contacts?"

"I don't know. Maybe. That's how I interpreted it."

"You don't sound very sure."

"I'm not." Lindsey uncrossed her legs and leaned toward White. "Jackson uses grass. There's no doubt about it. He's also used heroin in the past, although we don't know if he's an active user. But he has no known history with cocaine."

"Maybe he's just never been caught."

"Maybe. But I didn't see any signs of it, and he claims he wasn't using cocaine."

"So where does that leave us."

"I think Jackson knew something about the distribution of cocaine. He might even be involved in it in some peripheral way."

"So he could have something to trade."

"Yes. But I think that whatever he had would have been more valuable to a federal prosecutor in the Southern District than to Paul Parker."

White drummed his fingers on the arm of the sofa. "Why was Jackson so sure his case would go federal?"

"I can't say for sure. But he seemed to know about federal and state jurisdiction over drug cases and when the feds take over a state case. Why do you ask?"

White stood and walked to his desk. "Jackson was from West Palm Beach, and most of his life has been spent on the east coast and in the Keys." He spoke as if he was thinking out loud more than speaking to Lindsey. "If he wasn't worried about a federal prosecution, it means he had something to trade with the U.S. attorney in the Southern District."

"Maybe the reason Paul hadn't taken any action on your plea proposal was that he was trying to see what the information was worth to the U.S. attorney."

"It's a possibility."

"I suppose. Is there anything else I should know?"

"Lucius," Lindsey said before pausing. "Oh, hell. He's dead. I guess it can't hurt now."

"What?"

"I wouldn't have been surprised if it had been Shepard who ended up dead."

White felt his body stiffen. *David was right. He did have something to be afraid of.* "Why is that?"

Lindsey took another sip of her drink before responding. "When they were in jail, your client told Jackson that his father was a U.S. attorney and could get him out. Of course, that's a pretty stupid thing to admit to your partner in crime. Jackson told him that other inmates would think he was working for his father and might kill him."

"But Jackson might have wanted to kill him for the same reason."

"Jackson also thought Shepard was responsible for getting them arrested."

"Why was that?"

"Jackson swore that the cocaine found at his house, in his room, no less, wasn't his. He knew that they were being framed. He didn't think anyone had a reason to frame him, so he was sure he had just gotten caught in a frame-up that was intended to catch Shepard."

White leaned back and hesitated as he ran his fingers through his hair. Lindsey retrieved her glass and took another sip as she waited for White to continue. Finally, White said, "Jackson obviously had a run-in with someone after he was released—the person who killed him. And he was tortured before he was killed."

"I didn't know that. But it would be logical to conclude that he told his killer about the relationship between Shepard and Brochette."

"Which means that whoever killed Jackson has a good reason to kill David Shepard."

Lindsey finished her drink and started to stand. "It seems like you have your work cut out for you."

"Do you know anything else that might be helpful?"

"Nothing comes to mind, but I'll call you if I think of anything else."

"Thanks."

"Now can I go find an eligible male?"

White chuckled and shook his head. "You're a piece of work."

Lindsey laughed. "Hey," she said as they stood and she kissed him on the cheek. "I haven't gotten laid for a month. I have to line someone up for New Year's Eve."

&

Paul Parker was leaning against the wall when Lindsey left White's study.

"Merry Christmas, Paul," Lindsey said.

"And to you too," Parker said, his attention focused on Lindsey's ass as she walked away. "If I weren't married…" he said to White.

White laughed. "She'd kill you in one night."

"So I hear. But what a way to go."

They both laughed.

"Got a minute, Lucius?"

"Sure, Paul. What's a Christmas party if I can't do some business with the state's attorney?"

White followed Parker back into his study and closed the door.

Parker took a long swallow of his drink. From the color of the liquid in his glass, White concluded that whatever he was drinking wasn't watered down. White also knew Parker had been drinking heavily lately; enough so that it had become the subject of discussion in the legal community. White was tempted to suggest Parker come to one of his meetings, but the time wasn't right.

Parker stood by the window, gazing calmly at the river and the city waterfront to the northeast. Without turning, he said, "I was born here."

"I didn't know that," White said, uncertain where Parker was going.

"Yeah. When I was growing up, this place wasn't much

more than a pimple on the ass of progress," Parker said as he took another swallow of his drink. "Now look at it."

"No doubt about it. Things have changed."

Parker continued to stare out the window.

White wanted to return to Leslie and the party but couldn't avoid thinking Parker was trying to tell him something important. "Was there something you wanted to talk about, Paul?"

Parker paused, almost as if he was coming out of a trance, before responding. "I know it's a shitty time to bring this up, but I wanted to give you a heads-up. Ballistics came back on the slugs from the Jackson kid. They're from the same make and model as a gun owned by your client's father."

Damn. "Are you saying it was his gun?"

Parker slid onto the corner love seat. "We don't know yet. Brochette's gun is government-issue. They keep ballistics records on every gun they have. We're checking the FBI data files. We'll know in a couple of days."

"You don't think Graham had anything to do with the murder?"

"I don't think anything, but it's hard to imagine Graham Brochette as a suspect. Besides, the gun was reported stolen from Brochette's car on December 1."

White didn't need to be reminded that December 1 was the day of David Shepard's probable cause hearing.

Parker remained by the window, giving no indication he was ready to leave.

White understood he had something else on his mind and waited.

It took Parker a full minute to gather his thoughts and make up his mind what he was going to say. Finally, he looked directly into White's eyes and said, "Lucius... be careful on this one."

"Be careful of what?"

"I know these people. They're dangerous."

"What people, Paul? You aren't making any sense."

"I don't know who's involved. I just know there's more to this than either of us knows."

White waited for more. Instead, Parker returned his attention to the river and asked, "Do you ever feel like we're all wasting our time?"

"In what way?"

"Drug cases."

"What do you mean?"

"What's the point?"

White looked at Parker closely, wondering how much he'd had to drink.

"We prosecute them," Parker said, returning his attention to White. "If we get lucky enough to convict them, they're back on the streets in a few years doing the same thing. We spend hundreds of thousands of dollars keeping them in prison. And for what? It's a victimless crime, but it still ties up half the criminal court docket and fills half the prison cells."

"We don't make the laws."

"But wouldn't it be better if we only had to worry about the important cases?"

"You have discretion. You can decide which cases to prosecute."

"It's not always that easy."

"That reminds me of something. Diane Lindsey just told me that she had only been retained for Tom Jackson at his bail hearing, but she didn't know what attorney represented him. The jail logs don't show him making any calls. Do you know who told anyone that Jackson had been arrested?"

Parker turned away slowly and resumed his study of the river. "I'm sure it wasn't anyone in my office."

&

The musicians had departed. The caterers and bartenders were packing the last of the china and crystal glassware.

Amidst the holiday decorations, Lucius White leaned his elbows against the railing on the deck of his apartment. He was only vaguely aware that Leslie was suddenly standing beside him. They stood together in silence, gazing into the night.

White started to say something when the door opened and Horse and Sandra joined them.

After a moment of shared silence, Horse said, "Harry would have enjoyed the party."

White forced a smile. "Harry does like parties."

"We'll have another one for Harry when he gets better," Leslie said.

Sandra looked at Horse as if asking, *What should I say?* Horse shook his head imperceptibly. Sandra leaned against him and said nothing.

Another minute passed before Horse said, "Well, I guess we should be going." Then, turning to White, he asked, "Will I see you tomorrow?"

"I have a meeting with Manny Rodriguez."

Horse raised an eyebrow. Meetings with Manny Rodriguez were always important.

"We need help. If there's a drug connection, Manny is the man to find out about it."

18.

The Three Flags Marina was named for the flags flown by sport fishermen when they've scored a triple by landing all three of the major billfish: a swordfish, a sailfish, and a marlin. It was located on the Manatee River just west of Interstate 75 and approximately midway between White's office and his friend's home in Tampa. Mutually inconvenient, as Rodriguez had described it.

The warmth of the afternoon was beginning to yield to a cooling evening breeze. A jazz combo was setting up on a stage in the corner of the lounge. White was waiting at the bar when Manuel Rodriguez came in, alone, and signaled White to a table by the window overlooking the docks.

They first met when Rodriguez was charged with money laundering. He owned more than three hundred bill-changing machines located in laundromats, self-serve car washes, and video arcades throughout Florida. It was a near-perfect cover for couriers carrying large amounts of cash, and it justified the large cash deposits that banks were required to report to the government. Money laundering was undoubtedly the least of his wrongful acts, but it was the only one the U.S. attorney believed he could prove. The government lost the case to a hung jury, and White had been Rodriguez's attorney ever since. They were now more than just attorney and client; they were friends who exchanged favors on a regular basis.

Rodriguez had no illusions about his business. "We do what we do," he observed on more than one occasion.

Nonetheless, with some exceptions relating to his own business, he respected the law and frowned on the misdeeds of the common criminal element of society.

Rodriguez smiled and handed White a package wrapped in silver foil. "A little something to be remembered by during the holidays." White smiled as he retrieved a package from his briefcase and handed it to Rodriguez.

At first, the annual ritual seemed awkward. They were friends, sometimes close friends, but only within limits. During the yearlong investigation, and the three months of Rodriguez's first trial, they had come to know each other well. Each knew he could count on the other when necessary, but there was much they could never share. Their annual exchange of presents allowed them to confirm that they had a personal relationship that transcended their business ties.

"May I?" Rodriguez asked, holding up White's package.

"Be my guest."

Rodriguez withdrew a small knife and carefully cut the tape before unfolding the wrapping paper. As he opened the box, he smiled. Grasping the object in the box as if it were a delicate flower, Rodriguez withdrew a mounted gavel. A brass plaque proclaimed that it was the gavel used in the trial where White first represented Rodriguez.

"The judge retired last year and gave it to me," White said. "I thought you should have it."

"The judge would probably not appreciate your gesture, but I assure you that I do."

White responded with a smile and a slow, deep nod.

"And now," Rodriguez said as he tilted his head toward the package he had given White.

White ran a finger under the seam of the wrapping paper and tore it from the package. Inside was an autographed first edition of *The Making of a Country Lawyer*, the best-selling book by Gerry Spence. Spence was the Wyoming lawyer who came to national attention in his defense of Randy Weaver following the standoff with the FBI and ATF at Ruby Ridge, Idaho, during which government sharpshooters had killed Weaver's wife and daughter. White and Spence had met only once, but their shared background in the rugged West and their mutual distrust of government prosecutors created an instant bond.

White smiled as he examined the book and the inscription: "Lucius, the way of the West will prevail. *Non illigitimus carborundum.* (Don't let the bastards grind you down.)"

"Thank you, Manny. I appreciate this."

Rodriguez nodded. "But enough of this," he said. "We have things to discuss."

"As a matter of fact, I have a problem you may be able to help me with."

"If I can," Rodriguez said.

"I have a client who's been charged with drug dealing and is the prime suspect in the murder of his partner."

"I assume your client is David Shepard, Graham Brochette's son?" Rodriguez said.

"That's right. Has anyone shown any interest in him?"

"My men have been watching over him. They haven't seen anything suspicious."

"That's a relief. But that's not what I was going to ask about."

"You want to know about his partner, Tom Jackson!"

White struggled to suppress his surprise at the extent of Rodriguez's information. Little escaped Rodriguez's attention, but this was more than White expected. Now he was sure Rodriguez could find out what he needed to know.

"That's right. I have a name that may lead somewhere."

"Who?"

"Richard Barlow. He's an immigration lawyer in West Palm Beach."

Rodriguez laughed.

White looked confused. "What's so funny?"

Rodriquez stopped laughing and a serious expression came over his face as he looked at White. "You really don't know, do you?"

White stared at Rodriguez with a blank look. "I have no idea what's so funny."

Rodrigues chuckled. "Richard Barlow is Tom Jackson's stepfather."

White lowered his head and rubbed his forehead. "Damn! One simple case and I can't follow the players without a scorecard."

Rodriquez stopped chuckling and returned his attention to White. "Why is the father of interest to you?"

White continued to shake his head. "Bastard sons. Stepsons. Throw in a few dealers with aliases and we'll need a scorecard."

Rodriguez didn't laugh. In his world, the use of aliases was as common as carrying business cards was for bail bondsmen. He ignored White's apparent frustration and returned to the initial inquiry. "Why are you interested in Richard Barlow?"

White returned his focus to the subject of their conversation. "Right now, it's nothing more than a hunch. We know he served in Vietnam and represents a lot of clients from Southeast Asia. Beyond that, all Horse has come up with are rumors that the lawyer's representation of immigrants may go beyond getting visas and immigration papers."

"And you want to know if his interests extend to importing certain agricultural products?"

"Something like that."

Rodriguez looked at White with the sternness of a father who has caught his teenager smoking for the first time. "You understand that we do not deal in that product."

"I understand."

"Very bad," Rodriguez continued softly as if talking to himself. "Very bad stuff."

"Something else has been bothering me ever since this case began," White said.

Rodriguez waited without saying anything.

"My client was arrested when the sheriff got a tip that he and the Jackson kid were holding two kilos of uncut cocaine."

Rodriguez raised an eyebrow and nodded.

"But no dealer is going to waste two kilos of pure blow just to set up a couple of druggies unless it's damned important."

Again, Rodriguez nodded. "*Si.*"

White continued thinking out loud. "And I can't find any reason someone would want to set Shepard and Jackson up for a drug bust."

"Perhaps you're looking for an explanation in the wrong place, my friend."

"What do you have in mind?"

"Perhaps it is not a drug dealer who wanted to have your client arrested. Have you considered the possibility that it might be the authorities who arranged for your client's arrest?"

"What makes you say that?" White asked as he remembered the conversation with Harry Harris after Jackson was murdered.

"The authorities have seized much cocaine. They cannot sell it, but it would be of little consequence to them to plant a large amount to ensure an arrest, and possibly cooperation in a larger investigation."

"We've considered the possibility that something more than a drug bust may be involved."

Rodriguez waited while White thought. "We think it might involve a fight between rival distributors."

"That may also be true," Rodriguez said in a tone that was polite but didn't signify agreement.

White gave Rodriguez a puzzled look.

"There are those in our business who cooperate with the authorities when it suits their purposes."

"And," White said, as he wrestled with a thought he would have preferred to ignore, "There are those in law enforcement who occasionally find it advantageous to ignore the law when it suits their own interests."

"This is also true."

"Either way, I have to start somewhere. Can you help me with Jackson?"

Rodriguez nodded. "I can ask some questions."

&

As White pulled out of the parking lot and headed for Interstate 75, his cell phone rang.

"Lucius," Brochette began. "I'm glad I caught you."

White was suddenly tense. He had not spoken to Brochette since David Shepard's release. Now he felt a twinge of guilt over not calling to check on his client, but he somehow knew that David wasn't the reason for Brochette's call.

"I just received a call from Congressman Tierney."

"I wasn't aware you knew the congressman."

"It's hard not to. Politics and law enforcement is a small community."

White nodded before thinking how foolish his gesture was in a telephone conversation.

"Besides, I worked with the congressman a few years ago. He was on the House Ethics Committee, and I was with the Public Integrity Section of the Department of Justice."

"I assume he wasn't the target of an investigation."

Brochette forced a laugh. "Nothing like that. We were investigating the bribery of public officials in connection with government construction projects. One of the projects happened to be in the congressman's district."

"And what did the congressman have to say?" White asked, returning the conversation to the apparent subject of Brochette's concern.

"He wanted to give me a heads-up on a potential problem. He couldn't give me anything definite, but he's heard some rumblings of opposition to my nomination."

"What kind of rumblings?"

"That's the thing. He wasn't clear on specifics."

"Didn't know or couldn't say?"

"Probably the former. I think he'd have told me if he knew anything definite."

White chewed on his lip thoughtfully before asking, "Why are you telling me this?"

"Well… I know I don't have any right to ask…"

White knew what was coming.

"Dammit, Lucius. I want this appointment."

"And you want me to call Jack Lancaster and nose around?"

Jack Lancaster was chief counsel to the House Committee on the Judiciary. He was also, as Brochette had learned when he first worked with White, White's law school classmate and close personal friend.

"I don't know how much good it'll do. The confirmation of presidential appointments is the responsibility of the Senate."

"But I have a feeling your friend Jack knows everything that goes on in the Senate Judiciary Committee as well as the House Committee."

"That's probably true," White said. "I'm going to Washington on Wednesday on a securities fraud case. I'll see if I can connect with Jack while I'm there."

White ended the call from Graham Brochette and turned up the ramp to Interstate 75.

A blue Porsche with a Dade County license plate pulled into traffic three cars behind him.

19.

Outside the hotel on Connecticut Avenue, a light snow was falling. As usual, traffic in the nation's capital was at a standstill. No one in Washington knows how to drive in the snow. What they did know how to do was blow their horns.

Leslie was waiting in the hotel lounge when White returned from his meeting with the lawyers from the Securities and Exchange Commission. She smiled brightly as White crossed the room. White struggled out of this winter coat and sat down. Leslie leaned across the table and they kissed. The waitress made her way through the throng of partiers and took White's drink order, Diet Pepsi with two squeezes of lime.

As the waitress disappeared into the crowd, Leslie asked, "How did your meeting go?"

"Not as well as your shopping trip," he said, ignoring the question. No trip to Washington was complete without a major shopping spree by Leslie.

"I got something nice for Harry," Leslie said. She was just beginning to come to terms with Harry's condition. Recovery remained unlikely, but this was the first time she'd given any indication that she could even think about him without crying.

"I know he'll appreciate it."

Leslie bit her lip, fighting for control.

"Are you okay?"

"I'll be fine in a minute." As if to prove her point, she

touched a napkin to the corner of her eye, removing a tear. "See?"

White changed the subject. "I see you bought a new dress too."

"Do you like it?"

"Let me see."

Leslie stood and did a slow turn, allowing White to admire her new dress.

"Very nice."

"I have a few other things I think you'll like just as well. Some things for frolic time."

White smiled. "Maybe we should skip our meeting with Jack."

"Down, boy. I'm not going to miss a night on the town just so you can have your jollies."

"I thought you enjoyed it as much as I do."

"I do." Leslie laughed as she threw a peanut shell at him. "But unlike men, women have some self-control."

"Tease," White said, lofting the peanut shell back at her.

The waitress brought their drinks and a bowl of party mix.

"So how was your day?" Leslie said.

"About like any other day of dealing with bureaucratic lawyers."

"That good?"

"They all have too much power and no need to be reasonable."

Leslie nibbled at the edges of a cracker but said nothing.

White looked at her and smiled. "That's it. No more venting."

"You're getting better. A meeting with government lawyers is usually good for at least a few minutes of healthy bitching."

"I guess I'm getting too old."

"Older and wiser."

"Older, at least."

"Not too old to keep me happy." Leslie smiled as she leaned across the table and kissed him.

"Maybe you'd like to show me."

"Later," Leslie said, grinning. "It's time we went to meet Jack."

&

Three blocks east of the Capitol Building, in an otherwise nondescript neighborhood of restored brownstone row houses, is the least-known seat of power in all of Washington. The Hawk and Dove is the archetypical Capitol Hill bar where legislative staffers have, for more than a quarter century, gathered to talk politics and policies and gripe about their bosses—but never by name. Everyone knows who works for which congressman or senator, but custom and etiquette dictate that staffers always referred to their bosses as "my member." The Hawk and Dove serves Congress in much the same way that the officers' clubs serve the military; a place where rank is disregarded and issues of state are discussed frankly by the nameless and faceless people who really make government run.

Snow swirled around White and Leslie as they walked east along Pennsylvania Avenue, still jammed with rush-hour traffic. Christmas trees, lighted wreaths, and simulated candles filled the windows of storefronts and townhouses alike.

Leslie held onto White's arm and leaned lightly against him as she hummed along with the Christmas music coming from one of the boutiques. "This is what the weather is supposed to be like for Christmas," she mused.

As they approached the Hawk and Dove, they heard the clamor of voices from inside. As usual, the front room of the bar—it called itself a restaurant, but its most famous menu items were its fifteen variations of hamburger—was filled to capacity.

White led Leslie through the crowd, past the sunken fireplace at the back of the main room ,and into the pool room at the rear of the famous bistro. The pool tables had long since disappeared, much to the chagrin of the long-time habitués, and had been replaced by additional tables.

Jack Lancaster waved as he worked his way through the crowd, stopping every few feet to press the flesh with one or another Capitol Hill staffer or other Hawk and Dove regular.

"Sorry I'm late," Lancaster apologized. "Congress is recessing for the holidays on Friday, and there's still a pile of things to be acted on."

Lancaster threw his coat over the back of the booth, slid in opposite White and Leslie, and said, "Leslie, you're looking as beautiful as ever. Any time you want to leave Lucius and come to Washington, you just give me a call."

"And what," Leslie laughed, "will we tell your wife?"

"That's what makes her such a good lawyer," Lancaster said, addressing White. "She pays attention to nagging lit-tle details."

Everyone laughed.

"Paul," Lancaster shouted to the bistro manager over the din. "My usual… and another round here."

"On its way, Jack."

Lancaster returned his attention to White and Leslie. "To what grave misfortune do I owe the pleasure of seeing you?"

White scratched his ear, taking his time before responding to Lancaster. "What makes you so sure it's anyone's misfortune?"

Lancaster responded with a you've-got-to-be-kidding look.

"Okay. So maybe I've come to you with a little problem every once in a while," White said.

"Every once in a while."

White shrugged before admitting, "Maybe a little more often than that. You should be accustomed to it."

"Let's get it over with. Then we can go meet my better half for dinner."

Leslie put her hand to her mouth as if she was embarrassed to have committed a major breach of social etiquette. "We didn't intend to tie up your evening."

"Nonsense. My wife would kill me if I let you pass through town without getting together for dinner. Besides, you're new fodder for her pictures of our latest granddaughter."

"I hadn't heard. Congratulations."

Lancaster beamed. "I had nothing to do with it, but thanks."

"This is your fourth, isn't it?" Leslie said.

"Fifth."

"We *have* been out of touch."

"It happens," Lancaster said. "I've lost touch with just about everyone from our law school class."

"Yeah," White agreed. "Isn't it funny how we lose contact, but the alumni office always seems to know where to find us when it's time for the annual giving campaign."

Lancaster laughed. "You noticed that, did you?"

"It's hard not to."

"But we had some fun back then," White said, his face lighted by memories of old times and old friends.

"That we did," Lancaster concluded before turning to Leslie. "Did Lucius ever tell you about the time the dean—"

"No, Jack! Not that story!"

"Oh, come on," Leslie pleaded.

"No! No! No," White protested. "Some things past should be left in the past."

"Party pooper."

"I'll tell you later," Lancaster promised Leslie in a stage whisper before returning his attention to White. "Now, what's the problem?"

"It's not actually a problem," White said. "It's just something I'd like some information about."

"It wouldn't by any chance have to do with Graham Brochette's nomination?"

"You are good," Leslie said. "Isn't he good?" she asked White rhetorically.

"He's good," White agreed.

"Do you two run this routine on everyone?"

Leslie smiled. "Only on people we like."

"And people we don't like," White added.

"Yes. Them too," Leslie agreed.

Lancaster stared at them: first at White, then at Leslie, then back at White. "Are you two quite finished?"

White and Leslie looked at each other, then at Lancaster, before responding, in unison, "For now."

"Jesus. Of all the people I could have as friends, I have to choose a couple of Abbott and Costello wannabes."

White and Leslie laughed.

"So what do you want to know about the nomination?"

White's expression turned serious. "Graham Brochette called me yesterday. He'd just gotten a call from Congressman Tierney. Tierney mentioned that there were some rumblings of discontent over his nomination."

"And," Lancaster interrupted, "he wanted you to find out if there was a problem."

"I told him there wasn't anything you could do," White apologized. "But, yes, I said I'd ask."

"You know my committee doesn't have any involvement in the confirmation of presidential nominations?"

"I do, and I reminded him of that."

"But I can tell you there have been some rumblings."

"From who?"

"I'm not positive, but it's coming from the Florida delegation."

White and Leslie exchanged glances.

"Do you know who's behind it?"

"All I can say is that it's someone who doesn't want their position made public—yet!"

"What do you mean?"

"You know how things work around here, Lucius. Nobody takes a position on anything until they know which way the wind is blowing. The members get their staffers to talk with other staffers and drop hints about something they claim to have heard. Pretty soon the rumor takes on a life of its own. The staffers talk to their members, and all of a sudden it's an issue."

"So what's the issue?"

"I can't give you anything specific, but it seems to have something to do with Brochette's private life. There also seem to be some questions about his disclosure of his financial condition and other obligations."

"Nothing more specific than that?"

"Whoever is behind this is being secretive. They've leaked just enough to get other people talking and looking. If no one else comes up with anything concrete, they'll probably leak a little more just to point other people in the right direction."

"How serious is it?"

"It's too early to say. But there's one thing I can tell you. If he didn't give a complete and absolutely accurate financial disclosure, his nomination is dead."

"Isn't that a little harsh?" Leslie asked.

Lancaster shrugged. "The people elect morally degenerate, alcoholic wife-beaters to Congress. But as soon as they're here, they become holier-than-thou and demand perfection in everyone else."

"That sucks."

"Maybe. But Mr. Brochette has been nominated to head the agency charged with maintaining integrity in the judiciary. With all the scandals we've had around Washington lately, the president would be forced to withdraw his nomination at the slightest suggestion of wrongdoing."

"It still sucks."

"I don't make the rules."

"You said the problem seems to be in the Florida delegation," White said. "Do you have any idea where it's coming from?"

"I don't know if there's a connection to the other rumors, but a staffer in Congressman St. James's office asked me to look into something for the congressman."

"Is that the congressman St. James who represents Miami?"

"Yes. He's one of Miami's representatives."

"What did he want?"

"He wanted to know if the Justice Department has a formal policy on taking over drug cases from state authorities."

Beneath the table, Leslie squeezed White's leg.

"Isn't that a little unusual? Why didn't the congressman ask someone at the DOJ?"

"There was nothing unusual about the request. Congressman St. James isn't on our committee or any committee that would put him in touch with anyone at Justice. We get these requests all the time."

"Did the congressman say why he wanted the information?"

"I only talked to his staffer. But, no. He didn't say why he was interested."

White relaxed and waited for Lancaster to continue, as White knew he would.

"Although," Lancaster said as if the thought had suddenly occurred to him, "it might have something to do with the fact that the congressman is lobbying the speaker for an appointment to the Judiciary Committee."

White's eyes narrowed.

"Do you know something I should know?" Lancaster asked.

White told him the story of his representation of Brochette's son. When he was through, Lancaster drummed his fingers on the table for a moment before responding. "It sounds like you're about to become an enemy of a powerful politician."

"Like who?"

"Maybe you didn't know it, but Congressman St. James was a detective with the Miami Police before he was elected—a narcotics detective. Ever since he got elected, he's been on a crusade to fix both our drug laws and the laws relating to sentences for drug users. And he hates lawyers who represent drug dealers."

"I suppose that's a reasonable feeling for an ex-narcotics cop?"

"I'd agree if that was all there was to it. But St. James is vocal about his feelings. Almost too vocal."

"What are you saying?"

"Just that he never misses an opportunity to lash out at

defense attorneys. It's as if he wants everyone to know that he thinks we should do something to hamper them."

"What do you suppose that means?"

"I couldn't guess. But it does seem like he brings the subject up a lot more often than is necessary. As in, 'Methinks he doth protest too much.'"

"Do you think he has something in mind, or is he just trying to score political points?"

"I can't say. But if I had to guess, I'd say it's as much personal as it is political."

"As in, he's been burned by a defense attorney?"

"That could be part of it. But I think there's something more."

White took a sip of his Pepsi and thought about what Lancaster had said, before continuing. "What changes in the drug laws is he proposing?"

"I don't think anyone knows. I don't even think *he* knows what he wants done about the problem. All he's done is lobby for the creation of a committee to study the issue and make recommendations."

"Do I have to guess who he has in mind to head the committee?"

"You could guess, but you'd be wrong. He hasn't suggested that he should chair the committee."

"I wonder why not."

"Because there is no chance that the House and Senate can agree on what such a committee should have the authority to do. He doesn't really expect a committee to be established. He just wants the issue. Most of the marijuana and cocaine that reach the East Coast comes through, past, or over Florida. He gets lots of political mileage out of his issue without having to deliver anything."

"What's your point?"

"The senior senator from Florida has announced that

he won't seek reelection. I think Congressman St. James is positioning himself to make a run for the Senate."

"So what? Graham's nomination will have been voted on before the election."

"But not before the primary election. St. James can get a lot of mileage out of opposing Graham's nomination before the primary. As long as you're representing Graham's son, your investigation could get caught in the political crosshairs. Congressman St. James has a reputation for trying to destroy anyone who gets in his way."

20.

White pulled back on the yoke and the nose of his Lear 45, the *Legal Eagle*, rose from the runway at Ronald Reagan National Airport. The plane banked sharply to the left and headed northwest, following the winding course of the Potomac River. The snow-covered city sank slowly away as they climbed over I-495 and turned south. Below them, the highway was a parking lot of morning commuter traffic.

"I'll take over if you like, Lucius," his pilot, Captain John Atkins, USAF, retired, said as he began setting the controls for the flight to Tampa.

"How did I do?"

"For a lawyer, you're a halfway-decent pilot."

White had the hours, and the skill, to fly his largest toy solo. But he had the common sense not to do so when there was a risk of a blizzard en route. Captain Atkins was now employed as an independent flight instructor and charter pilot and frequently flew the *Legal Eagle* when White traveled. Atkins was an avid hunter, and the two of them had become close friends.

White released his harness and headed back to the cabin where Leslie was busy trying to figure out how to make coffee on an aircraft brewer. White took over the domestic chores as Leslie curled up on a leather seat beside the window. "What did you think about Jack's news?"

"His new granddaughter? I think it's great."

"You know what I'm talking about, smartass."

"Graham?"

"Of course."

"I'd like to know who has a bug up his ass about Graham's nomination."

"You don't think it's Congressman St. James?"

"He's put himself at the head of the list of suspects," White said as he poured coffee for both of them and sat down opposite Leslie. "The question is, why would he care about Graham one way or the other?"

"Who else could it be?"

"I don't know, but I intend to find out. We're going to stop in Tampa on the way home. I'm meeting Graham for lunch."

&

At nine-thirty, the *Legal Eagle* touched down at Tampa International Airport. By nine forty-five, they were parked at the civilian air terminal, and White was heading for his meeting with Graham Brochette. At ten-thirty, he arrived at the Causeway Restaurant.

It was too early for the lunch crowd, and the waterfront deck was still empty. A seagull landed on the railing, tucked its wings, and cocked its head to the side looking for a morsel of food. Seagulls were actually good-looking birds. The problem was there were so many of them, and they made so much noise that no one tended to notice how attractive they could be. It didn't help that they also shit on everything in sight.

The waters of Tampa Bay lapped at the pilings and the rocks along the shore. It was low tide, and the shallow waters under the deck released a profusion of mixed sea smells, dead fish and rotting vegetation trapped in the eddies and various bivalves clinging to the rotting pilings and seawall.

Someone at the bar threw a french fry onto the middle of the deck. A dozen birds descended on it in a flurry of thrashing wings and screeches. White watched as the victorious bird sprang into the air, the french fry in his beak, and headed out across the sand with the remainder of the flock in hot pursuit.

For the third time, White checked his watch. Traffic on the Courtney Campbell Causeway was light, and he wondered what was keeping Brochette. The Causeway Restaurant had been Brochette's suggestion. It was ten miles from Brochette's office in downtown Tampa, but White knew it was one of Brochette's favorite eateries. He also knew it was important for Brochette to get away from the office.

White sipped his Diet Pepsi and examined the long legs and firm ass of a waitress as she bent over to deliver drinks to the table across the deck.

"Better not let Leslie catch you doing that," Brochette said as he approached White, pulled out a chair, and took a seat.

"She doesn't mind a little window shopping," White said as he extended his hand. "She says it makes me appreciate what I've got."

"She's right. You'd be hard-pressed to find anyone better."

"Amen to that," White said as he raised his glass in a toast.

"By the way, where is Leslie? I thought she was traveling with you."

"She is. She had some shopping to take care of in town."

The waitress approached their table and slid a martini with three olives in front of Brochette.

"You sure you don't want one?" Brochette said, indicating his drink.

"Wanting one, and being able to handle one, are two different things."

"I'm sorry. I forgot."

"That I'm an alcoholic? Don't worry about it."

"I… Well… To our wives and lovers," Brochette said, touching his martini glass to the edge of White's glass of Pepsi.

"May they never meet," White concluded the old saying, smiling faintly as he recognized that his relationship with Brochette was moving closer to friendship. Under other circumstances, he would welcome the change. He admired and respected Brochette, one of the few prosecutors he felt that way about. But personal feelings couldn't be allowed to enter into the investigation. Besides, there were still too many questions about David Shepard for White to completely trust Brochette.

The waitress took their orders and disappeared.

Brochette looked hopefully at White.

White waited, examining Brochette's face as he considered what to say. He knew Brochette was becoming increasingly agitated over his son's case—and with White's refusal to tell him everything that was going on. White knew how he felt, but Brochette wasn't his client, and he wasn't entitled to know anything. More importantly, if Brochette knew too much, he might be tempted to do something, whether it was helpful or not. White's argument that Brochette's involvement in his son's case could endanger his own nomination was equally unsatisfactory, and Brochette's frustration was showing.

White leaned against the table, his gaze fixed on the plate in front of him as he considered, once again, how much to disclose. After a moment of thought, he returned his attention to Brochette. "Congressman St. James has been asking questions that may relate to David's case."

Brochette shook his head and shrugged. "Why would he care about David?"

"I'm not sure it's David he's interested in. He was asking questions about Department of Justice policy for taking over state drug cases. He may want to know if you're following policy in leaving David's case in state court. If he can show that you're not following policy with respect to David, he could muddy your confirmation."

"But my confirmation is up to the Senate. Why would he have any interest in it?"

"That's the big question. Have you ever had any run-ins with the congressman?"

"I've never even met him."

"Can you think of any reason for him to have an interest in your nomination?"

Brochette thought for a moment before responding. "Nothing comes to mind."

"Jack Lancaster said that one of the rumors about your nomination has something to do with your financial disclosures."

"I can't imagine what kind of problem there would be. My accountant filled them out, and I reviewed them thoroughly."

"What about David? You said you've been providing financial support for him. Did you disclose your support payments?"

"No. But they weren't court-ordered; they were entirely voluntary. Besides, I haven't provided support for him in years."

The waitress brought their orders, smiled, and turned away.

"What about your new position? Maybe there's some

legitimate reason he doesn't want you in that particular position."

"I can't imagine what it is. The position is new, but it's only a consolidation of functions that already exist under at least three different assistant attorneys general."

"What functions are being consolidated?"

"Well, first there's the office of professional responsibility. That office has principal responsibility for investigating misconduct by U.S. attorneys. Then there's the public integrity section. That office has responsibility for investigating misconduct by federal judges and public officials."

"And that's where you used to work."

"For five years."

"What else?"

"There's been a consolidation and expansion of enforcement activities relating to the conduct of elected officials, election fraud, and campaign funding and spending."

"What does that entail?"

"The scope of its activity is a little fuzzy. So far, it hasn't been the responsibility of any individual section. The president ran on a platform of campaign finance reform. He couldn't get the legislation he wanted, so he decided to beef up the investigation and enforcement of existing campaign laws."

White nodded and continued eating.

"Congress wasn't all that happy about the reorganization. They want to investigate everyone except themselves and preferred to leave responsibility for any ethical investigations scattered around the Department of Justice."

"Just as long as the left hand doesn't know what the right hand is doing."

"Something like that," Brochette agreed. "But no one dared take a position against the reorganization. That's why they demanded that the new functions be headed by a presidential appointee."

"So they could vote down any nominee they didn't like."

"Or who looked like he could cause them trouble."

"Why would St. James think you'd cause him any trouble?"

"You'd know better than I would."

White took a bite of his pastrami sandwich. "Maybe he's just questioning your decision to leave your son's case in the hands of the state's attorney when the feds should have taken it over."

"Is it possible that's all there is to it?"

"It's possible. It might be nothing more than a show. If it would make you feel any better, we'll look into it."

"I'd appreciate that."

White waited as Brochette continued to ponder the congressman's interest in his confirmation.

Suddenly, Brochette threw his fork on the table. "But dammit, I haven't done anything wrong. There's nothing that says we have to take over the investigation of every drug case."

White returned his sandwich to his plate and leaned forward. "This isn't just any drug case. It's your son."

Brochette clenched his jaw, a troubled look on his face.

White knew Brochette had something specific on his mind. "What is it, Graham?"

Brochette exhaled deeply before continuing. "Dwight Madison, the managing US attorney for the Fort Myers office —"

"I know who he is," White said.

"Of course," Brochette said, confirming White's knowledge of the obvious. "Anyway, Madison has also been asking why we haven't taken over the case."

"Does he know David is your son?"

"Yeah. He pointed that out when he made his argument… 'appearance of impropriety' and all that."

"We knew that was going to be a problem."

Brochette nodded gravely. "I may not have a choice."

White shrugged.

"It'll be awkward."

White nodded his agreement as Brochette continued. "I'll have to keep my distance, stay completely out of the investigation."

"You have to do that anyway."

"This'll be different. I'll have someone who is supposed to be reporting to me running an investigation I can't participate in."

"Maybe you should ask the attorney general to appoint a special prosecutor from outside the district."

Brochette nodded but said nothing.

White knew what he was thinking.

21.

White was leaning against the polished brass railing of the office mezzanine, thinking about Harry Harris, when Grace Matthews signaled that he was wanted on the telephone. "Mr. Rodriguez," Grace Matthews said icily. Matthews had never liked Manuel Rodriguez, but she would never tell White why. Calling him "mister" instead of "señor" was her way of showing her disapproval.

"I'll take it in my office." White strode purposefully to his desk and picked up the telephone. "Do you have anything for me?" White asked as the connection to Rodriguez was completed.

"I do not know anything that will assist you," Rodriguez said. "But there is someone who may be able to help."

"Who's that?"

"It is not that simple, my friend. I am going to give you a telephone number. It is a cellular telephone. The person who answers will ask what you want to know. He will pass your request on to someone who may be able to answer your questions. If he is so inclined, you will be contacted and told where you will meet."

"And if he is not so inclined?"

"You will hear nothing more."

"Why all the cloak and dagger?"

"The gentleman who may be willing to talk with you is of a different organization than my own."

It wasn't necessary for Rodriguez to say anything more. Common interests often required rivals to cooperate, and it was considered good business to maintain open channels of communication, and even exchange favors. But trust was an entirely different matter. Knowledge was a commodity like any other, something of value to be used only when something of value was received in return.

"If the gentleman is willing to assist you, you will be indebted to him."

"I understand."

There were times when White thought the people who inhabited Rodriguez's world watched far too much television. This was one of those times. The only thing that prevented White from laughing was the old adage, often cited to him by Rodriguez, "The fact that you're paranoid doesn't mean that no one is out to get you."

"What's the number?"

The telephone was answered on the third ring.

"Who gave you this number?" an accented voice demanded.

White couldn't avoid thinking of an armed sentry pointing a rifle at him and demanding, "Friend or foe?" In the history of man, he wondered, did anyone ever answer "foe"?

"Manuel Rodriguez."

"Who are you?"

"Lucius White."

"Your call has been expected. What do you want to know?"

For three minutes, White spoke, uninterrupted, summarizing his situation and the information he was seeking. When he finished, the voice said, "You will be contacted," and hung up. *Don't call us; we'll call you.*

White counted to sixty and then redialed the number. As he expected, after ten rings, it was answered by a recorded message, "The number you have dialed is not a working number." *These people are serious about their security.*

&

White returned the telephone to its cradle and was about to open the file on his securities fraud case when he was interrupted by Grace Matthews on the intercom. "Mr. Parker is calling for you. He's on line one."

"Thank you, Grace," White said as he quickly thought through the possible reasons for Paul Parker's call. Contacts between prosecutors and the defendant's counsel were common during the final stages of trial preparation when they were required to confer and attempt to resolve procedural and evidentiary matters between themselves before invoking the powers of the court. But any trial was a long time away.

White pressed a button on his telephone console. "Good morning, Paul."

"Not for long," Parker said.

"What's up?"

"I just got a call from the U.S. attorney in Miami. They're taking over your Shephard case."

For a moment, White remained silent as he reflected on his last conversation with Graham Brochette.

Parker interrupted his thoughts. "Did you know anything about this?"

"I expected it."

"Do you know why the case has been taken over by the Miami office?"

"Probably because Graham Brochette would have a conflict. It was hard enough for him to ignore the conflict when it was just a drug case. When it became a drug-murder case, he didn't have any choice."

"Uh-huh. I figured it was something like that."

"Is he just taking over the drug case, or is he also taking over the investigation of Tom Shephard's murder?"

"Both."

"How would he have been able to claim jurisdiction over the murder case?"

"They also claim to have evidence that Jackson was actually killed within the confines of the Southern District, and his body was merely dumped over here."

"Which is possible."

"I suppose I should be grateful."

"Grateful? Why?"

"It turns out that I was in law school with Jackson's father. Actually, it was his stepfather, Dick Barlow."

"That's quite a coincidence."

"I suppose," Parker said in a voice that made White think his mind was half a world away. "But I suppose I should be grateful. I hate prosecuting cases where I have any kind of connection to the victim."

White understood what Parker meant. Personal connections between the victim and the prosecutor were grounds for "rush to judgment" defenses. He had used the argument himself and knew how embarrassing it could be for prosecutors.

"When are they taking over?" White asked, changing the subject.

"I just got the call. A guy by the name of Lyle Wilson—he's the number-two guy over there—is taking over the case. He's sending someone over this afternoon to collect everything we have."

White suddenly understood the reason for Parker's call. State law requires prosecutors to disclose all their evidence to the defense attorney, but the federal rules aren't so liberal. Once a U.S. Attorney gets his hands on the evidence, they tend to keep it secret until the eve of trial. "Can we take a look at what you have before they pick it up?"

"That's why I called."

"I appreciate your concern."

"Once the feds get involved," Parker continued, as if he hadn't heard White, "you never know what's going to happen."

"I can't argue with that."

"This is one of those times we have to stick together."

What is he trying to tell me? White thought as his mind returned to his unusual conversation with Parker at the Christmas party. "Will one o'clock be okay?"

"Fine. I'll see you in my office at one."

"One other thing, Paul. Do you know anything about Wilson?"

Parker paused, seeming to sort his thoughts before responding. "He's okay."

"Have you ever worked with him?"

"Not really. But Congressman St. James likes him."

"How do you know Congressman St. James?"

"I worked with him a long time ago. I was with the Miami Police Department while I was going to law school."

"I forgot about that. And you've stayed in touch?"

It took longer than White expected for Parker to answer. "Occasionally."

The tone of Parker's voice suggested that there was something more than an old working relationship that connected Parker to St. James. White thought about pursuing the matter, but decided against it. There would be time to ask about that later.

&

White returned the telephone to the console and,

without thinking, pressed the intercom number for Harry Harris's office. After two rings, he realized his mistake. He leaned back and closed his eyes as feelings of his partner's absence suddenly overwhelmed him. He was just beginning to come to terms with Harry's condition. The loss of the law partner with whom he'd shared so much, and on whom he depended, was something else. Without thinking, he turned his chair to the wall behind his desk and looked at the picture of him and Harry fishing for bonefish in the Florida Keys.

White's reflections on his time with Harry were slowly replaced with thoughts about his appointment with Parker. Almost without thinking, he pressed the intercom button for his apartment.

Leslie answered on the second ring. "Home of the horny bimbo. Blow in my ear, and I'll do anything you like."

White laughed in spite of himself. "One of these days, you'll say something like that and it won't be me on the line."

"What makes you so sure I only say that for your benefit? Are you planning on inviting yourself up for a nooner?"

"Regretfully, I must decline. We have an appointment at Paul Parker's office at one."

"We?"

"I thought you wanted in on the case."

"Oh, I do." White could imagine the smile on Leslie's face. "Why are we meeting with Paul?"

"The feds have taken over David Shepard's case. We need to look at Paul's evidence before it gets taken to Miami."

"What do you want me to do?"

"Paul won't be expecting you. His guard will be down, and he may let something slip if he's dealing with you."

"Then I'll wear something extra sexy!"

&

Leslie followed White into Parker's office on the third floor of the Lee County Justice Center. When Parker looked up and saw Leslie, his lips parted, as if he was about to say something, then closed as he thought better of the idea.

Parker pointed to the conference table and sat down opposite White and Leslie. He pulled a stack of folders from a box on the floor and laid them on the table beside him. "These are copies of all the police reports, the crime scene reports, and the lab reports that have been finished."

Parker opened the first folder and studied it briefly before passing it to White. "This may be the most import- ant file. It's the ballistics report on the gun. The FBI con- firms that the gun that killed Jackson was the gun issued to Graham Brochette."

White took a deep breath as he examined the file, then slid it to Leslie and watched as she read it, shaking her head as her eyes moved down the page.

"I'm sorry, Lucius," Parker said. "I know Graham is a friend of yours, but it's looking more and more like his son is involved in the murder."

White nodded but didn't respond to Parker's observa- tion. *If Brochette's gun was used in the murder of Tom Jackson, Brochette must also be a suspect. Why is Parker only talking about his Shepard case?*

Leslie realized that White's delay must mean that he was thinking about something, so she asked, "Who knows about the ballistics report?"

"So far, only I do," Parker said. "But I have to give it to Lyle Wilson."

White nodded and rejoined the conversation. "What else do you have?"

One by one, Parker opened the files, slid them in front of White and Leslie, and summarized their contents. When he reached the last file, he hesitated, looking first at Leslie and then at White. "Are you sure you want to see the photos of Jackson's body?" He was facing White, but his eyes were on Leslie.

"Let's have them," White said.

Parker slowly spread the pictures on the table. Leslie stifled a gasp.

"The bullet to the back of his head blew away most of his face. We've confirmed the identity from his fingerprints."

White bent over to examine the pictures. "It appears that they burned him with a cigarette."

"Seventeen burn marks," Parker said without looking at the pictures. He continued to watch Leslie, waiting for a reaction.

"And the rest of these marks," White said, pointing to a series of fine bloody lines. "Knife wounds?"

"Or razor," Parker said. "Whatever it was, it was very sharp. But they're all superficial. They were intended to inflict the maximum pain without killing."

"Whoever did this is a vicious bastard with no conscience."

As Parker returned the pictures to the file, Leslie asked, "What's your theory of the murder, Paul?"

Parker looked from White to Leslie and back to White. He seemed to be asking why Leslie had suddenly taken over the discussion.

White responded by inspecting his fingernails. He understood Parker's expression, and the challenge it appeared to convey. Paul Parker was a good old boy in a community still primarily controlled by the old boy net-work. The real power in Lee County still rested in the hands of leaders born and raised locally, and Parker was as "old boy" as you could get. As often as not, significant decisions concerning the community—funding for parks, permits for new developments, and appointments to important boards and commissions—were made over beer and bour-bon at a fishing camp in the Everglades. Women were still not welcome at fish camps.

Leslie smiled at Parker, but her eyes, which never left Parker's face, had a coldness that conveyed a different mes-sage. When Parker didn't respond, her smile faded, and her expression grew sterner. "Paul?" she said in a tone that was not yet demanding but nonetheless conveyed her growing impatience.

"Uh…" Parker returned his attention to Leslie after apparently concluding that she was in charge. "I'm sorry. What was the question?"

"What's your theory of the murder?"

Parker opened the middle drawer of his desk and removed a bottle of chewable antacid tablets. Ignoring Leslie, he opened the bottle and removed two tablets. He returned the bottle to the drawer and continued to stare at the tablets in his hand before placing them in his mouth and returning his attention to Leslie. "Everything seems to point to your client."

"That's the evidence," Leslie said. "I'm interested in what your gut tells you."

Parker leaned back in his chair and found a spot on the ceiling that, for thirty seconds, demanded his attention.

"I have to go with the evidence," Parker finally said.

"But the gun is the only evidence pointing to David."

"It's what we call good evidence."

"Have you even considered anyone else?"

Parker shifted uneasily in his chair. "Like who?"

"It was Graham's gun. Why isn't he also a suspect?"

Parker seemed to think about the question before responding. "I don't think anyone believes that Graham would have killed Jackson. What motive would he have?"

Leslie ignored the question and White rejoined the conversation. "I understand the body was found as a result of a telephone tip."

"That's right."

"In fact, it was you who received the call, wasn't it?"

Parker hesitated before responding. "That's also right." His voice had a suspicious sound to it, something that White noticed and recorded for future consideration.

"Did you do anything to find out who called in the tip?"

"I dialed star sixty-nine."

"And?"

"Nothing. It was from outside the area."

"Didn't you think it's a little unusual for someone to call you with the tip?"

Parker moved uneasily in his chair. "What do you mean?"

"Isn't it more common for people with tips to call the sheriff?"

Parker adjusted his tie. "I suppose so."

"And you also got the call tipping you off to the drugs in the house in Matlacha, didn't you?"

"What are you getting at?"

"Oh, nothing," Leslie said. "It just seems like someone wanted to make sure that you knew about the tips."

"So?"

Leslie ignored his implied question. "I'm sure you get tips on cases all the time."

"Not as often as we'd like, but it's not uncommon."

"But is it common for you to get two tips, disclosing two different crimes that are apparently related and involve the same people?"

Parker looked from Leslie to White and back to Leslie before responding. "I don't suppose so. But that's no longer my problem, is it?"

"No, Paul," White said. "It's the feds' problem now." White stood and concluded, "Thanks for the help. We'll call you if we need anything else."

"Any time," Parker said. The tone of his voice indicated that he meant something else entirely.

&

As they walked from Paul Parker's office in the courthouse to their office, Leslie looked straight ahead, suppressing her smile and waiting for White to make some comment on their meeting with Parker.

White had still not said anything by the time they reached the warehouse, and Leslie was beginning to think she had done something wrong. *Dammit, Lucius White. Say something.*

They were just leaving the elevator on the mezzanine when White turned to face Leslie and said. "I guess it's about time you moved your things into Harry's office until he comes back."

Leslie smiled as she slapped him gently with a file.

&

White went directly to his office where he placed a call to Graham Brochette.

"Graham, what do you know about a U.S. attorney in Miami by the name of Lyle Wilson?"

"What do you want to know?"

"Do you know him?"

"Of course. He worked in this office for about five years before transferring to Miami."

"Why did he transfer?"

Brochette hesitated. "I think it had to do with some family issues."

"What kind of family issues?"

"Before he transferred, he went through a messy divorce. He was pretty much wiped out, both financially and emotionally. He may have been looking for a fresh start."

White nodded.

"Or it may have had something to do with my appointment."

"What do you mean?"

"He was also being considered for my position. He was acting U.S. attorney here, and he wanted it made permanent. He wasn't happy about being passed over, and things were a little strained when I first got here."

"Were they still strained when he left?"

"I don't think so. He worked for me for three years. When I took over the office, I put him in charge of all our drug cases and let him decide which state cases we'd take over. He had a little empire of his own, and he seemed perfectly happy."

"Do you trust him?"

"That's a strange question."

"He's taking over David's cases. I need to know all about him."

"Uh-huh. Well, I don't have any reason not to trust him. Of course, I haven't worked with him for a few years."

"Were you on good terms when he left?"

"I think so. He even stopped by to visit on the day of David's probable cause hearing."

"How do you know that?"

"My secretary told me."

"What was he doing in Tampa?"

"The office log shows that he was here to review some case files."

"Why would he have to review case files in the Tampa office?"

"It's not that unusual. Investigations by one office often require information on investigations going on in another office, especially when the offices cover neighboring districts."

"Why wouldn't he have just called to get the information?"

"Normally he would. But he used to live in Tampa. Maybe he was coming to town for some other reason."

"Uh-huh."

"Why do you want to know about Lyle?"

"He's in charge of your son's case."

"Yeah. I know. He called me when the matter came up. He told me he was going to ask for the case and he wanted to know if I had any problem with him prosecuting my son."

"And did you?"

"I felt a little awkward at first. But if it has to happen, I'd rather someone I know is in charge."

"What can you tell me about him?"

"I hate to admit it, but I don't know that much about him. He'd been with the office about a few when I got here. He was already supervising the work of younger assistant US attorneys. He didn't get into the courtroom much, so I can't tell you a lot about his trial skills."

"But you worked with him for three years. You must know something I can use."

"As I said, he was already a supervisor when I got here. He kept me informed on the status of cases in his section. As long as there weren't any problems, he pretty much ran his own shop."

"Did you ever have any disagreements with him?"

Brochette hesitated before responding. "That's an odd question."

"I'm just trying to get some insight into his personality."

"Well… now that you ask…"

"What?"

"He was generally hard-nosed about cutting deals, even with cases I didn't think were that strong. He'd rather risk losing at trial than cut a deal."

"But…"

"There were maybe half a dozen times I thought he should have taken over some state cases." Brochette paused as if trying to dredge up old facts. "The evidence was good, and the dealers seemed to be serious players."

"But isn't it your policy to let the state's attorneys prosecute their own cases?"

"That's right. And that was the problem. The dealers in the cases Lyle passed on seemed important. I thought he should have taken over. But his decisions were consistent with my policy."

"You didn't have to approve his decisions."

"They were judgment calls, and I try to support my people."

"So, you trust him?"

The silence on the other end of the line continued longer than it should have.

"Graham?"

"I don't have much choice, do I?"

But you know something you aren't telling me. What the hell is going on?

22.

It was Monday, the week before Christmas. Horse wasn't surprised to see that the judicial docket, posted on the notice board beside the bank of elevators, didn't show any trials commencing that week. Judges have no more interest in working over the holidays than anyone else. The judicial calendar only listed a smattering of hearings. Attorneys don't like to work over the holidays either.

"Would you be Mister McGee?" a voice behind Horse said.

Horse turned and introduced himself to Detective Peter Gordon, retired. Gordon was unimposing in every respect. Short, no more than five feet, seven inches, and small framed. His face was narrow, his hair gray and thin. It was hard for Horse to imagine him as the highly regarded narcotics detective Lou Hamilton described when he arranged the meeting.

"I hope you don't mind if we grab a quick sandwich in the canteen. I have the misfortune of being involved in one of the few cases being heard this week. The judge wants this case wrapped up today, and he only gave us forty-five minutes for lunch."

"What kind of a case is it?" Horse asked, just to make small talk as they walked down the hallway to the canteen.

"Divorce," Gordon said. "That's mostly what I've been doing since I left the force."

Horse resisted the temptation to say something. Surveillance in domestic relations cases was generally regarded as the bottom rung of the private investigation ladder.

Gordon seemed to read Horse's mind. "Running around seeing who's screwing who isn't what I figured I'd be doing when I retired and hung out my shingle..." Gordon paused to exchange holiday greetings with a uniformed policeman. "But Palm Beach is a little different. Sometimes I think everyone on the island is sharing sausages with someone other than his or her lawful spouse. Their divorces involve big money, and I mean big money. Scorned spouses are willing to pay very well for proof that hubby has a wandering dick."

They entered the canteen and Gordon dropped his briefcase onto a plastic chair. "What'll you have? My treat."

"Chicken salad on a kaiser roll and iced tea would be fine."

"Betty," Gordon called out to the elderly woman behind the counter. "Two bird salads on rolls and a couple of cold teas."

Gordon let his coat slip off his shoulders and laid it on the back of the chair where he'd dropped his briefcase. "Now what can I do for you?" he asked as he took a seat opposite Horse. "Lou Hamilton didn't tell me much."

"I'm interested in information on heroin trafficking."

"Ah, the good old days," Gordon said as if there was something nostalgic about the heroin trade. "I hear it's still a problem down in Miami. A lot of heroin was being spread around Liberty City, but not much up here. Designer drugs and cocaine are the mind adjusters of preference among the obscenely rich."

"What about a few years ago?"

"Now that's a different story." Gordon seemed to find something amusing in old memories. "Not that we had a big problem on the streets, but we had us a hell of an investigation into importing the stuff."

"Tell me about it."

"There isn't that much to tell. A lot of heroin was hitting the streets up in Jacksonville, over in Tampa, and down in Miami. The state attorney general put together a multi-jurisdictional task force to share information. The local authorities cut deals with a few users, got the names of some street dealers, and worked their way up the food chain to a few distributors, but that's where the trail ended. None of the distributors ever had direct contact with the top guy."

"None of them?"

"None of them would admit to anything. Whoever was bringing the stuff into the country was either very good or very careful. But most everyone we talked to claimed the stuff was being brought into the country by someone right here."

"Who?"

"We never did nail anyone. The task force was on it for about a year. Had a hell of a lot of leads, I'll tell you that. But we just couldn't nail the guy."

"Why not?"

"He was smart. Never got within two or three guys of the stuff himself. I gotta hand it to him. He had himself a slick network. We got close, but we never got anyone high enough to give us the big man."

"So, you don't know who he is?"

"Not that I could prove… but I had my suspicions." As he spoke, Gordon rearranged the condiment containers in front of him. "Trouble was, all of a sudden everything stopped. No more leads were coming from other cities. No more snitches. It was like whoever was the local kingpin, if there ever was one, packed up and vanished."

"Is that what you think happened?"

"No one much cared what I thought. But no. I don't think he left. I think he just moved on to something safer."

"Do you have someone specific in mind?"

"Yeah. There was a Cambodian guy who worked for a lawyer name of Richard Barlow. He's a—"

"Immigration lawyer," Horse completed the sentence. "He the guy you're looking at?"

"His name has come up."

Gordon nodded before continuing. "You know, immigration's not the biggest part of Barlow's practice. At least not anymore."

"Oh. What is?"

"He's the go-to guy for drugs."

"That's interesting. When did he start doing that?"

"I don't remember. It was a while ago. But I think it was about the time his kid got nailed for possession of heroin?"

"That could have an effect on a father. Did he handle the case?"

Gordon rubbed his hands, seeming to think about the question. "Yeah. I think he did. And he seemed to have the magic touch."

"How's that?"

Gordon shook his head. "A lot of his cases were thrown out for bad searches or some other technical reason."

"And you didn't like that."

"Well sure. No cop likes it when someone walks on a technicality, but..." Gordon paused and surveyed the room before leaning closer to Horse. "But I think Barlow won a lot of cases he had no business winning."

"Do you think cases were being fixed?"

"Those are your words, not mine."

Horse paused while he jotted some notes. When he

looked up, he asked, "Did you ever think Barlow's interest went beyond just representing drug dealers?"

"To tell you the truth, I don't remember him representing many dealers. Mostly just users."

"Didn't you find that odd?"

"I didn't think about it. But now that you mention it…"

"Yes?"

"At one point I thought he might be a dealer."

"What made you think that?"

"Well, it wasn't him personally. It was this Cambodian guy he had working for him. Supposedly he was Barlow's investigator. But I had some low-level snitches who claimed he did more than investigate."

"Like what?"

"No one would, or could, say anything definite. I just put a lot of little things together and got a bad feeling about the Cambodian."

"And Barlow?"

"Nothing definite. But if the Cambodian was involved, I figured Barlow had to have something to do with it."

"What do you have on Barlow?"

"Not much. We never had enough to even bring him in for questioning."

"Why not?"

"This guy has serious juice in important circles. He's cozy with the prosecutors in the state's attorney's office, and I hear he's got some politicians that owe him favors. You don't drag guys like him in for questioning unless you have something solid."

"Do you think he's still in the business?"

"I couldn't say."

Betty delivered their sandwiches. Neither of them said anything as they chewed and thought.

Horse washed down a bite of sandwich with a swallow of iced tea and resumed their conversation. "You said something about a task force looking into the heroin trade. What can you tell me about that?"

"There's not much to tell. Like I said, the brass figured there was a connection between someone here and the major distributors in Jacksonville, Tampa, and Miami. Each of the jurisdictions assigned someone to the task force. We exchanged leads and got together once a month to share ideas."

"Did anything come from the task force?"

Gordon chuckled. "I got some great out-of-town meals at taxpayer's expense… but nothing else."

"You didn't mention the FBI or the DEA. Were either of them involved in the task force?"

"When's the last time the feds cooperated with anyone?"

"Dumb question," Horse admitted.

"Damned straight."

"Do you remember anyone else on the task force?"

"Just one guy—and I wouldn't remember him except that he got himself elected to Congress."

"Congressman St. James," Horse said without looking up from his sandwich.

Gordon's eyes brightened. "There you go."

"What was your impression of St. James?"

Gordon stared at his plate before speaking. "I hate to say anything about another cop…"

"But he's not a cop. He's a congressman."

Gordon laughed. "Well, I don't mind saying anything bad about a politician."

"So you didn't like him?"

"Didn't trust him."

"Why?"

"He was worse than the feds. He'd take all the information we came up with, but he wouldn't share what he had."

"Why do you suppose that was?"

Gordon put down his sandwich and leaned forward, crossing his arms on the table. "I remember thinking about that one time after we all got together. We had met for dinner in Miami. As usual, St. James didn't bring anything new to the table. After dinner, I met for drinks with another guy I knew in the narcotics division. We were swapping stories when he started talking about some scumbag who was ready to cut a deal and rat out a whole heroin network."

"And St. James hadn't mentioned any of this?"

"No. But that's not all. It turns out the rat was released on bail, but he got himself killed before he could talk. A needle of pure smack in the arm."

"And you're sure St. James knew about this?"

"Know about it. He was responsible for keeping an eye on the guy. You know, making sure he stayed safe until he testified."

Horse perked up. "What happened?"

"The surveillance car went to the wrong address. Apparently, someone transposed the digits on the guy's location."

"And you didn't think anything of that?"

"Not at the time," Gordon said between bites. "Shit happens. And besides, I wasn't inclined to bust anyone's balls. St. James was a cop, for God's sake."

"Did you ever ask him about it?"

"Yeah. I mentioned it at our next meeting. He admitted the story was true, but he claimed the guy hadn't said anything useful."

"He must have said something to get a bail reduction."

"He gave up the names of some local bottom feeders. But he was still holding the good stuff when he was murdered."

Horse pushed himself away from the table, crossed his legs, and took a bite of his pickle.

"Do you know anything about the Cambodian who worked for Barlow?"

"Not really. Just some loose threads that may have linked him to some out-of-town dealers. Like I said, I wanted to look at him a little closer, but I didn't have enough to justify ruffling Barlow's feathers. Was he involved in moving the drugs?"

"He may have been. Have you heard anything about him?"

"Not for a long time."

"Anything else?"

Gordon continued to munch on his sandwich as he thought. For a moment he looked at Horse as if trying to decide how much to say. Finally, he swallowed and leaned forward. "There's one thing that bothered me about the way the task force was closed down."

Horse waited while Gordon took a swallow of iced tea. "Now, mind you, this is just instinct talking." Gordon swept his plate to the side with the back of his hand and leaned forward on his elbows. "I think we stumbled onto something the feds were interested in and we got called off."

"What makes you say that?"

"Like I said, I didn't have enough to bring Barlow in, but I had enough to ask for a wiretap."

Horse stopped chewing and waited expectantly.

"Nada."

"You didn't get the warrant?"

"No. And right after I asked for the wiretap warrant the task force was disbanded."

"What do you think it means?"

"You're going to call me crazy, but I think the feds already had a tap on the guy."

"Nothing the feds do would surprise me."

"You got that right," Gordon said. "But that's not all. I think their tap was illegal."

"What makes you say that?"

Gordon responded with a look that was somewhere between a smile and a smirk. "I got my sources."

Horse resumed slowly chewing his pickle as he considered Gordon's revelation. Finally, he swallowed and said, "And it was right after that when everything came to a stop?"

"Pretty much. What do you think happened?"

"Maybe he was warned that you were getting close."

"Anything's possible," Gordon said. "Whatever happened, I'd dearly love to know how much the feds knew."

"Just one last thing," Horse said. "Why was your task force focusing on the heroin trade. I'd think the cocaine would have been more appropriate."

"I wondered about that too. But this was a couple of years ago, and cocaine was mostly the drug of choice for the rich. I guess the bosses didn't want to go after them, or their dealers. Heroin was still a big-time street drug, so that's where they had us looking."

"But things are different now," Horse said.

"Yeah. In some ways. Coke is still the drug of choice among the idle rich, but crack cocaine is the scourge of the lower classes. That's where the cops are putting their manpower now."

"Whatever happened to the Cambodian, the guy who worked for Barlow?"

"I thought he might have had something to do with heroin trafficking. But like I said, he sort of disappeared."

"Did you ever think that he may have just moved from heroin to cocaine?"

"No. I can't say that the idea ever occurred to me. But that was about the time I retired from the force." Gordon swept the remaining dishes away from in front of him and leaned on the table. "Is that what you think happened?"

"It was just a thought," Horse said.

23.

From West Palm Beach, Horse drove south on Interstate 95 to Fort Lauderdale. At the first Fort Lauderdale exit, he turned off the interstate and headed east toward the county courthouse. As in West Palm Beach, downtown traffic was light, and Horse easily found a parking spot within a block of his destination.

As he entered the offices of Gereghty and Martin, Bail Bondsmen, a woman Horse guessed to be in her mid-thirties waved him to a chair while she chatted on the phone. Getting the final details on how some friend got dumped by her boyfriend was more important than tending to business. Horse used the time to examine the office.

Behind the low divider that defined the waiting area was a clutter of mismatched filing cabinets and cheap steel desks. The clients of bail bondsmen don't tend to be concerned with office accouterments, but the new Mercedes parked in the reserve spot outside the door suggested that business was good. Gereghty and/or Martin understood their fiscal priorities.

In the rear of the office room were two offices, separated from the front room by windows with vertical blinds. One of the offices was dark. In the other room, a middle-aged man with thinning hair, an open-neck sports shirt, and a serious aversion to exercise was talking on the phone. A thick cigar with a long ash protruded from his mouth. Each time he spoke, the cigar jerked up and down.

Horse's attention was focused on the ash, waiting for

it to fall, when his concentration was interrupted by the woman in the front room. "Can I help you?"

Horse handed her his business card. "I'd like to speak to someone about a bond you posted for Thomas Jackson over in Fort Myers."

The woman studied at the card suspiciously before turning and glancing toward the office where the man was just ending his call. She picked up the telephone, held the receiver close to her mouth, and pressed a button. Horse watched as the man listened to her whisper a message. The man looked up from his desk, inspected Horse with a look of disdain, and nodded.

"Mr. Martin will see you in a moment."

A minute later, the heaving bulk of Robert Martin crossed the office. He scowled as he examined Horse's card. "You want to know about Tom Jackson?" he said, without the benefit of an introduction. Personality isn't an essential quality in the bail bond business.

"Yes. I was wondering—"

Martin waived a hand dismissively. "He's dead, you know?"

"Yes. I know. But I was hoping you could tell me who paid for his bail bond."

"He had an attorney over in Fort Myers. Why don't you ask her?"

"I was in the neighborhood, and I thought I'd stop in."

The man wasn't buying it. "Since when is Fort Lauderdale 'in the neighborhood' for a private investigator from Fort Myers?"

"I had some other business over here."

"Something connected to Jackson?"

"Maybe. I'm not sure."

The man continued to inspect Horse. "What was it you wanted to know?"

"Who paid for Tom Jackson's bail bond."

"His attorney."

"Who was that?"

"You're the investigator. Check the court records."

"They only show the attorney who represented him at his bail hearing; the one you sent the bond to."

"Then I can't help you. The attorneys I work with don't want their names given out."

"Well, can you tell me if you write bail bonds for an attorney named Richard Barlow in West Palm Beach."

"Yeah. I done some other business with him and his clients. So if that's all…" Before Horse could ask another question, Martin had turned and was walking toward his office.

Horse was about to accept defeat when he had one last inspiration. "Have you ever had clients referred to you by Franklin St. James?"

The man stopped short and hesitated before turning around. "What are you suggesting?"

"I'm not suggesting anything. I'm just looking for information."

"Why do you care about St. James?"

Horse ignored the question. "I knew him when he was a detective for the Miami Police Department."

Martin leaned against a file cabinet and cocked his head. "Yeah? What division was he in?"

"Narcotics. Fifteenth Precinct."

"Okay. So you know St. James. So what?"

"He was always after the dealers. Never cared much about recreational users."

"Yeah. That was St. James."

"He said he had a bail bondsman he referred a lot of business to. Was that you?"

"Yeah, sure. He sent me some business from time to time. What's that got to do with the price of coffee?"

"I was just curious. St. James is a Miami cop. Why was he referring business to a bail bondsman in Fort Lauderdale?"

Martin's nostrils flared. "That's none of your business."

"In fact, why would a narcotics detective have any reason for helping anyone he had just arrested?"

"Ask him?"

"And why are you writing bail bonds for an attorney in West Palm Beach?"

Martin glared at Horse. "Mister. Ain't none of that any of your business?" Martin again turned and started toward his office. "And I've said all I'm going to say."

"Did it ever strike you as odd that half the people Mr. Barlow bailed out ended up dead?"

Martin didn't bother turning. "That's got nothing to do with me."

"How about conspiracy to commit murder?"

Marten abruptly stopped and turned. "What the fuck are you talking about?"

"If you knew what was going to happen to your clients when they got out of jail, you're just as guilty as the person who killed them."

The man glared at Horse for a moment before responding, "Get the fuck out of here," and returned to his office.

&

Thwump. The side of Leslie's foot slammed into the side of the heavy punching bag in the gym on the first floor of White's warehouse.

"One more," White urged her.

Leslie spun and threw the side of her foot against the bag. Her gray sweatshirt was dark with perspiration.

White released the bag and came to where Leslie was standing. His own sweatshirt was also dark, and sweat was dripping off his chin.

"Good workout."

"What's the matter, big boy?" Leslie said as she danced around the bag throwing feigned punches. "Getting too old for a little workout?"

"I think two hours is enough."

"You just want to save your energy in case you get lucky later."

"You caught me."

Their conversation was interrupted by the chirping of White's cell phone. "It's Horse," he whispered to Leslie as he answered. "What do you have?"

For five minutes White listened, nodding occasionally as Horse summarized his meetings with Detective Gordon and the bail bondsman. Finally, White said, "We need to dig into that," and hung up.

"Dig into what?" Leslie asked.

White lowered himself to the bench beside Leslie and gazed thoughtfully at the floor. "The congressman's name has come up again."

"As in the congressman who seems to be interested in Graham's nomination?"

"The same."

"What are you going to do?"

"I don't know," White said as he pulled a towel off the rack and began drying his face.

"Graham needs your help," Leslie said as they entered the elevator that would take them to their apartment.

"I'm not sure he wants it."

"That's irrelevant. You're going to help him whether he asks you or not."

"Probably," White said.

"And you think there's a connection between David's case and whatever Congressman St. James is doing?"

"If it weren't for David's case, and David's connection to Graham, there wouldn't be any reason for the congressman to be interested in Graham's nomination."

"That's not the same as saying that David's case is connected to the congressman."

White pursed his lips and nodded. "Someone has to figure out what the congressman is up to, and why he's trying to block Graham's appointment."

"Jack Lancaster didn't say St. James was the one who was blocking the nomination."

"No. But St. James is the logical suspect."

"And Graham can't very well investigate the congressman himself. You're the only one who can investigate the congressman."

"And you don't think I can handle two investigations at the same time?"

"You could be looking for two different things with contradictory consequences. What helps David might hurt Graham… and vice versa."

"But only David is our client."

"That's not going to stop you from looking into anything connected to Graham's nomination."

White smiled. "Uh-huh. And I suppose you have a solution in mind."

"Me?" Leslie said in mock surprise. "*You're* the boss."

"Uh-huh."

"What?"

"Why do I have the feeling you want to take over David's case?"

Leslie returned his smile. "You finally concluded that I'm a damned good attorney."

"And a fine lover."

Leslie snapped her towel at him and ducked off the elevator before he could respond. "If you promise to be a good boy, you can join me in the shower."

&

An hour later White and Leslie lay together on their bed, naked and spent.

"That was nice," Leslie murmured into his ear. "And you didn't even have to buy me dinner."

"But now I have to cook."

"It's a small price to pay for great sex."

"What makes you think it was all that great?"

"What makes you think you'll be getting more any time soon?"

"This is one of those times I should keep my mouth shut, isn't it?"

"You learn fast for a country boy."

24.

Leslie and Horse were hunched over the conference table in the War Room when White knocked on the door and wandered in. Something didn't feel right. It was the first time they had met in the War Room since Harris's stroke. The empty spot by the side of the conference table where Harry always parked his wheelchair left a void White could feel. For a moment, he stood in the doorway, lost in his own thoughts, before entering.

"I wondered where my top investigator had disappeared to."

Leslie looked up and smiled innocently. "I sort of borrowed Horse."

"So I see. What are you two doing?"

"We're going over the lab reports from the crime scene."

"Have you come up with anything?"

"We're sure Jackson wasn't killed where the body was found," Leslie said, handing White the report she and Horse had been studying. "There was grass caught in his shoes. But there wasn't any grass in the field where the body was discovered. We think the grass is from where he was killed. Probably when he was dragged to whatever vehicle took them to the dumpsite."

"Any leads on the vehicle?"

"Nothing that seems very promising. The sheriff's people made casts of the tire marks, but there were just too many. Same with shoe prints. The fresh prints all seem to be from the police and the police cars. The others had been pretty much destroyed as useful evidence."

"What else do you have?"

"There's something else in the crime scene report for the Matlacha house. In addition to cocaine residue in Jackson's bedroom, they found traces of marijuana everywhere, and a couple of marijuana roaches in the living room."

"David admitted that he used marijuana," White said.

"There's another thing that may help," Horse said. "If nothing else, it may be a connection between the Matlacha house and the murder."

"What?"

"The crime scene report for the Matlacha house says that they found butts from a French brand of cigarettes. A butt from the same brand of cigarettes was recovered from the field where the bodies were found. It's not likely that Jackson was given a last smoke before he was shot."

"So the killer had been at the Matlacha house sometime."

"It's a good bet."

"Is the grass from Jackson's shoe consistent with grass near the house?"

"Do you think Jackson was killed in Matlacha?"

"It wouldn't be my choice. But you better check on the grass."

Horse nodded and made a note on his pad. "It may also be important that this brand of cigarettes isn't sold anywhere in the Fort Myers area. The nearest place they're sold is Miami."

White nodded.

"There's one other thing," Horse continued. "The cigarette is a brand that's popular with the Vietnamese. Probably something left over from the French occupation of Vietnam."

"Or it might also be the brand of choice of a Cambodian."

"It could be. Anything else?"

"Any leads to who Shepard and Jackson were working for... or who else might have a motive for killing Jackson?"

"Not yet."

"So we're nowhere."

Horse shrugged.

"Maybe we're just looking at it wrong," Leslie said.

White and Horse returned the crime scene reports to the table and turned to Leslie.

"So far we've been trying to find a cause-and-effect connection between events. 'X' happens because of 'Y.'"

White and Horse nodded. They had no idea what Leslie had in mind, but nothing else was getting them anywhere.

"Maybe the events aren't connected... not to each other. Maybe the only thing they have in common is their connection to some scheme we haven't discovered.

"The point is," Leslie continued, "a motive might help explain what we know." Leslie twirled a lock of hair around her finger as she struggled for words to explain what she was thinking. "I know motive isn't an element of a crime, but everyone knows that motive is important to juries. Without a motive, a close case can become a not guilty, and with a motive, the same case goes the other way."

"That's true enough," White agreed. "But we're nowhere near trial."

"We're nowhere near anything," Leslie said. "The facts we have aren't enough to explain all the events. We know about more crimes than we have suspects, and we don't even know which of the crimes are connected. We're obviously missing something. If we can figure out why these things are happening, maybe we can figure out where to look for the missing facts."

"She's right, you know," Horse said. "Whatever else may be going on, the only thing we have to be concerned with is David Shepard. If he isn't being set up, all the rest of this is irrelevant."

"And if he is being set up," Leslie interrupted, "there has to be a reason for it. By himself, David just isn't important enough for anyone to want to frame him."

White chewed absently on his lip. "But we're really looking at two setups, the original drug bust and the murder."

"You don't think they're connected?" Horse asked.

"Oh, I'm sure they're connected," White said. "But I also think Leslie is right. They may not be part of a single plan."

White leaned back. The chair creaked as he rocked slowly and rubbed his chin. "Let's start with the drug arrest… and let's assume it was a setup. The only ones who get hurt are Shepard and Jackson. Somebody wanted them thrown in jail. That was the original plan."

"But why?"

"I still don't know. All I'm sure of is that somebody wanted leverage over them."

"But," Horse said, "if Jackson was in jail, he couldn't have been killed. And if Shepard was still in jail after Jackson was bailed out, he wouldn't have been able to kill Jackson."

"Okay. Then let's assume that Jackson's murder wasn't part of the original plan."

"Then why was Jackson murdered?"

"That depends on your perspective," White said as he picked up a colored marker and began tapping it on the table. "We can assume that Shepard and Jackson were set up, but we don't know who was behind the setup, or why it was necessary. The way the drugs were found, a single deputy coming out of the bedroom with drugs that David swears he never saw before, makes it look like they were being framed."

Leslie and Horse nodded as White continued. "The only likely reason the authorities would have for framing a couple of small-time nobodies is that they expected them to give up someone else, someone higher up the drug food chain."

Horse slapped his palm on the table. "And when Jackson was released, the higher-ups figured he'd made a deal and it was time to get rid of him."

"Them," Leslie corrected. "If someone higher on the food chain thought they had to get rid of Tom Jackson, they would have to get rid of David for the same reason."

"That's one possibility," White said. "And it means we're looking for two different people: the person who wanted Shepard and Jackson arrested for leverage and whoever wanted one or both of them killed, to keep them from talking. Under that scenario, both David and Jackson were victims of someone's plot, and both Shepard and Jackson were liabilities who needed to be eliminated."

"Do you have something else in mind?"

"Maybe," White said. "Suppose David was the target of the setup all along, and someone wanted to frame him on drug charges. When Jackson agreed to a deal, David suddenly had a motive for getting rid of Jackson. Whoever was after David in the first place saw an opportunity to pin Jackson's murder on him in addition to having him charged with possession of the drugs."

"Murder is an extreme step just to set David up."

"It depends on how badly someone wanted to frame him."

"I suppose," Leslie said. "But we can't ignore the possibility that someone else had to keep Jackson from telling what he knew."

White nodded. "We also can't ignore the possibility that Jackson alone was the target of a setup and Shepard was just a victim of circumstances. Sort of an innocent bystander."

"But who would want Jackson set up for the drug bust?" Horse said. "The only outside connection we have is to the Cambodian... and his only known connection, other than to Shepard and Jackson, seems to be to Jackson's father."

Leslie stopped making notes and turned her attention to Horse. "Are you assuming that Jackson knew something that could hurt his father?"

"He might have."

"But even if he did, we have to assume that his father isn't behind his murder. What father is going to go along with a plan to murder his own son?"

White stood and began pacing around the conference table. "Someone else connected to the father might not be so sentimental."

"Do you think the Cambodian was acting on his own?"

"That... or he was working for someone else... someone other than Barlow. It's time to start nosing around on the east coast."

"Fine. But where?"

"I don't know," White said. "We'll just have to start pushing until someone decides to push back."

"Well," Leslie interrupted, "while we're sticking our noses into interesting places, there's something else we need to consider. Jackson started talking about a plea while Paul Parker still had the case. Right?"

Horse and White nodded and waited.

"I'm just brainstorming... but Jackson offered information in exchange for a deal from Parker. That means he wasn't afraid of the consequences of talking to Parker."

Horse shook his head. "Not necessarily. It could be that he just didn't know enough to be afraid of talking to Paul."

"But Leslie may be on to something," White said. "According to Diane Lindsey, Jackson thought his case would be taken over by the U.S. attorney for the Southern District. She said he only started talking about a deal with Paul when he realized that, if the case was taken over by a U.S. attorney, it would be in the Middle District. He must have known that whatever information he had to trade wouldn't do him any good in the Middle District."

Leslie seemed to suddenly realize what White was implying. "So someone in the Southern District could have a reason to be afraid of what Jackson knew… and might be willing to trade for a deal."

"That's what I was thinking," White said. "But that alone doesn't narrow things down very much. We can agree that whatever Jackson knew probably only had value in the Southern District. But we still don't know if it concerned wrongdoing by drug dealers or the police or someone in the judicial system. Someone from any one of those groups could have a reason to shut Jackson up."

&

The rhythmic beeping of the heart monitor created a kind of peaceful background noise, like the chirping of crickets in the night. Leslie was the only visitor in the ICU. She heard the squeaky soles of the nurse's shoes approaching and looked up from her place beside Harry Harris's bed.

"He looks like he's asleep," Leslie said softly.

"He comes and goes," the ICU nurse said. "His eyes were open a little while ago."

"Was he…?"

"Alert?" the nurse prompted.

"Yes."

The nurse shook her head. "I'm sorry."

"It isn't your fault," Leslie murmured, still holding Harris's hand.

"He's being moved tomorrow, isn't he?"

Leslie fought back a tear. "We're taking him to the long-term care center in Miami."

"They're the best. If anyone can help him, they can."

"That's what Dr. Levenson said," Leslie said.

The nurse returned to her station, and Leslie sat down. "We're going to do everything we can, Harry," she whispered.

The ICU room's door opened, and White entered, followed by Dr. John Wiley. White headed directly for Harris's bed, and Leslie. Wiley retrieved Harris's chart from the nurse and joined them. "Hi, Leslie," Wiley said. "Are you doing okay?"

"I guess… Better than Harry."

Wiley scanned the chart before continuing. "He's holding on. That's a good sign."

Leslie looked up hopefully.

"He has a long way to go, but I didn't expect him to make it this long."

"Harry's tough," White said, to no one in particular. "If heart and willpower mean anything…"

They were interrupted by the nurse. "I'm sorry, but visiting hours are over."

Dr. Wiley was about to object when the nurse scowled at him. Instead, he merely said, "Thank you, nurse."

Leslie stood slowly. White wrapped an arm around her

and guided her toward the door. When they reached the waiting room, Leslie collapsed on a chair and began to cry.

25.

White was reviewing the final draft of a brief in his securities fraud case when his private line rang. Without looking up from the brief, White reached for the receiver and answered, "Lucius White."

"Please listen carefully, Mr. White."

The unusual beginning of the conversation seized White's attention. A quick look at the screen on the telephone console told him that neither the caller's name or number was identified. Out of habit, he looked at the clock on the corner of his desk and made a note of the time.

"I'm listening."

"On the southeast corner of the intersection of US 41 and State Road 997, there's a gas station and convenience store. There's a parking area on the north side of the convenience store. The man you want to talk to will meet you there at seven o'clock tonight."

"That's only three hours from now," White said, hoping his response didn't come out as the protest it had started out to be.

"That's enough time."

"How will I know you?"

"The man you want to talk to will know you. Come alone."

"It would be helpful, to all of us, if my investigator was there."

What White assumed to be a hand over the caller's mouthpiece muffled a brief conversation with someone else. Fifteen seconds later, the caller returned. "You may bring Mr. McGee. But no one else."

How the hell do they know Horse's name? "We'll be there."

"Seven o'clock," the caller confirmed and hung up.

&

Traffic on Route 41, known locally as the Tamiami Trail, the original road across the southern edge of the Everglades from Naples to Miami, was surprisingly light. Few people traveled the old road, the original Alligator Alley, since the interstate across the Everglades opened. There were no enclaves of significance between Naples, on the west coast, and Miami. What little traffic there was most likely stopped at Port o' the Glades, an upscale development midway across the Alley, or turned south to Everglades City or one of the isolated clusters of fish camps

Half an hour into the crossing, Horse signaled White to stop.

"What's up?"

Horse turned on the overhead light and unfolded a large-scale map between them. With his finger, he made a circle on the map extending from the road they were on south to Everglades City. "This area is one of the few areas where there's grass like the kind found on Jackson's shoe."

"How do you know that?"

"I checked on the grass stuck in Jackson's shoes. It wasn't like the grass in Matlacha, so I called the Department of Agriculture extension service. According to them, the grass found on the body is only indigenous to this area."

White retrieved a flashlight from the compartment on his door and shined it on the area of the map Horse indicated. "There aren't many ways in or out."

Horse grunted. "I think we just passed this road," he said, indicating a narrow line on the map.

White continued to examine the map. "Pretty isolated back there."

"Uh-huh."

"Good place to dump a body."

"Uh-huh."

"The gators wouldn't leave a trace."

"Uh-huh."

"But if this is where Jackson was killed, why was his body found fifty miles north of here in an open field near a busy highway?"

White put the truck in gear, and they continued east.

Horse broke the silence first. "They wanted the body discovered."

White nodded. "Why?"

"To send a message," Horse suggested.

"Maybe. But to who?"

Horse shrugged. "Maybe they wanted to be sure the bullet would be recovered."

"So that there would be proof that Graham's gun was the murder weapon."

"Could be."

"Or…" White paused, "to avoid a payoff on a bail bond. If Jackson disappeared, the bail bondsman would have to cough up fifty thousand. With a body, he has no liability."

"But why Alva?" Horse asked. "It would've been just as easy to dump the body along Alligator Alley, and there wouldn't be as much risk of being caught."

"Maybe it was for jurisdictional purposes."

"How's that?"

"If the body was found here, the case would be in the jurisdiction of the Collier County state's attorney. Bodies found in Lee County give Paul Parker jurisdiction over the murder."

"So someone wanted Paul to have jurisdiction."

White shrugged. "Or maybe Paul wanted it."

"Why would he want jurisdiction?"

"If he had it, he controls the investigation... and the evidence."

"You don't think..."

"I'm just listing possibilities."

Miles passed before Horse broke the silence. "Maybe someone just wanted to make David a viable suspect."

"How would moving the body to Alva do that?"

"David has to check in with the court officer at least every six hours, and he has to check in from a phone in Tampa. Alva is within a six-hour round trip of Brochette's house, but this area of the Glades isn't."

"Good thinking. That's why you're the investigator, and I'm just the lowly attorney."

&

At 7:02, a dark limousine, black or maybe dark blue, pulled off the Tamiami Trail and into the convenience store and gas station on the corner of State Road 997. It cruised slowly around the parking lot until the driver spotted White's gold pickup truck. The limousine made a wide arc and parked directly in front of White's truck. Its lights, on high beam, blinded White and Horse.

In spite of the glare of the limousine's headlights, White could make out the movement of the passenger door opening and a large man stepping out. For a moment, he remained standing beside the limousine. White assumed the man was somehow confirming his identity, although where the other man could have obtained a picture, or any other means of identification, eluded him.

The man nodded to someone still inside the limousine and walked toward White's truck. The limousine driver's door opened, and another man headed for the passenger side of the truck. When the first man reached the door, White rolled down the window. All he could see was the man's waist, broad chest, large forearms, and larger hands. White guessed the man to be at least six feet five and, if his forearms were a good indication, at least three hundred pounds. At a minimum, he was an intimidating bodyguard. More than that, White preferred not to consider.

White quickly examined the man's arms and hands. He wasn't wearing a watch or any rings and had no visible tattoos. Nothing that could be used to identify the man. White concluded that these people were very cautious and didn't overlook even the slightest detail.

A voice told White and Horse to get out and face the truck. They did as instructed.

"Put your hands on the truck," the first man ordered.

As they did so, powerful hands expertly patted them down.

"He's clean," the first man said.

"So's this one," the driver said.

"This way," the first man ordered, signaling White and Horse to the limousine.

The rear door opened as they approached. The inside of the limousine was as dark as a cave, made so by the black window tinting and the absence of any interior lights. White could only make out the legs of someone seated in the middle of the rear seat. His upper body and black face were lost in the shadows.

"Get in," the first man ordered.

White and Horse slid into seats opposite the other passenger and the doors closed. No one said anything as the limousine backed up and made several circles in the parking lot before pulling out into traffic.

White knew the circles were intended to confuse him. Unable to see out, and disoriented by the circles, he couldn't determine which direction they were going. It probably didn't make any difference. He assumed the entire conversation was going to take place in the car, but it confirmed White's assumption that his host was extremely careful.

"Which one of you is White?" the man in the rear seat asked in a deep baritone. His tone was neutral, neither demanding nor accusatory. The voice disclosed little about the man, except that he was probably African American.

Considering the ethnicity of the man and his associates, White was tempted to say, "We both are," but he doubted the man would find humor appropriate. Instead, he merely said, "I am."

In the shadowy darkness, White could vaguely see the man nod.

"So you must be Horse," the man said, the sound of his voice indicating that he had turned to face Horse.

"That's me."

"I've heard of you," the man said. "Both of you."

"Good things, I hope."

"If they weren't good, you wouldn't be here." The voice sounded mildly irritated as if stating the obvious was a waste of everyone's time.

The limousine pulled onto the expressway and accelerated. White tried to establish their location on a mental map but quickly gave up. A few minutes later, the limousine left the expressway and wound its way through backstreets with no apparent traffic. White sensed that the other man would continue in his own time, so he waited in silence.

"We have a mutual acquaintance," the voice continued abruptly.

White noted that the man had not said they had a mutual friend. He waited for the man to say something more, maybe something about their mutual acquaintances—or why he had agreed to the meeting. Anything to give a clue to his identity or his place in the pecking order of the underworld.

The man remained silent. White said, "Our mutual acquaintance believes we have common interests."

The man seemed to be considering White's comment when the limousine pulled off the road. White heard the sound of gravel crunching beneath the tires as they came to a stop. White realized that they had driven into some kind of building and strained to determine what, or where, it was. The last of the light from the outside streetlights was lost when the door to the building was closed.

The front door of the limousine opened. A moment later, the rear door was opened from the outside. Around them, there was nothing but darkness.

"Come," the man instructed. "We'll walk."

Where the hell are we going to walk to?

They left the car, and the door closed. A lighter flared in the dark, illuminating the face of the man from the front seat as he lit a cigarette and passed it to the man with White. *Talk about being careful.*

The man inhaled. A whiff of pungent, bitter smoke drifted past White. There was something familiar about the aroma, but White couldn't place it.

The ash of the cigarette glowed, but not enough to reveal the man's face. He held the cigarette between his thumb and forefinger with the ash hidden in his cupped hand—the classic positioning of a cigarette by a combat soldier. White immediately thought of Jackson's father.

Could this guy be connected to attorney Barlow? White was suddenly conscious that he was perspiring. The dark interior of an empty building would be an excellent place to get rid of any problem they might think they had with White and Horse. White could only hope that Manny Rodriguez had properly vouched for him, or whatever is done to assure safety in meetings such as this.

The man stepped into the darkness. Only the ash of his cigarette showed his movement. White and Horse followed. The man from the front seat remained standing beside the limousine.

Abruptly the man asked, "What do you need?"

White was suddenly aware of a sense of unease. The darkness, and the mysterious stranger, he understood. But there was something else, something in the stranger's voice, something he couldn't explain, that told him he had to be careful.

No sense playing games. "I need to know about any drug connections involving a lawyer in West Palm Beach."

"What kind of drugs?"

"I don't know. I suspect someone may be dealing in heroin or cocaine, but I'm not certain."

"You talkin' 'bout dealing or distributin'?"

White understood the difference between dealing and distribution and was suddenly struck by the fact that he had not been making the distinction. He knew that "dealing," the so-called street-level selling to users, was at the bottom of the drug distribution chain. But distributing occurred at many levels as drugs moved from the importer through various middlemen until they reached the street dealers. He knew that people who had been arrested on drug charges were being killed after they had made plea deals and been released on bail. But he didn't know if they had been merely users or street dealers or distributors. White thought about the distinctions but couldn't decide if the difference was of any significance to his case. *All pleas involve trading up. Everyone, users, dealers, and distributors alike, make deals by providing information on someone higher in the chain. Whoever was doing the killing would only be concerned with someone who had information about them.*

"It could be either… or both."

"You should ask Mr. Barlow," the man said without hesitation.

White was surprised by the suddenness of the response. *Are Barlow's activities that well known, or did the mystery man make inquiries before our meeting?* It probably didn't make any difference, but little things had a way of being important.

"Ask him what?"

"He the go-to man if you got a legal problem 'bout drugs. You're the attorney. You'll think of the right questions." There was now something cold and sinister about the man's voice. *There's something personal between him and Barlow.*

"Do you know him?"

"I know what you need to know. That's all that's important."

"What do you know?"

"Mr. Barlow used to get people into the country. People bring certain products with them."

"You said he used to get people into the country. Has he stopped whatever he was doing?"

"He's moved on."

"Before he moved on, how long had he been doing what he was doing?"

"That isn't important."

Or you don't want to say. White sensed he was close to something important, and dangerous. "When did it start?"

"That isn't important either."

If it isn't important, why aren't you telling me? "How is it distributed?"

The man paused. In the dark, White could only guess at his expression, and what he might be thinking. Whatever the answer was, it was significant enough to require some thought.

"Why do you want to know?"

What am I getting close to? What are you hiding? "I need to understand how large his operation is."

"Large enough."

"Is he still in business?"

The man stopped walking and turned toward White. In the darkness, the cigarette ash, which had been tracing the movements of the man's hand, stopped moving. "Things change."

White waited for more. When it became apparent that the man wasn't going to offer anything else, he changed the subject. "Does Barlow have a Cambodian working for him?"

For a moment, the man said nothing. Even in the darkness, White could visualize him thinking. *There's something important about the Cambodian.* "You're well informed."

"Is that a yes?"

"Yes."

"What's his name?"

"He has many names."

"What do you call him?"

"The Cambodian."

"Do you deal with him directly?"

"Sometimes."

The mystery man kicked at the gravel. It hit something a few feet away and bounced harmlessly to the ground. The man took one step, turned, and sat down. "Sit with me," he said. Oddly, it sounded more like an invitation than a command.

White moved cautiously forward, feeling his way with the toe of his boot. When he felt something solid, he reached out and touched what felt like canvas tarp coving a stack of something. It could have been anything, but White concluded that it was lumber. White sat and resumed his questioning. "Where can the Cambodian be found?"

"Miami."

"Not West Palm Beach?"

"Not anymore."

"What do you know about the Cambodian?"

"What do you want to know?"

"What does he do for Barlow?"

"Whatever needs to be done."

"And what does Barlow do?"

"Barlow looks out for him."

"For the Cambodian?"

"For everyone."

"Everyone? That doesn't narrow things down very much."

"Ain't supposed to."

It was evident that the man was not going to volunteer any information, and a direct approach was required. White found himself wishing that there was at least enough light to make out the man's face. He didn't need to be able to identify the man, but he did need some visual clues about the man's reaction to his questions. If he didn't know the truth, or wouldn't share what he knew, Manny would never have suggested the meeting. But the truth comes in many degrees, and facial expressions, and the look in a man's eyes often conveys more than his words. These were things that White relied on when examining a witness, and the darkness deprived him of this information. But there was nothing he could do about it.

"Is Barlow involved in fixing drug cases?"

"For some people."

"Who?"

"The folks who are willing to pay his price."

"Are these people who want to get out of jail."

"Sometimes the money comes from people who want out themselves. Sometimes it comes from people who want other people out?"

"Where is he involved in fixing cases?"

The man hesitated before responding. "Barlow takes care of things wherever they need to be taken care of."

"Does that include both state and federal courts."

"It means what it means."

"Does Barlow do anything for you?"

"It isn't in my interest to say."

"Does Barlow work alone?"

"No."

"Is Barlow the head of the operation?"

"Not anymore."

The response startled White, and for once he was glad that the man could not see his face. "Who is?"

"That depends on your definition."

"Who makes the final decisions?"

"Now?"

"Yes."

"You need to look close to home."

White pondered the man's answer for a moment before continuing. "What do you know about Tom Jackson's involvement in the business?"

"He is a fool."

"But what's his involvement?"

The stranger didn't seem to hear the question—or he chose to ignore it. "Barlow is too smart to do business with a fool."

"But the Cambodian did business with Jackson."

"The Cambodian used him. There's a difference." The bitterness in the man's voice suggested that his answer was based, at least in part, on some personal experience—probably not a pleasant one. The tone of the answer cried out for more investigation. But it also carried a warning. Too many questions about the Cambodian and Jackson might end the man's cooperation. That wasn't something White was willing to risk.

"Do you know that Tom Jackson was killed after he was released on bail?"

"Heard 'bout that."

"Do you know why he was in jail?"

"He needed to be taught a lesson."

"What kind of lesson?"

There was a long pause. White heard the man take a deep breath and felt him move on the stack of whatever they were sitting on. When he answered, there was venom in his voice. "Don't screw with the wrong people."

White was again overwhelmed with the feeling that he was venturing into a dangerous topic. But those were precisely the topics that would lead to the most valuable information... or an end of the interview.

"Who were the wrong people, and how was Jackson screwing with them?"

"Don' screw with the people who run things, an' don't want what ain't yours."

"That doesn't answer my question."

"Yes, it does. You jus' don't know it."

White couldn't understand why the man was being so circumspect. He had agreed to meet with White, but now he seemed to be talking in riddles. Or maybe he was telling White something that he just didn't understand. "Do you know who killed Tom Jackson?"

"No."

"Do you know why he was killed?"

"Got an idea."

"Why do you think was he killed?"

"He ready to talk to the wrong people 'bout the wrong things."

"Do you mean he was about to enter into a plea agreement with the state's attorney."

"Could be part of it."

"Only part of it?"

"That what I said."

White leaned forward, resting his elbows on his knees as he considered what he had learned, or not learned. For a moment he thought about Manny Rodriguez and why he had negotiated a connection between White and this particular man. He concluded that the other man must be someone high in one of South Florida's drug cartels, but there were many cartels. They coexisted peacefully only when their mutual interests required it. In other matters they were enemies, and their relationships were measured by the body count in the Dade County morgue.

There was one more thing that White needed to know. He was certain that the man wouldn't tell him everything he knew. But his reaction to the question White wanted to ask might, by itself, let him know what he needed to know.

"What is Congressman St. James's connection to Barlow?"

For a full minute, the man remained silent, but White could hear his heavy breathing. Whatever the man said, White now knew that Congressman St. James had some involvement in what Barlow was doing.

"St. James was a crooked cop."

It wasn't an answer to White's question, but it was enough to increase the flow of adrenaline.

"Is he in business with Barlow?"

Another long silence was followed by, "Could be."

"How do you know?"

After only a short pause the man said, "I introduced them." His voice was firm, but his tone was filled with reticence.

White was suddenly thankful for the darkness that hid the shock he knew was showing on his face.

White wanted to pursue the issue, and he was confident that the stranger knew something that would help his investigation. But the tone of the man's last revelation indicated that his cooperation, at least on that topic, was ended. White was tempted to press ahead, but he wasn't ready to offend the man and lose future access to whatever information he could provide. When a half minute passed without White asking any more questions, the man said, "Is that all?"

"For now. Can I contact you if I have any more questions?"

"That depends."

"Depends on what?"

"Depends on whether there's anything in it for me."

"How will you know?"

"I be watching what you doing. I'll know."

&

The limousine waited in the dark corner of the parking lot until Horse turned onto Route 41 and headed west.

"What do you think?" White asked.

"I think Manny's friend is a very careful dude."

White nodded. "Probably with good reason."

"Uh-huh. Do you think he's in business with Barlow?"

"He said he does business with the Cambodian."

"But the Cambodian works for Barlow."

"Maybe he also works for others."

"Like who."

For a minute, White drove on in silence. When he spoke, it sounded more like he was thinking out loud than talking to Horse. "It also sounded like he did business with Barlow independent of what he did with the Cambodian."

"So why didn't he tell us?"

"That wouldn't have been in his own best interest."

&

The western suburbs of Miami faded behind them, and they were engulfed in darkness. For twenty minutes, neither of them spoke.

Finally, Horse interrupted the silence. "There's something about the Cambodian's drug dealing that bothers me."

"Something has been bothering me too. But I can't figure out what it is. Do you have any ideas?"

"We've been assuming the Cambodian started out dealing heroin—"

"Smuggled into the country by Barlow's clients."

"Right," Horse said. "But our new friend said that 'things change.' What do you suppose he meant by that?"

"Your guess is as good as mine."

"Everything David had to say about offshore drug pickups screams cocaine. Do you suppose he meant that Barlow had changed from smuggling heroin to smuggling cocaine?"

"The Columbians aren't generally inclined to let outsiders in on their business."

"So someone else has to have brokered an arrangement between the Cambodian and the Columbians."

"Or the Columbians are behind everything," White said.

"What do you have in mind?"

"Maybe the Columbians were trying to get rid of the Cambodian by framing Shepard and Jackson and hoping they'd turn on the Cambodian."

26.

The exchanges with Manny Rodriguez's contact continued as the subject of the morning meeting of White, Horse, and Leslie. The man's meeting with White would not have been accepted if he wasn't willing to provide valuable information, and all agreed that the information he had provided was cryptic at best. But cryptic or not, White was convinced that his information was the key to unlocking some secret. All White had to do was determine what that secret was.

Leslie finished taking notes and was about to ask a question when they were interrupted by Grace Matthew's voice on the intercom. "Someone who says he's a U.S. attorney in Miami is calling for Mr. White."

"Thank you, Grace," White said. He switched on the speakerphone and answered, "Lucius White."

"Mr. White, this is Lyle Wilson. I'm an assistant U.S. attorney in Miami."

"Yes. I know. You've taken over the David Shepard case."

Wilson's pause suggested that this wasn't the greeting he expected.

"What can I do for you, Mr. Wilson?" White asked in a tone that said he had no concern for anything the prosecutor might have to say.

In federal criminal cases, the rules are stacked in favor of the government. U.S. attorneys and their investigators in the FBI and other federal agencies are accustomed to instilling fear in witnesses and opposing parties merely by virtue of their inherent power. Wilson, for whom White's apparent indifference was something unexpected, paused again before responding. "Call me Lyle."

"Fair enough. Call me Lucius. Now… what can I do for you?" White said, continuing to assert his control over the conversation.

"As I'm sure you know, I've just taken over the Tom Jackson murder case."

Wilson waited for White to make some response.

White said nothing.

Wilson gave up and continued. "I haven't looked into the whole matter yet…" White and Leslie exchanged "Yeah, sure" glances, knowing that Wilson wouldn't have called before he knew everything there was to know about the case. "But it seems to me that we have a pretty good case."

"Uh-huh."

"So you agree?"

"No. Just letting you know I haven't hung up."

"I see."

"Good."

Wilson was off balance.

White repeated, "What can I do for you?"

"I thought we could talk about a deal."

"What did you have in mind?"

"Well, as I assume you know, I'm a friend of Graham Brochette. I know this is hard on him, and I'd like to see if we can work something out for his sake."

"Graham Brochette isn't my client."

"No. Of course not," Wilson fumbled. "But…"

"What kind of deal did you have in mind?" White asked again.

"Look… ah… Lucius," Wilson began before pausing.

"We've got enough to indict, and I can probably convict your client of Jackson's murder. But there may be a way to avoid that."

White tensed, not sure he had heard Wilson correctly and unable to believe what he thought he heard. A deal without even an indictment? It wasn't unheard of, but it was far from conventional. "I'm listening."

"Until I go for an indictment, I have a lot of discretion and—"

White knew Wilson had some ulterior motive for shopping for a deal before he had even charged David. He just couldn't imagine what it was. "What makes you think you can convict David of Jackson's murder?"

"He had opportunity. He was out of jail when Jackson was killed. He had access to the murder weapon—his father's gun. And he had motive—Jackson had the cocaine that justified his arrest."

"Let's cut to the chase. You need my client for something. What is it?"

The silence on the other end of the line said Wilson was unaccustomed to dealing with attorneys like White. "We… We think Jackson was connected to a drug distribution network we've been investigating. Whoever is behind it has been very careful. Every time we seem to be getting close, our witness disappears. According to Paul Parker, Jackson was ready to make a deal when he was bailed out. With Jackson dead, your client may be the only one who can help us get these guys."

White tugged at his ear. "Let me get this straight. You think David Shepard and Tom Jackson were connected to a heroin network."

"I don't know about Shepard. I don't have anything connecting him to heroin. As far as I know, he wasn't ever a user."

"But Jackson's another matter?"

"That's right. He's got a record of using. And we're looking into links between his father and heroin traffickers."

"You do know they were arrested in Matlacha for possession of cocaine?"

"I'm aware of that. But that isn't my interest."

"I thought you had taken jurisdiction of David's whole case."

"Just Tom Jackson's murder. Like I said, I think they may have been connected to heroin trafficking over here. Their cocaine case is still with the state's attorney over there. But I may also take jurisdiction of that case if that's what it takes to make a deal."

"Paul Parker said you had taken over both cases and had taken all of his files."

"I don't know why he would have told you that."

White and Horse looked at each other and shrugged. Their expressions showed that they were both questioning what was happening. It took White a few seconds to realize that Wilson was waiting for him to speak.

"And you're willing to give my client a get-out-of-jail-free card in exchange for what he knows?"

"As far as I'm concerned, killing Jackson saved the government the cost of a trial. I'd be happy if the bastards who push drugs all killed each other off. Short of that, I'd make a deal with the devil to break up a major network."

"What makes you think my client knows anything?"

"He was working with Jackson. Jackson was ready to cut a deal when your client killed him. We assume Jackson knew something important, and your client had to kill him to keep him quiet."

"Assuming that what you say is all true, what makes you think Shepard would have had the authority to kill Jackson."

"For all we know, someone they were both working for ordered the killing."

"Do you think they were part of a larger drug distribution network?"

"I'm sure of it. But that's all I can tell you?"

White leaned back in his chair and swiveled toward the window. Something was wrong. The offer Wilson was making was too good. There had to be a catch somewhere.

"My client would require complete immunity."

"He won't even have a federal arrest record."

"And the drug bust?"

"It's too late to void the arrest, but I'll agree to a reduction of the charges to simple possession and probation."

"What if Shepard tells you everything he knows, and you think he knows more?"

"Nothing he says will be used against him."

Where the hell is the catch? "I'll get back to you."

&

"Graham. I just got off the phone with Lyle Wilson. He wants to talk a deal for David."

White heard Brochette take a deep breath.

"Graham?"

"Sorry. I… ah… that's great. You just caught me by surprise. That's not something I would have expected."

"Me neither."

"What's the deal?"

"We'll talk when you get here."

&

White, Leslie, and David Shepard were alone in the War Room. Shepard sat at the conference table. Leslie sat on a chair in the corner. White leaned against the wall opposite Shepard.

"Here's the deal, David," White began softly. Shepard looked nervously at White. He knew something important was coming, but White's tone wasn't encouraging. "The US attorney is willing to give you a walk and complete immunity in exchange for everything you know about what Jackson was up to."

"That's good, isn't it?" Shepard said hopefully.

"Too good," White said. "The only obvious catch is that Lyle Wilson, he's the U.S. attorney in charge of your case, gets to decide if you've really lived up to your end of the bargain."

"I don't understand." The look that had begun as one of hope was already becoming something else.

"You could tell Wilson everything you know, but he could still claim you haven't been completely honest and withdraw the deal."

Shepard bit his lip. "What if I don't know anything?"

"Wilson thinks you do."

"But what if I really don't?"

White looked toward Leslie as he took a seat opposite Shepard. She nodded imperceptibly and spoke for the first time. "He probably won't believe you."

"What happens then?"

"You won't have a deal, and he'll prosecute you for both the drugs and the Jackson murder."

Shepard looked around the room as if searching for some hint of what he was supposed to say.

"While you think about that," Leslie continued, "there are a few other things we need to know."

Shepard turned to her, apparently still not understanding where he stood.

"Where did you get the drugs that were found at the house?"

David made a fist and pounded the table with the side of his hand. "*Dammit*. I told you before. We didn't have any drugs. They were planted."

White responded with an equally commanding slam of his palm on the table. "Stop bullshitting us, David."

"I'm not. We never brought cocaine to the house."

White surged to his feet and leaned across the table, his face inches from Shepard's. "But you brought other drugs."

Shepard's lip trembled. "I don't know what you mean."

"I've about had it with you, David. Either you level with me, or you can find yourself another lawyer."

Shepard erupted from his chair, shouting at White. "Dammit. You said you didn't want to know what we did."

White stepped back. David had a point. That was what he had told Shepard at their first meeting. He waited patiently while Shepard calmed down. "You're right," White admitted. "I did say that. But now there are some things I need to know."

Shepard returned to his chair where he sat quietly wringing his hands. His eyes were still fixed on the conference table.

Leslie suddenly intervened and changed the subject. "Where were you when Jackson was killed?"

Shepard froze, staring at Leslie and seemingly unable to speak.

"Where were you when Jackson was killed?" Leslie asked again.

Shepard's fingernails suddenly demanded his full attention. Finally, he said, "I was at... my dad's house. I'm not allowed to go out unsupervised."

"And where was your father?"

"He was there too."

"What were you doing?"

Shepard shifted uneasily in his chair. "Eating a pizza and watching a movie."

"Where did you get the pizza?"

"Some takeout joint."

"Which one?"

"What difference does it make?"

"Those places keep records of pizza deliveries. I want to be able to check your story."

Shepard looked away. "Maybe it wasn't a takeout. I don't remember."

"David, I've been getting lied to for a long time. I'm starting to recognize a lie when I see one."

"I'm not lying," Shepard said as if pleading to be believed.

"If you don't know how to bluff, you shouldn't be playing the game."

Shepard continued to stare at the table.

"Wait here," White said. "I need to talk to your father."

&

Brochette stood as White and Leslie entered White's office. Leslie crossed the room and took a seat at the conference table. White leaned—half standing, half sitting—against the conference table and glowered at Brochette before ordering, "Sit down, Graham."

An expression somewhere between puzzlement and shock came over Brochette's face as he sank back to his place on the sofa.

White didn't give Brochette time to even think about what was coming. "Where were you when Jackson was killed?"

Brochette's head snapped up. "What the hell are you suggesting?"

"It's a routine question, Graham. You obviously qualify as a suspect. I want to know what you're going to tell the authorities when they ask you."

"You can't be serious."

"Do I look like I'm not serious? What would you be asking if it was your investigation?"

Brochette took a deep breath and exhaled. "I suppose you're right."

"So where were you?"

"I don't know." Brochette leaned back and stared at the ceiling. "As far as I know, they haven't established a time of death. Until I know when Jackson was killed, I can't tell you where I was when it happened."

"Answered like a lawyer. But you're avoiding the issue. Can you account for your time the evening before Jackson's body was discovered?"

"I went out to dinner with David early in the evening. I dropped him off at home and went back to the office to review some files."

"So the office pass card system will show the time you logged in and out."

"No. When I arrived at my office, I discovered that one of my other attorneys had taken the files home that night."

"Where did you go?"

"I stopped off for a drink."

"Where?"

"I don't remember. Someplace near the office."

"And I suppose you paid for your drinks in cash?"

"I usually do."

"Then there won't be a credit card receipt to prove where you were?"

"What's with the damned third degree? You know I didn't kill Jackson."

"But your story is vague. A verifiable alibi would be helpful."

"Lyle won't even consider me a possibility. He knows me too well."

"It was your gun. And if Jackson was going to make a deal for his testimony—"

"I'd have a motive… wanting to protect my son." Brochette looked away and began tapping his fingers on the arm of the sofa. "You don't honestly suspect me?"

"I would if I was a prosecutor."

"But it wouldn't make sense for me to use my own gun. I know that its ballistics are on file with the FBI. My gun could be identified in a matter of hours, and Wilson would know that."

"Which leaves David with a motive, no alibi, and access to the murder weapon," White said as if he was making a closing argument for the prosecution.

"I know it doesn't look good."

"Then why did Wilson offer your son a deal?"

Brochette stared at White, stunned by his violent outburst and unable to say anything.

"Dammit. Wilson doesn't make deals. You said it yourself. You said he'd rather lose a case than make a deal. Now he has a solid case against David, and he wants to talk about a deal even before David has been formally charged."

"Maybe…" Brochette began. "Maybe it's because we're friends, and he's looking out for me… and David."

"That's bullshit, and you know it. Wilson's an attorney, but he's also political and ambitious. He's not about to risk his future by showing obvious favoritism to you."

"Maybe he's more interested in the information he thinks David has."

"You know better than that. If Wilson isn't inclined to accept plea offers when he has all the facts, he's not going to suddenly start shopping for a plea deal just because David might have some useful information."

Brochette rested his head on the back of his chair and rubbed his eyes. White couldn't know what he was thinking, but he couldn't ignore an undeniable truth. Finally, Brochette spoke in a tone that suggested he was trying to rationalize the acceptance of a fact that he wanted to avoid. "Wilson has been gone from my office for a couple of years. Maybe he's changed."

"You don't believe that. Besides, Wilson can't just ignore Jackson's murder. If he's willing to talk about letting David off entirely, he must have someone else in mind as a suspect."

"What's your point?"

"If David didn't do it, you are the next logical suspect. If Wilson wanted to charge you, he knows enough to make a case."

"He'd lose."

"Maybe. But he'd destroy you in the process."

Brochette frowned and shook his head. "No way! Lyle wouldn't have any reason to hurt me."

"None that you know of."

Brochette recoiled at the suggestion that his old friend would have any reason to turn on him.

White ignored Brochette's response and continued thinking out loud. "The one thing we know is that Wilson won't act until he's sure who killed Jackson. If he indicts David, he'll create reasonable doubt for anyone else— including you. He can't afford to even indict David as long as he has any other suspect."

A look, something in Brochette's eyes, caught White's attention, but it was gone before he could interpret it.

White glared at Brochette. "Wilson can't wait too long. He's going to have to do something soon, and I want to know what the hell is going on before he does."

Brochette stared at the floor, breathing deeply. The growing silence finally became too much for him. "I'm sorry, Lucius. But I didn't have any choice."

White's chest tightened and his breathing became more rapid. "About what?" White demanded.

"I'm not sure where the beginning is… or how much I can tell you," Brochette said. White immediately understood, or thought he understood, Brochette's dilemma. Whatever Brochette was referring to had something to do with an ongoing investigation, and DOJ policy prohibited disclosure of such information.

White waited.

"About a year ago, the attorney general started hearing stories. It looked like something nefarious was going on in our Miami office."

"What kind of… nefarious?"

Brochette leaned forward with his head bowed and his elbows on his knees. When he finally spoke, his voice was soft and subdued. "We didn't have anything definite. A public defender in the Southern District contacted the attorney general. He said one of his clients had information on corruption in the system down there."

"Corruption? System? You're going to have to be more definite than that."

"What it came down to was a suspicion that cases, particularly cases involving drug dealers and users, were being fixed. He said his client wanted to make a deal in exchange for what he knew, but he was afraid to approach the local US attorney."

"Why did he contact the attorney general?"

"His client wasn't even willing to tell him everything.

But he seemed to think that someone in the US attorney's office might be implicated by whatever his client had to say."

"Is that all you know?"

Brochette turned his back to White. "No. They claimed to know of instances where suspects died under suspicious circumstances after agreeing to deals with local prosecutors. Apparently, his client had proof about things that were happening in some state court cases... but he was afraid that the same thing was happening in the federal courts in the Southern District."

"Seems like a good reason to be concerned."

Brochette nodded but said nothing as he sorted his thoughts.

"It's hard to believe that a U.S. attorney would do anything dishonest," White said. As he spoke, his eyes were locked on Brochette's own eyes. White's mocking tone was not lost on Brochette. Few attorneys in his office were not familiar with the story of White's father's arrest, conviction, and stabbing death in prison. White blamed the government, and overzealous prosecutors, for using fabricated evidence and paid informants for his father's conviction and death. Brochette was one of the few prosecutors against whom White did not exercise his hatred.

Brochette glared at White and started to respond, but thought better of it. Instead, he merely continued with his story. "The attorney general had to do something, but he had a problem. Some of the people in the Miami office had close ties to Washington—"

"And the AG was afraid they'd find out about an internal investigation."

"Something like that. That's why the attorney general appointed me to investigate. It would have been bad enough if there was corruption in the federal courts, but the Department of Justice also has jurisdiction to investigate corruption in state courts."

"How long had this alleged corruption been going on?"

"It's hard to say. There's some evidence that it had been going on for a long time in the state courts. We're still not sure about the federal courts."

"Why did the attorney general come to you to look into it?"

"You probably remember that I did a stint in the Public Integrity Section of the Department of Justice."

White nodded.

"It was all pretty delicate. I couldn't even let anyone in my office in on it."

"So how did your son get involved?"

"He… I'm sorry I couldn't tell you earlier."

"Go ahead."

"We started with an investigation of the federal courts. The idea was to set up a sting. We needed a clean case to give to our Miami office, but it couldn't be anything a federal agency was already involved in. It had to come from outside. That meant we had to have a state case the Miami office could take over. We thought about making up a phony file, but there were too many risks. Then someone came up with Tom Jackson. He was still on probation, for an old heroin plea from when he was in college. All we had to do was make a case for probation violation, and we had him. Then we were going to convince him that it was in his best interest to cooperate with us."

From the way Brochette spoke when describing the plan, White knew Brochette hadn't told him everything.

Brochette lowered his head, avoiding White's probing look, and stared at his desk. After a minute of silence, he continued. "About the time we were putting our plan together, David got busted for possession of marijuana when he was in the Keys. The state's attorney was looking for someone the help him gather information on people who were dealing drugs down there. He convinced the judge to give David a choice. Go undercover or go to jail. David agreed to go undercover."

"How did you find out about it?"

"David called his mother, and she called me. I called the state's attorney down in Marathon and found out the rest."

"What happened then?"

"After the state's attorney told me about the deal the judge had given David, I called him a few names I now regret. When I finally calmed down, I decided he'd probably done David a favor. We agreed that he would keep me informed."

"And?"

"A couple of weeks later, he called to let me know what was going on. He told me David had connected with Jackson."

"Because the sheriff had picked up David and thrown him into the same cell as Jackson for a weekend."

"Yeah."

White took a deep breath and did everything he could to control his rage. "Dammit, Graham!"

"I know. I should have told you, but there was too much at stake."

"What could be more important than keeping your son out of jail."

"Lucius, you have to understand. I'm part of a multi-jurisdictional task force on drugs. The U.S. attorneys for all the districts in Florida and some representatives of law enforcement are trying to come up with a solution to a problem that we're all facing."

"And what's that, other than the drug epidemic?"

"The information we got that started our investigation turned out to be accurate, or close to accurate. Anyone the drug bosses are afraid will turn state's evidence were being bailed out, and the crime families take care of their problems."

"As in permanently."

"Right."

"Is that all there is to it?"

"We can't prove it yet, but we think some of the state's attorneys are directly involved in the arrangement. We've identified at least five state attorneys who don't seem to have made very convincing arguments at bail hearings for over a dozen dealers who have made bail and ended up dead."

"Is that all?"

"I'm afraid not. We also think that at least one attorney is involved."

"In what way?"

"This attorney arranges the bail bonds for whoever the drug bosses want to be released."

"The attorney you're interested in wouldn't happen to be Richard Barlow, Tom Jackson's stepfather?"

"How the hell did you know that?"

"You're not the only one who knows how to conduct an investigation!"

"I don't suppose I have any right to ask, but please keep this to yourself. A lot of people would be in danger if what we've discovered became known by any of the drug bosses."

"Then I suggest that you start being straight with me."

"Absolutely."

"Starting with how many people know that David was undercover?"

Brochette ignored the statement and said, "I'm sorry, Lucius. My hands were tied."

White controlled the urge to say what he was thinking. "I don't give a damn about that. But I want to know who else knows about David."

"Only the U.S. attorneys for the three districts in Florida and our contact at the Department of Justice."

"Dammit! Do you mean that Wilson knows David is undercover?"

"No. Wilson is an *assistant* U.S. attorney. Only his boss knows about David."

"How can you be so sure?"

"I can only be sure that he wouldn't have been told. I know his boss well, and I know he wouldn't say anything to anyone… especially now that he knows David is my son."

White waited until Brochette's breathing slowed. "What else haven't you told me?"

Brochette took a final deep breath before continuing. "About a month after David and Jackson got together, we discovered that Jackson was actually involved in cocaine trafficking. We knew we were getting into something more serious than we originally expected. After the arrests in Matlacha we knew David was in over his head. He wasn't safe in jail, and there's no way I could have gotten him released without revealing our relationship."

"You could've told Paul what was going on."

"It was too big a risk. We didn't know who might be involved, and we couldn't risk anyone finding out that there was an official investigation going on."

"And that's when you came to me."

"We could have continued the original investigation," Brochette said. "But once my relationship to David became known, David was useless as an undercover snitch. We knew we'd never be able to get anyone else to pursue the drug angle on the inside. Then the attorney general decided we could play it out as a murder investigation. You could stick your nose into anything, and no one would think it was anything more than a routine defense investigation."

"I'm beginning to understand why you waited five days before coming to me."

"It's the bureaucracy," Brochette agreed. "Decisions like that don't get made overnight."

"And you didn't know anything about Jackson's father?"

"I've told you, Jackson was our only interest."

"And you don't know about any connection between his father and Congressman St. James?"

"Other than knowing his name, I didn't know a thing about St. James."

"Well, he certainly seems to know about you, and he's ready to do anything to block your nomination."

"How would knowing about my relationship with David help St. James?"

"Maybe he expected you to take a leave of absence to defend David. That would have forced you to withdraw your nomination."

Brochette exhaled and nodded.

"When you hired me, instead of trying to defend David yourself, he had to change his plans. He tried to use David's arrest to embarrass you into withdrawing from consideration. I think that was the problem Congressman Tierney was telling you about."

"It's possible," Brochette agreed.

"It's also possible he dug into your financial disclosures and found out that you hadn't disclosed the fact that you were supporting a child."

"What makes you think that?"

"Jack Lancaster said the rumors had something to do with your personal life, and your financial disclosures. At first, I didn't make the connection because we didn't know where the problem was coming from. Even though you disclosed your relationship to David at his bail hearing, there was no reason for that fact to go anywhere else. It wasn't until we came across a connection between you and Congressman St. James that I put it together."

"And when it became obvious that those parts of his plan weren't going to work, he decided to tie me into the murder investigation."

"I don't have anything connecting the congressman to the murder investigation."

"Then who?"

"I'm still working on that," White said. "Jackson knew something. I don't know what it might have been. What I do know is that when he started talking about a deal with Paul Parker, he became a liability. He had to be eliminated, regardless of anything else."

"But why frame David?"

"If Jackson was going to make a deal, and name David as a conspirator, David would have had a motive to get rid of Jackson. If they could pin the murder on David, no one would look any further."

"And using my gun created a direct link to David."

"Something like that," White said. "And while we're on the subject, how did you discover your gun was missing?"

"That's simple enough. I kept the gun in my car, but I knew there would be times that David would be driving the car. If he was stopped for anything, and the gun was found, his bail would be revoked. When we got home from the bail hearing, I went out to the car to get the gun. That's when I discovered that it was missing."

"Before that, when was the last time you saw the gun in your car?"

Brochette rubbed his chin. "A couple of weeks, maybe a month before. I usually go to the range for some practice at least once a month."

"Do you keep your car locked?"

"At home I do. I don't generally lock it at the office."

"Why not?"

"We have restricted underground parking in the federal building. I park in a portion of the garage that's only accessible to the U.S. Marshals, the attorneys from my office, and the office of the federal public defender."

"What about your staff and the court staff?"

"They park in a different part of the garage. Their passcards don't give them access to our part of the garage, and a guard keeps anyone from just walking in."

Leslie interrupted from across the conference table. "As interesting as it is to watch you two play 'what if' games, we still have to decide what to do about Lyle Wilson's plea offer."

"We can't take it," White said firmly.

Brochette looked from Leslie to White. "Why not? With the murder charge out of the way, we can reveal that David was undercover. He won't face any charges on the drug bust."

"Except that dropping the charges is contingent on David telling Wilson what he wants to hear. David doesn't know anything to give Wilson, so there's no assurance that Wilson will drop the murder charges."

"But if Wilson knows David is innocent, he won't indict him. Like you said, if he indicts David, he's giving any other suspect a 'reasonable doubt' defense."

"Which is why Wilson will wait. He has a rope around David's neck, and he can pull any time. But he won't do anything until he has to. That buys us time to figure out what's going on."

For a minute, no one said anything.

Finally, Leslie broke the silence. "Then I guess it's time I had a chat with Mr. Wilson."

&

"Wilson was less than thrilled by the news," Leslie said when she rejoined White, Horse, and Brochette in the War Room.

"He'll survive," White said. "But he's going to be under a lot of pressure. We better come up with something soon."

"If it helps," Horse began, "I'm beginning to think Manny may be right about the source of the cocaine."

White looked at Horse and waited. Horse thumbed the eraser on his pencil as he considered what to say. "First of all, we've never been able to explain why two kilos were found. We know a drug dealer wouldn't waste that much on a setup."

"That's yesterday's news. Where are you going with this?"

"Stay with me for a minute," Horse said. "We also know that only law enforcement agencies would have that much cocaine that could be used in a setup."

White waved his fingers in a "get on with it" motion.

"I've checked with my sources in all the jurisdictions in South Florida. I can't find any record of that much cocaine being used in a sting."

"That doesn't mean it wasn't."

"No," Horse agreed. "But it does reduce the possibilities. Think about this. If you were running an authorized sting, there'd be a record of your use of seized drugs… but there aren't any such records.

"On the other hand, if you were running an unauthorized sting, a lot of people would have to be involved to hide your use of two kilos of blow. You'd be taking a big chance, and whoever is behind this is too smart for that. The fact that there's no record of seized drugs being used in any sting tells me that the drugs didn't come from seized evidence."

"So where does that leave us?"

"There's one more clue we haven't been focusing on."

"What's that?"

"The cocaine they seized was pure, uncut."

White was suddenly interested. "Which means it was seized before it got into the hands of any dealer."

"More than that," Horse continued. "I think it was seized right off the boat."

White knew Horse wasn't just guessing.

"'Bout a month ago, ah read about a murder in Marathon. Some old guy wandered into a bar during the hurricane. No one paid any attention to him until the next day. That's when they discovered that he was dead from a knife in the chest. He didn't have any identification, but a waitress said he tried to say something to her in Spanish. The next day they found the wreckage of a deep-sea fishing boat. The old man's fingerprints were all over the cabin."

"This boat, could it have been a cocaine delivery boat?"

"It has the range to have come from the coast of a cocaine country. But big-time dealers usually use freighters and drop their goods for fast boats to pick up. The pickup boats can outrun the Coast Guard, but the fishing boat couldn't."

"And the Coast Guard probably wouldn't have even suspected it of transporting cocaine. That might have been the idea."

Horse did not immediately respond, but his expression suggested that he was thinking about White's proposition. "Or…" Horse paused again as if trying to focus his words. "What if a new operation was trying to get started in the trade. Someone who couldn't afford to use freighters and didn't have a network to use shore-based pickup boats."

Leslie scowled. "But David Shepard said that he and Tom Jackson used a fast boat to pick up packages that were dropped at sea. That doesn't sound like an operation that would be smuggling in a fishing boat."

"Unless…" White started before pausing and clicking his pen open and closed while thinking. "What if someone in the organization is branching out on their own?"

"We don't have any evidence of that."

"No, but it's a possibility we should keep in mind." White made a note on his legal pad and continued. "What else do you have?"

"Ah made some calls, and it turns out that authorities had a tip about a cocaine delivery being made in Marathon about the same time as the murder. The official story is that nothing came of it, or the hurricane changed everyone's plans."

"And you think someone intercepted the delivery and kept it?"

"Not just someone. The DEA and the FBI were responsible. But their activities were being coordinated by Lyle Wilson."

White stopped his idle doodling and came to attention.

"I thought you'd find that interesting."

"Frightening might be a better choice of words," White said.

"What do you have in mind?"

"Everything you've said is consistent with something David said about a cocaine pickup in Vaca Key. He even knew about the old man being stabbed by the Cambodian."

Leslie's face was quickly developing a confused expression. She was beginning to realize how much more complex White's criminal investigations were than the legal issues she was accustomed to dealing with. But she was determined to show White that she could be an asset. "Are you suggesting that the Cambodian is in bed with Wilson?"

"Ah think it's a possibility."

"But how? Is the Cambodian feeding information to Wilson, or is it the other way around?"

"She asks a good question, Lucius," Horse said.

White could see where the conversation was leading and didn't want to deal with it.

"You were going to look into Tom Jackson's father..."

"Richard Barlow."

"Yeah. Have you found anything useful?"

"Ah don't know how useful it is, but ah've come up with some things that I think are interesting. Ah've done some more digging into Congressman St. James. Who do you suppose the congressman's biggest financial backer is?"

White rocked backward and shook his head as if denying the possibility of a fact would make it go away. "I don't think I'm going to like this."

"Probably not. It's Richard Barlow."

"Damn!"

"Barlow established a political action committee. He's chairman of the PAC, and he contributes big money every year."

"It's interesting," White said. "But a PAC can't directly support a specific candidate. PACs are limited to promoting issues."

"Barlow's staying within the law, but just barely. The issues his PAC supports are almost word for word the issues the congressman campaigns on."

"Is Barlow giving money directly to the congressman's campaign?"

"He's the congressman's biggest individual contributor."

"St. James doesn't represent Barlow's district, does he?" Leslie asked.

"No, he doesn't. In fact, the issues that St. James has campaigned on aren't even the same issues that seem to be important in the district where Barlow lives."

"I don't get it. Barlow doesn't live in the district St. James represents. And Barlow doesn't seem to have any connection to St. James's former employer where St. James could help him? Why is he such a big campaign supporter of St. James?"

"That," White said, "is one of the things we have to find out.

27.

"I'm in the kitchen," White called as he heard the elevator door open. The sounds of a John Coltrane recording wafted through the apartment accompanied by the sound of a knife striking the rock maple of the cutting board on the pedestal island in the middle of the kitchen.

"Ah. Onions," Leslie murmured.

"If you knew as much about food as you know about sex, you'd know that these are shallots, not onions," White said. "Onions go on hamburgers, or on bagels with cream cheese, lox, and capers. They don't go into my famous chicken excelsior."

Leslie made no secret of the fact that she was domestically impaired. She justified her lack of skills in the kitchen with the simple observation that "I have talents appropriate to many rooms. The kitchen just isn't one of them." White conceded both points.

Leslie slid onto one of the stools by the breakfast bar and accepted the glass of wine White offered. Her major contribution to dinner was watching as White worked. She took her job seriously, and she was very good at it.

"Nice," she observed after taking a sip of wine. "New?"

"It's something a client gave me a while back." White slid a tray of cheese in front of Leslie. "Try some of this. It goes great with the wine."

Leslie nibbled on a piece of cheese. "Mmmm. You're right."

"I'm always right."

"We'll let that one go," Leslie said. "So what else are we having for supper?"

"Well, in addition to chicken excelsior, for your dining pleasure we have a mixed medley of yellow squash, zucchini, eggplant, mushrooms, Vidalia onions, and green, red, and yellow peppers."

"Ah. My lover, the cook."

"Damned straight. Eating well is one of life's great pleasures."

As White chopped his vegetables, Sherlock wandered to Leslie's side and stood on her hind legs. Only her quivering nose and front paws extended over the edge of the breakfast bar. White ignored Sherlock when she begged. Leslie was another story. The food lady could always be counted on for a treat.

Leslie stroked Sherlock behind the ear and snatched a mushroom from the cutting board. Sherlock snarfed it down and waited. Sherlock would eat anything.

"That's all," Leslie said to Sherlock.

Sherlock looked up with sad brown eyes. She could do guilt with the best of them. White was certain that Sherlock was part Jewish.

"Sorry, girl. That's all there is."

Sherlock looked toward White for confirmation.

"That's right," Leslie said. "He's the old meanie who won't feed you."

Sherlock gave White a last soulful look and lay down on the floor beside Leslie.

"That was quite a performance with Graham this afternoon."

White put down his chopping knife, took a deep breath, and exhaled slowly. "I think Graham is holding out on me. He knows something I need to know."

"How do you know that?"

"It's just a feeling. The way he says some things. How he looks when I bring up certain topics."

Leslie took another sip of wine and waited.

"It was all too convenient," White said, more to himself than to Leslie. "His son was undercover for the state's attorney down in Marathon."

"So?"

"I don't know. It's just…"

"I know how you feel," Leslie said. "But maybe Graham didn't have a choice."

White nodded. "It's possible. But something is going on that I just can't figure out."

"What's that?" Leslie asked as she sipped the remainder of her wine.

White leaned forward, resting his outstretched arms on the breakfast bar. "There are too damned many coincidences."

"Like what?"

White opened the refrigerator and removed the rest of the ingredients for their dinner. "Graham said Jackson was picked because of his heroin past. Then it turns out his father seems to have had his own past connection with the heroin business."

"I agree. That is odd."

"Then we find out that a congressman, who seems to be opposing Graham's nomination—is connected to Jackson's father."

"And has his own history that seems to be related to Barlow's activities."

White lit the gas stove and dropped a half stick of butter into a frying pan. "We're missing something."

"Such as?"

White filled a saucepan with chicken broth, added a pinch of salt, and put it on a back burner. "I don't know.

It's as if Graham and Lyle Wilson both want us to focus on one thing, but the facts want to take us somewhere else."

"What makes you say that?"

"Graham has an answer for everything, and it's always an answer that's contrary to our theories. It's all too convenient."

"Do you think he's lying?"

White leaned against the breakfast bar. "Would that I could discover truth as easily as I can uncover falsehood."

Leslie sipped her wine. "Shakespeare?"

"Cicero."

"I never was good with the old Romans."

White nodded absently as he patted seasoning into both sides of two chicken breasts, laid them in the frying pan, and returned his attention to Leslie. "The murder takes things way beyond the original drug bust, and whatever Graham was looking into when the bust went down. David's afraid of the guy with the blue Porsche, but that's only connected to the original plan. I think he's also afraid of something he knows about the murders."

"What makes you say that?"

White stopped dicing a green pepper and pondered the question. "The story David gave when I asked where he was when Jackson was murdered…"

"What about it?"

"David was evasive about what he was doing the night of the murders, but he was firm on the fact that his father was at home with him."

"But Graham said he was out at a bar, alone."

"Exactly." White turned the chicken breasts and emptied a container of chopped scallions and sliced portabella mushrooms into the frying pan. "David's story creates an alibi for Graham as well as himself, but Graham didn't even try to give David an alibi. He had a chance to tell me they were together, but he didn't."

"Do you think David suspects Graham of being involved in Jackson's murder?"

"I don't know what to think. They both had to know I'd ask about David's alibi. If they wanted to get their stories together, they had plenty of time to do it."

Leslie nodded. "So Graham knew he was undermining his son's alibi."

"That's what it seems like," White said as he checked the chicken, splashed some wine into the pan, and reduced the heat. "And there's something else."

Leslie put down her wine and waited.

White added a cup of yellow rice to the boiling broth and lowered the flame. "David claimed that the reason he and Jackson left the Keys was that the authorities in Matlacha didn't care about simple possession. But if that was the reason for the move, Jackson would have known better than to keep two kilos of cocaine in his house."

"Which means the cocaine must have been planted."

"Exactly."

"Hasn't that been your assumption all along?"

"It is. But we've also been operating on the assumption that the arrest had something to do with what Shepard and Jackson knew and could be forced to tell. I have a feeling we've been focusing on the wrong motive."

"Which is?"

"I don't know. White leaned against the breakfast bar and sighed. "This is one of the times I really miss Harry. He had an instinct that…" White stopped and bowed his head.

Leslie understood what he was thinking. After a minute, she interrupted him. "It isn't your fault, Lucius. Anything could have caused the clot to break loose."

"But I'm the one who sent him traipsing around Pine Island. If I'd just kept him in the office…"

"Harry was doing what he wanted to do."

"And it may cost him his life."

"There isn't anything you can do about it now."

"I can find out what the hell is going on. I owe Harry that."

"What are you going to do?"

"I'm not sure. I have a meeting with one of the sheriff's detectives later this evening. I'm hoping he has some answers."

28.

O'Malley's was a cop bar in the finest tradition of Irish cop bars. Owned by Sergeant Michael O'Malley, retired, formerly of the Philadelphia Police Department, O'Malley's was located on Fort Myers' main north-south artery, approximately equal distance from the courthouse, the central office of the Fort Myers Police Department and the Lee County Sheriff's Office. That made it a convenient place for both formal and informal meetings of officers from both jurisdictions.

The distinction between Irish and all others didn't have the significance in Fort Myers that it had in Philadelphia. In Fort Myers, the only relevant distinction between classes of people was the distinction between native rednecks and everybody else. Nevertheless, when they were in O'Malley's, all law enforcement officers accepted that, at least for the time it took to down a few brews, everyone who wore the uniform was an honorary Irishman.

From the afternoon shift change at four o'clock until early evening, and again late in the evening when the night shift came on, O'Malley's was populated mostly by law enforcement officers. It was undoubtedly the safest place in town to go drinking. Outsiders were tolerated, but not made especially welcome. Lawyers, at least those recognized as members of the criminal defense bar, were unwelcome and ignored.

It wasn't that law enforcement officers had any more loathing for lawyers than the general public, or even that defense lawyers occasionally got guilty scumbags off. Most cops accepted the proposition that their job was just to catch the bad guys. If the state's attorney couldn't get a conviction, that was their failure. What made defense attorneys particularly loathsome was that the "defense du jour" was that sloppy police work tainted all evidence, and law enforcement agencies were staffed by ignorant morons who had never heard of the Constitution. On the witness stand, rank and file law enforcement officers were sitting ducks for top-dollar lawyers. Ripping an officer apart in a public trial didn't tend to cause the welcome mat to be thrown out at their watering hole.

&

White sat at the end of the bar, facing the door, drinking his customary Diet Pepsi with two squeezes of lime, and watching faces as people moved through the short vestibule inside the large, solid wood doors.

Fifteen minutes later Tony Andrews came through the door and walked straight to where White was sitting. "Let's talk in the corner," Tony suggested. "We can have some privacy."

There was an unwritten rule in O'Malley's that the corner farthest from the bar, windowless and dimly lighted, was reserved for private conversations. Even when the bar was packed three deep and every table was filled, the corner would be empty, waiting for those who needed privacy.

Tony ordered a beer from a passing waitress and followed White. The men slipped into seats on the opposite sides of the corner booth. "It's been a while," Andrews began. "How have you been doing?"

"Same old thing."

"I heard you got Howard Marshall off on the wife's murder case."

"Word travels slowly."

"I was on vacation."

White took a drink of Diet Pepsi and waited for the inevitable barb. When Tony didn't say anything, White asked, "Aren't you going to say anything about defense attorneys getting scumbags off?"

"To tell you the truth, I never believed that he did it."

"Why not?"

"I don't know. It just didn't smell right."

White nodded.

"You know how it is when you get that feeling?"

"Yeah. I know. I get those feelings myself."

"Something tells me you have that feeling now."

White nodded. "Yeah. I do."

"The Matlacha drugs and murder case?"

"Yeah."

"What's your gut telling you?"

"I don't know. It's trying to tell me something, but it's in a foreign language."

"And you figured buying me a beer would help your translation."

White laughed. "I figured buying you a beer might get me some information."

Tony took a swallow from his bottle. "Like what?"

"Like any rumors you might have picked up about the case."

"Haven't heard anything. The feds took the case over before we got started."

"What about the tips?"

"What about them?"

"Didn't anyone think it was odd that both the tips—

the drug tip and the Jackson murder tip—were received by Paul Parker?"

Tony's attention shifted from his beer to White's face. "I hadn't heard that. But now that you mention it, it does sound odd. What are you getting at?"

"I don't know. Right now, I'm just pulling at loose threads… and hoping something will start to unravel."

"And the calls to Parker are a loose thread?"

"Anything out of the ordinary is a loose thread."

"I don't know what to tell you. The last year or so, we haven't been as close to Parker's staff as we used to be."

"Why's that?"

"All I know is… about a year ago, Parker and the sheriff got into a shouting match over the way Parker was handling some drug case."

"What was that all about?"

"The sheriff was pissed at the way Parker was letting defense attorneys carve up his deputies on the witness stand. The sheriff thought Parker wasn't preparing his men right. He even accused Parker of letting the defense have information on some things we'd rather the defense didn't know."

"Parker's required to disclose any potentially exculpatory evidence."

"I know. But there's exculpatory, and then there's exculpatory. The sheriff thought Parker was reading the rules a little too liberally."

"Did the sheriff think Paul was throwing cases?"

"He'd never say that… exactly."

"But did he think it?"

Tony hesitated before responding. "You'd have to ask the sheriff."

"What do you know about the plea Jackson was offering?"

"Just that he knew something important."

"About what?"

"I don't know, but it must have had Parker worried."

"What makes you say that?"

Tony shook his head. "Like I said, we haven't been close to Parker for a while. From what I hear, Parker didn't want to make a deal. But some of the other prosecutors in his office were about to revolt. They knew Jackson had something important and they were just itching to get whatever information he had."

"So what? They work for Paul."

"But he's up for reelection. He needs their support. Whatever he was worried about, his self-interest was more important."

"What do you think he was worried about?"

Tony shrugged. "I can only tell you this: he wasn't pushing the investigation of Jackson's murder."

"But that's been taken over by the U.S. attorney in Miami."

"This was all before that happened. Jackson agreed to testify about the drugs and Parker agreed to bail."

"What did Parker do after Jackson was murdered?"

"What could he do?"

"Did Jackson give Parker anything before he was released on bail?"

"Not that I know of. From what I hear, Parker expected the U.S. attorney in Miami to take over the Shephard drug case, so he hasn't pushed the investigation."

"Is that the only reason he was laying off Shepard's case?"

"I don't know. Should there be others?"

"Maybe," White said. "You'll let me know if you hear anything?"

"As long as you keep buying the beers, you'll be my first call."

29.

White and Leslie were wakened by the ringing of the telephone. Leslie rolled over and groped for the receiver. Horse greeted her with his usual, "I hope I didn't interrupt anything."

"Same old stuff," Leslie said in a bored voice, hoping to get a rise out of White.

White ignored her.

"Lucius is about to get lucky," she said to Horse. "He'll call you when we're through. That should be in about an hour."

The quality of the relationship Leslie and White shared was no secret, certainly not from Horse. Leslie enjoyed taking every opportunity to stimulate some kind of response from Horse. Horse had learned to return her teasing in kind. "So you finally surrendered."

Leslie continued the game. "I felt sorry for him. All that whining and begging. It was pitiful."

"Jesus, Leslie." White laughed and shook his head as he took the receiver. "What's up, Horse?"

"I may have a lead on our friend with the blue Porsche."

White sat up abruptly. "What do you have?"

"I just got a call from a guy I know out in Dunbar."

"Where you can buy drugs on any street corner."

"What can I say? Where else should I look for someone who can help our case?"

"I suppose you're right. What does he have?"

"He heard about our case and said he might have something useful."

"Like what?"

"He didn't say. He wanted to talk to us in person."

"When?"

"I told him we'd meet him at ten o'clock."

White rolled over and retrieved his watch from the nightstand beside his bed. "It's already eight."

"Nice to know you can still tell time."

"I'll ignore that. Where does he want to meet?"

"At the T&A down on the beach."

"Why there?" The T&A was better known as a place for viewing skimpily clad women, and where, in the wee hours of the morning, female companionship can be purchased by the hour. It wasn't known as a place where money was exchanged for drugs.

"It's outside his neighborhood. He'd rather not be seen talking to us."

&

The T&A had been a landmark on Fort Myers Beach for decades. In 1984, George Blake, USMC, retired, fled to Florida, intent on fulfilling his lifelong dream of having a place where he and like-minded veterans could congregate and swap lies. Taken by the beautiful teal-blue waters of the Gulf of Mexico and the clear azure skies overhead, George's wife had insisted on naming their little corner of the world the Teal and Azure Tavern.

True to George's dream, the little tavern had become a home away from home for the retired military population of Southwest Florida and, in time, it became a favorite spot to see and be seen. The T&A, as the tavern quickly came to be known, grew in popularity. By the early 1990s, the

T&A had become the place for the thong bikini crowd, and the tavern's nickname took on a new, but wholly accurate, meaning.

The waterside deck of the T&A was forty feet deep and stretched a hundred feet along the white sand beach. The decking planks were old and weathered to a silvery gray. A good pressure washing and some wood sealer would have restored the natural color of the wood, but George Blake thought that too much polish would make his little piece of the world look too much like a California fern bar. He'd seen more than enough fern bars when he was stationed at Camp Joseph M. Pendleton north of San Diego. Real men, by whom Blake meant marines and those like them, didn't go to fern bars. Blake preferred the weathered nautical look.

On any weekend afternoon or evening, the deck of the T&A was filled with suntanned bodies. Now, however, it was virtually empty. White and Horse found a seat at a table on the far corner of the deck, under the shade of the Tiki hut, away from the main bar. A few sparrows hopped from the railing to the various wooden tables and benches searching out scraps.

Less than five minutes after White and Horse arrived, a hulking black man appeared by the bar. A brief, but apparently friendly, exchange between the man and the bartender said he was probably a regular patron of the T&A.

Horse stood and raised a hand. The man wore a light blue suit and a dark blue silk shirt with the collar over the collar of his jacket. His shirt was open halfway to the waist revealing a dozen gold chains around his neck. His boots were made of the skin of a deceased reptile. He also wore a gold Rolex watch, and the diamond in his pinky ring could have been mistaken for an ice cube. White immediately pictured a gold-trimmed pink Cadillac convertible with lambskin seat covers sitting in the parking lot.

"Hey there, Pony," he greeted Horse, his smile revealing two gold-capped teeth. White smiled at the greeting, an apparent reference to the fact that, at six-six and a well-toned two-hundred-ninety, Horse was still small by comparison to the other man. One thing was certain: the man was someone to be reckoned with in his community.

The man grinned at White and said, "They call me Tiny."

"That would have been my guess."

Tiny laughed and took White's hand in his enormous paw.

A waitress in tight short shorts and a T-shirt knotted beneath her breasts brought White's Diet Pepsi and a beer for Horse. "Can I get you anything?" she asked Tiny.

Tiny gave her his toothiest grin. "Girl, just seein' you in that little outfit be all the refreshment I be needin'."

The waitress smiled and backed away.

Tiny turned his attention to Horse. "You been a busy boy, Pony."

"It's better than the alternative."

"Guess so," Tiny laughed. "But you also been makin' people nervous."

"Who?" Horse asked.

"People who'd rather you didn't ask too many questions about our business."

The reference to "our business" caught White's attention. He started to say something when a look from Horse silenced him.

"I wasn't aware of that," Horse said.

"You not aware of lots of things, Pony."

"Like what?"

"Like you seem to think your problem is on the east coast."

White couldn't control himself any longer. "What problem are you referring to?"

"What problem you investigatin', counselor?"

White considered the question, debating how much of the investigation he should reveal. The fact was, he still didn't know whether he was investigating trafficking in heroin or cocaine, or something else. Finally, he said, "You wouldn't be here if you didn't already know."

Tiny laughed. "That's good, counselor. You pretty sharp."

"Horse says you have information that may help us."

Tiny laughed again. "Got lots of information."

White waited.

The man leaned forward, resting his enormous forearms on the table. "You looking at the wrong connection."

"We're looking where the facts take us."

"You got the wrong facts."

"What are the right facts?"

"Shepard and Jackson got busted for snow, right?"

White's eyes narrowed and creases formed on his forehead. "That's what was discovered."

"They wasn't dealing snow."

White studied Tiny and wondered where the conversation was going. "How do you know?"

"'Cause I know everything." Tiny was no longer smiling.

"You're not being very specific."

"Gotta be sure I can trust you."

"You're the one who said you could help us."

"Got something that be helpful. Just not sure 'bout sharin'."

"What would make you sure?"

Tiny ignored him. "I hear you don't like prosecutors."

"Let's just say I don't think they all play by the rules."

"That be sure."

"What's your problem with prosecutors—aside from the fact that they'd like to see you in jail?"

"Don't like paying to stay out of jail."

Am I hearing right? White cocked his head. "And…?"

"Price of doing business is going up."

"Who's raising the price?"

"Don't know fo' sure."

"Who are you paying?"

"Pay the man who makes sure I got no problems."

"Who's that?"

"He drives a dark blue Porsche."

"With Dade County plates?"

Tiny made a gun with his forefinger and thumb and dropped the hammer.

"Do you know his name?"

"Most folks just call him 'the Cambodian.'"

"And he's collecting for protection from the authorities?"

"Ain't that what I just said?"

"And he's squeezing you for more?"

Tiny nodded. "Like I said, the price of business is going up."

"Who does the man with the Porsche work for?"

"Can't say. But he just the collector. He got to work for someone else."

"Is it possible that he works for an attorney?"

Tiny leaned back and relaxed. "I heard something about that. But I don' know anything I could prove."

"What else can you tell me?"

"If I were you, I'd be watching my back."

White's heart began pounding, and he fought to control his breathing. "Why's that?"

"The Cambodian been asking questions 'bout you?"

"Oh. What kind of questions?"

"The kind you ask 'bout folks you don't like."

White's fingers curled into fists. "That's good to know. Do you have any other information you'd like to share?"

"That be enough for now," Tiny said as he stood to leave. "Yo' have a happy Christmas."

White and Horse watched Tiny's back disappear through the sliding glass door into the dining room. "Interesting friend," White said.

"I have a diverse circle of friends."

"You like to stay in touch with the little people... figuratively speaking, of course."

"Of course," Horse agreed. "Tiny is also helpful when we get threats."

"You mean..."

"He's been known to watch folks' backs."

White nodded knowingly. "Tiny also likes to keep his secrets."

"He likes his freedom."

"Then why is he saying anything?"

"He wouldn't tell you anything if there wasn't something in it for him."

White considered the conversation with Tiny before continuing. "He's being squeezed."

"That's what he said."

"But who's squeezing him?"

"Sounds like it's the same people that Shepard and Jackson were working for."

White paused while he considered the possibilities. "What do you think they're squeezing the local dealers for?"

"Could be the suppliers raising the price of the product they're selling the local dealers."

White shook his head. "I don't think so. He was talking about the cost of protection."

"Maybe one distributor is just protecting his dealers from a rival distributor."

White pursed his lips. "It's possible. But I think there's something more to it?

"Like what?"

"I think dealers are being forced to pay the authorities to avoid being arrested."

"Maybe. But what do you think he expects from you?"

"He thinks that solving Shepard's problem will also solve his own."

30.

Two days before Christmas, Miami was engulfed in a shroud of heat, humidity, and haze. The crush of afternoon traffic, last-minute shoppers, and those leaving work early for the long holiday weekend only made matters worse.

Lucius White wiped the perspiration from his forehead as he trotted down the steps in front of the Miami Police Department.

A black limousine pulled to the curb. The driver stepped out and approached him.

"Mr. White?"

"Yes. Who are you?"

"Mr. White, Congressman St. James would like to see you."

How very interesting. "I'm a little busy just now."

The driver looked at White as if he wasn't sure he had heard him right. He was apparently not accustomed to having requests by the congressman rejected. He tried again. "Sir, Congressman St. James would like to see you."

"I heard what you said, and my schedule hasn't changed in the last ten seconds. Tell the congressman 'thank you.' If he wants to see me, he can make an appointment like everybody else. I'm at the Coral Reef Hotel."

The driver remained standing, speechless, beside the limousine, staring at White's back as he walked away.

&

Back at his hotel, White dialed the number for his apartment. When Leslie answered, he told her, "Something came up at the last minute. I'm going to spend the night in Miami."

"Did you find a slinky bimbo on South Beach?" Leslie teased.

"More like a slimy slug."

"Huh?"

"Congressman St. James sent a limousine to collect me for a command appearance."

"How did he find you?"

"I think he followed the trail of bread crumbs. I was checking up on him with the police and his limousine was waiting for me outside the police station."

"You're getting more important. Until now, the only people who sent limousines to get you were felons."

"I'm not sure anything has changed."

It took Leslie a moment to understand what White was implying. "If he already sent a car for you, why do you have to stay overnight?"

"I was too busy to see him this afternoon."

"And were you really? Busy, I mean."

"I wanted to see Harry. I went to visit him at the convalescent facility."

For a moment, Leslie didn't say anything. White understood what she was thinking and waited. Finally, she asked, "How's he doing?"

"According to the nurses, he seems to be a little more alert than he has been."

"Isn't that a good sign?"

White revisited the debate he had been having with himself since leaving the rehabilitation center. "Probably." Why ruin her holidays with the truth. "He isn't as responsive as they'd like, but it takes time." White hated lying to Leslie, but the truth about Harry's condition—he was completely non-responsive—wasn't something she needed to know. Not now. Not by phone.

"So, what are you going to do now?"

"Wait for the congressman to contact me again."

"What makes you think he'll try again?"

"Just a hunch."

"But how will he be able to find you?"

"I told him where I'd be staying."

"Are you always so generous with your assistance to the bad guys?"

"Only when I don't think they're smart enough to find me on their own."

"If you want to see the congressman, why didn't you go see him this afternoon?"

"I wanted to see what you've come up with first."

"I thought you'd never ask."

"Anything interesting?"

"Maybe. I spent the afternoon searching the online morgue of the Miami Herald and…" White heard the rustle of papers. "Most of what I found was just routine campaign stuff."

"But?"

"I came across some pictures of the congressman at campaign events and fundraisers. Some of the people the congressman is being chummy with are interesting."

"Barlow?"

"Among others."

"Who else?"

"The esteemed esquires Arthur Bell, Tommy Lester, and Don Wright."

"Interesting. A former narcotics detective being chummy with defense attorneys who represent big-time drug dealers."

"There were also some society page pictures of the congressman hamming it up with a few other politicians and, get this, Lyle Wilson."

"No shit?"

"Yes shit."

"When did he appear anywhere with Wilson?"

"Let's see," Leslie said as she shuffled through printouts. "There's one from the Fourth of July celebration with some veterans group… and another from a charity ball on December first. They must have had something to do with the gala because they were both in the receiving line."

"I might have something to discuss with the congressman after all."

"And there's something else. Horse got curious about any connections that might exist between Graham and the congressman. He spent a couple of hours playing with his computer and trying to find anywhere that both Graham's and St. James's names appeared."

"And?"

"He didn't find any direct connections between them."

"But?" White knew Leslie wouldn't have brought the subject up if they hadn't discovered something.

"He found a connection between Graham and the congressman's brother, Robert St. James."

White retrieved a legal pad from his briefcase and scribbled a note. "Interesting."

"I thought you'd like that," Leslie said. "And get this. Robert St. James spent some time as a guest of the federal government. He was released from the prison camp at Saufley Field a little over a year ago."

"What was he in for?"

"Horse is working on that, but I may have something even more interesting. I think Graham is still holding out on us."

"What makes you think so?"

"According to Graham, his investigation was supposed to be looking into corruption in the Miami office of the U. S. attorney."

"Yeah. So?"

"Graham also said that the investigation was being conducted under the auspices of the Public Integrity Section of the Department of Justice."

"And?"

"The Public Integrity Section doesn't investigate U.S. attorneys. It investigates corruption in the judiciary and public officials. Investigations of activities in the offices of the U. S. attorney are conducted by the Office of Professional Responsibility."

"Son of a bitch."

"Amen. Graham was never after the federal prosecutors. He was investigating corruption in the state judicial system."

"No wonder he wasn't concerned with Wilson."

"But where does that leave us?"

"I'm not sure, but I see a lot of water and no paddles."

Leslie laughed. "Will you call me after your meeting?"

"Nothing could keep me from doing just that."

"Not even a slinky bimbo from South Beach?"

"Well, maybe that."

&

The Conch Shell Lounge at the Coral Reef Hotel was indistinguishable from a thousand similar bars in a thousand hotels. The nets, floats, shells, and inflated puffer-fish were equally interchangeable with the faux maritime adornments of any nautical bar or seafood restaurant in the city. Even the artificial Christmas tree with blue and green lights had a standard stock number in a restaurant supply catalog.

White arrived at eight o'clock and took a seat at the ornately carved bar opposite the entrance to the lounge. The mirror over the bar gave him an unobstructed view of the entrance and anyone who might come in. The cocktail crowd had dispersed to their rooms or dinner, and the serious evening drinkers had not yet appeared in numbers. White ordered a Diet Pepsi with two squeezes of lime and settled in to wait.

Forty-five minutes, three Pepsis, a plate of complimentary peeled cold shrimp, and one trip to the men's room later, White was beginning to think he had misjudged the congressman. A commotion at the entrance to the lounge saved him from having to consider the possibility. The congressman, complete with a plastic smile and the obligatory minions in tow, greeted his constituents with back slaps and hearty seasonal wishes as he headed for a table in the corner of the room. Being the farthest location from the bar and the free food, it was relatively isolated. White watched as the congressman's staffers dropped bills on the nearby tables and said a few words, and the table occupants moved elsewhere.

Less than a minute later, a deep voice behind him said, "Mr. White, Congressman St. James would like a moment of your time."

White turned to face the voice. One look at the man behind him told White that the congressman learned quickly and knew how to send a more explicit message. Any correlation between the polite request and the man facing him was purely coincidental. The man was a thug. He knew it, White knew it, and he knew White knew it. Things were always easier when everyone knew where the other players stood.

White was tempted to ask a question about Faye Wray but thought better of it. Instead, he asked, "Is the congressman buying?"

Either King Kong had bad ears or no sense of humor—not that it mattered which. The firm grip on White's shoulder as he said, "Come with me, please," left no doubt that the congressman would not accept another refusal.

Congressman St. James nodded to his entourage as White approached the booth. The congressman's toadies found urgent business to attend to at the bar. King Kong sat at a table five feet away, his back to the congressman's table.

A row of bright teeth and a phony smile asked, "Can I order you a Diet Pepsi with lime, Mr. White?"

White smiled. "No sense playing games. Just come right out and let me know you've been investigating me."

"It simplifies matters," the congressman said, making no attempt to apologize.

"Did you find anything interesting?"

"I find everything interesting, Mr. White, or may I call you Lucius?"

"Lucius is fine. What should I call you?"

"Anything you like."

Several alternatives came to mind, but none of them were appropriate to the circumstances. "Why don't I stick with Congressman?"

"As you wish."

White's drink arrived. Congressman St. James thanked the waitress and indicated he was ready for a refill.

"You've been asking a lot of questions about me." The congressman's voice was pleasant. It was probably the same voice he used to thank supporters for their contributions to his campaigns. It was also the only thing about him that suggested he was in a good mood.

"I like to know about my elected representatives."

The congressman showed no emotion as he studied White's face. "I don't represent your district."

"You have me there."

"Now why don't you just tell me why you have been asking questions about me?" The congressman's bright teeth were no longer visible.

"I'm a curious guy."

The congressman's eyes narrowed. "Curiosity killed the cat."

"I've heard that."

"I don't like people asking too many questions about me."

"That can be annoying. But you're a public figure. You should be accustomed to it."

"Not when the questions are being asked by a criminal defense attorney."

"That is a little different. I'll give you that."

"You're something of a smartass, aren't you, Mr. White?"

What happened to 'Lucius'? "My father taught me to go with my strengths. Besides, the hours are good and there's no heavy lifting."

St. James's jaw grew taut, and the coloring of his face inched into the red tones. "Now listen to me, you son of a bitch."

"If that's your new campaign slogan, I suggest you reconsider."

St. James glared. "Let me tell you something, Mr. White. In the larger scheme of things, you are wholly irrelevant. You could disappear, and no one would give a damn."

"I sort of hope my girlfriend would care."

Self-control was becoming increasingly difficult for the congressman. "I don't know what you're up to, but I want to put a stop to it. If there's something you want to know, this is your opportunity to ask."

White couldn't help but admire his tactics. It was unlikely that the congressman would answer any of his questions, but the mere act of asking would reveal much about what White knew. "As much as I appreciate the offer—"

St. James interrupted. "Did you think I wasn't going to find out you were asking questions about my time as a narcotics investigator?"

"Actually, I was pretty sure you would."

"Then what the fuck do you want?"

White gave St. James a sardonic smile. "Is that any way to talk to your constituents?"

"Listen up, pissant! You're not one of my constituents. So why are you investigating me?"

"I want to know about your connection to Richard Barlow."

"Never heard of him."

"That's funny. According to your campaign finance reports, he's one of your biggest contributors."

"I have a lot of big contributors. It takes a lot of money to run for Congress."

"But Mr. Barlow lives in West Palm Beach. The last time I looked that isn't in your district."

"So what?"

"I just thought it was odd."

"Fuck you, you—"

"I guess that means you don't want to tell me what you know about drug cases being fixed."

The congressman clenched his jaw and gripped the edge of the table with both hands. "I wouldn't know anything about that, and I'll sue you if you say anything different."

White ignored the congressman's threat. He knew he

couldn't be sued for anything he said about a public figure. But he still wanted to know how far he could push the congressman. He slid his chair away from the table, casually crossed his legs, and clasped both hands behind his neck.

"Tell me about your business with Lyle Wilson."

"Why, you little—"

"I guess you don't want to talk about Lyle," White said with a mocking smile. "How about Graham Brochette's nomination? Shall we talk about that?"

St. James stiffened and propelled himself away from the table, tipping over his chair and spilling the drinks. "I'm warning you. Stop investigating my affairs."

King Kong stood, glared at White, and followed the congressman away from the table.

"Congressman," White called. St. James stopped and turned. "Give my best to your brother." The blood drained from his face as he started to say something. Apparently, he thought better of his impulse and turned and headed for the door, ignoring the greetings of his constituents.

&

White waited until the elderly couple who had shared the elevator entered their room and closed the door before inspecting the jam around the door to his room. As he expected, the thread he had placed between the door and the jam was missing.

Inside the room, there was little sign of an intruder. The casual observer probably wouldn't notice anything out of place, but a casual observer wouldn't have known how carefully White had arranged his briefcase and the files left open on the small desk.

All the documents were in the same order White had left them, even the ones he had purposely placed out of their natural order. White took a short ruler from his pocket and laid it on the table. Beside the ruler, White unfolded a sheet of paper containing the precise location of each document when he left the room. Whoever had been there was very good, but not good enough.

31.

The federal prison camp at Saufley Field Naval Air Station, west of Pensacola, Florida, bears little semblance to a prison. It's a collection of two- and three-story red brick buildings set amid pine trees on manicured lawns maintained by the inmates. There are no fences and no armed guards patrolling the perimeter. With its clean concrete walkways and numerous brick gazebos dotting the lawn, it looked more like a small college campus than a prison. The inmates housed at Saufley were mostly first offenders convicted of nonviolent crimes. A few were convicts with good records who had been transferred to Saufley from other prisons to serve out the final months of their sentences.

The visitor center was a one-story brick building that, on the inside, could pass for a school cafeteria: linoleum floor, plastic tables and chairs, and vending machines dispensing sandwiches, sodas, and miscellaneous snacks. The guard examined White's credentials and scanned the authorized visitor log.

"Your boy is in the yard. Follow me."

Behind the visitor center was a two-acre enclosed area with umbrella-shielded concrete picnic tables and benches. Inmates in green prison fatigues huddled with girlfriends, spouses, and families. A few babies cried softly. Young children from different family groups played together like old friends.

"All things considered, it's a halfway pleasant place," White observed.

"Yeah," the guard said. "Say what you want, the feds know how to run a prison." The guard pointed to a table.

&

Michael Drews embraced White and led him to a table in the corner of the yard.

Drews should never have been in a federal prison. As a first-time drug offender with only enough marijuana for his personal use, probation was the only rational sentence. Maybe a few months in a county jail on a misdemeanor charge was justified. But an over-zealous federal prosecutor was sure that Drews knew enough to help him make a case against a major dealer, so he was charged under federal law. Drews didn't know what the prosecutor wanted from him, but that didn't make any difference. So now he was here, and White was handling his appeal pro bono. Lawyers who provide their services at no cost are highly valued by convicts and tend to get a lot of cooperation in return.

White withdrew packs of cigarettes from each pocket and slipped them to Drews. "One of these days I'm going to get caught doing this."

Drews lowered himself to the concrete bench with his back to the guards.

"So? What are they going to do?"

"I'd rather not find out."

"But aren't you here on official business?"

White rocked his hand from side to side. "That depends on how you define 'official.'"

"Ah. That kind of official business?"

"Sort of."

Drews opened the pack of cigarettes and leaned forward as White held out a lighter. He took a drag and let the smoke out slowly. "Now. What can I do for you?"

"I understand you shared a dormitory with Robert St. James."

"Saint Bobby? That's a name I haven't heard for a while. Yeah, he was here for a couple of years."

"What can you tell me about him?"

"Bobby was a nice guy. Everyone liked him."

"Was he bitter?"

"About being convicted?"

"Yeah."

Drews took another drag and looked skyward, apparently savoring the smoke as he inhaled. "I don't know. He put in six or seven years at a medium-security prison before he got transferred here. He might have been bitter when he first went to prison, but he didn't seem too wound up about it when I met him."

"Did he ever talk about his conviction?"

"Not much. It's a subject we learn to avoid. Especially if your case is on appeal."

"Did he say anything?"

"It's not like this is his first choice of places to be. Given his druthers, he'd rather be somewhere else."

"But he never talked about getting revenge or anything?"

Drews rubbed his chin. "Just once."

"And?"

"It was just before he was released. A couple of us were talking about what we're going to do when we get out. Someone asked him about the first thing he was going to do."

"And?"

"It's kind of a joke around here. Getting laid is pretty much the first thing most of us plan to do."

White chuckled.

"But not Bobby. He just sat there… all quiet… like he

was picturing what he was going to do. Finally, he got this weird kind of look and said, 'I'm going to get someone's ass fried.'"

"What do you think he meant?"

"That's not the kind of phrase you explore."

White nodded.

"It's not a good idea to know too much, if you know what I mean."

"I understand."

"What's your interest in Bobby?"

"I honestly don't know if I have any interest in him. He's the brother of someone whose name keeps floating around the edges of another case."

"Congressman St. James," Drews said.

The immediate change in White's face showed his surprise. "I assume he talked about his brother."

"All the time."

"What did he say?"

"He was always bragging to the new guys about how he had a congressman in his pocket. They'd be all sorts of impressed… until he told them the congressman was his brother. He got a lot of laughs out of that."

"Is that all he said?"

Drews glanced around the courtyard before continuing. "There was this one time when he talked about his brother. Bobby claimed he was responsible for getting him elected."

Drews took another drag and exhaled. "He said he was owed big favors for not ratting out the people he did business with before he was convicted. He claimed he cashed them in for support in his brother's election."

"Did he name names?"

"That's something else we don't do around here."

&

When he returned from the federal prison camp that afternoon, White walked into his office, leaned back in one of the conference chairs, and propped his cowboy boots on the table. He looked up as Horse and Leslie came in.

"All right. Let's get this show on the road," Leslie said.

"Why?" White asked. "Do you have a hot date waiting?"

"I don't know. I may have to warm him up."

"I can see we aren't going to make much progress today," Horse said.

Leslie laughed. "Speak for yourself, Horse."

White looked at Horse. "See why I didn't want to put her in charge?"

"If you can't stand the heat…"

"All right, already," White moaned. "Let's get going."

"Whatever we're doing, we're getting someone's attention. Congressman St. James is pissed."

"That explains why we weren't invited for Christmas dinner."

"But not a lot else," White said. "There has to be a connection between the congressman and Barlow, and maybe Wilson."

"But what is it? All we know for certain is that Barlow is funneling a lot of money into the congressman's campaign."

"There has to be a reason."

"If I knew what it was, it would officially be a wonderful Christmas. All I know is that they're scared. Otherwise, St. James wouldn't have confronted me the way he did, and they wouldn't have taken the chance of breaking into my hotel room to find out what we know."

"But we don't know anything."

White ran the fingers of both hands through his hair. "No. But they seem to think we do. We must be getting close to something. I just wish I knew what."

"I have some more information on Barlow," Horse said. "But I don't know if it means anything."

"Nothing else is getting us anywhere. What do you have?"

"I looked into the guys who were bailed out by Jackson in West Palm Beach and later killed."

"And?"

"There's no apparent connection between any of them."

"Nothing?"

"Not that I could see."

"Not even race… ethnicity… where they live?"

"No, no, and no. Not even crime. Three of their cases were cocaine-related. One was heroin-related. Two were marijuana-related. And that's only in the last six months."

"Judges? Prosecutors?"

"Two different judges. Two different prosecutors. The only thing they had in common was that they had all made plea agreements and gotten bail reductions."

"And the fact that they were killed before they could testify."

"Yeah."

"So Jackson was arranging bail to get people out of jail where they could be silenced."

Before anyone could respond, the intercom sounded and Grace Matthews said, "Horse has a call from someone named Peter Gordon. He says he's a detective in West Palm Beach."

Horse picked up the receiver on White's desk and said, "Hello, Peter. Do you have news for me?"

For three minutes he listened, muttering only an occasional "uh-huh," as he scratched notes on White's desk pad.

Finally, he said, "Thanks, Peter. Let me know what else you come up with."

"What was that all about?" White asked.

"They found Barlow's body in his car at a rest area off of Interstate 95."

"When?"

"They found him about six o'clock this morning. According to Gordon, he died sometime between midnight and two o'clock."

"What was the cause of death?"

"Gunshot to the back of the head."

"Someone is getting seriously concerned."

"There's more," Horse said. "They already have the ballistics report. It's the same gun that was used to kill Jackson—Graham Brochette's gun."

White stood and began pacing in front of the marker board that spanned the width of the War Room. "Someone breaks into my hotel room and finds my file on our investigation of St. James. Four, maybe six, hours later Barlow is shot to death."

Before White could continue, the intercom buzzed again. "There's a call for you, Mr. White. He's very insistent. He says it's imperative that he talk to you now."

White, Horse, and Leslie looked at each other.

"What line is it on?"

"Line two."

White pressed the button for line two and switched on the speakerphone.

Without any greeting, the voice on the phone said, "You're sticking your nose into matters that don't concern you."

The voice had a metallic echo readily recognizable as computer-generated. Whoever was calling had sophisticated equipment and was going to great lengths to avoid identification.

"If you don't back off, something very unpleasant will happen to your girlfriend."

White's grip on the receiver tightened. "What am I supposed to back off from?"

"What happens on the east coast is none of your business."

"Who..." White started to ask when the line went dead.

White and Horse looked at Leslie. She was already biting her fist and breathing hard.

"Bastards," White muttered under his breath.

"I'll have Tiny here in twenty minutes," Horse said as he reached for the receiver and punched *69.

"Tiny?" Leslie asked from behind her fist.

"A mountain that walks."

Leslie wrinkled her nose.

"You'll be safe," White assured her.

Slowly, Leslie regained control of herself. "Who would threaten me?"

"I don't know," White admitted. "But we've obviously touched a nerve. Someone is starting to push back."

They both looked at Horse, who was still holding the receiver to his ear. He shook his head. "Nothing on star sixty-nine." He clicked the receiver and started punching other numbers.

"Who do you think it was?" Leslie persisted. Uncertainty and confusion filled her voice. Public interest lawyers don't get a lot of death threats.

"Not the congressman," White said. "He already warned me personally. Another warning would be redundant."

White was interrupted by a sudden "*Damn!*"

"What do you have, Horse?"

"No number. Just the area code... 239."

"But that's…"
"I know. The call was local."

32.

"Let's get a move on it, slowpoke. Sherlock is ready for a nice run. She can't wait forever."

Leslie peddled her new bicycle in small circles in the parking lot as White finished adjusting the seat of his own Christmas present.

"All ready," White shouted as he mounted his bike and headed for the path along the river. Sherlock trotted along, stopping to sniff at the trunks of trees and bushes, pissing on every object she came to, and going through the motions even after her supply ran out.

A light breeze blew off the river, tossing Leslie's hair. "This is great," she said. "We should have gotten bikes a long time ago."

"You have lots of good ideas."

"I do, don't I?"

For twenty minutes they laughed and talked as they peddled along the river and through the empty streets of downtown Fort Myers. As they crossed the Edison Bridge a mile from their warehouse, White's cellular phone began chirping. *Who the hell is this?* He was suddenly back at Clyde's on the evening he received the call from the emergency room. *Please don't be about Harry.*

White came to a stop, resting against the bridge railing. He was greeted by a voice that was vaguely familiar. "Counselor. Are you and your lady enjoying your ride?"

"Who is this?"

"How quickly they forget. I the man who's covering your ass."

"Tiny?"

"None other. And right now we all got company."

White fought the urge to look around. "Where are you?"

"Nearby. Ain't important. What's important is where your other friends is."

"Where are they?"

"One be sitting in the park you just passed. Other one be in the green Chevy that jus' went pas' the bridge."

"What are they doing?"

"Seems to be just watchin'."

"How long have they been here?"

"Showed up early."

"Are you sure they're watching us?"

"Sure as I know you a white boy."

"Do you recognize them?"

"They from out of town. Car got Dade County plates."

Leslie peddled back down the bridge, stopped beside White, and mouthed, "Who's that?"

"We're on our way back to the apartment," White said before ending the call and turning to Leslie and saying, "Let's head back."

"Who was that?"

"Tiny."

"Who?"

"Don't look now," White said. "We have company."

Leslie gasped. "Someone's following us?"

"And it isn't Santa Clause."

"What does he want?"

"He just wants to know where we go and what we do."

"Where do they think we're going to go on Christmas Day?"

"Hard to say. And he probably doesn't know either. He's just doing what he was told to do."

"Let's ditch him!" Leslie suggested. "It might be fun to play with him."

"That would only make him more curious," White said. Just the thought of Leslie playing spy and counterspy was humorous.

"What are you going to do?"

"I think Horse and I might give our new friend a Christmas surprise."

&

"Yeah, Lucius," Horse said after answering on the second ring. "I'm just about to head over to your place."

"We have a little matter to take care of."

"I know. Tiny just called. What do you have in mind?"

"I thought a little chat with our visitors might be useful."

"How many are there?"

"Looks like only two. One in the park and one in a green Chevy that's now parked up the street."

"What do you have in mind?"

"Can Tiny take care of the one in the park?"

"Does a fish swim?" Horse laughed.

"Do you feel like being a holiday jogger?"

"It works for me."

"Park up by the butcher shop on the corner and call me when you're in position."

&

White closed the gate to the yard behind his warehouse and began stretching as if preparing to go for a jog. As he expected, the man in the green Chevy slumped down behind the wheel, too low to see anything in his rearview mirror.

White began running in place when Horse came around the corner and started trotting up the street. The man in the green Chevrolet slid lower in the seat as he pretended to read the newspaper.

"Sherlock," White shouted, locking the man's attention on him as Horse approached the car from the rear.

Before the man was aware of him, Horse had the door open and a 9 mm Glock pointed at the man's face. The man didn't move as he stared at the barrel of Horse's gun. He also didn't respond when Horse said, "Merry Christmas."

White crossed the street as Horse gripped the man by the collar, pulled him from the car, and slammed him against the trunk. White circled the car, making a note of the Dade County license plates, and approached the man. "You're a long way from home. You should be with your family during the holidays."

The man glared at White but said nothing.

Horse pressed the barrel of his gun against the man's back as he searched for weapons. He removed a Beretta from the waistband of his pants and handed it to White. He continued to pat down the man's legs and withdrew a snub-nosed .38 Smith & Wesson revolver from his ankle holster.

"I hope you have a permit to carry these," White said.

"Better than that, you dumb motherfucker."

"He speaks," Horse said.

"I noticed."

"If you assholes are finished with your little routine, you'll find my carry permit and license in my jacket pocket."

Horse reached into the man's pocket and removed a

wallet containing a laminated card identifying the man as a private investigator. He slowly lowered his Glock as White removed the clips from the man's gun and put them in his pocket. "You won't be needing these."

Horse handed White the man's concealed carry permit and private investigator's license. "Miami, huh. You're a long way from home."

The man continued to glare at White.

"Now. Do you want to tell us what you're doing following me?"

"No."

"He's a man of few words," Horse said.

"So I noticed."

"Maybe we should throw his ass in the river."

"That would only add to the pollution."

"Maybe we should ask Tiny," Horse suggested, looking over the man's shoulder to where Tiny was prodding the other surveillance man toward them.

"He got no Christmas spirit," Tiny said, explaining the bruises on the man's face before anyone could ask. "And he don't seem to think much of my momma or my color."

"Shame on you," Horse said.

"If you clowns are through," the man from the car said, "I want my gun back."

"I don't think so," Horse said, taking the gun from White and hurling it into the river.

"You fucking son of a bitch. You better hope I never see you again."

"That's just what I was going to suggest," White said as he shoved the man into the car. "Tell your employer to back off."

"This isn't over," the man spat as he started the car and accelerated away. White, Horse, and Tiny watched them go. The man in the passenger seat turned and shouted something through the open window—probably not "Merry Christmas."

"As soon as they returned to White's warehouse, Horse went to his office and turned on his computer. A few minutes later, White followed and stood behind Horse and watched as he paged through a series of websites. Finally, he found the page he was looking for and began to scroll through a list of names. When he found the name of the private investigator they had just encountered, he pressed another key and the man's complete file appeared. Slowly Horse moved his finger down the page looking for anything out of the ordinary. Halfway down the page he stopped and turned to White.

"I'll be damned," White said. "He's an ex-Miami narcotics detective. I think I now know what client sent him to visit us."

"And," Horse said as he continued to read down the screen, "he left the force before qualifying for retirement benefits."

&

Leslie and Sandra looked up from the sofa when White and Horse stepped off the elevator.

"Our heroes return," Leslie announced.

"You might have at least shown some concern for our welfare," Horse said, indicating the glasses of wine and a tray of cheese sitting on the table in front of the women.

"Why?" Leslie asked. "There were only two of them."

"But they were very big," White said.

"And mean," Horse added.

"Yeah. Sure."

"Well, they could have been."

Leslie shook her head as she walked toward the kitchen. "Can I get you a drink, Horse?"

"Sure. A beer always goes down well after a hard day of chasing bad guys."

"How do you put up with these guys?" Sandra asked Leslie.

"It helps to remember that they're just a couple of pre-pubescent children playing out their fantasies."

Leslie handed Horse a beer and filled a glass with Diet Pepsi for White. "I generally ignore them when they get like this."

"That lasts until she gets hungry," White whispered to Horse. "Then she's completely in love with me."

"I heard that," Leslie scolded.

"But something smells wonderful," Sandra interrupted. "What is it?"

"Well, let's see," White answered as he checked the oven settings. "We have red potatoes roasted with butter and herbs, summer squash and roast venison, straight from Idaho."

"You killed Bambi?" Sandra exclaimed.

"Of course not. The deer died of natural causes on the front porch of my lodge… and she was smiling."

Sandra chuckled. Horse cracked up.

"And I helped cook," Leslie announced proudly.

Horse looked at her in amazement. "And what, may I ask, did you do to help cook?"

"I boiled the water."

&

"That was a fun day," Leslie said as she curled up naked in the bed beside White. "Aside from the visit from your snoopy friends."

"Isn't that about like Mary Todd Lincoln saying 'It was a wonderful play, except for that other thing'?"

Leslie hit him with a pillow. "You're horrible."

"But you love me."

"Only because I'm too old to start training someone else."

White kissed her on the forehead.

Leslie snuggled closer and muttered, "Horse and Sandra are a lot of fun together."

"Yes, they are."

"She's so different from the women he usually dates."

"That she is."

"I never thought Horse would find someone like her. Emergency room nurse. Combat medic in Syria."

"Uh-huh."

"I hope it lasts."

"That would be nice."

"Do you think it will?"

"Maybe."

"You're not being much of a participant in this conversation."

"I was just thinking about our uninvited guests."

"Well, I can take your mind off them," Leslie said as she slid under the covers.

33.

White took a sip of his coffee as he dialed the private telephone number for Graham Brochette. Brochette answered on the second ring. "Do you have any news?"

"Nothing new. But I need some help from you."

"You know I can't be officially involved in David's case."

"I'm not even sure that what I need is connected to David."

White envisioned Brochette reaching for a legal pad and searching the usual clutter on his desk for something to write with. Whatever other feelings he had, White admired Brochette for being a roll-up-his-sleeves attorney whose desk reflected a full caseload. "Okay. What do you need?"

"I need some crime statistics."

"Crime statistics? Why?"

"I'm just following up on a hunch."

"Okay." Brochette sounded dubious but resigned. "What do you need?"

"I need a breakdown of murder statistics for the past five years for the counties in the Southern District."

"That's all. That will be easy enough to put together."

"That's not all I need."

"I should have known that. What else?"

"I need to know how many victims had been arrested for drug-related crimes and had been released on bail."

"You can't be serious. I don't have the staff to compile this much data."

"Then call Washington and let them do it."

"And what am I supposed to give them as justification?"

"Tell them it has to do with your new job."

"But I don't have my new job yet."

"If my hunch is right, you'll get it."

"What do you need this for?"

"You don't want to know. At least not yet."

"Whatever you say. But while I've got you on the line, I have news from the eastern front. Earlier this morning I received a call from Lyle Wilson."

"And what news does Mr. Wilson have? Good or bad?"

"A little of both."

"Start with the good news."

"I don't know which is which, so here goes. Sometime this morning the Miami PD pulled a body out of the Miami River. The body had been in the water for at least twenty-four hours."

"Get to the good part."

"The body was identified from the driver's license photo. His name is Cho Wok Lo."

"Is that supposed to mean something to me?"

"It would if you knew the real name of the Cambodian who worked for Richard Barlow."

White gasped. "Damn!"

"Damn is right, but that's not all. The police chief in Miami is a friend of mine. He had the coroner recover the bullet from the body and send it to their crime lab for ballistics testing. Our friend was killed with my gun."

"So now your gun is linked to three murders. Does anyone have any idea who killed…"

"Cho Wok Lo. And no. They don't even know where he was killed."

"Maybe it will help if they can find his car. It's a blue Porsche."

"I suggested that to the chief. The registration was in

his wallet. It was soaked, but the crime lab was able to put it together."

"Who's the owner?"

"You better buckle your seat belt for this one. The car is registered to a political action committee established by Richard Barlow."

"The one he established to help Congressman St. James?"

"The same."

White bowed his head, put his elbows on the table, and rested his forehead on his hands. A minute later he raised his head and said, "We already knew that the Cambodian—"

"Cho Wok Lo."

"Whatever. We knew that he worked for Barlow. The fact that he drove a car registered to Barlow's PAC doesn't mean much."

"Maybe not. But something else the Miami chief told me does. I told him about our conclusion that drug dealers who make deals with the prosecutors have a way of getting killed."

"And?"

"He told me that this afternoon a dealer they had arrested a couple of days ago got bailed out and was shot as he left the courthouse."

For a moment White stopped breathing. "That pretty much destroys our working hypothesis. We thought Cho Wok Lo was responsible for killing Jackson and Barlow… and the dealers who had been bailed out after they had made deals to testify against others. He would have been my prime suspect for the killing of the drug dealer in Miami, but he has a perfect alibi for that one. He was already dead."

"That doesn't mean he wasn't responsible for the other killings."

"No. But Jackson and Barlow were killed with the same gun used to kill Cho Wok Lo. That certainly raises doubts about his involvement in the Jackson and Barlow murders."

34.

United States attorneys do not usually respond to the commands of defense attorneys, but these were not ordinary circumstances. White had called Graham Brochette early that morning and asked him to come to White's Fort Myers office. Brochette had not even suggested that whatever White had to say could be discussed on the telephone. Instead, now, only three hours later, Brochette was pacing nervously around White's office when White entered and told him to take a seat. "There have been a couple of new developments we need to talk about."

"In David's case?"

"I'm not sure. That's one of the things I wanted to talk to you about."

Brochette waited.

"Somebody called and threatened Leslie if I don't stop investigating."

Brochette was suddenly attentive. "*Jesus.* Why didn't you tell me?"

"It didn't seem to concern you or David. The caller just said that what happens on the east coast is none of my business."

For the next few minutes, Brochette remained silent as White recounted the circumstances of the threatening call and Horse's efforts to trace it. After White was finished, Brochette leaned forward with his elbows on the conference table and formed a pyramid with his hands. He closed his eyes and rested his forehead on his joined hands. After a minute Brochette said, "It'll be difficult for me to look into it without alerting anyone to our interest."

"They already know I'm interested."

"But if I started asking questions, they'd put us even closer together than we obviously are. If someone is pushing back, wouldn't it be better to keep them focused on you?"

"You may be right," White said. But I still need to find out who's doing the pushing. Do you have anyone who can ask around without anyone connecting things to you?"

"I'll see what I can do. What else do you have?"

"Does the name Robert St. James mean anything to you?"

"I assume he's related to Congressman St. James."

White nodded and waited.

For a moment, Brochette looked perplexed. Then a bemused smile crossed his face as he nodded. "Bobby the Saint. That's a name I haven't thought about in years."

"So, you know him?"

"I wouldn't exactly say I know him," Brochette said. "But I prosecuted him… it must be close to ten years ago—when I was with the Public Integrity Section at DOJ. Where did you come up with Bobby the Saint?"

"I was trying to find some reason why Congressman St. James might want to scuttle your nomination. Horse ran a computer search for anything that put your name together with anyone named St. James. This is all that came up."

"I'll be damned," Brochette mused again. "Bobby the Saint."

"What was he prosecuted for?"

"We nailed him for bribery of a public official. Ten counts, if I recall correctly. That was probably the least of his crimes, but we had a clean case."

"What else were you looking at?"

"Not all of the bribes were being paid in money. Sometimes he gave drugs. I'd like to have nailed him for the drugs too."

"Why didn't you?"

"He cut a deal and gave us the names of the people he'd bribed. Extra charges wouldn't have gotten us any more information, so we never pursued the drug issues."

"Who was he bribing?"

"Pretty much anyone who had a hand out. We convicted him for bribery in connection with contracts for the construction of federal buildings. In fact, the new federal courthouse in Fort Myers is one of them."

"Was this the case that got you connected to Congressman Tierney?"

"Yes. Is that important?"

"Probably not. Go on."

"As I said, bribery in connection with construction contracts was probably the least of his crimes. There were rumors he bought favors from some elected officials… and may have bribed a state prosecutor and a federal judge in Miami."

"What happened with those charges?"

Brochette shrugged dismissively. "By the time we had a provable case against Bobby, the judge was dead. We gave everything we had to the local state's attorney, but it didn't go anywhere. I guess they figured he was going to do enough time on his federal conviction."

"What kind of favors was he supposed to have bought from local officials?"

"We never got far enough to be sure. We knew about the money and the drugs he was passing out, but we could never connect them to favors being returned."

"Did it occur to you that the money was being passed

on to someone else, or that Bobby was just a conduit for money to buy favors for someone else?"

"We figured something like that was going on. But whatever it was, it was a state matter."

"Did you ever have the feeling that maybe someone didn't want the state charges investigated?"

"I can't say I gave it any thought one way or the other. What are you getting at?"

"Maybe nothing," White said.

"Besides, what does that have to do with Bobby?"

"Bobby is the congressman's brother. Bobby is familiar with the bribery of public officials. Bobby was paying bribes with drugs. What if the reason the drug charges weren't investigated was that Bobby's brother made sure they wouldn't be?"

"Congressman St. James?"

"He wasn't a congressman back then. He was a detective in the narcotics division of the Miami Police Department."

"It's not much to go on."

"I don't believe in coincidences," White said. "Look at the facts. The congressman was a narcotics detective when you gave the case back to the state authorities. The case never got investigated. Now I'm representing your son and asking questions about old drug cases, and the congressman seems to have a sudden interest in defeating your nomination."

"So the congressman is opposing my nomination as payback for convicting his brother."

"Partly. But I think there's more to it. When I talked with Wilson about a deal for David, he said his office had been keeping an eye on Jackson for some time. He also said he thought Jackson was involved in a major heroin network."

Brochette seemed confused.

"You picked Jackson because of his old heroin conviction. If your Miami office didn't know about your investigation of Jackson…"

Brochette suddenly understood. "How did Lyle Wilson know anything about a heroin connection?"

"And," White said, "why did he claim to have an ongoing investigation of heroin? Plus, if there was no federal investigation, why was Wilson willing to give your son a walk in exchange for what he knew about a nonexistent investigation?"

Brochette rose and walked to the window where he stopped and stood looking out at the peaceful river. "Whatever you're thinking, you're wrong about Lyle."

White ignored Brochette and continued. "I think Wilson knows something that isn't in the record. And I think David is the key to what he does next."

"Why would he need David?"

"I don't think he needs David to make a case. In fact, I don't think he has any intention of making *any* case. He knows there was a heroin investigation going on. When your relationship with David was exposed, he put two and two together. I think he wants to know how much David knows, and how much David might have told you. Once he knows that, David would have an accident."

"You're not saying…"

"These people aren't shy about eliminating obstacles. If they think David knows too much, they won't hesitate to kill him."

"Like they killed Jackson."

White nodded.

"So who killed Jackson?"

"I can't be sure, but I think Lyle Wilson set it up."

Brochette stared at White. "Lyle Wilson. I can't believe it."

"I could be wrong, but that's the way it looks. Wilson knew you had a government-issued gun. He also knew where you kept it, and you said he was in Tampa the day you discovered the gun was missing. Could he have gotten into the secure part of your office garage and stolen your gun?"

"You've got to be kidding. Why would Lyle steal my gun?"

"Unless you or David shot Jackson, somebody has to have stolen it. I'm only thinking about different possibilities."

"But what motive would he have for taking my gun?"

"I've got a couple of theories."

"Such as?"

"Wilson is acting U.S. attorney for the Southern District. Right?"

"Yeah. He's been acting head of the office for about six months."

"And he wants to be made permanent."

"Probably. But he was also acting U.S. attorney for the Middle District when I was appointed. He's already been passed over once."

"That might not happen if he has a political champion."

"Such as...?"

"Congressman St. James. The same congressman who seems to want to block your appointment to the Department of Justice. The same congressman who's been lobbying for an appointment to the House Judiciary Committee. If he gets the appointment, he'd also be in a position to assure Wilson's permanent appointment as U.S. attorney for the Southern District."

"You're stretching."

"Maybe. But what if Wilson is already in bed with St. James?"

"How do you mean?"

"I think we've come full circle."

Brochette searched White's face for a clue to what he meant. Suddenly, he burst out, "*No. It can't be Wilson.*" Brochette hesitated as he studied White. "You think Wilson is the rotten apple in the Miami office?"

"It all fits. Wilson knows about an investigation he shouldn't know about. How did he find out about it?"

"I—"

"Dammit, Graham. This isn't the time to be holding out on me. You were using Jackson to create a case the Miami Police Department could give to the U.S. attorney. But Jackson wasn't your only interest. You were still interested in his father's old heroin connections. No one outside the department was supposed to know about that, and yet Wilson seems to know. He could only have found out about it from someone who has close ties to the narcotics department of the Miami police. I think his information came from St. James."

"All right. Just for the sake of argument, let's assume that Wilson has a source, and knows about my investigation. What's his interest in it?"

"One possibility is that Wilson himself was involved with Barlow directly. So far, we haven't come across a connection, but if there is one..." White let his thought trail off.

Brochette furrowed his brow, a troubled look in his eyes.

"You knew there was a problem in the Miami office. That's what got your investigation started in the first place."

"But Lyle...?" Brochette hung his head. "I can't believe it."

White waited.

"You sure know how to ruin a guy's day."

"It gets worse."

Brochette looked up, not wanting to hear more bad news but bracing himself for the worst.

"I got a call from Jack Lancaster."

Brochette perked up.

"He said there's a hold on your nomination."

Brochette sighed as if the news was something he'd anticipated but hoped wouldn't come. He hung his head and exhaled. "Lucius," he said. "There's something I have to tell you about David. And you're not going to like it."

35.

Lucius White cleared the last of many files from his desk and was about to leave his office at six-thirty when the telephone rang. *Damn!* He wanted to ignore it and let the caller leave a message. What could be so important that it couldn't wait to be dealt with tomorrow? He was preparing to turn off his desk light when he had a sudden feeling, something between guilt and foreboding, that told him to take the call.

"Hello. This is Lucius White."

"Lucius. It's Graham. I'm glad I caught you."

"Graham…" The news that Brochette had conveyed in their last conversation, only hours ago, was fresh in his mind, and he was still seething. He heard his own voice and knew he had to exercise greater control. He took a deep breath, exhaled, and began again. "What can I do for you, Graham?"

Brochette had to understand how White was feeling. The collection of expletives he had been called had been deserved, and White could not be expected to be in a forgiving mood. But what he had to say couldn't wait. "I received some news that I knew you would want me to pass on."

White's indifference toward Brochette and anything he might have to say could not have been greater. White looked at his watch and stifled a yawn that had fought its way through his angst. "What is it?"

"I got a call from the Miami crime lab. They retrieved

some information from the cell phone on the body of Cho Wok Lo."

"The Cambodian?"

"Yes. He still had his cell phone when the body was discovered."

"What good was that after it had been underwater for God knows how long?"

"Not much," Brochette said. "But they recovered some data from the phone's call history."

White's breathing quickened as he leaned against the edge of his office conference table. He was tired and still not ready to forgive Brochette for withholding the information he had disclosed only hours earlier. But his curiosity got the better of him. "Anything interesting?"

"More than just interesting. We found cell phone numbers that could be traced to half a dozen major drug dealers over on the east coast."

"What's so interesting about that? You'd expect him to have those numbers."

"Yes. But we recovered other numbers we didn't expect him to have." Brochette was beginning to sound like a child who, on Christmas morning, was delivering a package he was particularly anxious to give. Open me first! Open me first! "He had the cell phone numbers for half a dozen narcotics detectives plus Congressman St. James, and a couple of state's attorneys—including Paul Parker."

White moved to the leather chair behind his desk and switched the call to his speakerphone.

"Do you know what this means?" Brochette said.

"I'd say your investigation of corruption has gotten a little more complicated," White said calmly, stating the obvious as though it was of no great consequence. But his pulse was racing, and only his years of experience in responding to surprise revelations in the courtroom enabled him to remain calm. As soon as Brochette had spoken White realized that the information recovered from the Cambodian's cell phone added vital pieces that were missing from the puzzle of his own investigation.

Brochette's silence suggested that he was waiting for White to say more. White knew what Brochette wanted to hear, but he was loath to oblige him. Not after what Brochette had revealed about David in their afternoon conversation.

An analysis of the implications of Brochette's newest disclosure could wait for morning. But White's mind was already roiling as he kneaded his left palm with his right fist.

"Lucius?" Brochette said.

"I'm still here," White said.

"There's something else."

"I'm not sure I can take any more of your news today."

"You'll want to see this. I'm faxing it to you now."

"What is it?"

"Just read it. It's something Lyle Wilson sent over late this afternoon."

On the corner of his credenza, paper began to flow from his fax machine. White retrieved the first page and began to glance over it. Before he had finished reading the first page, he stopped reading and reached for his legal pad and a pen. As he started to write, he suddenly realized the Brochette was still on the phone.

"Graham, I have something to do right now."

"I thought you would. I'll call you in the morning."

White leaned back in his chair with his boots on the desk as he read the remaining pages of the fax. When he had finished, he closed his eyes and ran the fingers of both hands through his hair. Then he dialed his apartment.

"Where are you, sweetie? Sherlock is looking for her evening treats."

"I received a call from Graham. I want to take another look at a couple of files."

"Can I help?"

"I think I need to work on this alone. I won't be long."

&

It was almost 10:00 p.m. when White stepped off the elevator into his apartment. Leslie laid down the book she was reading and rose to greet him. "You look like something Sherlock might leave on the sidewalk."

White stepped into her embrace and wrapped his free arm around her. "I feel like it too."

"What have you been doing?"

"I was going back over the evidence we have on David Shepard's case."

"I would have been happy to help."

White gave Leslie a quick kiss. "I know you would have. But I had to think about some things and Horse…"

As White spoke, Horse followed him off the elevator. "I was working late and just happened to stop by the War Room when Lucius was finishing up."

Leslie gave White a disappointed look that bordered on a glare. "Oh?" It was clear that she was feeling left out of something White and Horse had been doing. White understood everything that her tone conveyed, but he hoped that a report on his evening's activities would appease her.

"Well, sit down and tell me about it."

"First, I need a drink… a real drink."

"Do you want some wine or a beer?"

"Scotch. Single malt," White said, sliding his briefcase onto the breakfast bar and heading for a sofa.

Leslie frowned. "Are you sure? After seven years?"

"It's been a scotch kind of day."

"If you say so." Leslie selected a bottle from the bar and poured two glasses, lots of ice, and only a splash of scotch. She moved to the sofa, handed White his drink, and curled up beside him.

"Now tell me. What was so important that you had to work on it tonight?"

White took a sip of scotch and rested his head against the back of the sofa. When he spoke, his voice was soft and languid, as if he was merely engaged in a conversation instead of reciting the facts of a complicated murder case.

"The facts we know weren't getting us anywhere… but we know they're connected. I had to think about how they fit together."

"And have you figured it out?"

"I've filled some of the gaps in what we know." White closed his eyes, took a deep breath, and exhaled slowly. After a minute of silence, he said, "Biggest screw-up I ever saw."

When he didn't say anything else, Leslie asked, "And who was the screwee?"

"You name it… Me… The system… The country."

"Sounds complicated."

"You don't know the half of it." White sat up and took another sip of scotch.

"But have you made any progress?"

White glanced languidly at Horse and made a weak "go ahead" gesture with his free hand.

Horse shook his head slowly, suggesting that he, like White, was feeling a sense of disbelief. "We may never know the whole story, but we're finished with our investigation."

"That's wonderful!" Leslie said. She put down her glass,

curled her legs on the sofa, and leaned against White like a child eagerly waiting to hear a bedtime story.

White stared at his drink with unseeing eyes. Horse squeezed the bridge of his nose and slowly, almost methodically, shook his head again. Leslie watched, and waited, with growing anticipation. Finally, the silence became too much.

"Are you guys going to let me in on the secret?"

White rolled his shoulders and neck and sat up. His eyes seemed to be focused on something that remained just out of sight. When he finally spoke, his voice had a mixture of frustration and disbelief. "I should never have trusted Graham. He took advantage of me the whole time."

Leslie waited silently for White to continue.

After a minute, White said, "David Shepard isn't Graham's son. He's an agent with the Drug Enforcement Agency."

Leslie snapped upright and turned to face White.

"The whole thing was a lie... one big fucking lie."

Leslie reached for White and took his hand.

White shook his head slowly. "And I walked right into the middle of it... and kept on going."

For a minute, neither of them said anything. Finally, Leslie asked, "Do you want to tell me about it?"

"I hardly know where to begin."

"The beginning is usually a good spot."

"I'm not even sure where that is." White drained his glass and went to the bar where he poured himself another scotch—a full glass. With a wave of the bottle, he asked if Leslie was ready for more. She shook her head, and White returned to the sofa.

For a minute, White focused his attention on his glass as if it was an oracle from which he could draw wisdom. When he eventually spoke, his voice was tainted with his continuing sense of rage at having been so blatantly misled by Brochette.

"They *did* arrange for David Shepard, or whatever his real name is, to connect with Tom Jackson down in Marathon. But the story about David having been arrested and being given a choice of going to jail or going undercover was a complete fabrication."

Leslie gasped and gripped White's arm. In a halting voice, she said, "All of it was a lie?"

"Not all of it. The state's attorney for the Keys *was* making an increasing number of heroin arrests… they did think Jackson could lead them to some of the big dealers… and they did need someone to go undercover. David—and his first name really is David—was loaned to them as part of a joint operation. An arrest record for David 'Shepard' was fabricated and he and Jackson were locked up together—and eventually released together. Unfortunately, nothing came of the original plan because it was supposed to ferret out drug dealers in the Keys, and Shepard and Jackson moved to Matlacha soon after they got out of jail. Once they left Monroe County, the prosecutor in Marathon didn't have any interest in them. As far as I know, the Marathon prosecutor didn't know where they had gone, so he couldn't even tell Paul Parker about them or the arrangement he had made with 'Shepard.'"

Leslie seemed to anticipate where White was going. "But, if 'Shepard' was a DEA agent, wouldn't he have told someone where they had moved to?"

"Apparently he told his own superiors because the DEA called Graham and told him they had an undercover agent working in the district."

"How do you know all of this?"

"Graham told me. I'd told Graham that his nomination was being held up because of some problem with his past financial disclosures. When he disclosed his relationship to 'Shepard,' someone must have investigated and found out that he hadn't reported having any child support obligations. For some people, that apparently raised questions about his fitness for his new position. Graham wanted me to talk to Jack Lancaster about helping clean up the problem. That's why he finally told me the whole story."

Leslie nodded but appeared to remain perplexed. "Why did the DEA leave 'Shepard' with Jackson when Jackson moved to Matlacha?"

"That was Graham's idea. He was investigating drug-related corruption in the Southern District. They had planned to set up a sting with their own undercover agent. When 'Shepard' and Jackson were put together in the Keys, he decided to piggyback his investigation with the one set up by the state's attorney. They could do that because the Keys are in the Southern District."

Leslie seemed to deduce from White's demeanor what was coming next. "But that plan fell apart when Shepard and Jackson moved to Matlacha."

"Yes… temporarily," White said before taking another swallow of scotch. "Graham ran a background check and found out that Jackson was from West Palm Beach, which is in the Southern District. He probably assumed that Jackson would eventually go back to West Palm and could be used in his investigation of corruption in the Southern District."

"But why?" Leslie asked. "He didn't have any real reason for thinking that Jackson would go back to the east coast—or do anything that could help his investigation."

White suppressed a yawn as he strained to recall precisely what Brochette had told him. "Graham's investigation in the Southern District was being conducted at the request of the attorney general himself. The investigation itself was real, but it was also a sort of test. The attorney general had plans to reorganize functions within the Department of Justice. Offices responsible for the investigation of federal attorneys and judges and both state and federal public officials will all report to one deputy assistant attorney general. That will be Graham if his nomination is confirmed."

"That makes sense."

"I think so too. But the proposed reorganization wasn't a popular move in the Senate. As we dug deeper into our case, we found problems that would justify investigations by multiple offices of the DOJ. Graham used what we had discovered to focus on his investigation of corruption in the Southern District. He wanted to demonstrate the benefits of the proposed reorganization of DOJ functions. But that spread his resources pretty thin, and he missed some things. I think he may have let his personal aspirations color some of his decisions."

"That's a reasonable assumption. But what did he miss?"

"Even though the investigation of corruption in the Southern District was important, he had other responsibilities that he let suffer."

"Like what?"

"For starters, everything we know about 'Shepard' and Jackson happened in the Middle District, which is Graham's district. Once the DEA told him that 'Shepard' and Jackson moved to Matlacha, they became his problem, and he had responsibility for investigating their activities.

"One of his assistants is in charge of the Fort Myers office, which is responsible for federal cases in all of Southwest Florida… including Matlacha. Graham left it up to him to follow up with 'Shepard' and keep track of anything 'Shepard' and Jackson were involved in. Otherwise, Graham didn't do anything. When 'Shepard' and Jackson were arrested, his office should have taken over the case. All he had to do was recuse himself from anything involving 'Shepard.' When Jackson was murdered, he should have taken jurisdiction."

Leslie took a sip of wine and swirled her glass. Her eyes focused on the legs that formed on the inside of her glass, and if she would find the answer to a troubling question in the burgundy liquid. Whatever she was hoping to find, it alluded her. She shook her head, as if dismissing the mental search, and asked, "What was Graham doing in the mean-time?"

"He was focused on the investigation of corruption in the Southern District. He still didn't know whether the problem was in the state or federal courts. But he did do one thing right. Until Jackson was murdered, Graham still expected him to move back into the Southern District sooner or later, so he ran a more comprehensive background check on him. That revealed that Jackson's stepfather was Richard Barlow. Then Graham ran a background check on the father and found out that he was the attorney of choice in the local world of illegal substances. A little more look-ing and it turned out that Horse's contact over in West Palm Beach was right. Barlow had been a suspect in the heroin trade a few years ago, and the FBI had tapped his phones."

"And no one knew this before Graham's investigation started?"

White made a quiet snorting sound and shook his head. "It was an old investigation that hadn't gone any-where, and the wiretaps had been illegal. The investigation had been terminated and the file closed. But Graham had the file reopened."

Leslie seemed to know where this discussion was going

and guessed, "And the old taps were the key to solving the problem?"

White shook his head. His weak, enigmatic smile implied that he had hoped she would guess correctly. "I'm afraid not. The original investigation was looking for evidence of Barlow's involvement in the heroin trade. But the wiretaps didn't come up with any evidence to support that theory. I couldn't tell Graham everything we were finding in our investigation, but I was able to tell him enough for him the develop a new theory for the old Barlow investigation, so he had the recordings reexamined."

Leslie listened with rapt attention and fidgeted whenever White stopped. "And?"

"The wiretaps contained enough to prove that Barlow was getting certain drug users out of jail at the request of dealers. But because the original wiretaps were illegal, Graham couldn't use anything they had learned about Barlow."

"What they found is starting to sound familiar."

"It should," White said. "They were still a long way from understanding what Barlow had been doing. There were hints that Barlow has some involvement in the drug trade, but that's all they were, only hints. Then I told Brochette about Horse's interview with the private investigator, Peter Gordon. That gave him the insight he needed to refocus his investigation. His team put beaucoup hours looking into Barlow's record in Palm County and started putting together a complete picture of what Barlow had been doing."

Leslie bit her lip. "And was Barlow involved in drug trafficking?"

"Yes, at one time he was involved in drug trafficking. When his practice was limited to immigration law, he arranged for people from Southeast Asia to get into the country with small quantities of heroin. He brought it in, and the Cambodian who worked for him distributed it. It wasn't a huge operation, but it was big enough to get the attention of the local authorities."

"What about the federal law enforcement agencies?"

White shrugged and finished his drink. "Heroin was still a big concern up north. Cocaine-related investigations took most of the resources of the local authorities, but the state and federal agencies don't seem to have been on speaking terms. But the state put together the task force to deal with the heroin problem in Florida."

"That's the task force I heard about from the private investigator in West Palm Beach," Horse said.

"Right. When the U.S. attorneys found out about the state task force, they decided to look into the trade. That's what lead to the wiretaps. But that's also what got Barlow out of the business. The state task force was beginning to put pressure on his operation. But then things happened that changed his whole operation."

White laid his head on the back of the sofa and closed his eyes as if he was finished with his story. Leslie sat up squarer and poked him playfully in the ribs. "You can't stop now. What happened next?"

White rolled his head lazily and looked at Leslie. "When did you become a five-year-old?"

Leslie sighed. "You wouldn't have to tell me the story if you'd let me be more involved in the case."

Horse chuckled. "She has you there, Lucius."

White rolled his eyes. "We can finish the story in the morning."

Leslie pouted and gave White a pleading look.

White shook his head. "Why am I beginning to feel like a kindergarten teacher?"

Leslie laughed and clapped her hands. "Please! Please!"

"All right," White said before reluctantly returning to

the story. "About the time the state task force was beginning to make inroads into the heroin trafficking, Barlow's stepson—"

"Jackson?"

"Yeah, Jackson. He was arrested for heroin possession. Barlow represented his son and got him probation. That seemed to have gotten him interested in doing more work on drug-related charges. According to the records Graham dug up, Barlow initially only represented users who had been arrested. But that must have been enough to let him see how law enforcement was going after drug smugglers and dealers. What he learned must have made him realize how vulnerable his heroin network was. With the state task force starting to make inroads into his heroin business, and with a growing practice in defending drug cases, he got out of the heroin business."

Horse interrupted and said, "That's consistent with what my private investigator friend said. He said that heroin trafficking took a nosedive overnight."

White stood, put down his drink, and started to walk away.

Leslie frowned in an apparent show of annoyance until she realized where White was going. She shifted her position on the sofa so that she could look at White and said, "It's the second door on the left, in case you've forgotten."

White made a rude gesture and trotted down the hall.

"Okay, Horse," Leslie said. "Tell me the rest before the Grouch gets back."

Horse took another swig of beer and closed his eyes. He seemed to be trying to sort the facts of the story to be sure that they were in the proper order. Finally, he returned his attention to Leslie. "It turns out that Barlow was a surprisingly good negotiator. His clients were either getting probation or minimum jail time. He actually represented his clients well, and pretty soon he was the go-to attorney for Palm County for petty drug arrests. He was still only representing users and a few small-time dealers, but their money was green, and business was good. Then he started getting approached by people who had been arrested in other counties. Barlow was happy to oblige them and pretty soon he had clients from West Palm Beach to Key West."

"Then he started getting greedy," White called from down the hall.

"And stupid," Horse said.

"Yes. Very stupid."

"Very, very stupid," Horse said.

Leslie pursed her lips, and her expression began to show her impatience. "I get it! He was stupid. But what was he doing?"

Horse looked at White who shrugged and nodded. Horse settled back in his recliner and seemed to think for a moment before continuing. "At some point, Barlow decided that the information his clients were willing to give up in plea bargains was also worth money to the dealers he represented. Not surprisingly, they were willing to pay Barlow for what he knew. All of a sudden, clients who had made plea deals and been bailed out were changing their minds or were getting amnesia. Of course, Barlow could tell from his clients' casts and bruises what form the persuasion had taken, but no one was getting killed."

"Let me get this straight," Leslie said. "Barlow was negotiating plea deals... then he was telling the person who was named in the plea that Barlow's own client was ready to testify against him."

"That's about it. But he was only selling information to dealers who were also his clients."

Leslie shook her head. "I can't believe it. He was pond scum."

"No doubt," White muttered. "He had a highly questionable grasp of legal ethics."

Leslie moved to the edge of the sofa and leaned toward Horse. "What happened then?"

"Then fate reared its ugly head," White said as he reclaimed his place on the sofa beside Leslie. "A couple of Barlow's clients got real sweetheart deals by becoming informants or testifying against someone higher in one of the cartels. This, of course, did not make distributors happy. So they approached Barlow with an offer—"

"The kind of offer that can't be refused," Horse said from in front of the fireplace where he was beginning to stack kindling.

Leslie leaned forward as though getting closer to Horse would get information to her faster. "And what was the offer?"

"When Barlow was negotiating a deal that involved testifying against someone in the drug network, all he had to do was tell the subject of the plea deal about expected testimony and get his client bailed out before he testified."

"And since this was an offer that he couldn't refuse, he started doing what he was told to do."

"But isn't that what he was already doing?"

"Yes, he wasn't only reporting to dealers who were also his clients. Now he was working for people at the top of the drug cartels, and the people he was getting out of jail were never seen again."

Leslie rolled her eyes. "So now Barlow was himself a felon—an accomplice to the murder."

"I'm sure that fact was obvious to Barlow. But the money he got was more than enough to assuage his conscience."

"Was that all there was to it?"

"No, there was one more piece," White said. "And it wasn't even something Barlow did."

Leslie was becoming more and more impatient. Complex criminal cases were not new to White, but to Leslie the sorting out of facts was taking on all the features of a television drama. White had barely finished talking when she was demanding, "What was it?"

"Patience, dear."

"Patience, my ass. What happened next?"

"Patience, your ass. What's that supposed to mean?"

Leslie frowned and gave White her most serious look. "It's what you won't be getting any of if you don't hurry up."

"Ah. Well, now that you've explained the benefits." White cracked his knuckles and put on his best "I'm thinking" look before continuing.

"About this time Barlow made a deal for a client to testify against a major dealer from Miami who had been arrested in Palm Beach. But the prosecutor wouldn't let Barlow's client out until after he had testified. And the prosecutor demanded some absurdly high bail—cash only, no bond—so Barlow couldn't get his clients out of jail. For a while, Barlow was in a quandary. Then the prosecutor approached Barlow and explained that he was a 'reasonable' man and, for a price, the prosecutor would reduce his bail demand."

"You mean the prosecutor offered a bail reduction in exchange for a bribe?" Leslie said.

"That would be the legal term for it. His client was desperate to get out of jail, so Barlow paid the bribe and arranged for bail. But Barlow also reported the arrangement to the person who was the subject of his client's proposed testimony. This time the client was also found shot in the head after he had been bailed out."

"But," Horse added while adding logs to the growing fire, "Barlow had discovered a new way to get his clients out of jail—bribe the prosecutor. He started slowly, with the prosecutor who had first approached him. But that only helped him in one county. That was fine for him, but it wasn't good enough for his new clients who had problems all over southeast Florida."

"So what did he do about it?"

"The only thing he could," White said. "Barlow had to find a way to bribe other prosecutors who wanted high bail for people his clients wanted to get out of jail. But that, alone, didn't solve his problems. He knew that some of the people he bailed out were going to be killed. But unless there was proof that they were dead, and hadn't simply run from the jurisdiction, the bail bondsman was liable for the whole amount of the bond. All of a sudden, no one was willing to issue bonds for his clients. He had to find a way to ensure that the bodies were found."

"And that is where Franklin St. James, Congressman St. James, comes into the picture."

Leslie's hands shot to her mouth. When her initial surprise dissipated and she was able to speak, she asked, "How did Barlow go from managing his little scheme in West Palm Beach to being connected with St. James?"

"They were connected by a drug smuggler in Miami. This was back when St. James was a narcotics detective with the Miami PD. But he was a crooked cop. St. James was taking bribes from dealers to avoid being arrested, and he was taking money from distributors to keep their dealers in line by arresting the ones who made any trouble."

"Okay. But how did St. James connect with Barlow?"

"One of the distributors who was using Barlow was also bribing St. James. He must have seen the benefit of having both a narcotics cop and an unethical defense attorney on the payroll. He brought Barlow and St. James together."

Leslie's eyes narrowed, and her face took on a quizzical look, "Let me get this straight. A narcotics detective in Miami arrests someone… then he refers that person to an attorney and bail bondsman who can get him out of jail."

White nodded. "Yes. Of course, there were a lot of people being arrested by other cops. Some of those cops were recruited to join in the scheme. In the end, there were a couple dozen cops involved."

"And how many drug distributors?"

"That's hard to say."

"For that matter, how did drug distributors benefit from the arrangement?"

"For them, it was a dream come true. First of all, users and petty dealers could get out of jail cheaply. That kept the dealers' businesses going. But if anyone didn't want to play along with their plan and tried to get out of jail by making a deal with prosecutors—"

"Those higher up in the system would find out about it."

"Right. Then they would arrange for the wayward prisoner to be released on bail, and they would be persuaded not to testify—or they'd be eliminated."

"Killed?"

"That's right."

Leslie tugged on a strand of her hair. "It's hard to believe. The police and prosecutors were actually helping the drug lords keep their people in line?"

"Exactly!" White said. "And it wasn't long before the major players in the trade knew how the arrangement was working. But I couldn't figure out how so much money was moving around without it becoming obvious that some prosecutors were being bought off."

Leslie continued to play with her hair. "I don't get it. Why was that a problem?"

White leaned forward until he was resting his elbows on his thighs and turned his head to face Leslie. "The first indicator of corruption is usually when a public official starts spending a lot more than they're supposed to be earning. But Horse couldn't find any obvious evidence of that. I didn't put it all together until Graham told me about Congressman St. James's brother, Bobby the Saint."

"What about him?"

"Bobby had been convicted of bribery of a public official in connection with some federal construction projects. If someone that he was bribing hadn't been caught and agreed to testify against him, Bobby would probably still be in business."

Leslie pulled her knee to her chest and wrapped her arms around her legs. "What was Bobby doing that was so interesting?"

"Bobby was setting up three-way and four-way bribes. Instead of bribing anyone directly, he arranged for officials to get favors from a third or fourth party, someone Bobby was paying to provide whatever the target wanted. Whoever wanted a favor paid Bobby, Bobby paid the middleman, and there was never any link from the target to Bobby or whoever wanted the target to do something."

Leslie closed her eyes and pursed her lips as she seemed to struggle to keep track of the mounting collection of facts. "And what did Barlow and St. James do?"

White took a deep breath and exhaled. It was one thing to know the individual facts. It was quite another to see what they meant when they were all put together. Even as he was explaining the facts to Leslie, pieces were falling into place.

"It took a while, but eventually they put together a network of crooked prosecutors in all the counties along the east coast that were in the Southern District of the federal court. Barlow was the conduit for the money. He got paid by drug dealers and distributors, and he used Bobby's model to pay prosecutors, and maybe even some judges. He'd find out something they needed, and then he'd arrange through some third party to provide it. Then he and St. James would split the remainder of whatever they collected for their efforts."

"Is St. James still involved? I mean, now that he's a congressman?"

"By the time they had all the pieces of their plan in place, St. James had already decided to run for Congress... although God only knows why. Barlow started paying St. James's share of the bribe money into a political action committee he set up for the congressman. That way there was no direct connection to the congressman."

Leslie seemed to understand the essential parts of the arrangement White was describing, but she apparently wanted to know more of the details. "Why did they only do this in the Southern District?"

White rolled his shoulders, rested his head on the back of the sofa, and closed his eyes. "St. James knew the narcotics detectives in all the counties in the Southern District." He paused and rubbed his eyes. He didn't really know the answer to Leslie's question, at least not all of it. But he knew enough to guess. "It took him a little while, but he managed to recruit some of them to participate in their scheme."

Leslie stretched and wrapped another lock of hair around a finger. "But federal prosecutors can assert jurisdiction over drug cases that originate with arrests by state law enforcement officials."

"To keep control of the cases against the people in their

organizations they needed to keep the cases in state court. So they started bribing federal prosecutors to leave cases in state court."

"Couldn't they simply bribe federal prosecutors the same way they were bribing state prosecutors?"

"They could. But it was easier to bribe them to not take jurisdiction over state cases in the first place."

"What about the cases that started out with arrests by federal agencies? Didn't they have to stay in federal court?"

"At first, there wasn't anything they could do about that. But then Lyle Wilson transferred to the office of the U.S. attorney for the Southern District where he could have federal drug cases assigned to him. Then he would handle it the same way cases were being handled in the state courts."

"How could he have done that with Graham investigating corruption over there?"

"I hate to admit it, but I completely misunderstood what Graham was doing."

Leslie's quizzical expressing asked her question for her.

"When Graham first told me about his assignment, I thought he would be conducting investigations in both federal and state courts. But as soon as we stumbled onto the Barlow–St. James scheme, Graham started to put all his resources into the investigation of state cases. Then I remembered that his investigation was being conducted under the auspice of a DOJ office that only investigates corruption by state officials."

Leslie shook her head and sighed. Her eyes showed only confusion. "You mean he was never supposed to investigate whatever Wilson might have been doing?"

"I don't think so. But even if it had been part of his assignment, I doubt it would have made any difference. Graham knew Wilson from their time together in the Middle District, and he trusted him. It seems that Wilson was free to do whatever he wanted."

"Your analysis seems to be based on a lot of assumptions," Leslie said. Her tone suggested that she was beginning to have doubts about White's story.

"I never would have put it together if Barlow hadn't been murdered."

Leslie looked from White to Horse and back to White. "Are you guys having a little fun at my expense? This story is getting too crazy to be real."

White gave a Boy Scout salute. "Scout's honor. Truth is stranger than fiction."

Leslie looked suspicious but settled back to hear the rest of the story.

"Now, where was I?" White said.

Leslie wrapped her arms around a throw pillow and mumbled, "You were about to make up some story about Lyle Wilson."

"Ah yes. Well, Lyle Wilson took over the investigation of Barlow's murder. That murder should have just been a state matter. But Wilson claimed that it was connected to his own investigation into drug trafficking. The state's attorney was only too happy to let him have the case."

"What does that have to do with your analysis of how the Barlow–St. James operation worked?"

"When Jackson was murdered, Barlow concluded that some of the people in his organization were behind it. Jackson had already tried to get a payoff to keep quiet about what he knew and some people in the Barlow–St. James operation had discussed eliminating him. Of course, Barlow was opposed to killing his own stepson. But when Jackson was murdered, Barlow threatened to find out who ordered it and get even."

"That was pretty stupid of him," Leslie said.

"You're right. And that's why he was eliminated. But what the organization didn't know was that he had compiled an insurance policy—a detailed summary of everything. After Wilson took over the case of Barlow's murder, he got access to Barlow's office and found documents outlining the whole scheme. Names. Dates. Amounts paid. The whole thing. Apparently, Barlow actually was going to go to the authorities and had compiled documentation to give them. He must have thought that he could make a deal for what he knew and stay out of prison."

"How do you know all this?"

"Wilson gave Graham what he found in Barlow's office. Those documents filled in all the gaps in our investigation and we were able to understand everything about the operation of the Barlow–St. James organization. Graham sent me the file this evening. That's what I've spent the evening analyzing."

"Well, way to go, boyfriend," Leslie beamed. "You solved Graham's corruption case for him."

"Not really. He did most of the work. I… Horse and I only provided some leads and filled in some gaps. I called him as soon as I put it together and he's ready to start making arrests."

"But you haven't said anything about the Matlacha arrests and Tom Jackson's murder."

"All in good time, my dear."

"Tease!" Leslie said and playfully hit White with a pillow.

White smiled and stood up. "I'm hungry. Would anyone like an elk burger with all the fixings?"

Horse raised his hand.

Leslie said, "I want the rest of the story."

"Then you'll have to join me in the kitchen because I feel a need to cook."

36.

Horse and Leslie sat at the breakfast bar as White burrowed into the refrigerator selecting ingredients for his famous burgers: elk meat, shitake mushrooms, bacon, Vidalia onions, and blue cheese.

At the breakfast bar, Horse's hands were wrapped around a bottle of beer. A glass of Merlot sat untouched in front of Leslie.

White stood by the open refrigerator contemplating something that only he understood. Finally, he reached for a can of Diet Pepsi, closed the refrigerator door, and moved his burger ingredients to the island in the middle of his gourmet kitchen. He popped the top of his can of Diet Pepsi and took a long swallow. "Now, where was I?" he said to no one in particular.

"You were about to tell me why anyone wanted to frame 'Shepard' and Jackson for having cocaine in the first place."

"No, I was looking for this," White said as he pulled a cutting board from the shelf under the island and selected a knife to begin preparing one of his favorite light meals. As he prepared to chop the mushrooms and onions, he returned this attention to Leslie. "Now, what was your question?"

"Why did anyone want to frame 'Shepard' and Jackson?"

White put a cast iron skillet on the stove and lit a gas burner before responding. "That's a two-part question."

"Okay, then why did anyone want to frame 'Shepard'?"

White considered the question for a few seconds before responding. "'Shepard' was merely in the wrong place at the wrong time. If he hadn't been home when the house was raided he would never have been arrested in the first place. But once he was in the system, they had to do something with him."

"Couldn't Graham have told Parker that he was a DEA agent and gotten him released?"

"They couldn't do that because then 'Shepard' would be useless to the DEA as an undercover agent. Graham and the DEA had to protect his identity as long as they could."

"How is that any different than letting Graham claim that 'Shepard' was his son?"

"The difference was mostly bureaucratic. Graham didn't need the DEA's permission to disclose that 'Shepard' was his son. In any event, by the time we had to disclose that fact, the risk that he might be harmed while in jail had increased."

"How?"

"We think that Jackson was getting suspicious of 'Shepard.' He knew that the cocaine the sheriff found wasn't his, but it was found in his room. He had started telling other inmates that he had been arrested because of something that 'Shepard' had done. When he heard about that, Graham just didn't think 'Shepard' was safe in jail."

As White continued to chop the onions and mushrooms, Leslie pondered his explanation. White glanced in her direction. Her brow was furrowed and her lips pursed. White concluded that she had decided to try to decipher the remaining clues herself. He smiled at the thought and waited for her to proceed.

"Well, if 'Shepard's arrest was just a mistake, why was Jackson framed?"

"Probably because he knew about the Barlow–St. James plan. Most likely he was threatening to tell the authorities about it if he didn't get a part of the income."

"What makes you think that?"

White stopped what he was doing and leaned over with his elbows on the breakfast bar. "We know Jackson knew about the Barlow–St. James scheme—at least the Palm County part of it—because he told 'Shepard' about it. We also know that he specifically told 'Shepard' that snitches got killed. That's why, when I interviewed him in jail, 'Shepard' made a point of telling me that he wasn't going to make any kind of plea agreement. He was afraid that I had been sent by someone in a drug cartel."

Leslie's eyes narrowed. "Are you saying that Jackson was blackmailing his own father?"

"And, indirectly, everyone involved in the Barlow–St. James scheme. But the other people involved in the scheme—mainly the prosecutors Barlow was bribing—had to know that money alone wouldn't keep Jackson shut up."

"How could they know that?"

"Blackmailers are rarely satisfied that easily," Horse said. He spoke in a voice that didn't seem to require any thought, as though what he was saying was self-evident. "They always want more."

"Then what was their plan for dealing with Jackson?" Leslie said.

White stood, chuckled, and resumed preparation of the elk burgers. As he worked, he explained, "That's probably the only rational decision they made. They decided to have Jackson arrested and charged with something that carried a long prison sentence. That was intended to send Jackson a message. He had to know that he was being framed. They wanted him to know what they could do to punish him if he didn't stay in line. Two kilos of cocaine would be enough to send Jackson away for a long time if he was convicted. But, more importantly, it was enough to ensure his bail would be so high that Jackson would have to stay in jail until they decided to get him out.

"Whoever arranged for him to get arrested wanted to keep him in jail for a while. Once they were satisfied that Jackson would stay in line, he'd have been released on some technicality. They thought he was smart enough to know that they, or at least his father, would eventually get him out. They hoped that by showing him that they could have him arrested the experience would be enough to scare him into keeping his mouth shut."

Leslie suddenly sat up straight and smiled as if she had received a divine revelation. "If Jackson had already told 'Shepard' about the…"

"Barlow–St. James scheme."

"Yes. Thank you. If Jackson had already told 'Shepard' about the scheme, why didn't you put all the pieces together before you got Barlow's 'insurance policy'?"

White smiled. "That's a good question. You might make a half-decent criminal attorney after all."

Leslie started to scowl and looked as if she was about to say something but seemed to change her mind. "Then answer the question."

White scooped up the ingredients he was chopping and put them in a bowl before turning and leaning against the island. "It turns out that Jackson only knew what his father was doing, and that's all he told 'Shepard' about. Graham investigated and confirmed what Jackson had said. But Graham knew that the arrangement was much bigger—so he kept digging."

"Wait a minute," Leslie said. "How do you know the Barlow–St. James people didn't intend to kill Jackson from the beginning?"

"If that was all they intended, they would have just killed him—or arranged for him to be killed. But as I said, Barlow wouldn't agree to that."

"Then it was the people on the east coast who planted the cocaine that got them arrested."

"Yes. At least indirectly."

"How did they do that?"

"I'm coming to that."

"Well, come a little faster."

Horse, who was taking a drink of beer, burst out laughing. Beer came out of his nose. "Now there's a phrase that I'll bet you don't say often."

White strained to stifle a laugh of his own. Leslie pondered his statement for a moment before blushing and giving him a playful punch on the shoulder. "You have a dirty mind."

Horse responded with another laugh. "You're the one who said it."

"Well, harrumph to you," Leslie said before taking a sip of wine and returning her attention to the story of the investigation. "Then what went wrong with the plan?"

While White busied himself at the cooking island, Horse picked up the story. "The attempt to scare Jackson into keeping his mouth shut appeared to have backfired when he started trying to bargain his way out of jail. The people who ran things on the east coast had to assume he was offering to tell the authorities what he knew about the Barlow–St. James operation."

"But you said Jackson knew that people who tried to make plea deals were being killed when they were released from jail."

"Jackson must have assumed that his father would never let him be killed. Besides, he probably never intended to tell anyone about his father's operation."

"Then what information was he going to give Paul Parker?"

"It could have been anything."

Leslie took a sip of wine and returned her glass to the breakfast bar before asking, "Such as?"

"Well, for instance, Jackson knew that his father's organization had never framed anyone. And since he knew that he hadn't brought any cocaine to Matlacha, he must have assumed that 'Shepard' had brought the cocaine to the house—or that 'Shepard' was the one being framed. Whatever deal Jackson was trying to make with Paul must have involved testimony against 'Shepard'—not his father's organization."

"Or," Horse interjected, "he might also have planned to tell what he knew about the Cambodian and the protection racket *he* was running."

"What racket was that?"

"That's a whole different story, but we'll get to that."

"Well, get a move on it!"

"Don't get your undies in an uproar."

Leslie gave White an oral razzberry.

White narrowed his eyes and considered several responses of marginal propriety before continuing. "When Jackson offered information to Parker as part of a deal, the people on the east coast didn't know about the other things Jackson could testify about. They must have assumed that the only thing he was ready to talk about was their operation."

"So, they got him bailed out."

"That's right. But the fact that he had been ready to make a deal to get out of jail made it clear that he hadn't learned his lesson. But they still had to find a way to deal with his blackmail demands."

"How do you know they didn't already have a plan?"

"Do you mean, 'why didn't they plan to kill him as soon as he was released?'"

"Yeah. I guess that's what I was thinking."

"By the time Jackson was in jail, the organization that was operating on the east coast involved more than just Barlow and St. James. Like all organizations, sometimes it takes time to make decisions. Some of the people in the organization must have believed that Jackson could never be trusted and had to be eliminated. If Jackson had been anyone else, they would have just had them killed. But Barlow wouldn't have wanted to let his stepson be killed, so the others had to find another way to deal with him."

Leslie swirled her wine and watched absently as its legs formed on the inside of the glass. She seemed to want to say something but was unable to decide what it was. Finally, she asked, "Wasn't one of our problems that we couldn't figure who would be willing, or able, to use two kilograms of pure cocaine just to frame 'Shepard' and Jackson. I mean, we've always assumed that it was a frame-up. And we've always assumed that no dealer would use that much cocaine to frame anyone. That meant that the drugs had to be from a supply controlled by law enforcement authorities."

White chuckled as he removed plates from the oak cabinets.

"What's so funny?"

White turned and leaned against the kitchen island. "I can't prove it now, but I don't think there ever was any cocaine."

"What? What makes you think that?"

"Whatever was supposedly recovered in the raid was never tested, so there is no proof of what it was. And since the plan was only to arrest Jackson, and hold him for a few days to scare him, there was never going to be a trial. To do what they wanted to do, which was scare Jackson, all they needed was something that looked like cocaine.

"I always had my doubts about the amount of cocaine that was found. We got the charges against 'Shepard' dismissed at the probable cause hearing, so I never had to make the state prove that their evidence was really cocaine. But that would have been my next challenge."

Leslie made a "T" with her hands and said, "Timeout. If the east coast people had so much control over things in Miami, why were 'Shepard' and Jackson even arrested over here?"

Horse looked toward White who said, "You're doing fine."

Horse turned his barstool so that he was facing Leslie. "The whole point of having Jackson arrested was to scare him. If he'd been arrested in Miami, he would have known his case could be fixed. That's why he was hoping that his case would be taken over by the U.S. attorney for the Southern District."

"Didn't he tell Diane Lindsey that he had something he could bargain with in the Southern District?"

"He didn't get that specific. All he said was that he expected the case to be taken over by the U.S. attorney. Then, when he was told he was in the Middle District, he wanted to try to make a deal with Paul Parker. Besides, what else would you expect him to tell Diane: 'My father can fix my case if it's in the Southern District'?"

"I get your point. But what was he going to tell Paul?"

"As Lucius said, there are a number of things he could have offered Paul without talking about the Barlow–St. James operation. But the people on the east coast didn't know that. In fact, neither Diane nor Paul knew what he was going to offer in exchange for bail and his release. But the east coast people feared the worst."

"So they hired Diane to get Jackson out on bail. And Jackson's efforts to plea bargain his way out of jail ended up getting him murdered."

"I don't think that a decision about Jackson's immediate future had been made by the time he was released. But a unique opportunity presented itself, and someone decided to act."

"What was the unique opportunity?"

"Jackson was bailed out on a Wednesday morning, and 'Shepard' got out on bail that same afternoon. When 'Shepard' was released, someone, or maybe more than one person, decided that Jackson could be killed and the blame put on 'Shepard.' That way Barlow wouldn't blame his death on anyone in the organization. And they got lucky."

"How so?"

"To get 'Shepard' released, we claimed that he was Graham Brochette's son."

"That must have shaken them up!" Leslie said.

White stood at the cooking island patting the elk meat into thick uniform patties. Without looking at the others, he said, "I'm sure it did. And since Jackson had been threatening to expose their operation, they had to assume that Jackson had talked about it to 'Shepard.' They didn't know how much 'Shepard' had learned, but it didn't matter. As far as the Barlow–St. James people were concerned it was enough that he was the son of a U.S. attorney. I don't think they had a plan for 'Shepard' at first. But—"

Leslie's eyes brightened as she appeared to realize how the next part of the story must have unfolded. "The people who ran the operation knew they had to do something about 'Shepard.' But no one was ready to kill the son of a U.S. attorney. So, they did the next best thing. They tried to destroy the credibility of 'Shepard' as a witness against them by framing him for murdering Jackson."

"You catch on fast," White said when he realized that Leslie had figured out the plan. "They decided to get rid of both of their problems by killing Jackson and framing 'Shepard' for his murder."

Leslie's demeanor became more animated as she began to understand how the plan had evolved. "And they used Graham's gun so that they could get a ballistics match and argue that 'Shepard' must have taken the gun from Graham's car."

White smiled. There was a hint of pride in his eyes as he watched Leslie demonstrate her grasp of the abstract ideas they were working with. "That was the plan."

"They must have acted fast. Jackson and 'Shepard' were released on bail on the same day, and Jackson was killed, with Graham's gun, sometime that night."

White added a slab of bacon to the frying pan. While it began to sizzle, he returned his attention the Leslie. "Since you're now so smart, tell us how they got Graham's gun."

"Are we still sure that Lyle Wilson stole Graham's gun?"

White shook his head. "We only assumed that because Lyle Wilson was in Tampa the day the gun disappeared from Graham's car. We know he had an opportunity to steal it, but we don't have any proof that he did steal the gun. That's what threw a curve into both investigations."

"Both?"

"Our investigation of Jackson's death and Graham's investigation of corruption in the Southern District."

Leslie pulled her feet onto her barstool and wrapped her arms around her knees. "How did the theft of Graham's gun affect Graham's investigation?"

"At first, Graham and I were both certain that Wilson had stolen Graham's gun. But once we thought about it, we started to question that assumption."

"Why was that?"

"If Wilson had stolen Graham's gun, that would have made him the prime suspect in Jackson's murder. But neither of us believed that Wilson was actually involved in Jackson's murder… so we both had a loose end. We both thought he was guilty of something, but we had different concerns. I had to find out who Wilson gave the gun to, and Graham had to investigate the extent of Wilson's involvement in any corruption scheme on the east coast.

"When Wilson took over the Jackson murder case, Graham questioned his motives because we still recognized that he might have stolen Graham's gun. Then Wilson said he was ready to take the case of the drugs in Matlacha if he could wrap that into the disclosure of information he wanted from 'Shepard.' Graham had to know that he probably didn't have jurisdiction over the drug case and went back to thinking that Wilson might be involved in corruption. Once he saw how the corruption was being conducted in the state courts, he realized how easily Wilson could implement the Barlow–St. James plan in the federal courts."

"Why would Wilson do that?"

"Patience, my dear," White said.

"You're enjoying dragging this out, aren't you?"

"Not at all. But telling the story is cathartic, and I want to get it out."

"Okay, so you were talking about Graham's investigation of Lyle Wilson. But didn't you say that Graham was only investigating corruption in the state courts?"

"That's what the attorney general had assigned him to investigate, but Graham wasn't sure that the problem was limited to those courts. The complaint that started his investigation wasn't specific. The corruption it referred to could have been in the federal or state courts. It wasn't until he understood the Barlow–St. James plan that he concluded that his initial tip concerned wrongdoing in the state system."

"But he was still investigating Wilson, wasn't he?"

"No. He dropped that side of his investigation."

"Why? I thought you were still operating on the assumption that Wilson stole the gun that was used to kill Jackson."

"Because Lyle couldn't have stolen Graham's gun."

"What? Why not?"

"Do you remember the newspaper picture you found of Wilson and Congressman St. James at the charity ball on December 1?"

"Yes. It was a picture of the receiving line."

"Well, the reason we thought that Wilson had stolen Brochette's gun was that we knew that Wilson was in Tampa the day 'Shepard' had his probable cause hearing. We didn't have any other suspects, and we assumed Wilson had taken the gun from Graham's car when Graham returned to Tampa. But the last flight from Tampa that would have gotten Wilson to Miami in time to be in the receiving line left Tampa at 4:25. 'Shepard' and Graham didn't leave our office until after three, so they couldn't have been back in Tampa until after five. Wilson couldn't have taken anything from Graham's car, because he would have been on his way back to Miami."

"Maybe Wilson drove from Tampa to Miami."

White shook his head. "If he did, he'd have had to leave Tampa even earlier to be at the ball in time to have to his picture taken in the receiving line. Either way, he couldn't have stolen Graham's gun."

"Then who did steal Graham's gun?"

"We'll get to that."

Leslie pressed her lips together like a child about to throw a tantrum. "You keep saying that."

"It's a complicated case. If you want to hear all about it, you're going to have to be patient."

Leslie pouted at White, to which he responded, "That's not going to make us go any faster."

"Oh, all right."

White removed the bacon from the frying pan and laid the crispy strips on paper towels to drain. Then he added the chopped mushrooms and onions to the bacon fat in the frying pan and turned down the flame.

Leslie leaned on the breakfast bar and crossed her arms. "Well?"

"Well what?"

"The case…"

"Oh, yeah. What else do you want to know?"

Leslie cocked her head and wrinkled her forehead. Finally, she said, "Lyle Wilson. There must have been some reason Lyle Wilson wanted to take over the 'Shepard' case?"

"There was, but it seems to be just what Wilson said it was. He claimed that he had jurisdiction because Jackson was killed in Dade County. By itself, the murder was a state court matter. But the quantity of drugs found in the raid in Matlacha was enough for federal jurisdiction. Wilson contended that the crimes were sufficiently connected to give him jurisdiction over everything related to Jackson."

"Could he pursue the drug charges after you got them suppressed in the 'Shepard' case?"

"He wouldn't have pursued the drug charges. All he wanted was jurisdiction over the murder case. He was sure it was connected to drugs, and he wanted a reason, any reason, to investigate drug trafficking. He had run the drug prosecution division of Graham's office before transferring to Miami. Graham trusted him and let him take over after Graham had determined how the Barlow–St. James organization worked."

"What was left for Wilson to be investigating?"

"Basically, nothing. Until Graham started his investigation, Wilson didn't know any of the details about the Barlow–St. James organization. But he knew there was some such organization."

"And he wanted to break it up!"

"Good guess. But he wanted just the opposite. He wanted to take over the operation."

"Oh my God. So he's not one of the good guys after all."

"He's not only dirty. He's filthy. And once he found the file that Barlow had compiled before his murder, he had everything he needed."

"Then why did he turn the file over to Graham?"

"He knew that Graham was investigating corruption, and he knew how valuable the files were to that investigation. He must have figured that Graham would take down the organization and leave a vacuum that he could fill. After all, who would suspect him of anything after he had helped eliminate a corruption network?"

"Very clever."

Leslie emptied her glass of wine and reached for the bottle. "Go back to your analysis of Jackson's plea negotiations. If your analysis is right, Jackson was never going to expose his father's organization. Jackson was going to either expose the Cambodian or turn on 'Shepard.' Is that right?"

"That's what I think."

"But he was killed because someone in his father's organization thought Jackson was going to expose them in a plea arrangement with Paul Parker."

"Right again."

"But how did anyone know that Jackson was talking to Parker about a deal?"

White took a deep breath and exhaled. For a minute

he stared at his Pepsi without saying anything. Then he said, "Parker was part of the Barlow–St. James operation for years."

Leslie suddenly sat up. "Paul! How did Paul get involved in something like this?"

"He knew St. James from when they were both narcotics detectives in Miami. Apparently, they were friends." White paused, thinking about what he was going to say. "When St. James realized how much money could be made fixing cases, he let some of his friends in on the deal. Paul had also been a dirty cop, and St. James thought he could trust him. They all referred prospective clients to Barlow, and he arranged for bail through the guy in Fort Lauderdale."

Leslie shook her head. "It's hard to believe that about Paul."

White made a bobbling nod of agreement. The difficulty of accepting the idea that someone he considered a friend could be involved in such an activity made him queasy. His deep feelings of betrayal were evident in his eyes. Leslie could see that he was having difficulty concentrating on what he was telling her. But she had been with White long enough to interpret his looks and knew that there was more to his story. Finally, she said, "What else is bothering you?"

Without moving, White said, "Paul isn't just involved. He's in charge."

Leslie gasped and put a hand to her mouth as White continued. "Even though the operation on the east coast was being run by a committee, St. James still had the controlling vote. Barlow had been in charge of routine operations, like managing the money and arranging for local attorneys to cover bail hearings. But St. James must have started getting concerned about Barlow when his son began making demands for a piece of the money. There didn't seem to be any urgency in dealing with Jackson, but St. James must have decided that something had to be done. Things were just getting too hot on the east coast to leave Barlow at the center of the operation, so St. James decided that the safest thing to do was move things out of the counties in the Southern District. That's when he turned the day-to-day operation of the scheme over to Paul."

"So Paul Parker is the head of a… I don't even know what to call it."

"Call it a crime syndicate. That's all it is."

"Then Jackson…" Leslie suddenly stopped. There was a question there, but she didn't seem to know what it was.

"When Jackson started talking about a plea deal, Paul knew he had to do something. I think that's when he decided that Jackson had to be eliminated. When he saw the opportunity to frame 'Shepard' for the killing, he had to act fast. He didn't even bother consulting with anyone."

"Not even St. James?"

"Especially St. James! St. James was too close to Barlow, and Paul didn't want to put him in a compromising position. Besides, he knew how St. James felt about Graham Brochette, and he knew that St. James would be happy about anything that cast an embarrassing light on Brochette."

"Then that's why Paul set a low bail for Jackson… so that Jackson could be released and then…" Leslie let her voice trail off.

"'Murdered' is the word you're looking for," White said. "But he had a problem because, as soon as he was released, Jackson must have tried to run."

"Where was he going?"

"He was probably headed for the Keys, but he was killed somewhere along Route 41, Alligator Alley."

"How do you know that?"

"The forensic evidence, some grass on his body, shows that Jackson was killed somewhere in the Everglades. But the only place that grass grows is in a part of the 'Glades that's in Dade County."

"And how did he get there?"

"I can't be sure. He didn't have a car. And he couldn't have walked that far. So maybe he hitchhiked."

"Or maybe he was riding with his killer," Horse said.

"It's a possibility."

"I don't understand," Leslie said. "I thought his body was found in eastern Lee County."

"It was. Paul needed jurisdiction over the murder case so he must have had the killer bring Jackson's body up here. Then he claimed to have received the tip that led to the discovery of the body."

"If Paul arranged for the killer to bring the body to Lee County, Paul knows who Jackson's killer is."

Leslie slumped over the breakfast bar, seemingly unable to believe everything she was hearing. She remained silent while White took another sip of his Pepsi and thought about what he had discovered. Finally, Leslie spoke. Her voice was weak but full of concern. "What did Paul tell Barlow?"

"He probably blamed Jackson's murder on 'Shepard,' or maybe even Graham. He was killed with Graham's gun, so they were both plausible suspects. When Lyle Wilson started his own investigation of the east coast operation, he initially concentrated on Barlow's past drug connections. Then it appears that drug dealers who were looking for deals started telling him about the new operation. Someone was squeezing dealers for 'protection'—pay me, and I'll see to it that the police leave you alone. It seems that the protection racket was being run by the Cambodian, Cho Wok Lo.

That wasn't part of the Barlow–St. James operation, but the Cambodian was still working for Barlow. Naturally, the drug dealers and distributors thought Barlow was behind it. This was all discovered about the time St. James transferred control of the operation to Paul. The 'clients' in the drug networks were happy to go along with the change in control because they thought Barlow was squeezing them for higher fees."

"Let me get this straight. Barlow was running the main operation, and he was demanding higher fees from the dealers and drug lords to get people out of jail. But at the same time, the Cambodian was running a protection racket to keep dealers from being arrested in the first place."

"Actually, it was Paul who started demanding more from the dealers and drug lords. And that was something he was only doing in Lee County—where he had complete control over drug enforcement policy."

"But he must have had help. I'm sure Paul didn't do something like that personally."

"You're right. He had the Cambodian."

"The Cambodian!"

"Yes. The Cambodian got mixed up with the cocaine dealers through the Barlow–St. James network. With Paul as his guardian angel, Lee County became his exclusive territory. He and Paul could do virtually anything they wanted."

"But how did the Cambodian get involved in cocaine trafficking?"

"As Barlow began dealing with people higher up in the drug networks—smugglers and distributors—the Cambodian put his talents to work as a cocaine distributor. He was ruthless with the competition, and it wasn't long before he was in charge of a few parts of the smuggling operations. Jackson was still in the Keys, and he was also in constant need of money. The Cambodian got him involved in picking up shipments of cocaine. The Cambodian was dealing directly with the drug lords who were involved in the scheme Barlow and St. James had set up.

"He was running his own operation on the side. He was collecting money from street-level dealers to avoid being arrested. He knew who the crooked cops were, so he bribed them to prevent them from arresting the dealers in the first place or for doing something else that a prisoner could capitalize on to get released.

"Forget to read someone their Miranda rights. Fail to voucher the evidence properly. There are any number of things they could do to taint an arrest. Then they just had to make sure that the prisoner used one of the attorneys in the organization to get them out. Running a protection racket in Lee County was one thing. Paul had enforcement authority, and he was getting a share of what the Cambodian collected. But when the Cambodian started to try his protection scheme on the east coast, without giving a share to the higher powers—"

"That's what got the Cambodian killed."

"But what about Jackson. Who killed him?"

"That's the part that hurts the most."

Leslie waited.

"When Graham was here for the 'Shepard' probable cause hearing, Paul Parker must have arranged to have his gun stolen from his car. Using Graham's gun to kill Jackson seems to have been St. James's idea. He hated the idea of Brochette getting his appointment with the Department of Justice. He was especially concerned because it would have given Brochette jurisdiction over corrupt practices in the federal courts and by elected officials. And he also wanted to get even with Graham for sending his brother to jail. Just the fact that he was a murder suspect would have forced the president to withdraw his nomination, or he would have done it himself."

"But why was Jackson killed?"

"Jackson showed that he was ready to tell what he knew when he started to talk to Paul about a plea. No one knew how much he could tell the authorities. But they had to assume he was ready to disclose everything he knew about the Barlow–St. James scheme if it would keep him out of jail. His life expectancy was already limited."

"Then who actually killed Jackson?"

"We may never know. Paul might have done it himself, or Paul gave the gun to the Cambodian, and he killed Jackson. With the Cambodian dead, Paul will at least be able to establish reasonable doubt if he is ever charged."

"Did you ever suspect that Paul was involved in something like this?"

"Not really. At least I didn't want to. But I did have a nagging feeling that I was overlooking something that should have been obvious."

"Why?"

"There were two things. The first was that the tips that led to the drug bust and to the discovery of Jackson's body were both received by Paul. Those calls were both unusual, and I should have paid more attention to them.

"Then there was the arrest of Shepard and Jackson. The police arrested them as soon as they got to the house in Matlacha. They already had an arrest warrant. But they didn't find the drugs until after Shepard and Jackson had already been arrested. In hindsight, it should have been obvious. Someone had to know that the drugs would be found before the arrest warrant was issued. That should have made me suspect Paul. But I guess I just didn't want to believe it."

Leslie sighed. After a minute she asked, "What about Graham's nomination? Where does this leave him?"

"According to Jack Lancaster, the only holdup on his confirmation was his apparent failure to report a child support obligation on his past financial disclosures. Now that the facts surrounding that are out, his nomination should sail through."

"But I thought the Senate didn't want to approve the creation of the position he was nominated for."

"It didn't. But the results of the investigation he was conducting down here proved that it was a good plan."

Leslie hugged him. "Way to go," she said. "He couldn't have done it without you!"

White smiled. "And I won't let him forget it."

&

White transferred the elk burgers to waiting buns and covered them with the sautéed onions and mushrooms and added a dollop of blue cheese and strips of bacon. "And now, my friends, dinner is served."

Leslie leaned over her plate and inhaled deeply. "It smells delicious."

Horse, who was already vigorously chewing his burger, raised a hand with an "Okay" sign.

Sherlock observed the events at the breakfast bar with a forlorn look. Leslie took pity on her and tossed her another piece of cheese.

White sat on a stool on the side of the breakfast bar opposite Horse and Leslie. His arms rested on the bar surrounding his plate, almost as if he was guarding it. But he had an absent, faraway look.

"What are you thinking?" Leslie asked.

"I was just thinking about the case."

"We've talked about it for the past hour. What more is there to think about?"

"I was just thinking about how it evolved. We started with a simple drug arrest and ended up with a case involving two murders and the exposure of a conspiracy between prosecutors and drug organizations throughout southeast Florida."

Leslie asked, "What do you think is going to happen now?"

White shook his head and smiled. Then he laughed.

Leslie adopted a puzzled expression and said. "What's so funny?"

"Irony of ironies."

"What's that supposed to mean?"

White continued to laugh and struggled to speak. "Graham can't let these crimes go unpunished!"

"Of course not. But what's so funny about that?"

"The only way they can get convictions is to get some of the clients of Barlow and the others to testify against them."

"I still don't see what's so funny."

Suddenly Horse understood what White found so funny and joined in his laughter.

Leslie grew increasingly frustrated. "Will one of you please tell me what's so funny?"

"Graham…" Horse started before convulsing in laughter. "Graham is going to have to make deals with the bad guys to prove his political corruption cases."

"Ooooh. Now I get it," Leslie said. "That sucks."

"It's not that bad. Graham's already negotiated deals with some of the minor players, and he's filled in some of the gaps in what he knows from our investigation. But Congressman St. James, Lyle Wilson, and a few state's attorneys, including Paul Parker, will be prosecuted."

"And that will be the end of it?"

White nodded. "Officially, that will be the end of it, as far as Graham is concerned. But I doubt it's over."

Leslie cocked her head.

"The bad guys have been squeezing a lot of the wrong people for a long time. They're no longer in a position to be helpful, but they know enough to be liabilities."

"So they're going to have accidents."

White shrugged. "Nothing would surprise me."

"And what are you going to do?"

"I don't know. Brochette has issued an arrest warrant for Paul and Paul is being given until tomorrow to turn himself in. After Brochette called Paul, Paul called me."

"That must have been an interesting call."

"He wanted me to represent him."

"You have to be kidding!"

"Would I lie to you about something like that?"

"No. I suppose not. What did you tell him?"

"Paul knows a lot about drug dealers and corruption in the state's attorneys' offices and police departments on the east coast. I think he knows enough about dealers to make some kind of deal. I'm going to talk to him tomorrow."

Before White could continue, the telephone rang.

"Lucius White," he said.

Leslie stood and headed toward the bar while listening to one side of the conversation.

"Yes… When?… I'm sure you did."

Leslie knew from the sound of White's voice that something was terribly wrong and hurried back to his side.

"Well, thank you for calling. I'll call back tomorrow."

White continued to hold the phone long after the caller had obviously hung up.

Leslie's hands covered her mouth. She knew what White was about to say.

"Harry died an hour ago."

Leslie buried her face against White's chest and began sobbing.

37.

Good evening, ladies and gentlemen. This is Lynn Thomas with the evening news.

In today's headlines, State's Attorney Paul Parker apparently committed suicide last night. His body was found by his housekeeper early this morning. A pistol that the sheriff has confirmed fired the fatal shot was found next to his body. Ballistics tests prove that the gun used by Parker is the same weapon used in three other murders: a drug dealer whose body was found in Alva two weeks ago; an attorney from West Palm Beach whose body was found last week in a rest area off Interstate 95, and a third man whose body was found in Miami earlier this week. Anonymous sources in the sheriff's office have told Channel 11 that there were no fingerprints on the gun.

In other news, the Senate has confirmed Graham Brochette, US attorney for the Middle District of Florida to be assistant deputy US attorney general.

White turned off the bedroom television, laid back on the pillow, and looked vacantly at the ceiling.

Leslie snuggled into the crook of his arm and laid her head on his shoulder. "I guess Paul couldn't face going to jail," she said.

"I don't think that's it," White said. His voice sounded distant, as if he was deep in thought.

Leslie propped herself up on one elbow and studied

White's face. "You have that look," she said. "What are you thinking?"

For a minute, White did not speak.

Leslie waited patiently.

"There weren't any fingerprints on the gun," White said.

"That's what the newscaster said. What of it?"

"How does someone commit suicide and not leave any fingerprints on the gun?"

THANK YOU READERS

Thank you for buying and reading my book and I sincerely hope that you enjoyed it. As an independently published author, I rely on my readers to spread the word, so, if you like my book, please tell your family and friend. And if it's not too much trouble, mention me on your social media pages and **post a review on Amazon**. If you would like to tell me your opinion directly, please visit my website – **www.alanpwoodruff.com** – and send me a message. If you have a question, I will respond as soon as possible.

Turn the page for an excerpt from

TRIPLE CROSS

THE NEXT BOOK IN THE

LUCIUS WHITE NOVEL SERIES

1.

Criminal attorney Lucius White's clients were among the biggest targets of federal prosecutions, and he had been successfully defending them for almost three decades. The money no longer mattered; he was already wealthy. Now he was pursuing a personal vendetta against the government, and he only accepted cases where the stakes were the highest and a win would be most embarrassing to the prosecutors. He knew what was driving him, just as he knew what it had done to his psyche.

That afternoon the jury had returned a verdict of not guilty in a multimillion-dollar securities fraud case. The government had tried every tactic in its arsenal—from offering arguably fabricated documents to using disputably perjured testimony—and he had beaten them. It was time to celebrate.

White still felt the glow of victory as he stood by the cooking island in the middle of his restaurant-grade kitchen, chopping the shallots for his celebrated Chicken Excelsior. He had a vast repertoire of gourmet recipes, but this was his favorite form of celebration.

§

At the far end of the converted loft in the Civil War-era warehouse that housed White's apartment and law office, Horse McGee, White's investigator and right arm, pressed a cell phone against his ear. Slowly, he paced the length of the apartment, oblivious to everything but the caller's words. Occasionally, he paused to concentrate on a particularly significant part of the conversation. As he passed the glass door leading to the deck, he saw in his reflection an uncharacteristically gloomy face and narrowed eyes showing every sign that the news was not good. It didn't really matter, but he knew he was being watched and was going to have to explain his reaction.

White put down his knife and strained to hear Horse's conversation. It wasn't any of his business, but Horse was his friend, and something was obviously very wrong.

Leslie Halloran, White's live-in girlfriend, sat opposite him at the breakfast bar sipping a glass of merlot and tossing an occasional cube of imported Swiss cheese to Sherlock, their mixed-breed retriever. She started to say something, but White cut her short with a raised hand. She turned and followed his gaze to Horse, who was leaning against one of the barrel chairs clustered in front of the fieldstone fireplace.

"Did he tell anyone he'd be going somewhere?" Horse asked. A short silence was followed with, "Are you sure?"

White and Leslie exchanged questioning glances.

"Is that all you know?" Horse said. He listened to the answer and nodded once. "I'll let you know what I come up with." With that, he pocketed his cell phone and for a few seconds stood as motionless as the abstract brass sculpture that dominated the center of the room. Absently, as if some force outside himself controlled his movements, he crossed the room and, without speaking, slid onto a stool beside Leslie and reached for his can of Budweiser. His face was fraught with concern, and his eyes had the vacant look of someone consumed by his private thoughts.

White's long friendship with Horse had taught him

to read the signs. Something was wrong, but White knew Horse couldn't be hurried.

Leslie turned toward White and shrugged in a way that indicated she wanted to say something but didn't know if she should. White shook his head. It was an almost imperceptible movement, but her quiet, frustrated sigh made it evident that she understood.

White returned to the task of preparing their dinner—going through the motions while waiting for Horse to speak.

Horse leaned forward, crossing his arms on the bar and hanging his head. Finally, he spoke—softly, more to himself than to the others, as though giving voice to the facts he'd just learned would somehow change them. "David Parker has disappeared."

White raised his head and glanced toward Horse. "Isn't he the guy you worked with at the National Security Agency?"

"Uh… yeah… that's him." Horse seemed to be only vaguely conscious of what White had said. "But that was a long time ago. He's been working at Oak Ridge for the last couple of years."

White strained to suppress his sense of foreboding. "That's still a top-secret facility, isn't it?"

"Yeah. Mostly," Horse responded. The absence of emotion in his voice indicated Horse's thoughts were still elsewhere.

As he waited for Horse to continue, White removed a utility knife from its oak holder and began slicing portobello mushrooms. Most of a minute passed before he said, "Are they still in the nuclear weapons business?"

"Huh?" Horse muttered as if he had suddenly become aware that White was talking to him. "Oh, yeah. They still build bombs… but they also do other classified work."

"What about David? What does he do?"

"He works in cybersecurity. His department analyzes foreign intelligence data."

The words struck White with the force of a divine revelation. *Cybersecurity. Foreign intelligence.* There were few more significant terms in the lexicon of national defense. The disappearance of someone from one of the nation's most secretive installations was enough to chill even White. Already he knew what Horse's mysterious call was going to lead to.

"Do you have any idea what's happened?" White said, still struggling to sound calm as if he was merely curious.

Horse took a swallow of beer and returned the can to the breakfast bar's marble countertop. "I don't know. The last time we talked was a few months ago. He'd been called up for duty in Syria."

White waited for more, but Horse remained silent with his eyes focused on his beer. After more than a decade together, White could read his expressions and knew Horse was trying to divert his thoughts, however briefly, from the news he couldn't ignore.

White turned up the flame under the iron skillet on the stove and added a stick of butter.

"Is there anything I can do to help?" Leslie asked White.

White knew she was trying to help take his mind off Horse. "Not right now." His monotone response said he was thinking about something other than her question.

Leslie took the last sip of her merlot. As she reached for the bottle to refill her glass, the shiny brick-red hair that cascaded in soft curls halfway down her back swung around her shoulder. She tossed her head and, after filling her glass, reached across the bar for another tidbit for Sherlock.

As she always did when meals were in the making, Sherlock had rooted herself at her customary post at the end of the bar, from which she could watch both White and

Leslie. Snacks could come from anywhere, and it paid to be prepared.

White retrieved a bulb of garlic from the wire basket hanging over the bar. He tore loose a couple of cloves and began shaving them into razor-thin slices. "Why would they send someone who worked in cybersecurity to Syria?"

Horse shrugged in a way that suggested he was only vaguely aware of the question. When he responded, his voice was flat and distant. "He spoke fluent Arabic, and we worked on intelligence analysis in the region when we were at the National Security Agency."

The melted butter spattered and crackled as White added the garlic. "And you say he went to Syria several months ago?"

Horse looked up from his beer. "Four, maybe five. He's been back for about a month."

"He didn't stay long."

"I thought about that. A normal rotation's at least six months, usually longer."

The mushrooms and shallots joined the garlic in the skillet, and the kitchen soon filled with their rich bouquet. "What was he doing back here so soon?"

"I don't know. We only emailed once since he got back. That was a couple of weeks ago. He was secretive about what went on over there, but he said he'd pulled some political strings and gotten released before his tour was over." Horse took another swallow of beer before continuing. "He also said he'd come across something that could shake up the peace negotiations."

"What kind of political strings would someone like him have?" Leslie asked.

Horse responded with an abbreviated snort. "I thought he was pulling my leg. David isn't at all involved in domestic politics. He's about as politically connected as Sherlock."

White chuckled at the idea of Sherlock being politically active—unless peeing on campaign lawn signs constituted a political activity. "What could he have found in Syria that would affect the peace negotiations?"

"I can't think of a thing. Politics bored David. Only something he thought was earthshaking would catch his attention."

"Then why didn't he tell you more about what he'd found?"

"I don't think he understood what he had found." Slowly, Horse's expression changed from one of angst over Parker's disappearance to a narrow-eyed look that said he was thinking about what Parker had revealed. "But he did say something I thought was odd."

Leslie put down her wine. White put his hands, one still holding a spatula, on the bar, extended his arms, and leaned forward.

"He said someone in Syria didn't want to let him do a complete analysis of some documents he'd found, but he was going to research them now that he was home."

"Why did that seem odd?" Leslie asked.

Horse wrinkled his forehead as he thought about the question. "Document analysis isn't part of his job. He only manages the computers that search digital records and identity documents for others to examine. But he said that *he* was going to analyze the documents he'd found in Syria."

"How'd he get documents out of the country?"

"I don't know. And I didn't pay much attention to it at the time. But *now* I think he was giving me a hint about what to investigate if something like this happened."

"And what *did* happen?" White said.

"I don't know that either. He and Terry Hardwick—that's the guy who just called—had an arrangement. They sent e-mails to each other every day. If David didn't send an e-mail for two days, Terry was supposed to call me."

"It sounds like he was expecting something to happen to him."

Horse cocked his head. "Sounds like!"

Leslie slid her glass to the side and put a gentle hand on Horse's forearm. "Was he afraid of anything specific? Anything that made him think something might happen to him?"

Horse paused, his face was once again taut and troubled as he stared at his beer. "Wish I knew. David wouldn't have disappeared without making any effort to contact me himself."

White laid down his cleaver and spread his hands on the bar. "And since he wanted *you* notified, it must have been something he didn't think the authorities would act on."

Leslie glanced at White over the rim of her glass. White knew she could see the fluttering tic over his left eye that betrayed the tension he was feeling. At the same time, White watched Leslie's expression transition from cautious concern to grim apprehension. He knew what she had seen, just as he sensed what she was thinking.

White returned his attention to Horse. "If he wanted *you* told about his disappearance, why didn't he tell you what was going on? Why did he rely on Hardwick to call you?"

Horse swallowed the last of his beer before crumpling the can in his massive hand. "Don't know. Whatever it was, it must have happened so quickly that he didn't have time to avoid it—or something prevented him from contacting me."

"Why would David want *you* notified?" Leslie said. "If

he thought he was in trouble, couldn't he have gone to the authorities?"

Horse pursed his lips. "Maybe it was something he couldn't go to them about or something that happened so fast that he couldn't go to them, but he knew he could count on me."

Leslie's eyebrows rose. "Count on you for what?"

"To help him," Horse said as casually as if going to the aid of an old friend was an everyday occurrence.

"That's *it*?" Leslie said, her tone somewhere between surprise and exasperation. "He expected you to drop everything and come running just because you're friends?"

"It's more than that." A reflexive smile replaced the strain on Horse's face. "It's part of a pact we made."

"A pact? What kind of a pact?"

Horse's features morphed into a reflective appearance. "We were more than friends. We were like brothers in our days at the National Security Agency. We were enlistees in a place where everyone else was an officer or a civilian with at least a couple of degrees. We were the outsiders, so, naturally, we got together. I don't remember what got us onto the topic, but it had something to do with the fact that neither of us had any family we could go to when we got into trouble. We each promised we'd be there if the other one ever needed help."

Leslie shook her head and frowned. "You guys and your macho promises."

"It's important in the security business. When you have a top-secret clearance and a job like David had, you're always a potential target for enemy action."

"Isn't that why we have police and other agencies to protect you guys?"

"They don't have the resources to give every case the

attention it needs, and government agencies can't do some of the things I can do."

"But it's really just a chromosome thing," White whispered to Leslie as he removed the shallots and mushrooms from the skillet and replaced them with the marinated chicken fillets.

Horse gave White a sour look suggesting that he was not in the mood for their customary exchange of irreverent banter. "Leslie, you have to understand that it's something the Army beats into you. You have to be able to count on your buddies, and they must be able to count on you."

Leslie made a face that indicated she pitied the male of the species. Finally, she rolled her eyes. "Men!"

"Yeah. It's a guy thing, but a promise doesn't mean much unless it's honored. I know I can count on David if I need him."

Leslie swiveled her bar stool and looked into Horse's eyes. "So, Mister 'Guy Thing,' what are you going to do now?"

"There's only one thing I *can* do. Find him—or find out what happened to him."

"When do we leave?" White said.

After more than a decade together, they were more than merely an attorney and an investigator. White understood the bond that existed between Horse and Parker. He also understood what Horse had to do and why he had to do it. Asking him if he wanted help was unnecessary. Horse would have refused, and White would have insisted. In the end, White would have prevailed. If their roles had been reversed, the discussion would have gone the same way. That was the way it had always been. Now, it was easier to ignore the polite dance and move on.

Horse nodded the slightest hint of acceptance of White's

offer. "We should go to Knoxville first thing in the morning."

"Then you'd better start packing," Leslie said.

White looked toward Leslie. "Don't you mean *we'd* better start packing?"

"What? You want me to come with you? This doesn't sound like something I could be any help with."

"I don't have any idea what we might be getting into, but I suspect we'll need all the brainpower we can muster. I know you're busy, but you've said you wanted to be more involved in what Horse and I do."

"I'd like to be more involved in your *cases*. Running around the country looking for missing people isn't what I had in mind. Besides, I have briefs due in two of my own cases in two weeks, and I have a ton of research to do."

"Can't you do it at the cabin as well as here?"

"I suppose so."

"Look on the bright side. You'll be able to spend a week at the cabin when the leaves are changing colors."

"Well… I could use a little time off."

"Good. Then let's start packing."

"What about Sherlock?"

"What about her? She needs a vacation, too."

Leslie smiled. "Did you hear that, Sherlock?" she said, reaching down and scratching the dog's ear. "We're going to Tennessee."

At the sound of Leslie's voice, Sherlock looked up and wagged her tail. She knew that something was happening but was unwilling to abandon her post at the end of the breakfast bar. It could be a trick to distract her from a tasty morsel.

§

White stood motionless by the open bedroom window, looking out at the faint light of the coming dawn. Outside, the wind picked up, and the silk curtains billowed as drops of rain—the outer edges of the storm moving over the Florida Keys—assaulted the windows.

Leslie rolled over, yawned, and propped herself up on her elbow. "You're up early." She allowed the sheet to fall from her shoulder, revealing her uninhibited nakedness. At five feet, six inches, and one hundred twenty pounds, she still had the body of the tennis star she'd been at Wellesley and a look that was seductively erotic.

White glanced toward their bed and ran his fingers through his long hair. "My mind seems to have woken up before the rest of me was ready."

"Do you want to talk about it?"

When White responded, his voice was low and thoughtful. "Talk about what?"

"Whatever you were thinking about."

"What makes you so sure I was thinking about anything important?"

Leslie shook her head. "Come on, Lucius. You know you have a tell. You run your fingers through your hair whenever you're deep in thought. So, tell me what you were thinking about."

"I was," White paused and rubbed the back of his neck. "I was thinking about Horse's friend."

"Do you know him?" Leslie asked in a concerned voice. "The way you talked to Horse tonight, I thought…" She let her voice trail off. Her hopeful expression said she expected White would fill the silence with an explanation.

"We've never met." His emotionless voice suggested that his thoughts were somewhere else. "I only know that he and Horse have a history."

White turned from the window and moved toward the

bed. "Horse has mentioned him a couple of times over the years." He spoke as if he was trying to recall something from past conversations that might shed light on their coming quest. "I always had a feeling there was something he couldn't share… or didn't want to share."

"Horse isn't the only one who's like that," Leslie said as she sat up in bed and pulled the blanket around her. "And I don't think that's all there is to your concern."

There was a sad, distant quality to White's voice when he responded. "You might be right. The ghosts seem to come more and more often."

It wasn't necessary for him to describe his inner turmoil any more than that. Leslie knew what he meant and how it affected him. As he extended his aimless stroll around the room, he continued to give voice to his buried thoughts. "Cases aren't just about finding the truth anymore."

"I know. You've let them become battles between you and the government. You're more interested in beating them than in winning for your client."

"I'm doing what every defense attorney does. I make the government prove its case."

"You know you're doing more than that. You're putting the government on trial."

"*Damn it!* They *should* be put on trial!" White's voice was filled with venom.

"Lucius…" Leslie paused, trying to find the right words to respond to White. She knew how painful it was for him when his ghosts returned. "Prosecutors can only make the case that the law and the facts allow."

"Prosecutors aren't the only problem. The agencies that make the rules, and the agencies that claim to be enforcing the rules, are just as guilty. They also have to follow the law, but too many times they don't."

"But the law isn't always clear. Things aren't always black and white."

White sat quietly on the edge of the bed, breathing deeply as he let his feelings about the government subside. "Tell that to my father," he said in a melancholy voice as if speaking to an imaginary listener from his long-ago life.

A tear formed in the corner of Leslie's eye. She understood what White was feeling, just as she knew that there was nothing she could do about it. Usually, the demons appeared only as memories, often painful but still manageable. But there continued to be times when, with increasing frequency, they emerged as uncontrollable compulsions.

"David Parker isn't your father. You don't even know if David's disappearance represents a real case… or that the government has *anything* to do with it."

"No. The *facts* don't tell me any of those things, but my *guts* are screaming loud and clear. If something has happened to Parker, the government is either behind it or is going to have an interest in our efforts to find him. Either way, there's going to be a clash between us."

Leslie slid further under the covers while considering whether she should say what she was thinking. She knew there were times when White's compulsions interfered with what he wanted most. Winning was what he was paid to do, but beating the government was what he now lived for.

"Lucius…" she said. "Have you considered the possibility that Horse's friend disappeared because he wanted to?"

White sat down beside her on the bed. "What are you thinking?"

Leslie hesitated, the troubled expression on her face suggested she wanted to ask a question whose answer she wasn't sure she wanted to know. Finally, she said, "What if

Horse's friend did something that he's running away from? What if that's why he didn't call Horse?"

White's answer came more swiftly than she expected. "Then he needs a lawyer. He needs *me*. But it doesn't change what we have to do. Before I can help him, we have to find him."

"Is that really what you want… or what you *need* to do?"

White left the bed and wandered slowly, almost aimlessly, toward the open window where he again stood silently, breathing in the fresh night air.

Leslie left him alone with his thoughts until he turned and started back to the bed. "What will you do if the government doesn't have anything to do with David's disappearance? Will finding him, and defending him if necessary, be enough?"

White returned to the bed and lay down beside her with his head on the pillow, but his eyes remained wide open. "I don't know. I honestly don't know."

Leslie reached out and held White's hand. She had other questions, but she knew this was not the time for them, just as she knew White was probably not ready, or able, to answer them.

ABOUT THE AUTHOR

Alan Woodruff was born in Pittsburgh, Pennsylvania, raised in Cleveland, Ohio. He holds bachelors and masters degrees in chemical engineering (Virginia Tech), a doctorate in administration (Harvard), a law degree (Florida State) and a post-graduate degree in tax law (Univ. of Washington).

Before going to law school, Alan was a researcher and consultant to local, state, federal and international agencies and organizations and the founder and CEO of multiple companies.

As a lawyer, Alan has twenty years of experience as a trial attorney. He has more than fifty published articles and professional papers and is the author of one legal reference book.

Alan lives in North Carolina. He can be reached through the "Contact" page of his website at **www.alanpwoodruff.com** or at **alan.jd.llm@gmail.com**.

Made in the USA
Coppell, TX
23 July 2021

59376926R00229